"A h

Viktor wonder[...] the telephone conversation. He was honest enough to acknowledge the spasm of disappointment that flashed through him.

Natalie concluded her call and turned to Viktor. "We should go eat." She spoke as if she were biting off the pin of a grenade. Clearly Frank—the man on the other end of the phone—had set her on edge, and Viktor felt a twinge of exultation. At the same time he reminded himself that he was not in a contest with Frank. He must fight the primitive urge to compete with a man he didn't know over a woman he had just met.

So he had better not look at her too much. "Yes, it would be good to eat," he replied. And once he had fed himself, he would sleep off his jet lag and be better prepared in the morning to cope with everything. He needed to be functioning at his best.

His twelve-year-old son's life depended on it....

Dear Reader,

In the military there is a group of soldiers whose duty is to plan—down to the smallest detail—everything necessary to ensure that a visit by or to a foreign dignitary goes off without a hitch. These protocol officers are more often than not the first representatives of their nation with whom the leaders of our world interact. They are relied upon for living accommodations, information, scheduling and attention to the issues such as who outranks whom and how that affects each phase of a visit. It takes a special kind of person to balance the many cultural and personal needs of such important individuals.

In this world I have set Army protocol officer Captain Natalie Wentworth and her latest assignment, Russian Colonel Viktor Baturnov. He isn't one of the high-ranking heads of state she's used to dealing with, but she's determined to do her best to get him started in his training program with American counterparts at the Pentagon. This means she must show him around, help him get settled and make certain he's properly in-processed and introduced. Although she's responsible for ensuring his comfort, she needs to remain detached and professional, no matter how attractive he may be.

Please be aware that this novel was written prior to the terrorist attack committed against the Pentagon on September 11, 2001. Facts in the book reflect how things were in a more innocent time. As you read this story, please remember all the men and women who lost their lives while defending their country, and the loved ones they left behind. The military and civilian personnel of the U.S. Department of Defense stand watch every day to keep us safe. Their vigilance and sacrifices must never be forgotten.

Elizabeth Ashtree

P.S. Please visit my Web site at www.e-ashtree.com and write me at eashtree@aol.com. I'd love to hear from you.

The Colonel and the Kid
Elizabeth Ashtree

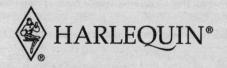

HARLEQUIN®

TORONTO • NEW YORK • LONDON
AMSTERDAM • PARIS • SYDNEY • HAMBURG
STOCKHOLM • ATHENS • TOKYO • MILAN • MADRID
PRAGUE • WARSAW • BUDAPEST • AUCKLAND

ISBN 0-373-71036-4

THE COLONEL AND THE KID

Copyright © 2002 by Randi Elizabeth DuFresne.

This edition published by arrangement with Harlequin Books S.A.

® and TM are trademarks of the publisher. Trademarks indicated with
® are registered in the United States Patent and Trademark Office, the
Canadian Trade Marks Office and in other countries.

Visit us at www.eHarlequin.com

Printed in U.S.A.

For my sister, Lori Gilmartin, whose skillful editing of the initial manuscript made this story so much sharper.
For Ruth Glick and the other members of her long-standing critique group, who hone writing skills with hammer and anvil—and lots of encouragement.
And for Robert Wall, who was, as always, indispensable regarding the critical research.

And to the men and women who lost their lives while serving at the Pentagon September 11, 2001.

CHAPTER ONE

THE AEROFLOT FLIGHT had touched down on the tarmac an hour ago. Natalie stood at the gate inside Dulles International Airport, waiting for her latest assignment to show up. If he was wearing his uniform and keeping his papers at the ready, as he'd been advised, he should have sailed through Customs. Instead, he was late. Very late. She shifted from foot to foot, imbued with an unbecoming impatience that warred with her military bearing.

Trying to stay focused, Natalie quietly practiced the Russian words with which she'd planned to welcome the Colonel. *"Zdrastvuytye, Polkovnik Baturnov. Minya zavut Kapitan Natalie Wentworth."* She hoped she had the pronunciation right and that she was saying "Hello, Colonel Baturnov. My name is Captain Natalie Wentworth." If that wasn't what the words meant, she hoped they didn't translate into anything embarrassing. But she was prepared to take the risk. In her more than ten years of protocol work for the Army, she'd found that people responded best when they were greeted in a reasonable facsimile of their own language.

She eyed the door through which the Colonel should emerge. People jostled past her, anxious to catch their connecting flights or in a hurry to find their luggage. She practiced the difficult words again, wishing that *hello* in Russian was not a multisyllabic word beginning with the impossible *zdr* combination.

Another problem had become increasingly apparent in the last half hour. She glanced toward the nearby rest room and decided to take care of the matter now. There was no telling how much longer the Colonel would be. With the sure strides born of forced marches with weighted packs, she quickly made her way.

Unfortunately, there was a line. Of course. There was always a line for the women's room. With a sigh of resignation, Natalie got in the queue.

"Captain Wentworth?" called a female voice from the sink area at the head of the line. "Is that you, Natalie?"

She craned her neck around the considerable width of the woman in front of her to see who had called. "Yes," she replied, and then wished she hadn't when she saw who it was. Captain Constance DiSanto came toward her in the same class A Army uniform that Natalie wore. It was just plain bad luck to run into Constance on a Saturday night at the airport. Given her uniform, she must also be picking up an assignment. Constance smiled, but the friendly gesture left Natalie cold. There was a rivalry between the two of them that made it hard for Natalie to warm up to DiSanto.

"Who are you here to meet?" Constance asked as if she didn't already have a pretty good idea.

Natalie shrugged. There was no hiding her new assignment even though it wasn't a type of job she was used to. After ten years of hard work perfecting her craft as a crack protocol officer, she normally spent her time dealing with generals, ambassadors and heads of state. But not this time. "I'm meeting Colonel Baturnov, a Russian officer coming to learn about supply movements with the Materiel Command."

"I see," Constance said, barely hiding a smirk. "Whatever did you do to deserve *that?*"

Natalie wished she'd been given some explanation as to why she'd been assigned Colonel Baturnov when one of the less experienced officers, such as Captain DiSanto, could have done it. "This guy needs someone with experience to get him settled in and working productively."

Natalie had queried her mentor, Deputy Director of Protocol Colonel James Freeman. But he'd sounded exasperated and frazzled—not uncommon in the protocol business—and had told her to get the job done instead of questioning it. Leaving his office, she'd reminded herself that she was a military officer trained to do whatever needed to be tackled. Rank did not always have its privileges.

The next person in line moved forward, and Natalie followed, grateful to see that there was only the heavyset woman still ahead of her. Though she had a funny feeling she would be happier not knowing the answer, basic politeness compelled Natalie to ask Constance, "Who are you here to greet?"

Constance smiled. "General Marco," she said lightly. Marco was the equivalent of a four-star general and an important connection to the Italian military. The fact that Constance was fluent in Italian made her an obvious choice to take care of him. Still, by nightfall Constance would be crowing to their mutual colleagues that she'd been assigned to a high-ranking officer while Natalie had been relegated to a Russian colonel.

"That's good." Natalie nodded and hoped she sounded sincere.

"Yes," Constance agreed as Natalie saw a stall door open. "I'll let you go. See you back at the office."

Natalie gave the other woman a wave over her shoulder but turned her attention to taking care of business. Within minutes, she exited the women's room and headed toward the customs area.

She spotted the Colonel immediately. He was standing beside two luggage carts, talking to an older gentleman. He wore an olive-green military uniform, trimmed in red. His epaulettes announced his rank. Her Russian Colonel had finally appeared.

The first thing she noticed as she began to weave her way through the crowd toward him was that he looked haggard. The long flight from his native country must have been grueling. The second thing she noticed was that he didn't look Russian. Then she silently acknowledged the prejudice of that thought. She knew better. Russians were as varied in appearance as Americans. This one looked very European with his finely wrought features and classic brow.

The older man said something to him as she approached the huge space between them. Suddenly the pair laughed together, and Natalie hung back, observing them curiously. Though she'd still been in college when the Soviet Union had fallen, she couldn't help a twinge of uneasiness when she noticed the old man hold out a small carry-on bag. The Colonel took it and then slid one of the two heavily loaded carts he'd been pulling in the man's direction. What was this? Why did Baturnov accept a carry-on bag from the other man?

At last, the frail-looking man waved farewell and Colonel Baturnov turned to scan the area, presumably for her. She gave herself a mental shake—she wasn't going to allow herself to harbor some absurd notion that her assignment was up to something. She walked toward him, telling herself not to let her imagination run away with her. Natalie could see this was no ordinary, run-of-the-mill Russian soldier. At least, not by the look of him. Colonel Baturnov held himself very tall and straight with a self-assured bearing that bordered on arrogance.

Despite her resolution, she couldn't keep from eyeing the nylon bag in his hand. The word *spy* popped into her head before she could talk herself out of it. Just because the two countries were no longer enemies didn't mean espionage was dead. But even if the Colonel was up to no good, Natalie's job was to keep an eye on his activities until she could report to her superiors. She wasn't trained for spy-catching and she'd be in big trouble if she tried. But her concern evaporated when she came to a stop before him. His expression was open and direct, even mildly curious. Not the cagey look she would have expected of a bad guy. As she admired his fine European features, she remembered her carefully prepared Russian greeting.

"Zdrastvuytye, Polkovnik Baturnov," she managed to say without tripping over her own tongue. She snapped her hand to her brow for a precision salute. He might not be in *her* Army, but he definitely outranked her. And his chest was bedecked with many ribbons and medals. He deserved the appropriate respect even though they were inside where salutes were not required. He returned her gesture with a very formal smile—the barest upturning of the corners of his mouth.

She opened her mouth to give the rest of her speech but forgot it all when he clicked his heels together and bowed to her like a pre-revolutionary Czarist instead of a post-Soviet Russian. It wasn't a very deep bow, and he kept his gaze locked on hers as he executed it, but the unexpectedness of the maneuver threw her off balance. She wondered if he'd done it on purpose. She glanced at the bag again.

"Kapitan Wentworth," he said after the barest glance at her epaulettes and name tag. He had given due deference to her rank and she was relieved by this sign of respect. It could be tiresome when her assignments treated her like a plaything. Setting them straight was always a delicate procedure.

"Um. *Da, Polkovnik, Kapitan Natalie Wentworth. Kak byl bam palyot?*" She hoped that she'd confirmed her identity and that she'd followed with a polite inquiry as to how his flight had been. She was rapidly departing the zone of her Russian competence.

This time his smile was more genuine. His brown eyes brightened with interest or amusement. As if playing along with a game he said, *"Kharasho, spasiba. Ochin' priyatna."* He put out his hand, and she shook it, pleased with the firmness of his grip and wondering if he'd told her that his flight had been "fine, thanks," and "nice to know you," or something to that effect. Then, with a shrewd but good-humored expression, he launched into a spate of Russian she had no hope of recognizing.

She smiled and shrugged helplessly as she let go of his hand.

"You speak a little Russian," he offered in clipped English that sounded heavenly, given that she could understand it perfectly. "That is very good of you, to learn some of my language to greet me. *Spasiba.* That is 'thank you.'"

She nodded, then repeated after him, "*Spasiba.* Thank you. I'll try to remember, sir. But you've found me out. We're at the end of my Russian. I'm glad you speak English so well."

He inclined his head, accepting her compliment. "We learn English in school, but it is easy to forget. I have practiced of late. I will be in your country for a month, I thought to better understand the language before I arrived. Or how will I learn from my American comrades about supplies?" Now the smile in his eyes was even warmer. "So, you will be my escort today," he said.

Escort. Now there was a noun with widely disparate meanings, she thought. "Yes, Colonel, I've been assigned to show you around and help you settle in." She moved to walk beside him as he pulled the cart that held his luggage. "I'm sorry I couldn't bring anyone to help with your bags. We'll have to get them to the car on our own."

He turned to her and the light of amusement had returned to his eyes. "I am but a colonel. I have never had anyone carry my bags for me."

"Really? A colonel in this country would have an enlisted person available to worry about luggage."

He shrugged slightly. "In *my* country, colonels are not so...mmm...." He seemed to search his mind for a word and as he did so, his free hand moved upward to indicate a high level. "Superior, perhaps? Yes? We are not so superior that we would have someone to carry our property."

She smiled at him. He carried himself like a prince, but had the sense not to put on the airs of one.

"This way, sir," she said. "May I carry this for you?" She indicated the carry-on bag he had received from the old man. It hung from his shoulder as he pulled the luggage cart with him. She reached out for it, thinking to help.

"I manage it well," he said, without any outward sign to indicate there might be something significant about the bag. But Natalie couldn't keep from wondering about it. She was empty-handed, but he didn't want her to help with the small case.

The last thing she wanted was to remain suspicious of that piece of luggage for the rest of the time she spent with him, so she took a chance. Conversationally, she said, "I noticed you accepted that bag from that elderly gentleman. Was there some problem?"

He gave a half smile, but now she detected an undertone of tension and a slight deepening of the color in his cheeks. "Ah. He and I were placed together, seat by seat. We talked. I walked with him as he passed through Customs. They didn't wave him through easily as they did to me. His luggage was searched and left in some disorder. I helped him.'' He spoke, using the hand that was not pulling the cart—pantomiming the act of putting things back into cases. "When I offered to pull his heavy trolley for him, I could see in his face that he is, mmm…proud, yes? So I ask him to carry my small *bagash* while I pull his trolley along with mine.''

Natalie felt ashamed of her unkind thoughts about spying. There was nothing nefarious about helping an old man with his luggage. "That was very nice of you.''

His eyes became solemn. "The elders in my country struggle in these changing times. It is a strategic error not to respect them.'' He stopped suddenly and looked off to his left. "Ah, and there is my old friend now, with another need of my help.'' He began to move off in the direction he'd been looking, leaving his own cart with her.

"Wait,'' Natalie called, but he kept on going. The elderly man stood beside his luggage carrier. Several of his heavier suitcases had fallen off. No one moved to help him as he struggled to lift one back into place. Baturnov greeted him in Russian and she saw the fatigue wash away from the Colonel's face. She realized he was handsome and refined when he smiled. Not at all over-bearing or arrogant in his appearance, as she'd first thought.

The Colonel and his elderly friend exchanged a few Russian words that she could not understand, then Baturnov set down the carry-on bag he'd kept slung over his shoulder so he could begin hefting the fallen suitcases back onto the carrier.

She moved closer, pulling the Colonel's cart, and eyed the nylon case sitting on the floor near his feet. Curiosity urged her to pick it up, but when she leaned toward it the Colonel slid it closer to himself with one foot. Even the elderly man noticed and eyed the bag with interest.

"It is not to worry,'' Baturnov assured her with a brief gesture that suggested she should stay back. "I have a small computer and…supplies.'' She heard the slight hesitation in his voice and wondered what he was hiding. Natalie felt an unwelcome spark of alarm again. What was inside that was so important he wouldn't even let her hold the thing for him?

She decided to simply observe what she could. She'd inform her superiors if things were still suspicious by the time she returned to the Pentagon. The tone of the conversation between the two men seemed casual enough, but she couldn't understand the words, so she couldn't be certain.

What happened next stole her breath. Baturnov bent to lift the last of the old man's suitcases into place, leaning away from where he'd placed his computer bag beside his own feet. In that instant, another man dressed in a white, button-down shirt and dark slacks pushed between the Colonel and Natalie, nearly knocking her over. When she regained her equilibrium, she saw that the man, already halfway across the wide area, had Baturnov's case swinging from his hand. In disbelief, Natalie looked stupidly at the Colonel's feet and confirmed that the case was no longer there.

"Hey!" she yelled. The thief glanced over his shoulder, made eye contact, then bolted. "Hey!" she yelled louder. Then she gave chase, jostling bystanders. Several people saw her coming and got out of her way. But no one tried to stop the guy, even when she shouted, "He's got our bag!"

"Na-tal-ia!" she heard a deep voice call from behind her. She didn't turn. She had to catch the bad guy who was making for the exits. If he reached them, that bag would be lost forever. And somehow that case had become very important.

"Stop!" she called, running faster. She thought she was gaining on him. But then someone streaked past, the olive-green uniform with its red trim supplying immediate identification. She heard the jangle of medals as he went by, making her feel as if she were standing still instead of running full tilt. If her Russian Colonel couldn't stop the thief, then the bag was a goner. She slowed her pace slightly, scanned the area and shifted her trajectory sharply to the right and through a nearby set of double doors.

She was out on the sidewalk in the May sunshine, squinting against the glare and running for the other exit she thought the thief would come through if the Colonel didn't manage to stop him. A whistle blew, probably airport security, but she didn't stop. A huge porter's cart piled high with luggage moved into her path, and she veered around it—just in time to see Colonel Baturnov leap over a similar cart like a gazelle and bring down his quarry.

The bag slipped from the thief's hand and skidded across the cement toward the road. Natalie grabbed it, barely snatching it from beneath the onrushing cars just as the Colonel shouted *"Nyet!"* with a hopelessly out-of-range outstretched hand.

While Natalie and the Colonel concentrated on the bag, the thief regained his footing and took off at a fast sprint again. A policeman gave chase along the street, but then a car door flew open, the criminal jumped inside, and the vehicle sped off. Even in her out-of-breath condition, Natalie felt as though she were in a scene from a movie. The policeman shrugged and asked the Colonel if he wanted to file a report, making it clear by his tone that it wouldn't be worth the trouble, given that the bag wasn't actually taken. Baturnov waved him off with a "Thank you."

He reached for the bag, but Natalie jerked it away and shook it a little. She felt the weight of the laptop and heard the clatter of something that sounded like plastic pellets, loose in some sort of container. Her stomach constricted as her mind whirled with suspicion. She glanced at the man she wanted to like. The Colonel looked back at her, expressionless.

"That was quite a takedown, sir," said another police officer who had walked up to them. "Looks like he got away, though."

Baturnov nodded, looking pained at his failure to detain the man. Then he ran his fingers through his hair.

The young police officer sized up the Colonel. He scanned Baturnov from head to toe. "Interesting uniform. Where you from, big guy?"

It was probably the *big buy* that brought the congenial smile back to the Russian's face. "I am from Russia," he said amiably.

"No kiddin'?" The cop looked impressed. "They teach that kind of stuff in Russia these days?" He gestured to indicate the all-out pursuit followed by the athletic leap and spectacularly efficient takedown.

That brought a laugh out of the Colonel, and even Natalie, as tense as she still felt, had to smile. "Yes," Baturnov said. "They teach that kind of stuff to, mmm…" He thought for a moment and looked at Natalie. Using his hands to communicate again, he set them sideways as if preparing to do karate. "Highly trained military—what is that?"

She was puzzled. "You mean like Special Forces? SEALs?"

"Yes, that is it," he crowed triumphantly. He looked back at the policeman and patted himself on the chest.

The cop's eyebrows shot up. "You're Russian special forces? Cool!"

Colonel Baturnov had the grace to look down in humility— or a reasonable imitation of such. Natalie tried to think back to what she'd read in the man's dossier before she'd driven to the airport. Had it mentioned a past career in some sort of Russian special forces?

"Well, I hope you two have a better day from here on out. Welcome to America!" said the cop. Then he moved back down the sidewalk the way he had come.

"Tak," Baturnov said in an expectant tone that made her think he'd said "So." He gazed at Natalie. "Excitement, yes? Perhaps I go inside for the suitcases before old Mr. Zurtin must defend against other thieves. I will return." He turned as if to go, making no move to reclaim his precious carry-on from her possession.

"Wait," she said. He stopped and looked at her, perplexed. "We should make sure nothing was broken inside, right?" She lifted it slightly.

The Colonel looked back at her, and she watched his features lose any hint of expression. Devoid of animation, his countenance would have chilled her except that a hint of warmth returned to his eyes almost immediately. "Perhaps after the adventure we shared today you will call me Viktor. And may I have your permission to call you Natalia?" He said it low and soft, with a *ya* at the end and with the emphasis on the middle syllable. The way he said her name sent a little shiver up her spine.

But she gathered her wits and remembered to remain calm and professional. She wanted him to trust her so she could get a look inside the case she held.

"Certainly, Viktor," she said, noting the strong sounds in his name. "Let's just make sure everything's okay in here." She shook it a little and she heard the pellet-like sound again.

If she hadn't seen it with her own eyes, she would not have believed that Viktor Baturnov was capable of being afraid. But his face drained of color and his right hand rose as if to still her.

Natalie's heart began to beat faster. Surely the containers she could hear inside the case did not contain anything dangerous. She recalled her routine briefings in bio-warfare and she resolved not to shake the bag anymore.

He took a measured step closer to her, holding her gaze steadily while slowly reaching for his bag. "There is nothing inside to concern you," he said reassuringly.

He would have gently removed it from her hand, except that she turned her back to him abruptly, set the thing on the ledge under the window and unzipped it. She heard him mumble, "Please, it is nothing," but she paid him no attention, half surprised he had not tried to wrestle the thing from her or make a getaway now that he was about to be found out.

Inside, a sleeve held the laptop in place. On the other side there were a bunch of plastic jewel cases for CDs. Then she noticed the many small orange plastic containers with white lids. They appeared to be prescriptions bottles.

Carefully, she lifted one of the containers and examined the inscription. It was in Russian, of course. The Cyrillic lettering confounded her, but she thought one of the words looked like it might read Baturnov in Russian. There were pills inside. Natalie had never heard of bio-warfare being delivered in tablet form. Her tension eased, but not her curiosity.

She looked at the Colonel, still standing motionless next to her. She saw a muscle clench in his jaw and realized he was not at all happy about her prying. Still, he was not behaving like a foreigner whose sinister plot was in the process of being discovered.

"What is all this stuff?" she asked, peering in at the other bottles, all with similar labels.

He stared at her and held out his hand as if she should give the bag into to him. "It is only medicine, Natalia. For my…for a relative. I have brought them for him—a personal matter. Now, give it back to me."

HE CONCENTRATED ON KEEPING his hand steady as he held it out, waiting for her to return his property. It would not do to show any sign of fear.

She hesitated, staring at him with uncertainty in her clear blue eyes. Viktor regarded her a moment, thinking how important it was to gain her trust. With a force of will, he dropped his hand to his side and shrugged.

"Keep it if you are more comfortable so. Provided I get the medications in time to give them to my relative, I do not mind." He spoke the words far more casually than he felt. Inside, his nerves screamed with tension. "If anything happens to my computer, your wealthy American government will provide money to replace it. Perhaps I could upgrade, yes?" He smiled warmly. He needed to soothe her; he could not risk having the medication confiscated. If she only knew what those vials contained…

"No. That's okay. I shouldn't have…" She looked slightly embarrassed as she zipped the bag and handed it to him. "Let's go get the rest of your luggage," she said, heading for the doors. He followed her, thinking that her back was almost as appealing as her front. For Viktor, she had become Natalia the moment he had heard her very Russian first name. And he had liked her almost immediately. About the time he had become certain her ability to speak his language was extremely limited, he had also registered the fact that his American escort possessed other attractive attributes. But now he schooled his features to show none of this. He must give this woman all due respect.

Mr. Zurtin stood next to a trolley, valiantly guarding the luggage upon it. In Russian the old man said, "I have watched over these for you, though my relatives have come for me."

"I am in your debt, Mr. Zurtin," Viktor replied in the same language, with a slight bow of his head. He picked up the cap to his uniform, which he had tossed on top of his luggage. He had felt naked without it.

"My daughter and her husband took my things to their car and will expect me on the curb momentarily. Did you catch the thief?" Zurtin asked.

"He escaped."

The elderly man glanced at Natalia. "Why is she carrying your case?"

"She wanted to. Women are as independent here as they are at home."

Zurtin nodded and looked over at the Captain. By the expression on her face, Viktor knew she did not like being left out of the conversation.

"Forgive me, Captain Wentworth," he said in English. "Where are my manners? This is Mr. Zurtin, the gentleman from the airplane of whom I spoke."

She produced a smile for the older man and managed to get out the words *"Ochin' priyatna,"* or "pleased to meet you." Mr. Zurtin beamed at her, clearly pleased by her efforts to speak his language.

"She could be Russian in no time at all," he concluded in his mother tongue. "You must keep this pretty one for yourself, Colonel."

His comment was so unexpected, Viktor actually felt his cheeks grow hot. The thought of "keeping" her for the few weeks he would be in her country—as if she would let him— was very appealing. But he did not want to think such things. Not when he had so many obligations. Later, perhaps he would allow himself to dream…

No, he must remain focused. Think only of the secret mission he must accomplish in the next few weeks. The one he had planned so carefully.

He bade farewell to Mr. Zurtin, who ambled off to find his

daughter, and then Viktor and Natalia pulled his luggage trolley to the glass doors.

"I will wait by the exit as you go for your car."

She nodded. "It might take me a little while to get back."

He watched her don the black beret that had been tucked inside the outer pocket of the small black purse she carried. It must be necessary for her to wear headgear outside when in uniform, just as it was in the Russian military. She looked very well turned out in her dark green skirt and jacket and the beret atop her golden hair.

"My car is red. Stand close to the door so I can see you through the glass. Okay?"

"Okay," he agreed, trying out the word for the first time outside of a classroom. All he wanted now was to get settled into his rooms in time to phone the elderly Russian couple he'd made contact with prior to his departure from St. Petersburg. They had agreed to help him with Alexander, whom he still thought of by the childhood name, Sasha. And he needed to let Dr. Brennan know he had arrived and that Sasha would be coming soon. Appointments had to be confirmed. Plans had to be finalized. If anything went wrong, he would be at the mercy of his American colleagues, who might not understand this course he had been forced to take.

But nothing would go wrong, he told himself as he spotted Natalia's car edging to the curb. He had planned everything too carefully, sacrificing every waking hour to developing his strategy. He could not let anything stop him from accomplishing what he had to do.

Shaking himself out of his morbid reverie, Viktor fitted all of the pieces of luggage into Natalia's little car. "Where are we going?" he asked, once they were on their way.

"There's a room waiting for you at the BOQ at Fort Drake. That's bachelor officers' quarters. You'll be staying there as a guest of Uncle Sam for the duration of your time here."

"BOQ," he repeated, thinking that this did not sound like anything he had been told to expect when he had planned this trip. He had imagined a flat or hotel suite. "What is it like, this BOQ?"

She shrugged. "Pretty much like an upscale dormitory."

Viktor immediately pictured what that would mean in his own country and fought back a scowl. It would be bad form to show distaste for what these Americans had very kindly offered him. "It is open for guests? I am free to come and go whenever I like?"

She glanced at him, her brow knit. "There are some restrictions. Not many. It depends on the guests, I suppose." He noticed color rising to her cheeks and he wondered what sort of guests she imagined he might want. "There are rooms where you can entertain, I think." He could tell she wanted to ask him more. He decided against volunteering any information at this early stage.

Although he had planned everything to the last detail, he did not forget that—as the saying went—a good strategist never poisons the well from which he might later need to drink. Captain Natalia Wentworth might turn out to be just such a well if anything went wrong. If he had to involve her—and he hoped he would not be forced to—he would need to gain her trust first.

Unfortunately, he did not have an unlimited number of hours. His son, Sasha, would arrive in two days. And the living accommodations were putting a twist in the program already. He did not like such surprises. When it came to his plans for his son, he could not afford unexpected problems.

Viktor had hoped to keep the boy with him until Sasha was admitted into the American hospital. But quarters on a military base would not allow him to keep the boy hidden, which was imperative if Viktor's activities were to remain a secret from the Americans. And they must remain secret from the Russian Army as well. His superiors would not appreciate the reasons for the desperate measures Viktor had been driven to take. So Sasha could not stay with him in the BOQ.

Instead, he would have to impose upon the elderly immigrants, Mr. and Mrs. Petrov, for more than daytime child care. He would have to ask them to let Sasha live in their home for a while. He knew they would agree, though there would surely be an additional fee which would be difficult to manage. Worse than the financial problem was the thought of being separated from his son any more than he already had been. The idea made Viktor's heart ache so much that his hand slipped to his chest as if the gesture could somehow ease the pain. When his palm came to rest on the hard coldness of the medals he wore on his uniform, he remembered that he must be stronger than this. Weakness of spirit would not see him through this very special mission.

"When will I begin work?" he asked.

"Well, you have a few days to settle in and sign papers. You'll need a Pentagon badge, for one thing." She showed him hers which hung from a dog-tag chain around her neck. It was a terrible picture of her. "You have to wear it so people can see it when you're inside the building, but it's supposed to be out of sight when you're in public." She tucked it back beneath her jacket.

He looked at Natalia, and wondered if she had children of her own. If she did, she might be better able to comprehend his quest on Sasha's behalf.

"It will be a...mmm...difficult surprise for people to see me in my uniform and also wearing that badge," he commented. She smiled and then changed lanes, fitting her car expertly between two others in a line of tight traffic. "When I was a child, I would never have thought this exchange of knowledge would be possible between our countries."

He was rewarded for his attempt at conversation by a friendly glance from his escort. "It is amazing how allegiances change," she said as she eased the car to the right and onto an exit ramp. "So we have a few days to get you in-processed and settled. On Monday we can take a tour of the Pentagon and I'll introduce you to the people you'll work with."

Monday night, he would need to pick up his son at the airport.

"I can show you around the city in the meantime, if you like," she offered.

"That is kind of you," he said. It would be no hardship to tour the city with the beautiful Captain Wentworth.

"This is Fort Drake," she announced moments later as they made a turn into a drive that led through an open wrought-iron gate. "The Quartermaster's School is here. You might be able to take a class or two during your time in America. And it's close to the Pentagon."

Two military police officers stood watch at a small guardhouse on a median between the entry and exit drives. Viktor looked on with interest as the MPs examined Natalia's credentials, eyed him suspiciously for a moment, then waved the car through. Past the guard house, the vista of the fort came into view. It was very pleasing to look upon. The grounds were meticulously groomed, flowers bloomed in neat rows of color, hedges were trimmed to perfection along a side road. It contrasted severely with the military bases at home where flowers and hedges would be considered unnecessary. This place seemed more like a dacha than a military installation.

"It is quite…" He searched for a word. *"Krasivy,"* he said. Then his jet-fatigued mind remembered the word in English. "Beautiful, yes?"

"Yes, the Army really takes good care of its posts. You should see the golf course."

Golf was not something he had ever had time for. Running was more to his liking. Glancing sideways at Natalia's athletic legs—which, he suddenly realized, he could see a very nice length of now that her skirt had ridden up a bit during their drive—he wondered if she was a runner, too.

She parked the car outside an old but perfectly restored brick building with many trees lining the walkway in front of it. "We'll get you your room assignment and stow your gear," she said as she pushed her car door closed, placed her beret on her head and looked at her watch. "The office where we have to get your identification card is closed now, so we'll need to do that Monday morning."

She led him toward the building, past a young man in a camouflage uniform working his way across the grassy expanse with a rake. The man saluted, and both he and Natalia returned the salute automatically. Although he had done it without thought, Viktor decided he should carry on this way from now on. Waiting to be saluted and then returning it in the manner of an American officer might help the local soldiers understand that he outranked them, despite the unfamiliar uniform. It would not do to allow a breakdown of respect, even in this Army that was not his own.

"After we bring your things inside, I'll take you to the Officer's Club and get you something to eat. You're tired, I know, but you'll need to eat before calling it a day." These kind words from Captain Wentworth reminded Viktor of how insidiously his weariness had numbed his ability to remain alert. It had been a very long trip. He was hungry and he was tired. Perhaps a stiff cup of tea—or coffee, as he had been told Americans preferred—would improve his condition. Surely a good night's sleep would repair his state of mind.

With military efficiency, Captain Wentworth spoke to the young soldier who manned the front desk until she had secured a key to one of the rooms. Viktor signed his name in the register, certain that the Cyrillic script would be unrecognizable to any American who might try to decipher it. Then he followed her up some stairs—there appeared to be no elevator—and along a corridor until she came to a stop and held out the key to him.

He took it from her, opened the door and saw a neat, well-appointed room. Quite nice and nothing at all like the military dormitories in his own country. He nodded his approval and stepped farther into the space. He saw a large bed and a chest of drawers. There was a desk with a clock and telephone upon it. He reminded himself that he must call both the Petrovs and Dr. Brennan first thing in the morning. He noticed the glass doors leading to a small balcony with a chair and table for enjoying the spring weather.

"Will you be comfortable here?" asked Natalia from behind him.

He turned and said, "Yes." Then his mind tumbled over the sight of her, standing next to the bed, examining it critically.

And, to his embarrassment, his body immediately began to react, joining his mind as both considered the possibilities that this picture of a beautiful woman and a bed presented.

She glanced up suddenly and caught him staring at her. A nearly forgotten primal tension quivered through him, and he did not seem to be able to drop his gaze. She stared back at him as her cheeks went slightly pink, and he thought how pleasant it was to see her blush because of him. It was particularly pleasing to see an officer in the United States Army blushing because he looked at her in this way.

As if realizing a vulnerability, Captain Wentworth retreated a few steps. Employing a strategy Viktor thought might be well practiced, she pushed aside one flap of her uniform jacket and plucked a pager from the waist of her skirt. "Oh, look at that," she said with admirable sincerity. "I need to make a call. I'll just go—"

"Use the telephone here," he offered before she could say that she would go back down to the front desk. "I will collect my luggage. It requires several trips, so privacy is yours."

"Um, *spasiba*," she said, remembering the Russian word for "thank you."

Nodding, he slipped past her, careful not to touch her. All the way to the car and back again, he reminded himself that he was not to touch her at any time. Because once he did—assuming she would ever allow him to—he would become seriously distracted. Besides, he needed to keep the relationship pleasant and professional in case his plans for Sasha went awry. He and his son might be forced to request her assistance.

He knew he must avoid relying upon her, no matter how good it would be to have help. He had to work alone, given the importance of keeping Sasha's presence here a secret from the Russian military. And even if Natalia turned out to be sympathetic to his cause, he hoped not to put her in any compromising position with her own superiors.

Setting the first group of bags outside his door, he let out a frustrated breath and contemplated how difficult the next few weeks were likely to be. Then he went down again to fetch the rest of his things. This time the soldier manning the front desk was no longer on the phone.

"Can I help you, sir? To carry your suitcases, I mean." The young man appeared eager to be of service, so Viktor accepted his assistance even though it would have been nothing to bring the remaining luggage upstairs by himself.

"I'm Specialist Murdock. I work the front desk most nights. You're the one from Russia, is that right, sir?"

"Yes. I am here to study the movement of supplies." Best to remind people of his official purpose so as to deflect attention from the other activities in which he would be engaging while in America.

"That is excellent, sir. It's great that you're here and that our countries can exchange knowledge nowadays." They reached the door to Viktor's room. Murdock put down his load next to the other bags and surveyed the large collection. "You need help with any of this, sir? I can send someone up to help you unpack."

"No, thank you. I will manage."

Murdock shifted uneasily. Then he spoke in a rush. "I just want you to know, sir, that me and Sergeant Citallio—he mans the desk during the weekdays—we both want you to know that we are one hundred percent behind you for the duration, no matter what some others might say about Russians and such." He paused as if waiting for some sort of acknowledgment of this heartfelt pledge, but Viktor did not know how to respond.

"The Sergeant asked me to tell you that if there is even the slightest hint of trouble, you should let one of us know right away so we can set things right. You are not to be bothered by anyone who might have a memory that's a mite too long. We want your stay here to be incident-free...." He trailed off as if he was not certain how much more he should say.

But Viktor thought Murdock had said quite enough. Suddenly, he felt the danger of allowing his usually sharp military wariness to be lulled by jet fatigue and the kindness of his escort. He could not afford to forget even for an instant that he was in a foreign country where some people might resent his presence for any number of reasons. Viktor was alone in the land of his former enemies. He would forget that truth at his own peril—and his son's.

"All right, then. You have a good evening, sir." The young man snapped to attention briefly, then turned sharply on his heel and retreated down the hall.

Tension made Viktor grind his teeth until he remembered he was trying to break the habit. He took a deep breath, forcing his body to unwind. Eyeing the luggage at his feet, he wondered if he had given Natalia enough time to complete her call. He listened at the door a moment to learn whether she was still in conversation. Then, against his better judgment, he kept listening when her words piqued his curiosity.

"Frank, I already explained why I can't have dinner with you tonight," she said in a peeved tone. "I'm working. I can't just leave the man to his own devices his first day in-country. His embassy doesn't normally pay attention to people of his rank and they said they didn't have the manpower, anyway. So it's up to me."

There was a pause during which Natalia undoubtedly listened to Frank. Viktor gleaned one important fact from her conversation—there was a man in Natalia's life.

Loath to eavesdrop, Viktor raised his hand to knock on the door. Then he heard her voice again and stayed his hand another moment.

"This may not be the important kind of assignment I'm used to, but I will give it my best regardless. Even a lowly Russian colonel, as you called him, doesn't deserve to be abandoned a few hours after setting foot on American soil." There was a slight pause, then she said, "What could possibly be so important about you having dinner with me, anyway? You see me all the time."

A husband or a lover, Viktor concluded. He was honest enough to acknowledge the spasm of disappointment that flashed through him. He consoled himself that because of Frank, it would be easier to keep his mind off Captain Wentworth.

Natalia's side of the telephone conversation devolved into single-word responses. Viktor knocked on the door and opened it. As she concluded her call, he slid his bags inside the room.

"We should go eat." She spoke as if she were biting off the pin of a grenade. Clearly, Captain Wentworth was primed for battle. Frank had obviously set her on edge, and Viktor felt a twinge of exultation. At the same time, he reminded himself that he was not in a contest against Frank. He must fight the primitive urge to compete with a man he did not know over a woman he had just met.

This is what comes of being too busy for women, he thought ruefully. The years had slipped away so rapidly, he had not had time for feminine companionship. Until now. Looking at her, even more vibrant and interesting when she was flashing with anger, he could understand perfectly why the primal juices were flowing through his veins.

So he had best not look at her too much, he concluded. "Yes, it would be good to eat." And once he had fed himself, he would sleep off his jet fatigue and be better prepared in the morning to cope with everything. He needed to be functioning at his best.

His twelve-year-old son's life depended on it.

CHAPTER TWO

DINNER WAS A DISASTER.

The minute Natalie walked into the dining room with Viktor, every eye turned toward them. This military installation did not commonly have foreign visitors, especially visitors wearing be-ribboned Russian military uniforms. She had only chosen Fort Drake because of the Quartermaster School. And because it was closer to her own apartment in case Viktor needed something. But those reasons suddenly didn't seem very important as they stood there with the attention of so many people trained upon them. This sort of unpleasantness was exactly what she, as a protocol officer, was supposed to prevent. It was her job to be sure that things went smoothly and that everyone, even her Russian Colonel, felt at ease. Instead, the American officers and their guests were staring blatantly, and she sensed that Viktor was bristling with tension, though he hid it well beneath a stoic exterior.

Hoping to recapture some semblance of control over the situation, Natalie glanced around the large room, searching for a familiar face. At last, her gaze fell upon a full colonel sitting with his wife and some others. "There's someone I should introduce you to," she told Viktor. She led the way to the table with the people she'd marked.

Smiling, she put out her hand as the senior officer stood. "Colonel Maglin, I'm Natalie Wentworth from the Pentagon protocol office. We spoke on the phone the other day."

"Yes, I remember." He sounded wary and shook her hand with little enthusiasm, probably unhappy to have his meal interrupted.

"I don't want to interfere with your dinner, sir, but I thought you'd want to meet Colonel Baturnov, who has just arrived from Russia. He'll be living on post here while he studies supply movement techniques at the Pentagon."

Colonel Maglin turned his cool gaze to Baturnov. "Welcome," he said without warmth as they shook hands.

Viktor gave a quick nod. "Thank you." There was no use of the word *sir* from either man.

She squared her shoulders in front of Maglin. "We'll let you get back to your meal, sir." She nodded cordially to the others seated at his table, turned on her heel and headed directly back toward the hostess waiting to show them to their own seats. She didn't look back to see if the Russian followed. Yes, there was the flash of olive-green with red trim in her peripheral vision. He'd taken his cue from her and was close behind her.

As they made their way to the indicated table, Natalie noticed that most of the others in the room had gone back to their food as soon as she'd concluded her brief exchange with Maglin. That was what she'd hoped would happen and precisely why she'd picked the highest-ranking officer in the room to approach. His handshake, tepid as it was, made the foreign officer acceptable to the others.

"You won't get this kind of reaction at the Pentagon, where everyone is more used to seeing foreign uniforms. They don't get too many Russians here."

He nodded. "Escorting me, it is not the usual assignment for you?"

Natalie looked up from her menu and wondered how he could possibly know that. His perceptiveness made her even more edgy. And there was that quirky little word again. She would probably be doomed to think of herself as the Russian's "escort" for the duration. "It's true I'm used to different assignments. But this one is a nice change. And it gives me a chance to brush up on my Russian." She ventured a smile, hoping it didn't look as forced as it felt.

He did not smile back, but simply gazed at her with those knowing eyes. She let her smile slip away and found herself looking back at him without pretense. It seemed natural, for some reason. Unlike Frank, the Colonel didn't seem to expect her to be anything but the person she was.

Or at least that's how it seemed in those long moments when their gazes locked before the waitress arrived. As they gave their orders—the Russian sticking to basic steak and potatoes—Natalie remembered the other long look that had given her pause. She'd been examining the bed in his room, wondering if it would be adequate for a man of Baturnov's size, when she'd found him staring at her. The hungry and dangerous glint to his eyes had spoken of unrequited needs that Natalie recognized. She'd grown used to living with such unfulfilled feelings herself. How long had it been since she'd been out with a man? She couldn't count Frank because it seemed she'd known him forever. And their relationship had only recently managed to stumble beyond a fraternal friendship into something like courtship. Natalie wasn't certain how she felt about that change.

"What made you join the military, Natalia?" Colonel Baturnov asked.

"My father was a career officer, so I pretty much grew up with the Army. My mother despairs, but I never doubted that I wanted to serve my country."

"And your father, he is still in the military?"

She shook her head, surprised that talking about him after all these years could still give her a pang of sorrow. "He died years ago."

Viktor's left eyebrow dipped, a thing she'd noticed he did when he assimilated new and important information. "I'm sorry."

"It was a long time ago," she said. Then she did what any good protocol officer would do and turned the conversation away from herself and onto him. "And what made you decide to be an officer, sir?"

His eyes glinted with something like determination as he gave her another one of those penetrating stares. "I hoped we agreed to be done with 'sir' between us, Natalia. Will you not call me Viktor?"

She was flustered at the notion of calling him by his first name. It seemed very intimate. Yet, she'd already done it once at the airport and could think of no reason not to continue. "Yes, of course. Perhaps it will be easier tomorrow when we're in civilian clothes." She smiled at him and it felt more genuine this time. "It's just habit to call a man with so many ribbons and medals 'sir' at all times. My father instilled it into me from just about the moment I said my first words." Oops. How had she ended up talking about herself again? "So what about you, Viktor?"

The waitress arrived with their salads and he leaned back in his chair to give her room to set the dish before him. Natalie wondered if he would use the interruption to once again avoid speaking of himself.

But he surprised her again.

"I joined because I had a wife to support," he said perfunctorily.

"Oh." That one simple word seemed so heavily laced with dashed hopes that Natalie felt her cheeks flame. Good heavens! It wasn't as if she had any business caring one way or the other about the marital status of this man! "Surely there were other things you could have chosen to do that were..."

She stopped herself midsentence because she had no idea how she could possibly end it in any polite way. She had been about to say "less violent," but had realized that the term might sound insulting to his masculinity, his military and his country—as if his nation were overly aggressive. The only other ending she could think of was "better paying," but that was equally insulting.

Viktor saved her from embarrassment. "How do you say it here? It seemed like a good idea at the time. I was particularly pleased with being away from home for training and military exercises much of the time. In my youth, I thought this would provide me with the perfect balance between family and freedom," he said with a rueful grin.

She was amused, as he clearly meant her to be. She couldn't

resist asking the next obvious question. "And what do you think now, in your maturity?"

With his smile, his face lost some of its sternness and weariness. "I think it is foolish to believe a man can have both a family and the life of a bachelor at the same time. A marriage is doomed to failure under such conditions."

She longed to ask if his own marriage had failed. But she couldn't do that. It was far too personal. And what difference would it make? Married or not, he would be here for such a short time. So she nodded her acceptance of this bit of wisdom and turned to another subject she burned to know more about. "You said you've brought medicine for a relative of yours. Does he live here in the U.S.? May I help you get it to him?"

Viktor didn't answer immediately, and she began to wonder if he would respond at all. "You may be able to help me. I will need to make some phone calls first. I am not certain how I will do this."

"Oh. Yes, of course."

"I will know more tomorrow," he assured her as if he didn't want her to believe he was purposefully being evasive.

As she searched for another safe topic of conversation, she noticed a gray-haired man in civilian clothes who seemed to glance their way from across the room a few too many times. What was his problem? she wanted to know. She tried to look away, but he was hard to ignore. Finally he came to stand beside their table.

"Saw the uniform from over there." The man indicated the table where a woman still sat, looking both worried and mortified.

Viktor looked up and gave the older man that formal smile he'd bestowed upon Natalie when they'd first met. With grace befitting a prince, and with something she thought might be a hair-trigger wariness, the Colonel stood and identified himself politely.

"I'm Brigadier General Roscoe P. Schwinn, U.S. Army retired," said the old man with a grin. "Wanted you to know that I know who you are, where you're from and what you're up to.

I'll be watching your every move." The retiree smiled so congenially he might have succeeded in distracting Natalie from the fact that he'd just delivered a challenge as effectively as slapping a gauntlet across Viktor's face. But she didn't miss the draining of color from Viktor's cheeks, the steely glint of his eyes and the sudden chill of the smile he kept firmly in place.

"You are courageous to alert me to this, General Schwinn. I will remember it well."

If Natalie had been on the receiving end of Viktor's calmly delivered comment, she would have been quaking. The Russian was formidable to behold. His spine was very straight, his expression impenetrable, his entire being coiled with a barely contained tension. But General Schwinn was either obtuse or self-destructive, because he took no heed of the warning.

"I won't tolerate any spying or other shenanigans on my post," Schwinn asserted with that same incongruous smile.

"General Schwinn is the former commander here," she told Viktor, emphasizing "former." She remembered hearing about the General and that he was suffering from some kind of senile dementia.

Viktor must have come to an understanding of the situation. She detected a minute easing of his taut muscles. He nodded slightly to the older man. "There will be none from me, sir," he said, clearly attempting to diffuse the awkward moment.

Colonel Maglin sauntered toward them then. He put his hand on the General's shoulder. "How are you today, Ros?" he asked congenially. "Good to see you back on post after your hospital stay. Did they treat you right over there?"

The General allowed himself to be distracted and led back to his own table. Colonel Maglin shot Natalie a look over his shoulder that confirmed her doubts about Schwinn's mental stability. As Viktor took his seat again, she took a stab at apologizing. "I'm sorry for that. I recognized his name and remembered hearing about his decline. As you can see..."

Viktor held up his hand to stop her. "I understood that he was not in full command of himself. No need to explain. He is old, as we all will be one day."

She nodded, grateful for his understanding. "It must be hard on his wife." She glanced in the direction of the beleaguered spouse and saw her gently take her husband's hand.

Viktor did not respond, but concentrated instead on consuming the entrée, which had been set before him during the unpleasant exchange. For once, Natalie felt no compulsion to make small talk. It didn't seem necessary. Somehow this man made it amazingly simple for her to give up trying to be the perfect hostess. It was a relief to let go of that particular strain and simply be herself.

But the few moments of relaxation turned out to be the highlight of the evening. General Schwinn continued to stare at them, the food was mediocre, and the coffee was bitter. Viktor was clearly preoccupied. By the time the bill arrived, she was more than ready to go.

"I will be receiving a daily allowance for meals while I am here. Your government and mine worked this out between them. I was told to retain all receipts. Is this the first of them?" He held up one of the two cash register tickets the waitress had brought.

"Yes, that's right. I know it complicates things, but we each have to pay for our own food so we don't confuse the travel office when it comes time for them to pay you your per diem." His brow knit slightly. "That's the term for the daily food allowance the military will pay while you're here."

He smiled. "Yes, I understand. Thank you. Is it proper for me to leave an additional amount for the serving woman?" He pulled his wallet out of a back pocket and looked exactly like an ordinary American male as he did so—at least until he took out colorful bills that had no likeness to American money at all.

"Uh-oh. We'll have to get you to a bank in the morning."

He held up a finger in the universal sign for "wait one minute" and reached into an inside pocket of his uniform jacket. From there, he pulled out some neatly folded U.S. currency. "I remembered to exchange money before departure from *Sankt Pitirburk*."

She watched him set out enough money to cover his meal

and a tip. Natalie doubted she could have figured out the precise amount of rubles to set out at a table in St. Petersburg—or *Sankt Pitirburk,* as he'd called it. Obviously Viktor had taken the time to learn some basics about living in America before he'd left his homeland. That would make her role easier and might even shorten the time she would be required to spend with him. Somehow that thought cheered her less than she would have expected.

Walking back to the BOQ, Natalie found herself thinking about General Schwinn and wondering if he would cause trouble for Viktor.

As if he had plucked the thoughts right out of her mind, he said in solemn tones, "I will deal with the General if necessary." He came to a stop in front of the building.

She nodded her head, vowing not to lose sleep over the General. "I thought I could show you around the city a bit tomorrow. Would you like that or do you plan to spend time with those relatives you mentioned?"

He smiled that warm, open smile of his—the one that contrasted dramatically with the formal one he could produce at will. "I would very much enjoy touring the city with you, Natalia. But what of you? Do you not have people who will expect you on a Sunday?"

She thought of Frank and dropped her gaze to the sidewalk. "No, I set aside tomorrow for you in case you needed—"

"An escort," he supplied helpfully when she hesitated. She nodded, still unable to meet his eyes. "Are you sure?" he asked gently.

"I'm sure. Good night, sir." She stepped back a pace and saluted, which seemed to startle him. By the glow of the streetlight, she saw amusement suddenly spark to life in his eyes as he returned the gesture. She stepped away, down the walk, across the curb, over to her car. At last, she was able to get away and be alone. She'd longed for that ever since the unnerving experience of meeting Captain DiSanto in the rest room at the airport. But now that she was by herself, she realized she was glad she'd be with Viktor tomorrow. It had been a long while since she'd spent time with a nice man other than Frank.

As if conjured from her thoughts, Major Frank Lezinski was waiting for her when she arrived at her own apartment a while later. He had used the spare key she'd given him and had made himself at home.

"What are you doing here?" She tried to sound cheerful, but she couldn't forget the way he'd reacted on the phone over her having dinner with Viktor. Frank had no reason to behave with jealousy. He had no way of knowing that Viktor was handsome and charming and intriguingly exotic. And even if he had known, Frank had no claim on her.

"I'm waiting for you," he said as he stood up from the easy chair he'd made himself comfortable in. "You're the one who gave me the key to your apartment. I thought I was welcome here." It sounded as though he might be on the verge of a little sulk, like the ones he sometimes slid into when she wanted to go out for a movie and pizza with her friend Marie.

She sighed. The key had been so that he could water her plants on the many occasions she went traveling for the government. But she couldn't bring herself to say that to him. He'd been a good friend to her. "Of course you're welcome here," she said.

She tossed her car keys and beret onto the table by the door and went to kiss him on the cheek. All at once, his arms snaked around her waist and he drew her in for a real kiss. Natalie tensed but didn't pull away. This was not the first time he'd kissed her. He'd made it clear he was in love with her and wanted to move their relationship in a more intimate direction, but Natalie wasn't ready.

Still, there was a familiarity to him. They'd attended Officers' Candidate School together many years ago. Frank had gone on to serve a year in the Balkans and had been promoted quickly as a result of that tour of duty. They'd lost track of each other for a while after that. But two years ago they had both been transferred to the Pentagon, unexpectedly finding themselves in offices near each other. In the beginning, she'd been there for him as he'd mourned the disintegration of a love left behind at his previous station. After that, he'd been there for her when she'd needed furniture moved or work done on her car. He was as familiar to her as Viktor was foreign.

She eased away carefully, not wanting him to pout over her lack of attention. "Whew! I'm exhausted."

"We can sleep in tomorrow and catch up."

Uh-oh. His words implied he meant to stay. They also indicated he meant to spend tomorrow with her.

"Um, I'm working tomorrow. No sleeping in for me." As she said this, she made her way casually to the kitchen, resisting the urge to make a dash for it before he engaged her in a serious quarrel. She made it all the way to the refrigerator before she heard him speak.

"What was that? Did you say something?"

Irritation crept through Natalie. How was she supposed to make herself fall in love with a man who didn't listen to her? But she knew the answer before the question had finished forming. She wasn't supposed to *make* herself fall in love with anyone, regardless of her dreams of marriage and the ticking of her biological clock. She stifled a groan as she unbuttoned the outer jacket to her uniform and stripped it off. It wasn't fair of her to generalize—as if Frank *never* listened to her. He could be very attentive sometimes. But communications seemed a bit strained these days. Although she used to be able to be honest and straightforward with him, something about the recent change in their interactions made her think she should tread gently. She really couldn't afford to offend Frank, a superior officer with power to help her career if she needed him. It was all very confusing, she thought as she slung the jacket over the back of a kitchen chair and loosened the collar of her shirt, letting the black necktie dangle loosely from one side.

Then inspiration struck.

She moved to the archway between the kitchen and living room and leaned her shoulder against the doorjamb. "Hey, do you think I could be coming down with something?" She put her hand to her throat where she'd just unbuttoned her collar and rubbed back and forth. The truth was, her throat did feel a little tight, probably from trying to say all those Russian words in a vaguely competent accent. "Could I have caught strep or something? I mean, didn't Barb Dwyer have strep last week?"

That got his attention. He looked up and blinked a few times. The light from the television did an eerie dance over his handsome face. He stood up. "If you're feeling sick..."

He rubbed his palms against the front of his shirt as if they'd suddenly gone sweaty. Then he rallied, took on a resigned and stoic expression and squared his shoulders. "I can make you some tea or something. How about some Tylenol?" She was touched. Frank Lezinski hated illnesses of all kinds, especially when they might attach themselves to him. But he seemed prepared to valiantly overcome his idiosyncrasy in order to take care of her. Natalie's heart swelled with fondness. She only wished it could swell with love and...

She sighed, recognizing that she shouldn't allow herself to languish in the land of wishes. "You know, all I really want is to go to sleep." That much was true.

"Well, if you're sure...." he said.

"Yeah, I'm sure. I could sleep forever. But I have to work tomorrow."

He hesitated in the center of her small living room, not moving toward the door anymore. "Work? On a Sunday? Doing what?"

She looked up sharply, wishing she hadn't mentioned work again. Too late. "You know. I told you before. Colonel Baturnov's sponsor from Materiel Command had a family emergency and can't meet with him until next week. His embassy can't spare anyone to look after a mere Colonel. So I'm looking out for him for now."

"Colonel Bad-Enough should be able to take care of himself," he growled. Ever since he'd heard the name of her Russian assignment, he'd been distorting it that way. Frank thought it was particularly funny once he saw how much it annoyed her. For once, though, she had the sense not to react.

"Well, I'm sure he'll be fine after a few days, but I promised I'd show him around a little tomorrow."

Frank shook his head in disgust. "Why would you work so

hard over a colonel? It's not as if this is one of your usual assignments to some European prince or something. You're used to dealing with heads of state. I thought you and I could…'' He stopped himself midsentence, and Natalie thought it was a good sign that he resisted turning the issue into an argument about the two of them. ''You don't need to give this guy another minute of your time.''

''I wouldn't feel right leaving him on his own when he just got here.''

''I just wanted to spend a little time with you,'' he added quietly. ''It's supposed to be a great day. Maybe we could go see if there are still any cherry blossoms or drive out to Baltimore's Inner Harbor. I could take you out for a nice lunch. You know…''

Natalie *did* know what he meant. He wanted to go out on a romantic day-long date like two potential lovers. It was a lovely thought, but…

''You've always been there for me, Frank,'' she said in an effort to mollify him. ''And I've always been there for you. But we've never, ever interfered with each other's careers, right?'' She watched a slight deepening of color come to his cheeks and she wondered if she'd made him angry. She hadn't meant to sound so condescending, as if he'd somehow needed a reminder of the rules.

''Right,'' he agreed, with an edge to his voice. She *had* made him angry. She watched him pick up his keys from the table by the door and relief warred with sorrow in her heart. She hated to have him go when there was this unpleasantness between them.

''Make yourself some tea,'' he said. It sounded like a peace offering and she gave him a relieved smile. ''You know that always makes you feel better, no matter what.''

''Yeah.'' She gazed at him from her position across the room, suddenly remembering all the nice things he'd done for her in recent months.

He gave her a wave and went through the door, leaving her

to contemplate how her dear friend had turned into a man who wanted to kiss her on the mouth.

She sighed and glanced around her small apartment. He'd left his glass dripping on her table. The TV still murmured and its screen still glowed. There was an open bag of pretzels on the floor near where his feet had rested. But at least she was alone. Blessedly alone.

VIKTOR SAT BESIDE HER on the Metro as they made their way into the city the next morning. Taking the subway was nearly always easier than trying to find parking downtown.

"I wondered if you might like to hear whatever military band is playing today on the Capitol steps. I think there's a concert there every Sunday afternoon. Maybe we could go later."

"Your military musicians play for no reason?" He had that incredulous expression on his face again. The one he'd worn when she'd complained that their Metro station looked pretty shabby these days. He'd asked her to define *shabby,* as if he didn't know the proper meaning of that English word. But when she'd confirmed his understanding of the term, he'd chuckled and explained that *she* must not comprehend the definition of the word. She'd taken that to mean that the subways were worse where he came from.

"Well, the concerts aren't for no reason. They play for the people. You know, government for the people, by the people, and all that. The military is a part of our government by the people." He looked interested and bemused by her patriotic speech. "Anyway, they're really good and they draw quite a crowd. At least they used to back when I had the time to come into the city to listen to them."

He nodded as if he understood what she meant, but she could tell he didn't. His reaction made her decide that it was imperative that she expose him to the military band concerts.

Glancing sideways at her companion, she couldn't help but notice his physique, which she could see much better now that he wore civilian clothes. The polo shirt and jeans did an amazing job of softening his formerly stiff posture, although he still moved with the air of authority she'd noticed right off. Or maybe it had been the good night's sleep that had eased his severe disposition. The dark circles under his eyes were gone. He still seemed a little guarded and he watched everything around him—including her—very closely. But all in all, he appeared to be a new man. And he smelled good, too.

The Metro train eased away from another station and suddenly pulled into bright sunlight. After the tunnels, Natalie had to squint against the glare. "This next stop is Arlington Cemetery, where many of our soldiers are buried. We can stop there on our way back, if you're interested."

"I am interested." He said it with just the right amount of reverence to be respectful without being maudlin. He might not always get the right English words, but he seemed to be able to find just the right tone. Frank could be clever with words but sometimes overdid the sarcastic inflections.

The train ducked back inside a tunnel, plunging them into darkness once again. The sudden change brought her to her senses. Making comparisons between Viktor and Frank could not be healthy. She must stop it at once.

"What would you like to see first in the city?" she asked.

"The Air and Space Museum," he promptly replied, though with a bit more solemnity than she might have hoped for. He was supposed to be having a good time, after all.

"Always a favorite," she agreed, wondering what troubled him. It seemed as if something weighed on his mind. She silently vowed to do what she could to put him at ease about being in a new country and about his work here. "We'll start there and make our way along the Mall until we're tired."

After disembarking, they approached the long escalator. "We have the longest escalator in the world in my country," he boasted as he stepped on.

"Really," she said, noting that he seemed very tall when she stood so close to him, even though he wasn't much over six feet. "I always thought the escalator at the Rosslyn Metro station was the longest in the world."

"No," he said simply. He smiled fleetingly. As he turned his attention toward the top of the long, moving stairway, his eyes took on a faraway look again. He didn't seem able to relax.

"Here we are," she declared as they rose to ground level and then stepped out onto the grass of the Capitol Mall. "This is the heart and soul of America right here."

She watched as Viktor looked carefully, turning three hundred and sixty degrees, slowly taking in all that he could see from where he stood. She thought he might have even sniffed the air. She wouldn't have been surprised if he'd stomped the ground to satisfy himself of its firmness, much like a guy might kick the tires of a car he was considering. Watching him, she couldn't shake the feeling that Viktor had a secret. And Natalie dearly wanted to know what it was.

VIKTOR COULD NOT GET HIS MIND off the fact that he had not been able to reach Mr. and Mrs. Petrov by phone before leaving with Natalia this morning. He had called repeatedly, letting the phone ring numerous times. He could have enjoyed this day so much more if he had been able to settle the matter of Alexander's living situation. He had been trying all morning to shake off the edge of anxiety.

The wonders of America's capital city helped. And the fact that his escort had left her hair loose and wore khaki shorts and a white button-front blouse for their outing. One wayward thought had involved the sensual unfastening of one button at a time. Now he wondered which was worse—his morbid fears about where the Petrovs could be or his fantasies about Natalia.

Walking through the Air and Space Museum reminded him of both. There were children everywhere, making him think of his own son. And while viewing the Apollo-Soyuz mock-up, he realized how much like lovers the two vehicles appeared. They were entirely dissimilar and yet joined together, like a Russian man and an American woman making love. He shook his head at the direction of his thoughts and decided they should move away from this particular exhibit.

As he led the way, through the next bay of displays, she said, "It's cool the way that venture helped to bring our nations to-

gether. From Apollo-Soyuz to the space station…and beyond!"
She smiled as if she had made a joke, but he did not understand
it. "Haven't you seen the movie *Toy Story?* You know, 'to
infinity…and beyond!' It's what Buzz Lightyear says."

He looked at her, even more puzzled than before. He had seen
many American-made movies, but not *Toy Story.* "Nothing is
beyond infinity," he said.

"Um." Her smile faded, so he immediately regretted his
words. Perhaps there was some other meaning to the English
word *infinity.*

"It's from a kid's movie—it's a joke, really," she said. "I'll
just have to play the video for you sometime." To his relief,
her smile returned.

The mention of a kid's video reminded him of his own child
again. His thoughts drifted to wondering what Sasha was doing
right now. He wished he knew how his boy was faring at the
St. Petersburg home of his cousin. Had she given him his medication on time? Had she ensured he did not overdo his physical
activity? Was she insisting that he read or was she just letting
him idle away his time?

"I would be glad to watch this video with you, Natalia. At
the moment, however, I need to find a telephone. The people I
must contact were not home earlier this morning."

"Oh, certainly." She fished in the small purse she carried. "I
have a cell phone you can use."

He smiled his gratitude to her and gestured toward a path
leading out of the crowd so they could seek a quieter place. He
put his hand upon the small of her back to guide her and keep
from losing her. Once through the crowd, he found himself reluctant to remove his palm from the delicate curve of her spine.
In the brief moments of touching her, he had felt a firmness to
her flesh that he liked. But in truth, he suspected he simply
longed for human contact in these difficult times.

That admission served only to make him shake his head again
in disgust at his own weakness and to bring his thoughts back
to the concern he was trying hard not to dwell upon—where

could the Petrovs be? They should have been at home, expecting his call.

"Perhaps out on the steps would be best," Natalia suggested as she eyed the tiny lights on her cell phone. She led the way through the glass doors. Her blond hair shone brightly in the spring sunshine. It dazzled him for a moment and he did not see that she was offering him her telephone. When he finally took it from her hand, she stepped a few feet away, giving him privacy.

"Are you not concerned I might call someone in Russia?" he teased. He watched in fascination as she hiked herself up to sit on the low wall along the steps. The lean muscles of her thighs and calves flexed as she did so. She closed her eyes and turned her face up to the sun.

"I trust you," she said, without looking at him.

Ah, he certainly hoped so. But would she continue to trust him if she learned his secrets?

CHAPTER THREE

HE DIALED THE NUMBER to the Petrovs' home, a number he had memorized and could have punched in without looking at the keypad. As he listened to the endless ringing on the other end of the line, he fought back the panic gnawing at his stomach. He found himself grinding his teeth again. Where the hell had they gone? Even if they had been to church or to run errands, they would be home by now. The fact that they liked to stay at home had been one of the reasons Viktor had chosen them for his son.

"Not there?" Natalia asked. He opened his eyes to see her standing nearer to him, staring up into his face with a slightly wrinkled brow. Was she concerned for him? She should be. He and his son would be in terrible trouble if this part of his plan fell through.

"No, it seems they are not. I will try again in a few hours." He forced a smile for her, telling himself the Petrovs must have simply gone out for brief periods and he had called at the wrong moments. Or perhaps they were in their garden and could not hear the phone. He would try not to worry.

"Is there anything I can do?" she asked with concern in her voice.

"No. They will undoubtedly return home soon. Perhaps you would allow me to call again later."

"Sure." She put the phone away. "Do you want to go back inside?"

He nodded. "I want to see the model of the small ship that began it all." He spread his arms to encompass the entirety of the space museum.

"Yeah, we didn't go into the section with the Mercury capsules yet."

He let his arms fall to his sides as her comment both amused and deflated him. He eyed her askance and said, "I refer to Sputnik."

"Oh. Sorry." But she grinned at him. She had a wonderful smile.

They toured the rest of the Air and Space Museum, then walked to the Museum of Technology. On the way, he breathed in the clean air of spring and practiced relaxation techniques he had used during missions when he had needed to keep his mind off danger of the situation. In the center of the grassy expanse of what Natalia called the Mall, he stopped and looked first in one direction and then in the other.

"Your government building is grand and beautiful," he said, facing the domed Capitol building. "I have studied your two-sided way of making laws with a House and a Senate. It is based on ancient Rome and this has always interested me." Viktor glanced away from the view of the Capitol to find Natalia staring at him as if he were the tourist attraction.

"I've grown up with it all, so I've never given it much thought," she said. "I always find it interesting to see how people from other countries see my nation."

He thought for a moment about how he might sum up his impressions so far. "Your country is very clean, very wealthy, the people are very certain of their comforts." He turned again and looked at the spike of stone at the opposite end of the Mall. "And you have great humor!"

Natalia looked at the enormous obelisk, too. She blushed slightly. "I'm not certain anyone meant to be funny when building the Washington Monument."

"No?" He could not suppress a chuckle. "It is possible for you to build a large *huylo* in the middle of your city without meaning humor?"

"I do *not* want to know what that Russian word means," she said, but she was smiling broadly now, almost laughing.

He grinned and raised his eyebrows at her. "It is an important word. Are you certain I should not define?"

To his delight, she laughed out loud. "I'm certain. And maybe it really is funny to have a monument of that particular... um...shape and...uh...size," she said, sounding as if she might choke on her words, and this made Viktor want to laugh all the more. "It represents the 'father of our country,' after all."

This was too much for Viktor. Forgetting all of his worries for a moment, he let go of his restraint and burst into guffaws. "I had...not...heard this...before! Father of your country!" he managed to say between chortles. He wiped his eyes and tried to regain control, fearing he might offend her.

Then he noticed that Natalia was laughing hard, too. And blushing. She looked stunningly beautiful to him in that moment. Time seemed to slow and his vision compressed until he saw only Natalia, standing in the sunshine, her face beaming.

All at once, she seemed to notice him staring at her. Her jubilance faded but was replaced by an amused expression that seemed to say she knew what he was thinking and did not find his thoughts offensive. This woman made him feel very young at times. It was not a bad feeling.

"Forgive me, please," he said, regaining control of his humor if not his libido. With a wave of his hand, he indicated the monument that he had found hilarious. "I should not have used that particular Russian word in your presence."

She shrugged. "I'm sure I've heard worse. I'm in the Army, after all."

They began to walk toward the technology museum again. "Do you like what you do?" he asked, genuinely interested.

"Oh, yes! It's fascinating to meet so many different kinds of people. And I get to arrange important meetings and huge conferences and formal dinners and..." She stopped herself and glanced at him out of the corner of her eye. "It's fun. And you?"

"I have done many things for the Army. My current work is interesting because it is different. And I am not away from home as much."

She did not say anything to that and they walked on to the technology building.

The displays at the museum kept Viktor's mind busy. He did

not want to dwell on how much he had enjoyed laughing with Natalia any more than he wanted to think about the absence of the Petrovs. He could not remember the last time he had laughed out loud. Probably before Sasha's condition had begun to deteriorate. It felt good to be playful again. Soon, when his son was well, he would insist on laughing with him every day.

"So, do you have kids?" Natalia asked when they were sharing sandwiches and colas in the sunny museum cafeteria.

Viktor nearly choked on the bite he had just taken. It was as if she had gone inside his head and discerned his thoughts. *"Mmm, da. U menya est' syn,"* he said, forgetting to speak English. He shook his head and repeated, "I mean, I have a son."

She nodded but looked a little sad. Perhaps she wondered how he managed being separated from his child. He wondered the same thing, especially at night, when he longed to be able to check on Sasha, to place a palm gently against his chest to feel the beating of his heart.

"Where do he and his mother live while you're traveling for the military?" she asked, looking pointedly at her sandwich.

"Alexander and I currently live in Yaroslavl, northeast of Moskva on the Volga River. His mother is…mmm…*myortvy*… gone."

"Myortvy," she repeated, as if the words was unfamiliar to her. "I'm very sorry." Her eyes darted away again. Her irises were intensely blue and she had delicate, arching brows that made her appear innocent. But there was an intelligence and burning intensity in those eyes that reminded him that she was a capable officer, not someone to be trifled with.

"It was a long time ago and she was not a happy person, always sickly. She is happy now, yes? And what of you, Natalia? Do you have a husband and children?"

She favored him with a brief glance and then shifted her eyes away again. "No, not yet. I'd like to someday. I have to find the right man first."

This was pleasing to his ears, though he knew he should not allow it to be. "A successful woman such as you will not have difficulty finding a husband when the time comes, I think."

She smiled and this time her attention settled on his face. "That's nice of you to say, but you'd be surprised how difficult it can be." She finished her sandwich and then suggested they head over to the Museum of Natural History.

Outside, Viktor stopped at a vendor who had clothing, hats and sunglasses laid out for sale. He eyed the selection with interest. The shirts were each emblazoned with American slogans or captioned pictures.

Natalia came to stand beside him. "Would you like to buy something? For your son, perhaps?" She picked up a shirt with a photograph of a youthful blond man in solid black attire who stood in a warrior's pose, holding a light saber. The caption read Anakin Skywalker—Star Wars—Episode II. "How old did you say he was?"

"Twelve years old." As he said it, he silently added to himself that in some ways Sasha was many times older than that. The only sport he could play was chess, the only activities he could engage in were sedentary. In this way, he was like an old man.

She scanned the stack of red-and-yellow shirts with Washington Redskins written across the chests. "How about football? Does he like that?"

Viktor smiled. "We do not play American football in Russia. But he might enjoy having such a shirt." He caught the vendor's eye. "The price of this?"

"It's a steal, my man, an' jus' f' you, three f' twenty." Viktor tried to puzzle out the meaning of this statement, but then Natalia stepped forward.

She leaned over the display and began sorting through the Redskins shirts. His gaze immediately went to the curve of her backside and the taut length of thigh below. "Twelve years old?" she asked. "Does that make him a small adult size?" She held one up so that it unfolded for his inspection.

The shirt would probably fit a normal child of his son's age. However, Sasha was not a normal child. This shirt would be far too large for him. Viktor's face must have betrayed his feelings, for Natalia grew very serious and let the shirt fall to the table again.

"What's wrong?" she asked as she leaned forward and almost rested her palm against the center of his chest. She stopped herself just before she made contact.

Viktor thought that was for the best. He knew her touch would be so soothing. He thought he might not be able to bear it without some unmanly display of emotion. Yet he had difficulty preventing himself from stepping forward against her palm. Pathetic. To his relief, she took the chance away from him when she slowly pulled back, as if she had become aware of the sudden intimacy between them.

He should give her an answer, he supposed. This was a perfect opportunity to see which way she would lean, but he decided he should not reveal too much just yet. "Forgive me," he said as he arranged his features into what he knew to be an unreadable expression. "It is nothing. He wears a smaller shirt. This reminds me that my son has been sick. I did not want to leave him in Russia but could not avoid it."

"Oh" was all that she said. Her tone conveyed that she understood how much he missed his son, how much he worried about him. He found comfort in her sympathy. How long had it been since someone had cared about him and his child?

"It is the nature of the military life, yes?"

Natalie nodded and led the way to the history museum. Her somber mood matched his own. But after a while, he was able to gain some semblance of control while they quietly strolled through the echoing corridors of historic displays. He promised himself that he would bring Sasha to this place when he was well. His boy was a history buff and this was the sort of activity he would enjoy. Perhaps he would be able to walk through the building without a wheelchair.

"What do you say we go see if we can find that military band concert?" Natalia suggested after she had shown him the Hope diamond in its thick glass case. "I'm ready to get off my feet for a while."

It was a perfect afternoon to be outside. As promised, the band played for free to a large crowd, and the music was very good. It was the Marine Corps Jazz Ensemble playing this time, Natalia reported. Sitting on the grass beside her, Viktor had the urge to sidle closer, but of course, he did not. This was not a woman he had asked out on a date, no matter how much it felt like one.

The band played its last tune. When it was over, they applauded with the others and then brushed themselves off. There was a bit of grass on Natalia's backside, but he only *thought* about brushing it off for her.

"We should head back," she said. "If we go now, we'll have just enough time to stop at Arlington Cemetery on the way."

He nodded, sorry that their day together was coming to a close. He had found moments of peace and joy with her. Those were rare commodities in his life these days.

This time, their Metro ride did not include much conversation. Viktor simply had no heart for idle chatter, even with the lovely Natalia. Every passing minute seemed to be weightier than the last, and he longed for the moment when he could call Mr. and Mrs. Petrov again and finally settle his plans with them. When the train pulled alongside the platform at the cemetery, Viktor eagerly led the way out.

As they walked toward the white grave stones, he asked, "May I use your telephone again? Perhaps now I will reach the people with whom I must speak." He looked at his watch, reassuring himself that it had been hours. The elderly couple would be home by now.

"Of course," she said. She reached into her purse, plucked out the phone and scowled at it. "It's been on all day. I hope the battery lasts."

He flipped it open and punched in the numbers. He listened to the ringing with his heart hammering. Then suddenly, there was a woman's voice on the other end of the connection.

"Allo?" she said, sounding older than she had during previous conversations. But relief flooded through him when he heard it.

"Mrs. Petrova, this is Viktor Baturnov," he said in Russian. "I want to confirm our arrangements."

"*Okh!*" she said. That one syllable conveyed a great deal of dismay. "*Oy, okh!*" she added, making his heart beat rapidly again.

"Is something wrong, ma'am?"

"Oh, my. Dear, dear *Polkovnik* Baturnov. I do not know how to tell you..."

Now Viktor's entire body felt hot and sweaty. "Go ahead," he urged.

"It is Yuri Ivanovitch," she said, her voice breaking.

"Did something happen to your husband?"

"He is in hospital, *Polkovnik*. He broke his hip." She emitted a wretched sound, almost like a half-hysterical laugh. "It should be me who breaks the hip, yes? I am the old woman and it is always the woman with the weak bones. How could it be Yuri Ivanovitch?" She broke off on a choked sob.

"I'm so sorry, ma'am." What else could he say. He wished he could help her, but he had problems of his own.

"Oh, so am I," she wailed softly. "Oh, so am I, dear *Polkovnik*. What will we do about your sweet little boy? I will be needed at the hospital for Yuri Ivanovitch. My children, all grown, are coming to see him. Their families will stay in my home, you understand? How could I also take care of your—"

"No, of course not. Please do not burden yourself so. I have other options for Sasha. You must not worry. Yuri Ivanovitch needs you now, and you must remain focused on him."

"Yes, but I am so sorry. We were greatly looking forward to having Sashyenka with us for a time. We do not see our grandchildren as much as we would like to even though we emigrated to this country to be near them."

"Yes, I understand. But you will see them now that they are all coming to stay with you awhile. You are not to worry about Sasha, Mrs. Petrov." He felt desperate to get off the phone so he could think. He must think!

"Please bring your Sashyenka to visit us after he is well again."

"Yes, of course. Give Yuri Ivanovitch my wishes for a swift recovery. *Da svidanya.*"

Viktor snapped the phone closed. He glanced around for a place to sit down, because he knew that falling to his knees in weary despair would alarm his escort. He must be strong, even now.

Before he could move, he felt a small, warm hand on his

shoulder. "Are you all right?" she asked from directly behind him. She rubbed her palm consolingly over his shoulder blade.

"I have received some unexpected news, that is all." He stood straighter, fighting the urge to give in to defeat.

He turned and looked at Natalia. Somehow, between now and Monday evening, he had to persuade her to take a chance on him and his son. Because Captain Natalia Wentworth had just become his one and only hope of saving Sasha.

NATALIE COULD SEE HE WAS distracted, but he walked through Arlington Cemetery with her and commented on the grimness of so many white stone crosses lined up row after row. He made conversation about the tragedy of war. But it was obvious the phone call he'd made earlier had upset him. She longed to know why.

"Hey, come over here," she said. "I want to show you something." He followed her up a slight rise and onto a sidewalk, then out over a narrow paved overpass. She pointed into the distance. "There's the Pentagon."

He spent a long moment gazing at the view of the vast five-sided building. "I've seen pictures, but this is the first time I've seen it...mmm..." He seemed to search the sky for the English words he wanted.

"...in person," she supplied. She was rewarded with his smile. But his eyes looked haunted.

"It is very large," he observed.

"Huge. And complicated to find your way around inside. I'd be glad to show you around tomorrow after we get your identification badges taken care of."

Somehow he managed to look both pleased and worried at the same time. "Perhaps you'd like to head back to Fort Drake now. It'll be past dinner by the time we get there. We can walk over from the Pentagon to see the changing of the guard at the Tomb of the Unknown Soldier some other time."

He nodded but shuffled his feet a bit as if he weren't ready to leave. She waited. "Tomorrow, it will be my first workday?" he asked.

"No, not really. You'll need a few days to sign in at various offices inside the Pentagon and get all your paperwork done. I'll introduce you to some people I know and to the people you'll be working with. But you won't start your training for a few days.''

He considered this. "What time is the day ended for me at the Pentagon, then?''

"Oh, I see. Um, probably we could be flexible. Were you hoping to meet your relatives tomorrow?''

His eyes brightened but he still seemed agitated. "Yes, that is exactly so.''

She nodded. "Well, just let me know, and we'll work it out.''

They walked back to the subway station and boarded a train that took them to her car in the parking lot at the Huntington Metro stop. In no time, they were headed in the direction of his BOQ. "Do you have Burger King where you come from?'' she asked, remembering something about McDonald's opening up Russian franchises. She pointed toward the fast-food joint.

"I have never seen one. But it looks much like the Mc-Donald's in Moskva.''

"Well, let's stop. I'm hungry.'' She turned into the drive-thru.

"You like food,'' he commented.

She smiled. They ate a picnic dinner on one of the tables outside. He was hungry and ate in silence. She wished he would confide in her—helping foreigners work out problems was what she did for a living—but she didn't press him. Still, his tension played upon her nerves.

After she'd returned Viktor to his BOQ, Natalie felt coiled tight as a spring. Particularly strange were the few minutes during which they'd said good-night. It had felt almost like the end of a date and there'd even been a moment when he seemed to be about to give her a good-night kiss. She almost wished he'd dared. Something about the sensual curve of his lips and the expressive way he used his mouth told her he'd be an excellent kisser.

But he hadn't tried. After finding out what time to be ready in the morning and confirming the type of uniform he should wear, Viktor had hesitated only a heartbeat or two before climbing out of her car. As she watched him walk away, she sighed deeply. The man did things to her insides. She couldn't make herself drive off—or turn her gaze away—until he finally passed through the doors of the BOQ and out of sight. The spell was broken and she reminded herself of the reasons she should not lose her head over the Russian Colonel.

VIKTOR SPENT A GOOD PORTION of the night calling to hotels listed in the thick yellow directory he had found inside his desk drawer. Though several were conveniently located between the Pentagon and Montgomery County Memorial in Takoma Park, Maryland, where Sasha would have his surgery, they were all fully booked. In addition, they were far too expensive. He would have to deal with this in the morning. And he would need help. Reluctantly, he made a list of things to do the next day and then went to bed.

By morning, Viktor felt less rested than when he had gone to bed. At first light, he rose and decided to go for a run in the hope that he might clear his head. He had plenty of time. Natalia would not arrive for him until 0800 hours. He ran on the roads and carefully noted all of his turns so he could easily backtrack. When he finally managed to run hard enough to evacuate the clutter from his mind, he turned back. By the time the BOQ came into sight again, sweat dripped from him in huge droplets and his lungs felt well exercised.

But when he saw who stood on the sidewalk in front of the building, his lungs nearly ceased working altogether.

General Roscoe P. Schwinn, U.S. Army retired, had planted himself like a sentinel by the door of the BOQ. He was alone, but clearly waiting for something—or someone. Viktor cursed rapidly in Russian.

The man had not seen him yet, so Viktor stopped, breathing hard and wishing he could keep moving to cool down slowly. But stillness was required at this moment. He assessed the situation, rapidly considering and rejecting options. The main problem was that he had no idea whether or not there was another entrance to the building. He berated himself for not thinking to check before leaving this morning. He should be treating his stay in this country as he would any other military operation. Finding a back door should have been second nature.

In the end, he decided he would have to go straight to the front door and hope that Roscoe would not make too much noise. If Viktor simply saluted the man, perhaps the General would not recognize him in his shorts and T-shirt. If he did not speak, the old man might mistake him for an American officer. Viktor's hand began its assent toward his brow.

"I've been waiting for you, Red," announced Schwinn before Viktor completed the salute. The old man wore that same inappropriate smile. This time he had on his camouflage battle fatigues. There were two stars on his collar and cap.

Viktor dropped his hand to his side and tried a greeting. "Good morning, General."

"I'm watching you. I saw you leave this morning and decided to make sure you didn't come back with a pack of American secrets in your hands."

Viktor splayed his hands outward to show that he had nothing in them, nor anywhere else. He tried a smile. This man was not entirely in his right mind, he remembered. Perhaps kindness would ease the situation. "Your vigilance should be appreciated by your country, General Schwinn. I must go now, sir." Viktor let his hands drop and jogged up the steps.

"I know you're up to something," Schwinn asserted. "If I see any little thing out of the ordinary, I'm going straight to the authorities about you. The CIA wouldn't listen to me before, but by God, they will if I get the goods on you."

Viktor kept on going even though the man continued to talk in this fashion. There was nothing to be gained from speaking to Schwinn further. And the General's words were so disturbing that Viktor could not stay and listen to them a moment longer. He could not afford to have people watching him closely. Had the man really contacted the CIA? God help him.

"Sorry about that, sir," said a sergeant from behind the reception desk. "I asked him to leave, but there's no telling the old General what to do. You want me to call the MPs?"

Viktor shook his head. Letting the General speak his concerns to military police was the last thing he needed. One of the MPs might decide to watch Viktor's activities, too. Viktor eyed the name tag the Sergeant wore, deciphered the Roman letters into Cyrillic for the purpose of pronunciation, and said, "Thank you but no, Sergeant Citallio."

"Colonel Baturnov, is that right, sir?" asked Citallio.

"Yes, Sergeant. I appreciate your efforts on my behalf." He gestured toward the door to indicate General Schwinn. "I'm told he intends no harm."

"Yeah, I think he's harmless. He's having a hard time. Thinks he's still in charge sometimes. Can't seem to stay clear that we're not in the middle of the Cold War anymore."

Viktor nodded. "We will do our best to give no attention to this, yes?"

Citallio agreed. As Viktor went up to his room, he wondered what he would do tonight after Sasha arrived. He had hoped that his son could stay here with him for a night or two, giving them a few more days to come up with a new plan. He had thought to tell everyone that Sasha was an American cousin, visiting briefly. His son was old enough to play along with such a ruse if the situation was explained to him. He was mature enough to amuse himself quietly with books and television during the workday so as not to draw attention. But now that General Schwinn had decided to personally scrutinize Viktor's every move, there was no doubt that his son's presence would be questioned. They could not risk that someone would realize that Sasha was his child.

A shower did little to soothe his roiling guts, and before he had finished rinsing himself off, he realized he was grinding his teeth. He would have an ulcer and cracked molars before this was all over. Still, those would be small prices to pay if Dr. Brennan could perform this miracle for Sasha. And thinking of Brennan reminded Viktor to call the doctor.

By the time Viktor finished checking with the doctor, it was time to go down to meet Natalia. General Schwinn was no longer standing at the door and Natalia was dressed like Captain Wentworth again and looked very attractive in her uniform— dark green skirt hemmed an enticing few inches above her knee, a snug-fitting light green shirt with epaulettes indicating her rank, and a tiny black necktie at her throat. Her name tag was pinned directly onto the right side of the blouse. She wore no ribbons or other medals. Although it was not a requirement to wear them all the time in Russia, the number of decorations on an officer's uniform could make a difference in the level of respect received. But things were different here, and Viktor did not want to seem pretentious. He would forego wearing his today.

"Good morning, sir," Natalia said with a cheerful smile. "We'll go get your Army ID so you can come in and out of Fort Drake, then we'll walk over to the Metro station so you can see how to get to work on your own in the future."

An hour later, he had a U.S. Army identification card in his wallet, though not the type given to American military officers. Still, it was odd to have it. "I am a...mmm... Is *contradiction* the right word?"

She laughed as they walked along the sidewalk away from Fort Drake. "Yes, you are a contradiction with your Russian uniform and your American identification. This way." She indicated a turn to the left and they traveled several more blocks.

Gone were the grassy lawns of Fort Drake. Here there were concrete sidewalks and black pavement next to buildings made of blocks and glass. Occasional trees set into grates along the sidewalk provided intermittent shade. They found the Metro station and Viktor assured her he would be able to find his way again the following day. What he failed to tell her was that there would be a small obstacle named Alexander that might prevent him from making this trek the next morning.

As they boarded the train, Viktor mulled over how to broach the subject of his son's imminent arrival but could not think of what to say without risking too much. He could feel himself drifting toward the cowardly approach of simply asking her to take him out to the airport to pick up a relative. She would meet his son and that might go a long way toward winning her assistance. It seemed unforgivable to give her no warning ahead of time, but at least at the airport, he could gauge her sentiments and he and Sasha would have an opportunity to come up with a plan if she went against them.

On the Metro, they were forced to stand, clinging to hand railings, which were certainly an improvement over the often broken leather and plastic straps on the trains he was familiar with at home. At least it was an improvement for him, given his height. Natalia, on the other hand, had to reach up, and this produced a very distracting tightness to her blouse across the buttons at her breasts. Viktor forced himself to look elsewhere.

"Today is for the workers," he observed, seeing the many dark business suits and dresses around them.

She smiled up at him, and Viktor realized how close they had been forced to stand. Her shoulder was more often than not pressed to his side. She was pleasantly warm against him. And he could smell a light scent wafting from her whenever she was jostled nearer. "You're right. And here we are. The Pentagon's not too far from Fort Drake."

This Metro station was nothing like any of the others he had been to the day before. The weekend crowd had been small, but this station was teaming with people moving like ants in long lines through the huge tunnels. He followed Natalia onto the platform and paid close attention as she indicated the signs and the proper direction to go toward the entrance into the Pentagon.

A very long escalator ride brought them to glass doors and a row of gates with guards watching who entered. Natalia did not hesitate but went straight to the guard desk at one side. Presenting her own Pentagon badge, she explained that she would be taking him to acquire one of his own. The guard didn't even blink at Viktor's uniform as he gave Natalia an escort badge and Viktor a visitor badge. They swiped their badges at the turnstyle and were inside the enormous military complex.

It was as simple as that.

"They did not seek confirmation. They asked no questions, checked no records," he said, hoping he did not sound breathless.

She pondered this a moment. "Well, I'm an officer in the U.S. Army. They have to trust me."

Viktor snorted at this illogical concept. It amazed him that her nation had managed to survive as long as it had with this sort of security. But then he shook his head in disgust, remembering that her country had outlasted the Soviet Union by many years.

In no time, Natalia helped him acquire a Pentagon identification badge, complete with his picture. This would allow him to enter the building without an escort. It boggled his mind. At least the identification clerk had checked first to be sure he was supposed to have a badge. But as soon as she had found his records in their computers, he was processed without so much as a raised eyebrow.

"You said to me that people here were more familiar with foreigners. No one seems to think my presence is unusual," he observed as they walked along an enormously wide corridor lined with shops and cafés, then an office building hallway. The pungent aroma of coffee beckoned to him, and he was grateful when Natalia veered to the right in the direction of a little pastry shop called Greta's. Caffeine would be a blessing.

"We have foreign visitors here a great deal," Natalia said. "People might eye your uniform with curiosity, but you won't find any animosity here. Let's get coffee. We have some people to meet this morning so we don't have time for breakfast in the cafeteria or restaurant. I'll show you those at lunchtime."

From the little coffee shop, Viktor looked out onto the Pentagon concourse, as Natalia had called it, and said, "This is a city inside five walls."

She smiled. "Pretty much. There are two large cafeterias and a full-service restaurant. There's a gym with everything from weights to basketball courts. Oh, and a center courtyard with huge flowering magnolia trees. It's really pretty this time of year. We'll have to go out there sometime soon."

They paid for their drinks—coffee for Natalia and, to his delight, tea for himself. Then she took him out to stand in the center of the huge concourse again. It looked to be about a quarter of a mile long.

"At that end is the bank. You can exchange money there if you need to and access your paychecks, I'm told." Natalia pointed to the other end. "Down there is the medical clinic I hope you won't need to use. Are you supposed to have a physical before you start work? I'll have to check on that." She searched inside the pocket of her purse where she had stashed her folded garrison cap and pulled out a white card. "I almost forgot. I picked up this little map for you. We're standing here."

She pointed and Viktor felt relief wash through him. Everything she had shown him so far fell into place like pieces of a puzzle. "Thank you," he said with a smile, careful not to let on just how grateful he really was.

"Let's go meet some people," she said as she led the way toward a large ramp. She looked at her watch. "You know, it's a little early for our meeting with your office chief. We could go over to where I work for a few minutes. You can see where I am in case you need me in the days to come. My office is here on the third floor. The stairs are in the center." Viktor consulted his tiny map to see what she meant. "You'll be on the fourth floor," she added.

As they walked, Natalia pointed out exhibits and displays along the hallways through which they walked until Viktor realized that the inside of the Pentagon was not only a huge military office building, but a gigantic museum as well. Every corridor was dedicated to something—a military era or campaign or hero.

"Here we are." As she turned into an office suite, she collided with a tall man with light brown hair. "Ooph!"

She crashed backward against Viktor, who resisted the urge to keep her pressed to the length of him for a moment. He steadied her and then dropped his hands.

"Frank!" she said.

Viktor's entire body went rigid. This was Frank, to whom she was not married but who had some claim on her. It should not matter, he told himself, but he could not shake the urge to compete with this American.

"So this is your Russian Colonel?" Frank said. He held out his hand and his smile was broad. But Viktor was certain the light in his eyes was not friendly.

"Viktor Baturnov," he offered as he clasped the man's hand briefly. Frank grinned wider, as if Viktor had made a joke.

"Major Frank Lezinski," he said, even though his rank was

obvious from his uniform. Clearly Lezinski liked to flaunt his status.

Unfortunately for Frank, a colonel would always outrank a major in any game of power and in any army. "Major," said Viktor as if he found the word slightly distasteful. He dismissed the man by turning his attention to the others in the room. There were four women and two enlisted men. Two of the women were officers who stood on the thresholds of separate offices. The others were seated at desks in the common room in which he stood.

"This is Emmy, our secretary," Natalia said, introducing the young woman at a desk near the door. Viktor stepped forward toward the secretary and gave her a smile and his hand.

"Emmy, like the award," she said, but Viktor did not understand the reference. 'Emmy, like the award,' he repeated in his mind. What did that mean?

"I was just looking for you," Frank said from behind them. Natalia held up her index finger, asking him to wait a minute.

"Emmy can get you anything you need in the entire Pentagon. She's a genius." The young woman preened under the praise. "So if your own secretary has any problems, just give Emmy a call."

"It is a pleasure to meet a woman with such important ability," Viktor said to her. He held her gaze and watched her turn soft and misty. It was his accent, he knew. With men, his accent could be a liability, but he had noticed that women adored it. He suddenly wondered if Natalia liked the way he spoke....

"Natalie," Frank said with a note of impatience.

"Hey, that's okay, Nat. You go ahead and talk with the Major. I'll finish introducing the Colonel around." This came from a woman with dark hair and features. She smiled at him coyly, and Viktor resisted the desire to take a step back from her. "I'm Constance DiSanto." She held out her hand and shook his a little longer than necessary.

Viktor saw Natalia hesitating at his elbow. But between Frank urging her to go with him to her office and Constance pushing her away with the considerable force of her body language and facial expression, Natalia moved off. "I'll be right back," she said.

But Viktor suddenly felt very alone in this room full of strangers.

CHAPTER FOUR

"WHERE'VE YOU BEEN?" Frank demanded the instant they were in her office behind the closed door.

"I've been with Colonel Baturnov. I told you…"

"You weren't home all day yesterday and you never returned my calls. Did you spend the night with him?"

She gasped, shocked that he would make such an accusation—and embarrassed that she'd fantasized about it during the previous night. "Of course not! How dare you ask such an insulting thing!"

He pivoted away from her and passed his fingers through his hair. She heard him let out a long breath. "Sorry. That was uncalled-for."

This was more than she expected from Frank. It was hard for him to express regret. That he'd done so now must mean she was special to him.

He turned back to her. "I was worried, that's all. I came straight here this morning hoping to reassure myself that you were all right. I mean…" He gestured toward the reception area past the closed door. "You don't even know this guy. He could be a spy or a nutcase or something."

Natalie forced her shoulders to relax. "Well, I'm fine and he's not a nutcase or anything else to worry about. I showed him around town and when I got home I was too tired to do anything but go to sleep. I forgot to return your call. Sorry."

He gave her a coaxing smile. "I'll forgive you if you forgive me…."

She returned his smile, thinking how much like her old friend he sounded. She decided to confide in him. "Well, it's good you came by, anyway. I wanted to talk to you about something.

Saturday night, I ran into DiSanto at the airport, and she said some things that got me thinking."

"Like what?"

"She hinted that maybe this assignment to the Colonel was arranged by someone who wanted to give my career a setback. Do you think that's possible?"

His brow creased in puzzlement. "Who would do something like that?"

"Well, DiSanto, for one. And Barbara Dwyer could stand to gain some ground if I was suddenly not in favor with our superiors. All of us want that assignment to NATO. All of us would give our eyeteeth for promotion to Major."

He cocked his head to one side. "Don't you think you're being a little paranoid? Maybe Colonel Freeman just thought you should slow down a little—not that it worked," he added. "You do too much, Nat. The boss is just looking out for you."

Now he was sounding exactly like her mother. "Let me guess who you've been talking to," she said. "My mom called you, right?" Natalie's well-meaning, but meddling mother had taken to calling Frank every now and then. Natalie suspected her mom was encouraging Frank's romantic endeavors.

"I haven't talked to your mother in weeks. But if this is the sort of thing she tells you, you should listen to her. You work too hard and have no time for anything—or anyone—else."

Natalie closed her eyes and searched for patience. This was not a conversation she had even the slightest desire to have right now. And she refused to be any more defensive than she already had been. "So you think maybe Colonel Freeman just wanted me to take a breather from the usual stuff?"

Frank shrugged. "He made the assignments, right?"

Natalie nodded.

"Why don't you ask him about it?" he suggested.

"I did. He didn't have time to talk to me then, and I'm half-way through what I need to do for Viktor, so there's no sense in belaboring it further. You're probably right. It's nothing to worry about."

Frank's eyebrows had gone up in the middle of what she'd

said. At first, she didn't understand why, but he clarified quickly enough. "'Viktor,' is it? Doesn't he outrank you by a mile?"

She felt the heat rising to her cheeks. And Frank noticed. Before she could respond, he blurted, "You have a thing for the Russian!"

"Stop it, Frank. You know that isn't true. He asked me to call him by his first name, and yesterday while we were in civilian clothes, I got used to doing so. I'm embarrassed I forgot to revert back to formalities this morning, that's all." As excuses went, Natalie thought this one seemed reasonably plausible. But Frank wasn't buying it.

"Yeah, right." Although his congenial expression barely changed, she knew him well. She noted that he'd gone very still and that the temperature around him had dropped about ten degrees.

She smiled at him, hoping to thaw the moment. "Seriously, Frank. He'll be gone back to Russia in a matter of weeks. Surely you know I'm not the kind of woman to get involved with such a man."

The Major nodded. Then he smiled sheepishly. "Guess I'm sounding jealous," he admitted. Then he moved toward the door. "Hey, I'll see if anyone has anything to say about your assignments. I know how important your career is to you," he said.

She looked at him, thinking he was a nice person, so reliable and helpful. Maybe in time she would come to feel for him the way...

Someone knocked on the door.

"Come in," she said.

Frank stepped aside, and Barbara Dwyer entered Natalie's small office. "Oh, sorry. Didn't know you had someone with you."

"That's okay, I was just heading out," Frank said. He turned his gaze back to Natalie. "I'll let you know if I hear anything." With a wink that only she could see, he left.

"What's up?" Natalie asked, trying to catch sight of the Russian in the outer office. She didn't want to leave him out there alone if no one was looking after him. But then she heard his laugh and two feminine giggles, so she figured he'd be okay for another minute or two.

When she looked back at Barbara, she was surprised by the change in her demeanor. The other woman's eyes were cold and hard.

"I just want you to know that if you screw around with my assignments again, you'll be sorry you ever messed with me." She said this in a low, seething voice.

For a second, Natalie was stunned silent. But anger quickly helped her to regain the use of her tongue. "What the hell are you talking about, Dwyer? No one has interfered with your assignments."

But Barbara didn't back down. "No? Then why have I been put in charge of the Secretary's European tour? You're the only one who has the kind of influence necessary to get anyone assigned a prime gig like that. You know I can't go. I have my kid to think of. How's it going to look when I have to go into Freeman and request a change?"

Now Natalie was confused as well as angry. "When did this happen?"

Barbara looked as if she might explode any second. "You know very well that the roster was changed last week. But you haven't been around so I couldn't discuss it with you until now."

"Dwyer, you have a hell of a nerve making these wild accusations. Who had the assignment before you?" None of this made sense. She needed a lot more information.

"DiSanto did. As if you didn't know that already. You get to hurt both of us at once with this move."

Natalie leaned forward, bracing herself on her desktop with stiff arms. She glared at the other officer. "I didn't have a thing to do with it. Your accusations are out of line."

"You think I'm pretty stupid, don't you." Barbara stepped back from Natalie and paced the narrow confines in front of the desk. "Who else could it be, if not you? You must want that NATO tour pretty bad." She paused to glare at Natalie.

"Meaning, you think I screwed with the trip to Europe so you two wouldn't be able to compete so closely with me."

Barbara threw her hands into the air. "See! You're so sure of yourself you even admit it!"

"Give me a break, Dwyer! I haven't admitted anything because I haven't done anything. In fact, I should be asking you if you know anything about how I got assigned the Russian Colonel!"

Captain Dwyer went very still. The satisfied smirk on her face told Natalie a great deal. The woman pointed a finger directly at Natalie's face. "Don't mess with me, Wentworth. Or this is going to get very ugly."

Natalie's back went ramrod straight. Then she briskly moved to her door and stood by it in an obvious invitation for Dwyer to leave. "You talk to me like that again, and I'll have you up on charges, Captain. Now, get out before I decide not to give you a second chance."

Barbara had the sense to look worried for a brief moment. Then she marched away, through the reception area and out of the suite of offices.

There was silence in the outer room. Before she could sort out exactly what had just transpired, Natalie realized her tiff with Barbara had probably been overheard. If not the actual words, then at least the tone and volume. Certainly, Captain Dwyer's angry retreat would be enough to set the tongues wagging. Time for damage control.

She stepped into the reception area and surveyed it with a critical eye. Viktor stood near Emmy's desk staring in silence at the door through which Barbara had made her exit. The others in the room were similarly transfixed. Collectively, their gazes shifted to Natalie.

"She's having a really bad day. You know Barbara…" She trailed off, allowing the others to draw their own conclusions. "Colonel Baturnov, we should be going."

He nodded and followed her out into the corridors of the Pentagon again.

VIKTOR PLACED HIS TRAY onto the table they had selected. "The people I will work with seem very nice," he said as they finally sat down in the oversized cafeteria to eat a late lunch. Natalia had kept him moving from one introduction to another all day. It was 1400 hours, and he was very hungry.

"Yeah, they seemed nice enough. The work seems pretty boring, though." She looked up from her sandwich with a startled expression. "Oh. I shouldn't have said that. It's what you do. I guess you don't think it's boring."

He chuckled. "Yes, I do."

She eyed him as she took a bite. "Well, then why do you do it?"

He shrugged and thought of his son. Transferring to working with supply transport allowed him to stay home and keep regular hours. Doing the special forces work he had been trained for kept him away on assignments and fieldwork nine months out of the year. When Viktor's mother had died, leaving Sasha without his babushka to look after him, Viktor had been needed in Yaroslavl. "I was tired of being away from home so much."

She seemed to accept this explanation and went on with conversation about the people they had met. As Natalia talked, Viktor glanced at the clock on the far wall. The minutes were ticking by and his tension doubled with the passing of each one. Sasha's plane would be landing in a few hours. Yet he still had not broached the subject with Natalia. There had not been time and now he felt tongue-tied.

"I must speak to you," he said suddenly, forcing himself to begin. He realized he had jumped into the middle of her sentence and he felt his face heat. He would not win her assistance by being rude.

She put down the remains of her sandwich and folded her hands on the table. It was as if she had been expecting this moment. She gave him her full attention and waited.

"I must go to the airport soon." The knots in Viktor's stomach tightened as he tried to think of how to explain. If she balked and went to the authorities, who would take care of Sasha? The stakes were so very high, this moment so very critical. Words simply would not come.

"To the airport? Are you meeting someone?"

"Yes. A relative is flying in to see me." Though he longed to trust her, he could not bring himself to take the chance of telling her more. "I thought you would want to know where I have gone. Is a taxi expensive? I will need to depart soon. This is why I asked yesterday about my work schedule today."

She looked at him, puzzlement creasing her brow. "The Metro goes straight to the airport. That would be better than a taxi. Are you meeting this relative to give him his medication?"

Ah! He had forgotten about her obsession with his bag of medication. This was the excuse he needed and he leaped upon it. *"Da! Meditatsiya!* To my relative I give. I am to meet him at the airport. I did not know the Metro would go such a great distance."

"Distance? Oh! You must mean you need to go back to Dulles. You should have had him fly in to Reagan National Airport. It's just across the river." She got that look in her eyes, the one Viktor had come to realize meant she was working on a strategy, solving a problem. "It's way too expensive to take a taxi out there. I'll drive you."

Viktor was relieved beyond measure to have free transportation to fetch his son. But what would Natalia say when she saw the boy? "That is very kind of you."

"What time is he flying in? What airline?"

"Mmm…" He glanced at the clock again. He had a little less than three hours to collect his bag and get to the airport. He could not be late. "Seventeen hundred hours, but I will also need to get the medication from the BOQ," he said.

"Well, my car is parked over there, anyway, since we came on the Metro. We'd better get going." She sipped the last of her drink. The intrepid Captain Wentworth did not appear to be troubled by this turn of events. She was prepared to take this detour with him and did not even press him with questions. He told himself this was a good sign.

On the drive to Dulles, he avoided saying anything compromising by telling her all about Yaroslavl. He described the beauty of the river Volga and the majesty of the city's hundreds of churches. One of the oldest cities in Russia, it had retained its air of antiquity. He enjoyed seeing the light of wonder in her eyes as he talked of his home. Suddenly, he was homesick. And he missed his boy. When he could hold Sasha again, then he would be all right.

"Here we are," Natalia said, bringing him out of his reverie. "We have plenty of time."

Time to worry, Viktor thought. Time to wonder whether this woman walking into the airport with him would be the American Captain Wentworth or the woman Natalia. He did not know her, could not necessarily trust her. But in a few moments, he would be forced to give her great power over him.

"Which airline is it again?" she asked as if he had mentioned it before and she had forgotten.

But he had not told her that part yet. Once he told her, she would begin to suspect. But he had little choice now. "Aeroflot. He is coming in from Russia," he admitted, then he waited for her reaction.

She looked into his face, searching. He could see her mind working. Her brow furrowed slightly. "Is this all on the up-and-up?" she asked.

"I do not understand this 'up-and-up.'"

"Why is someone coming from Russia to meet you here?" she asked, unsuccessfully trying to hide her exasperation. "You just left there. It seems strange, and I want to know if it's all been approved by your superiors."

Ah, so here at last was the moment he had been dreading. "You will know soon enough" was all he could manage to say. Then he strode off in the direction of Customs, hoping he would not have to wait for Sasha. Captain Wentworth was not likely to be put off for long.

He knew Natalia was close behind him. He checked his watch. Sasha had no baggage to declare. He carried his passport and his temporary medical visa. Viktor had arranged for a flight attendant to see to his Customs documents when they landed. So his son should get through Customs very quickly.

"Are you going to tell me what's going on here?" demanded Natalia.

He turned and surveyed her face but could not read her taut features. "Wait, please," he requested in a quiet voice. "Trust me in this."

She tapped her foot impatiently and glared at him.

"At least tell me if I'm going to get into trouble," she demanded. "Because if I am, I'm taking you with me. Sir." She spat out that last syllable as if it were poison.

"Please give me a little time," he asked. He looked at his watch and saw that it was ten minutes past 1700 already. "In a moment, I will be able to explain everything. I would not involve you if I had a choice."

She bristled at that, and he thought she would walk away without another word, leaving him stranded at the airport. He would not have blamed her for doing so.

"This is starting to get creepy. I can't be a part of it," she began, edging back from him with her hands splayed apologetically. "I have a career to consider. You can catch a taxi back...when you're done with whatever it is...."

But then the double doors to the customs area opened and a throng of passengers came through. Viktor's attention turned to them, and he craned his neck, trying to catch sight of his child. His heart beat so hard at the prospect, he was certain everyone around him could hear it.

The crowd thinned and he saw Sasha. The boy was laughing at something the pretty flight attendant had just said to him as she wheeled him forward. Those enormous brown eyes of his danced with mirth, his animated features outshone everything around him. Pride swelled in Viktor's heart. Not even the sight of the wheelchair could dim the fullness of his joy.

Sasha saw him and waved.

"*Sashyenka*," Viktor whispered as he realized how terrified he had been that something would go wrong, that Sasha would not make it here, that Viktor would not see him again. But he was here now. Safe. Viktor walked toward him, oblivious of anything else.

"Papa!" Sasha called out as he neared. Then he stopped the turning of the wheels with the flat of his hands and pulled himself from the chair. He walked to his father, who put the bag of medicines on the floor and went down on one knee so he could open his arms wide.

"I'm here at last!" Sasha said in Russian. Then the child

wrapped his too-thin arms around Viktor's neck and hugged. Out of the corner of his eye, Viktor saw that Natalia stood staring at them with wide eyes.

"Yes, Sasha, you are finally here with me." Viktor pulled his son close to his heart. He breathed in the youthful scent of the boy, pushing his nose against the soft skin of Sasha's neck. But when he realized his eyes were stinging, Viktor reined in his emotions at once, loath to allow anyone to see such weakness. Sasha needed him to be strong.

"You have to sign these papers, sir," the attendant said as she held out a clipboard.

When he lifted his face from Sasha's shoulder, he was composed and smiling. Reluctantly, he let go of his son and stood.

"Of course." He signed where she indicated and produced his identification card to prove he was Sasha's father. "Thank you," he said to the woman as she handed back his card and headed back to her other duties.

"Let me look at you, son," Viktor said with mock sternness. He grasped the narrow, youthful shoulder, needing to touch his child but not wanting to embarrass the twelve-year-old with another hug. "Did they not feed you?"

As he had hoped, Sasha laughed, wheezing a little in between the chuckles. "I am starving!"

It was an old joke between them. Viktor's mother had always complained about how thin Sasha was. The two men of the house had taken to declaring that if she would only *feed* him, then perhaps Sasha would gain weight. It was silly of them, because Sasha's babushka had cooked almost constantly, baking and roasting and tempting her *vnuk* every day until the poor boy could eat no more.

But there were other reasons unrelated to food that kept Sasha so small for his age.

"Excuse me," came a feminine voice from behind him. Viktor turned, only just remembering that he must explain things to his American escort. There was a decidedly vexed expression on her lovely face. But she was there. She had not left him.

Not waiting for an introduction, Natalie put her hand out to the young man who was clearly Viktor's son. The kid was skinny, but he was the spitting image of his father. And "papa" sounded pretty much the same in Russian as it did in English.

"*Privyet,*" she tried—this was her newest Russian word and she thought it meant "hi," a vast improvement on that horrible *zdr* word that meant "hello." "*Minya zavut Kapitan Natalie Wentworth,*" she said to the boy.

He shook her hand firmly, drew his heels suddenly together and gave her a short bow. His thinness and the wheelchair would have been indication enough, but the fact that Viktor had risked bringing the boy to this country made it clear that there must be a very good reason. There was something very wrong with this child.

"I am named Alexander," he said in a thick accent. "I speak English," he added proudly. A charmer, Natalie thought. Just like his dad.

"That's good because I don't speak Russian very well."

Alexander looked up at his father with a glint of mischief in his eyes. "*Krasavitsa,*" he said, and raised and lowered his eyebrows suggestively. Natalie didn't need a translation. The child had just commented on her looks.

Her assumption was confirmed by the fact that Viktor's cheeks flushed a bit as he laughed nervously. "She speaks a little Russian, Sasha," he admonished as he pulled the boy's head playfully into the crook of his arm and made as if to cover the outspoken mouth with his man-sized hand as Alexander squirmed and giggled. "And do not speak Russian in front of people who cannot understand. It is not polite."

Alexander nodded but seemed so cheerful about the rebuke his father had just delivered that Natalie knew Viktor was not a stern parent.

"And what are you doing in America, Alexander Viktorovitch?" she asked, using his patronymic, as was the custom in his country.

The young man grew serious for the first time since he'd appeared. He turned his face up to his father's and the pair exchanged a look, man to man. "I am here for heart surgery," he announced.

"Heart surgery..." Natalie was stunned. She looked from the

young, earnest face to the stoic, older one. "Heart surgery?" she asked, bewildered.

Viktor didn't take his concerned eyes off of Alexander. "Are you tired, Sasha? It is a long flight."

The child shook his head. "I am sleeps London to America," he said. "I must medicine soon." He tapped the face of his watch.

"Come," Viktor said as he moved to stand behind the wheelchair. "We will find a restaurant here. Are you hungry, Sasha?"

For some reason, this made the boy laugh again. A private joke, no doubt. Then he nodded and took his seat in the wheelchair.

Viktor looked at Natalie. "We will sit and eat together and I will explain it all to you, Tasha."

He called her Tasha. Natalie knew that in Viktor's country, this wasn't a separate name but an affectionate form of her given name. She recognized the intimacy of it and her heart beat a little faster in response. Insanity. This whole thing was insanity. But she followed where he led—again—even though her better sense urged her to head for the exit.

Before they'd gone far, though, that better sense caused her steps to slow. His secrecy and the fact that the boy traveled separately from the father led her to surmise that the Russian authorities didn't know what Viktor was up to. That would upset the American authorities, too. Natalie could have no part of that. She should go now, before she became any more entangled in this madness. She did not want to know any more about this child's need for heart surgery. She didn't want to care.

But just as she began to lag behind, Alexander turned his youthful face to her, peering around his father, who pushed his wheelchair. He looked as if he were checking to see if she still followed. His smile was so angelic, she found herself quickening her pace to catch up. She was smitten. That boy's smile was as irresistible as his father's. And these guys needed her.

"This will do," Viktor announced at the entrance to a sit-down restaurant.

Natalie allowed herself to be seated and even managed to order food. She listened to Alexander's broken English as he tried to tell his father about his flight in a language he had not yet mastered. Viktor encouraged him as he doled out medications from the supply in his carry-on bag. Every now and then he offered an English word to fill in for terms Alexander couldn't remember. But when the food arrived, Viktor's countenance turned somber. He moved his food around on his plate, then looked up at Natalie.

"We will need your help, Tasha."

She wished he wouldn't call her that. She tried to focus on the issue at hand, rather than on Viktor's deep voice sluicing over the softened syllables of the nickname he'd given her. "What kind of help?" she managed to ask.

He glanced at his son. "Take your medicine, Sasha." Then he turned to Natalie again. "My son has a heart condition. He had rheumatic fever as a very young child—this is not uncommon in Russia. But the result is somewhat rare. He has Mitral Valve Stenosis, something that is not common in one so young. The problem with his heart developed more rapidly than usual. He needs surgery to correct the problem. But he is very young and small, say our doctors. And one must have money in my homeland in order to receive such unusual care. The medical professionals are fine with diagnosis, but treatment is mediocre at best. No one will do this operation on him in my country, until he is larger and we can pay. But there is a doctor at Montgomery County Memorial who is willing to do this procedure for Sasha now, without waiting for him to grow."

"That hospital is in Maryland, I think. Just over the D.C. line. How did you manage to find such a doctor?" she asked.

Viktor looked surprised. "World Wide Web, of course."

Well, that made sense, she supposed. She nodded, remembering that his file had indicated he was adept with computers.

"We corresponded for a time over the Internet regarding Sasha's condition. He was very kind, and we became friends. He agreed that it would be best for Sasha to have surgery now instead of building him up with vitamins and managing his condition with beta blockers and antibiotics." Viktor swept his hand toward the array of medications he'd doled out to his son. "The surgery is a common thing here, even on a small person. Dr.

Brennan felt sorry for our situation and offered to do it for a reduced fee. The hospital specializes in heart surgery and also agreed to lower costs.''

"So, do the Russian authorities know you've brought him here for this surgery?" She was pretty sure she knew the answer, but confirmation of her worst fears seemed necessary.

Viktor looked down at his untouched plate. "We came separately to avoid being associated with each other by our authorities. They know I am here for the purposes of learning about supply movements. And Alexander has a valid passport and medical visa. But…''

"But if they find out you've brought your son here while you're on a military assignment, you'd be in a world of trouble,'' she finished for him.

"She intelligently also,'' observed Alexander, who seemed to understand English better than he spoke it.

"Do not talk with your mouth full,'' Viktor said to his son without looking at him. His gaze was locked with Natalie's. "What will you do, Natalia?''

Ah, now that was the million-dollar question. She should go directly to her superiors and tell them all the details, washing her hands of the whole mess. Let *them* figure out what to do about these two. It didn't have to be her problem.

"That depends on what kind of help you need from me,'' she heard herself say. "If you just want me to drive you somewhere and drop you off so you can get on with your clandestine activities, then I can do that. As long as I'm not responsible for you, I don't feel any particular need to tell anyone about your plans.''

Viktor let out an audible sigh, as if he'd been holding his breath. Had he been thinking she would rat him out? She still wasn't certain she wouldn't. But Viktor's cause was a worthy one, after all. Who could blame him for wanting to cure his son's heart condition?

"I will need a different place to stay, Tasha,'' he said softly, as if he feared he would upset her if he did not speak gently. "Alexander cannot be seen with me at Fort Drake. Schwinn is watching me. He was outside the BOQ this morning, threatening to call the CIA if I did anything out of the ordinary.''

"A place to stay..." she repeated, dumbfounded. Her heart began to race as her subconscious latched on to where this was going to lead her. Into the deepest trouble she could imagine, no doubt.

"An inexpensive hotel or apartment," he added. "I was not able to find anything I could afford by telephone. But surely you could help us with this."

She put her head in her hands, pushing her hair back from her brow and applying pressure with her palms to the headache that had begun to hammer inside her skull. "Why didn't you work this out before you came here?"

He pushed away so his back went up against the seat cushion. His severe expression told her a great deal about his frustration. "I worked everything out to the last detail. But first I am put into a dormitory on the American military base instead of the hotel I was told to expect. Then the place I had arranged for Alexander to stay during the days—with a Russian couple who had emigrated here..." He threw his hands into the air to indicate that this part of the plan had gone up in smoke. "The husband is in hospital, and so I have no help."

Natalie groaned. Every word he uttered seemed like another nail in her coffin. She could feel herself being pulled into his life, into his problems. She looked at Alexander, eating steadily while he listened to every English word they uttered. How could she turn her back on this child?

Viktor leaned forward across the table again. "I would not involve you if I had a choice. I will do everything in my power to prevent trouble for you."

His concern for *her* welfare on top of everything else on his plate only made it harder for her to be sensible. He'd planned everything so carefully. She remembered how worried he'd seemed yesterday after he'd spoken in Russian to someone on her cell phone. He must have been getting the bad news. No wonder he'd been so distracted.

There was no hope for it. If it was in her power to help, then she'd have to do it. She considered the cost of hotels and understood why Viktor could not afford one—especially if he had to pay even limited medical expenses out of pocket. She thought about offering to pay for a room herself but knew with deep certainty that Viktor would never accept charity from her.

She contemplated her list of friends and wondered whether she could impose upon them. Frank was out of the question. He and Viktor had already eyed each other with the special male animosity that meant they would not deal well with each other. Most of her women friends were also in the Army and would have the same misgivings as any other sane military person.

One possibility after another was considered and discarded as she picked at her food. She noticed Viktor didn't eat much, either, as he awaited her verdict. Even Alexander had grown quiet, occasionally eyeing the two adults who sat so pensively on either side of him.

By the time Alexander was served his dessert, Natalie knew what she would have to do. Stomach churning, she announced her decision. "I'll stay with a friend. You two can use my apartment for a few days until we figure out what to do."

The relief that washed away the tension on Viktor's face was nearly worth the terrible risk she was taking.

CHAPTER FIVE

SASHA'S WHEELCHAIR DID not fit easily into the boot of Natalia's small car. Viktor struggled with it for a few minutes, before Natalia produced a flexible cord with hooks on both ends. In seconds, she secured the boot in an open position over the protruding handholds of the chair.

"Thank you," he said simply. He wanted to convey so much more. Where to start? He could not begin to know. He only hoped she understood.

Her smile—the first he had seen since he had told her of his problem—lifted his spirits. "Yeah, well you owe me big time," she said. "I expect royal treatment when I visit Russia someday." Then she turned to get behind the steering wheel.

He assured himself that Sasha was buckled up in the back, then got into the passenger seat. "You plan to visit Russia?" he asked, a little alarmed at how the idea made his mind reel with all that he would like to show her.

"Well, I can't let all this Russian I'm learning go to waste, now can I?" She grinned and pulled onto the highway. "Assuming that you're not in Siberia, I figure you can make up for all this by showing me around."

He went very still at the mention of Siberia. He had seen those prisons once. The thought of being sent to one as anything other than a visitor made his blood run cold.

"I was kidding," she said. "They don't really send people to Siberia anymore, do they?"

He did not say anything. Much better to concentrate on the passing scenery until he could regain control of his thoughts. The buildings rushing by were modern, the road evenly paved with heavy railings along the sides for safety. Cleanliness and order persisted as far as he could see.

"Papa, what about Mr. and Mrs. Petrov?" Alexander asked in Russian. "What happened to them?"

Viktor explained briefly about Mr. Petrov's accident and how he had to go to the hospital. Then he summarized the exchange for Natalia. He did not want to offend her by speaking in a language she could not fully understand.

He saw her glance in her rearview mirror at his son. "You'll be staying at my place for a while. You'll like it. For one thing, there's a nice little elevator so you won't have to worry about stairs. For another, you'll have everything you need while your papa works."

"We must stop at the BOQ to get Sasha's clothes," he said, just remembering himself. "I brought them with me so he would not be burdened with luggage."

"Okay."

But as they drove toward the building, Viktor saw Specialist Murdock on the front step speaking with another man. Murdock's hands were splayed as if to plead with the other person. And then Viktor recognized the situation.

"Stop here," he said abruptly.

"But why...?"

"Stop!" He said it quietly but firmly and she stopped the car immediately, pulling alongside of the curb. They were about a hundred yards from the front of the BOQ. "Schwinn," he whispered to himself, but Natalia heard him.

"At this hour?" she said. "That man is crazy."

"I must do what I can to relieve the situation." He pulled the handle but did not open the door all the way. His mind ran over details and possibilities with the rapid precision he had honed during his many peacekeeping operations in Africa and Europe. "Captain, take the car to the parking lot near the bank. Turn off the lights and engine and wait for me there."

"But that's a couple of miles from here. How are you going to...?"

The look he cast her way stopped her in midsentence. This

might not be a military exercise, but he could not afford to shift his concentration to explanations. She was an officer and he needed her to act like one. "Back up to the turn just behind you and retreat the way we came. Circle to the parking lot from there. I will not be more than forty minutes," he assured her.

"Yes, sir." She softened this by adding, "Be careful."

"What happens?" Sasha asked, realizing that something serious was taking place.

Viktor turned a smile to his son. Speaking in rapid Russian, he said that this was one of those times they had talked about when they had planned things while still in Russia. They must all be very careful and alert.

Sasha nodded. "Captain Wentworth and I will be fine," he said firmly, taking on the role of an obedient soldier.

Viktor let himself out of the car, wishing he did not have to ask so much of his son. Bravery would be required in good measure once he entered the hospital. He should not have to be anything more than a child before then.

Certain that Natalia would obey his orders, Viktor donned his cap and strode to the entry of the BOQ.

"You see, sir," Murdock said to Schwinn when he spied Viktor's approach. "Here's the Colonel now. Nothing to worry about. Probably just went out for dinner or something."

"Good evening," Viktor said to the pair.

"Where have you been, Red?" Schwinn said.

Viktor's head screamed with a sudden lust to simply slug the bigot and drop him unconscious right where he stood. Instead, Viktor clenched his fists at his sides. He turned and glared at the old General. "I have not been ordered to explain my personal activities to anyone, sir. I will simply assure you that I have no ill intentions toward you or your country. Now, if you will excuse me..." He began to turn toward the door.

Schwinn grabbed his arm. "Just who do you think you're talking to, sonny!"

Murdock lifted a hand as if to intervene, but Viktor stopped him with a glance. The young man shifted back slightly but remained watchful.

The glint in the General's eyes showed the mettle with which he had once commanded troops, and Viktor suddenly felt sorry for the man. He had been in command, had known the glory of leading men of valor, had borne the weight of life-and-death situations. Now he lived a very different existence. It was not dissimilar to the way Viktor himself had struggled with the transition from special forces to the supply command.

All anger gone, Viktor looked down at the gnarled fingers holding his arm and wanted to give comfort. But he knew this would only enrage the General further. Instead, he straightened and looked at the man evenly. "I mean no disrespect, General."

"I could have you court-martialed!" declared the General. He took several steps back but did not take his eyes off of Viktor. "Lock him up, Murdock," he ordered. "We'll see if he has a cooler head after a night in the stockade."

"Uh, yes, sir," mumbled the Specialist, clearly uncertain as to what his next move should be. With a slight nod of his head, Viktor indicated that Murdock should take him inside the BOQ. "I'll lock him up inside, sir," Murdock told Schwinn.

The General took on a satisfied expression and he nodded regally. "I'll be staying awhile to see that everything is in order out here," he assured the young soldier. "Carry on."

Viktor went inside with Murdock, who slipped behind the reception counter shaking his head in dismay. "We're going to have to do something about him if he keeps bothering you like that. My apologies, sir."

"He is a confused old man. Harmless. Are there others who may be unhappy with my presence here?"

Murdock looked uncomfortable. "Not that I know of."

"That is good to hear. I will retire now. Good night, Specialist."

Viktor mounted the stairs, resisting the urge to hurry. He had been resisting that urge since he had left Natalia's car. Sedately, he made his way to the floor where his room was located. When he was certain no one could see him, he broke into a sprint down the hall.

He gathered a few things for himself and stuffed them into a small case. He pulled together his son's bags, two large ones with shoulder straps and a smaller valise with a handle. Hoisting the bags securely onto his frame, he maneuvered out of the door, turning this way and that so as not to make too much noise bumping the luggage against the jamb. On silent feet, he made his way to the back stairway, went through another door, and then rushed down the stairs. He knew now that the back door was at the bottom of the stairs, having done a circuit of the building from the outside after his encounter with Schwinn this morning. Sure enough, a door with a small window led into the darkness outside.

Just before he pushed the bar to open it, he noticed large black lettering proclaiming this exit was for emergencies only. Glancing up, he saw a metal box affixed to the top of the door frame. It bore a red sign that indicated an alarm. Damn!

Dropping the bags to the cement floor, he patted down his pockets for something with which he could disarm the mechanism. But he was wearing his office uniform and was not prepared for such eventualities as he might have been in his camouflage gear with its pockets full of small equipment like wire cutters and locksmith tools.

Finding nothing on his person, he decided he would have to go back to his room to get what he needed. What would Natalia do if he did not arrive in the prescribed forty minutes? he wondered. Climbing the stairs two at a time, he became conscious of a sound that made him go up an extra flight, even though he was not sure what he expected to find. Sure enough, there stood a row of vending machines, humming quietly in the landing of the upper stairwell.

He had American coins in his pocket, and one of the machines sold candy and snacks. Quickly, he purchased a pack of gum. Opening the outer wrapper he cursed to find that instead of the aluminum packaging he was used to, this brand contained white paper. Only in America, he muttered in exasperation as he purchased a different kind.

This time, his efforts yielded the expected aluminum inner wrappers. As he hurried down the stairs to the alarmed exit, he examined the brand name so as to avoid making the wrong choice again, should the need ever arise. *Chort poberi!* He hoped it never would.

He had two wrappers freed before he came to a halt in front of the door. Popping the gum into his mouth and chewing it rapidly, he folded the foil wrappers and attached them one to the other to make a long, flat strip. He was tall enough to reach up and easily position the length of aluminum on the bottom portion of the alarm housing, slipping it between the magnetic juncture. He secured the strip with the gum from his mouth. After inspecting his efforts to ensure that the foil would maintain contact between the upper and lower parts of the mechanism even if the door were opened, he stood back.

He was running out of time, so if this did not work he would simply have to outrun whoever came to investigate the siren the open door would set off. Holding his breath, he pushed carefully on the bar, felt it click as the latch gave way, then slowly eased the door open—all the while watching his handiwork to see if the wrappers would do what he hoped.

No alarm sounded, so he poked his head through in order to ensure no one was in sight on the other side of his escape route. All clear. He pushed the stacked luggage through the narrow space, then sidled through himself, letting the door ease closed.

Without waiting another second, Viktor slung the luggage straps over his shoulders and took off at a rapid lope, all the while maintaining an awareness of his surroundings. If someone spotted him streaking full-tilt with several suitcases, he would surely raise suspicion.

He reached a wooded area without incident. Scanning the perimeter and seeing no one, he checked his watch and saw he would be about five minutes later than he had promised. She would wait for him, but he hated to worry her. So he broke into a run, glad he had not let himself become less fit just because he no longer took part in special operations.

Circling around to where the car waited, he slowed to a walk and then stopped altogether before approaching the vehicle. The parking lot appeared to be empty except for Natalia's car. He walked to it, listening to the crunch of his footsteps on the gravel and straining for any other sounds that might spell trouble. Just before he reached the vehicle, he saw a movement from the corner of his eye. Someone stood watching from the sidewalk. Darkness obscured the person's identity but Viktor could see it was not General Schwinn.

There was nothing left to do but carry on as if his activities were not extremely strange. Sliding quietly alongside the vehicle, he knocked on the window to indicate Natalia should unlock the doors so he could put the bags into the rear seat with Sasha. She jumped at the sound. The minute his head was inside the back of the car she complained that he had scared her by coming from an unexpected direction and chastised him for being late. He did not say anything. No sense explaining the delay. The information would only alarm her unnecessarily.

When he climbed back into the passenger seat, Natalia eyed him expectantly, but he concentrated on looking for the man who had been on the sidewalk. There was no sign of anyone. Viktor turned to Natalia.

"All is well. I left by the back way so that Schwinn and Murdock undoubtedly believe I am asleep in my room. Let us be gone from here."

As she drove them off post, Natalia resumed her conversation with his son—an obvious attempt to put the boy at ease. Natalia explained that he could watch television and any number of videos while staying at her house, and Sasha seemed excited at the prospect.

"A computer, do you hold?" Sasha asked in his thick accent.

"Yes, I have a computer." Natalia glanced at Viktor as though he might have something to say about the boy getting free rein over the Internet, but Viktor did not have it in him to worry much about such things. There were so many other more difficult problems to overcome in the next few days. "You can use it if you're careful."

Viktor translated this so there was no misunderstanding. Then to Natalia he said, "He can be trusted with your computer. He is proficient with mine and is careful about where he wanders on the Web. One adventure into forbidden territory was enough, is that not right, Sasha?"

His son understood enough to look embarrassed by the memory of being caught and disciplined—no computer use for a month. Viktor smiled to himself. Sasha was a good boy. He could be trusted to take care of Natalia's things. But then his thoughts turned to more immediate issues.

"I have another favor to ask, Natalia," he said.

She shifted in her seat uncomfortably and adjusted her grip on the steering wheel, holding the thing tightly enough to make her knuckles turn white. "What is it?" she asked cautiously.

"I must take Sasha to his first doctor appointment tomorrow. It may take a good part of the day. Will you make an explanation for me at work?"

Her hands on the wheel eased. "That won't be a problem. You're still being in-processed. Next week will be harder, though. You'll need to be at work, so we'll have to come up with a plan. Maybe I'll be able to find someone to stay with him during the days." She paused and seemed to be thinking.

"You have been very kind to us," he said gently.

She shrugged. "Today is easy," she said as she turned into a driveway where a small apartment building stood. "But the next few weeks are going to be dicey."

"Dicey," he repeated, trying out the new word.

"Here we are." She turned off the engine and glanced to where Sasha sat in the back seat. He had fallen asleep.

"He does that more often these days. He tires so easily." He opened the back door and stood gazing down at his sleeping son. When he turned to head for the back of the car, he saw that Natalia was staring at him with softness in her eyes.

He might not have been able to move except that she looked away suddenly, as if she realized she had been staring. Both he and Natalia went around to the back of the car, and she knelt to unhook the cord. He leaned forward to grasp the handles of the wheelchair just as she let go of the cord. The boot lid flew up and smacked his head. He closed his eyes and reeled back a step with a grunt.

"Oh! Are you hurt?" she asked.

Cracking his eyes open, he became immediately aware that she stood very close, peering up at him with the streetlight revealing her concern. She looked worried and sweet and lovely all at once. He glanced at her mouth but quickly looked away again, alarmed at where his thoughts had drifted.

He reached up to touch his head where it hurt and contacted wetness. Looking at his fingers, he saw a drop of blood. His own blood.

His stomach turned over. If anything could get his mind off Natalia's attractiveness, it was seeing his own blood.

"Let me see," she ordered, going up on her toes and reaching for his head. She placed her warm palms on his cheeks and tipped him forward a bit to inspect his brow. Relieved to be distracted from the image of dark red fluid on his finger, he let her have her way.

"You've cut yourself," she announced. "It's not bad, but you must have hit your head pretty hard. You look positively green."

"It is nothing," he insisted. He would never admit that although other people's blood did not bother him in the slightest, the sight of his own made him quite sick.

She looked into his eyes, still holding on to him. Those wayward thoughts about her came crashing back, blood or no blood. Warmth pooled in the pit of his stomach, and then he heard her say, "It's hardly bleeding at all. Your eyes don't look dilated or…" She hesitated and seemed to become aware of how close they were to each other. For the barest second, her glance strayed to his lips. "Or anything," she finished very softly as she eased down onto her heels and let her hands slip to his shoulders.

She might have pulled back altogether except that he suddenly needed her to keep touching him. He clasped her wrists and held her palms against his chest while he searched her eyes for signs of protest.

"Tasha," he whispered, drawn to her by something far stronger than the common sense that had helped him keep his distance until now. He had known her for only two days, and yet every moment of that time had been filled to the brim with high emotion—worry and comfort, trepidation and laughter, frustration and wonder. He had shared his secrets with her and she had not disappointed him. And now the urge to show her what he felt seemed impossible to resist. He leaned forward.

She could have turned from him, but she did not. So he brought his lips into contact with hers. Ah, warm and sweet and very, very soft. Flooded with a yearning that overcame sanity, he would have wrapped his arms around her and drawn her closer, except that her pager went off just as he swept his tongue over her lips. Viktor lifted his mouth from hers reluctantly. She groaned softly and shifted slightly, then pulled the offending device from her waistband.

"My mother has excellent timing when it comes to interfering in my life" she said with a wry smirk. "At least she hasn't put in the code requiring an immediate call back, so—"

"Papa?" came Alexander's sleepy voice through the open back door of the car.

"One moment, Sasha," he called to his son as he looked down into Natalia's eyes. Once again he searched for the right words. "Natalia..." he began, but she lifted her fingers to his lips.

"Shh," she said softly. "Let's just get Alexander into the house."

He stepped back from her, feeling overheated and unsettled. He could offer her nothing of himself except momentary pleasure. She deserved more, yet he could not make himself regret the kiss he had stolen.

Forcing himself to turn away, he lifted the wheelchair to the pavement and moved it to where his son sat sleepily inside the rear of the car. He leaned forward and ran his fingers through Alexander's hair and over his cheek. In Russian, he told him that he should ride in the chair to Natalia's flat and then he watched with love swelling his heart as his son yawned and stretched widely. By the time the boy climbed out of the car and into the chair, Natalia stood nearby looking composed.

As Viktor walked into Natalia's building and rode the elevator up to her flat, it was impossible to forget his brief taste of her.

As he pushed Alexander's wheelchair toward the door to which she led them, his senses went on high alert. This was her home, her personal space. He would learn a great deal about her when he entered.

She fumbled with the key a minute—perhaps she was nervous, too—then swung the door open and stepped in. He followed and was struck by the homey scent inside. The aroma of vanilla and something that made him think of fresh sweet rolls permeated the place. He could see that Alexander noticed, too. A smile creased his son's sleepy face.

"Um, the kitchen is over there." She moved through the apartment, spacious by Russian standards, and indicated various amenities. "The bathroom is down this way and there are two bedrooms."

"One of the bedrooms is yours, yes?" he asked, fighting off the memory of their kiss.

"Yeah, but you can sleep there," she said with a slight blush rising to her cheeks. "Why waste a comfortable bed? I'll set out fresh sheets. And I can leave the phone number to my friend's house where I'll be staying—in case you need anything and can't find it. Feel free to rummage, but I don't mind if you call me." She looked over at Alexander with that same motherly expression most women took on when looking at the boy's sweet face. "I want Alexander to be comfortable."

Viktor smiled and shook his head slightly. Sasha would never go long without a female to coddle him. Although he had not given himself time to think of such needs for many months, Viktor realized now how much he needed a little coddling, too. He looked at Natalia and a surge of longing swept through him. The strength of it jolted him into action. If he got moving, he would not succumb to such thoughts.

"To bed with you, Sashyenka. Let us find your room and get you settled." He pushed the wheelchair down a little hallway to the second bedroom. It was a pleasant room with a thick, brightly colored quilt on the bed and old, sturdy furniture that made the space look cosy and comfortable. A stack of towels rested on a wooden armoire, waiting for Natalia's next guests.

An unlit candle stood on a swatch of lace near the towels, ready to fill the room with its scent. In one corner, there stood a wooden rocking chair with cushions on the seat and tied to the back. Viktor decided he would sit there while he read aloud to Sasha, as was their habit before bed. Then he would stay there awhile until his son fell asleep. He would plan what he should do next to begin Sasha's medical treatment while also keeping himself out of trouble with his superiors. And he would not allow himself to think of kissing Natalia.

He heard her footsteps on the wooden floor of the hallway. She set down one of the suitcases inside the door and looked at each of them as if she were happy to have people staying in her home. "The drawers are empty so you can put his things in them, if you like."

"Can you look through this bag for what should be unpacked while I gather the other things?" he asked his son.

When the boy nodded and began to unzip the bag, Viktor turned to get the other suitcases that contained Sasha's necessities. He realized he would have to move sideways through the doorway to get past Natalia. As he began to do so, the space between them suddenly seemed very narrow.

"Come to the bathroom and let me wash your cut first," she said as if she had just remembered it.

"Yes," he said, allowing her to lead the way. They passed a washroom off the corridor near the guest room. He knew before they crossed the threshold that she had brought him to her bedroom. Her scent was here. He passed her bed and tried not to let his mind wander. She led him into a different washroom where her personal things resided. Everything was neat and clean. Two bathrooms for one person, he marveled. Such luxury.

"Sit," she said, indicating the toilet where she had just lowered the lid.

He did as he was told, silently watching her withdraw a bottle of something from beneath the sink and then collect a number of square swabs from a drawer.

"This might sting," she warned just before she brought a soaked square to his cut. It hurt like hell, but he managed to keep from flinching. Pain had never bothered him. It was only his own blood that made him ill. No matter how many times he told himself that there was nothing to be ashamed of, given the horrific experience that had started his phobia, he still felt embarrassed by it. He had the sense to close his eyes so as not to catch sight of the reddened swab.

"All done," she announced a moment later. "You don't even need a bandage. It didn't bleed much." She held out the swab, but he turned away and closed his eyes again, hoping to settle his stomach once more.

"For a tough Delta Force type, you sure don't like blood much," she commented in a bland tone.

This impugning of his manhood forced him to open his eyes. He stifled a sigh of relief when he saw that she had already disposed of the swab.

"I have seen more than my share of blood, Tasha. Spilled blood is never a good thing." She stopped putting her medical supplies away and turned to look at him as if she might comment. But her eyebrows rose slightly and she did not speak. When his gaze met hers, the small room seemed to grow warmer. He knew he should say something about what had happened in the parking lot, but an apology would be a lie.

"I should not have kissed you," he admitted, unwilling to say more.

She looked startled at this change of topic, but then she gave him a crooked smile. "I should not have kissed you, either," she said, imitating his tone and accent.

He nodded, still looking into her eyes. This should be the end of what they had begun outside, but he knew it would not be. There was something between them now. He gazed up at her and wanted...

She took a step back. "I'll just...I should just...um...pack a few things. To...to take with me," she stammered as she escaped through the door.

He passed her in the bedroom, where she was putting clothes into a bag. He forced himself to keep walking until he was out in the hallway and in Sasha's bedroom. He busied himself with helping his son find pajamas and toothbrush and bringing the rest of the luggage to the guest room.

"Here is the washroom, Sasha. Change for bed and brush your teeth. Then come to say goodbye to Captain Wentworth, who has been so kind to us." Viktor tousled his son's hair as he left the boy to these tasks.

He made his way back to the living room, noting the family photos on the walls and the fresh flowers on a sideboard. He ran his fingers over the clean, aged wood of the narrow table and wondered if she polished it herself. It was clear she cared a great deal for her home.

"There's food—such as it is—in the refrigerator," she said as she came to stand beside him with a small bag in her hand and a pressed uniform on a hanger. "Help yourself."

"Goodbye, Captain Wentworth," said Sasha from behind her. She turned and looked down at the boy with a smile.

"Goodbye, Alexander Viktorovitch." She tipped her head toward the television. "You know how to use the VCR?"

He grinned widely and nodded. "VCR I understanding," he said.

"I will not let him break anything," Viktor assured her.

"I'm not worried about him breaking it. I just want to be sure he doesn't have trouble making it work."

"He is quite good with technology."

She nodded, satisfied. "Here's the phone number where I'll be." She handed him a piece of paper.

He wondered who she might be staying with and was relieved to see the name Marie written across the top. He did not want her to be staying with Frank, though he knew he had no right to an opinion on the matter.

"Will I find you more?" Alexander asked, and Viktor winced at his son's contorted English.

Natalia laughed. "Of course you will see me again. I'll come by tomorrow to see how you're doing and to figure things out with your father about where you can live."

"Live here," Alexander suggested enthusiastically.

Viktor felt a tug of yearning. Yes, it would be perfect if they could stay in this lovely apartment with all its warmth and comfort and where he could feel Natalia's presence. But instead of agreeing with his son, he strode to the door and opened it for her. "We are grateful and promise to find more suitable quarters tomorrow."

With another nod, she followed him to the door. Her smile had disappeared. She paused a moment on the threshold and glanced up at him.

Viktor had an overwhelming urge to lean forward and kiss her goodbye. Not a seductive kiss, but a light caress to express his gratitude and to wish her farewell. His guts tightened as he resisted the need.

She must have seen something in his eyes, for she took a step back and then turned to walk to the elevator. Without another word, she disappeared behind the sliding metal doors and was gone. His thoughts turned to settling down to sleep for the night. In her bedroom.

He groaned softly.

NATALIE DROVE STRAIGHT TO Marie's house, trying not to think too much about how it felt to kiss Viktor. Instead she thought about how it felt to have Viktor and Alexander in her apartment. The father had taken up a great deal of space, it seemed to her. And the son had simply filled up the place with his amiable spirit and youthful exuberance.

She'd been glad to get out of their way. She'd been sorry to leave them.

And that seemed to be how she was going to feel for as long as she continued to be tangled in their lives. Divided, uncertain, confused.

As she pulled into Marie's driveway, she wondered if she'd find her friend at home. She'd called her from her cell phone, of course, but there had been no answer. She knew where the key was hidden and was sure there'd be no problem about spending the night there even if Marie was out of town.

She left her bag and uniform in the car—she could come back for them after she talked to Marie—and walked to the door. She rang the bell. No answer. Through the narrow windows at the side of the door frame, she could see lights were on in the kitchen. Marie would not have left them on if she was away. Natalie knocked. Hearing the sounds of activity from an upper floor, she waited but heard nothing more. Reluctant to let herself in with the key when she knew Marie was inside, she rang the doorbell one more time. This brought the distinctive thump of feet. The outside light flicked on suddenly, nearly blinding Natalie. A shadow crossed over the small window and the lock turned with a clatter of small metal parts.

"What!" demanded the woman who appeared on the other side of the swiftly opened door. "Oh. It's you." Marie's expression grew a little sheepish, but she didn't invite Natalie inside. She looked as if she'd just tumbled out of bed. Her hair was mussed and she was still tying her bathrobe.

Natalie shifted from foot to foot as she explained her presence. "I wouldn't bother you if I didn't really need a place to stay...." She stopped when she heard someone moving in the kitchen.

A man's voice came to them from there. "Everything okay, Marie?" he said.

"Um, I'm sorry. I should have called first," Natalie said, as if she hadn't tried to call ahead. "I'll just..." she began to back away.

Marie followed her out onto the front stoop. "I'd let you stay, but... What's wrong with your place, did you say?"

"I just...it's nothing really...only for tonight, but..." She knew she wasn't making any sense but couldn't seem to make herself speak coherently. "You know, I can just find a hotel...."

Marie looked apologetic. "Really, I'm sorry, Nat. Any other time, I'd be thrilled to have you bunk here with me. But this guy, he's... You introduced us at O'Malley's a few weeks ago. Didn't you notice me going gaga over him?"

"Missed that," she said with a grin. She backed a little farther down the sidewalk. "I'll call you." As quickly as she could, Natalie climbed back into her car and drove away. The embarrassment of intruding into Marie's romantic night was only just now beginning to heat her cheeks.

Natalie drove to the nearest hotel, too tired to try to think of which other friend she might stay with. Frank would have been glad to let her stay with him, but with the way he had been urging her to a deeper relationship, she didn't feel comfortable going there. This made her a little sad. As she walked to the registration desk, her mind was so focused on her own thoughts, she didn't even notice the activity all around her.

"I'd like a room for the night," she said to the clerk.

"Name?"

"Wentworth. I don't have a reservation."

The clerk looked up and blinked. She stared a long moment and then said, "I'm sorry, ma'am, but we're booked for the whole week."

"Booked?" Natalie hadn't expected this.

In a gentle voice that implied Natalie must have been recently released from an institution of some sort, the clerk explained. "The Special Olympics are taking place here. Combine that with the AMA convention and I think you'll have a hard time finding a room anywhere around D.C. without a reservation."

"Not even at a little motel or something?"

The clerk looked sympathetic but helpless. "I could call around for you, but I doubt you'll find anything suitable." From her tone, Natalie inferred that any motel with an available room would be the kind people paid for by the hour rather than the night.

"Uh, never mind. I'll figure out something else. Thanks."

Weary to her bones, Natalie returned to her car. She noticed the multitude of vehicles parked in the lot and all around the semicircular driveway. The place was packed. And it would be the same everywhere, unless she went a good distance. To hell with that, she thought as she drove to O'Malley's. It was a weekday, so it would be quiet there. She would be able to sit and think of what she should do. No one would bother her there.

Except that when she walked inside her favorite watering hole, there sat Constance DiSanto sipping a beer and talking to a man whose back was to her. Natalie would have pivoted on her heel and walked back out again, but Constance saw her. The woman would have undoubtedly taken offense if Natalie had departed so abruptly. She didn't need to make an enemy of Constance right now.

"Hey, look who's here on a weekday!" Constance said to her companion.

The man turned. "Well, well, if it isn't Na-tal-ya. The prodigal returns." Frank's tone seemed light and teasing, but Natalie had the distinct impression he was annoyed. And his pronunciation of her name had not escaped her. Clearly, something was up.

CHAPTER SIX

"WHAT ARE YOU TWO DOING HERE?" she asked. Better to ask questions than to answer them, she thought as she tried to come up with a good reason to leave quickly.

"Actually, we were talking about you," Constance said with mock pleasantness.

"And Viktor Bad-Enough." Frank said it with a distinctly Transylvanian accent.

At least this explained why Frank had said her name the way Viktor did. One of them must have heard him refer to her that way while they'd been at the Pentagon today.

"Come. Sit. Tell us about the handsome Russian," Constance urged as if the two were friends.

Natalie didn't think she had much choice. Frank would be more suspicious if she departed so soon. "There's nothing to tell," she said as she took a seat at the little table.

"Well, tell us where you've been all night," Frank suggested.

"I don't answer to you, Frank," Natalie said gently.

"Enough, Frank" Constance declared. "I want to hear about the Russian." She turned to Natalie. "He's a hunk. And that accent! Tell me everything."

Natalie thanked the waitress for the fresh bowl of pretzels and the wine cooler she'd ordered. Taking a sip from the tumbler, she mumbled once again that there was nothing to say. Frank stared at her sullenly.

Constance squinted at her. "You're not going to hold out on me, are you? I mean, you wouldn't want to keep him all to yourself or anything. Would you?"

Natalie was appalled at how quickly she could conjure the memory of Viktor's kiss and how accurately she could recall the warmth and taste of his lips. Worse still was the blush she could feel creeping up over her face. If she didn't figure out a way to regain control, her companions would know more about her feelings for the Russian than Natalie cared to admit—even to herself.

"I have no interest in keeping Colonel Baturnov to myself, Constance," she stated firmly.

"See, Frank, you had nothing to worry about. Now that we have that settled," Constance said, "is he as charming as he seems?"

Natalie decided the best way to extricate herself from this situation was to give Constance what she wanted and say goodnight. Otherwise, the woman would likely hound her for days. "He's nice enough. He speaks English very well." And kisses with a warmth and sincerity she couldn't remember ever experiencing before, she silently acknowledged.

"Details, Captain, details."

Natalie sighed. "What do you want to know, exactly? You can look at his file, if that will satisfy you."

Constance impatiently waved her hand as if a pesky fly were buzzing in front of her face. "Is he married? How long is he here for? Did he say anything about meeting me?"

Two emotions washed over Natalie as Constance made her predatory intentions clear. Jealousy reared its green head to a degree that shocked Natalie to her toes. And a deep sense of protectiveness for the man and boy she'd left in her apartment rose within her. It wouldn't do to have Constance nosing around Viktor's business while he was trying to get help for his son.

"Married with children," Natalie said. It worried her that she felt no shred of guilt at the way she used the truth to deceive. Failing to mention that Viktor's wife was deceased didn't seem like a crime with so much at stake.

Constance sighed. "Too bad, though. I wouldn't have been opposed to a quick affair with someone like him," she admitted. "But I don't do married men."

"It's good to see you have some standards," Frank remarked with a slightly disgusted smirk. "Come on, Nat, let's get out of here. I'll walk you to your car." He dropped money on the table.

It annoyed her that he assumed she would depart now simply because he had decided to do so himself. But she was tired and needed to figure out what she was going to do for the night. And she wasn't about to stay and chat with Constance if she could help it. So she put some money on the table to cover her bill and left with him, leaving Constance alone to finish her drink.

Outside, Frank walked slowly. "So how's Marie?"

Her guard went up. He had never shown any interest in Marie before. In fact, he'd always seemed a little resentful of the time she spent with her close friend. "Fine," she said cautiously.

"Been there all evening?"

She was on the verge of making up some sort of reasonable answer about how they had ordered pizza and watched a movie when Natalie remembered that she didn't want to start lying and she didn't owe Frank an explanation of her whereabouts. And her military senses told her this wasn't a time to be defensive.

She stopped in her tracks. "You don't need to know where I am every minute," she reminded him for the second time. Was he trying to trip her up?

He glanced at her and looked as if he might retort. Then he shrugged. "I've been worried about you, Nat. You seem distant lately. Your mother was worried about you, too."

"You called my mother?" She hadn't moved from her spot, and now she felt as if she'd turned to stone. She remembered then that she hadn't returned her mother's page yet. So much had happened, and her mother hadn't indicated she needed a return call right away.

"Actually, she called me. She was looking for you and thought I might know where you were."

"What could be so important she felt she needed to call you to find me?" Eager to get inside the privacy of her car so she could use her cell phone to call her mother, she got herself moving again. With a flick of her thumb, she unlocked the car door with her key-chain remote and walked purposefully toward it.

Frank kept pace with her. "I don't think it was anything in

particular. She just knows we're close and thought she could catch you at my place.''

Natalie closed her eyes. The fact that Pauline Wentworth was making a habit of chatting by phone with Frank Lezinski didn't bode well. But some of the urgency to return her mother's call seeped away. ''You're sure it wasn't urgent?''

''Yeah, I'm sure. She just called to find out how you're doing. She knows how much I care about you. Says she can't always be sure you tell her everything.'' He chuckled over that, then leaned past her and opened the car door for her. ''I'll follow you home to make sure you get there okay.''

Still distracted by the thought of her mother and Frank with an ongoing relationship all their own, Natalie climbed into her car without really hearing what Frank said. ''Okay,'' she muttered, not thinking at all about what she'd agreed to.

But as she left the parking lot and headed home, she noticed Frank's lights in her rearview mirror, tailing her just as he'd said he would. That's when she realized her error. She wasn't supposed to be going home at all, never mind with Frank at her heels. But all she could do now was pray he didn't expect to come up with her to the apartment. She glanced nervously at the clock and saw that it was well after midnight. No wonder she was so tired. At least the late hour would be a good excuse for sending Frank on his way.

Her mind seemed to tumble over and over all that had happened in the last twenty-four hours. She couldn't seem to focus on any one thing. Worst of all, she kept remembering that brief kiss. Then she recalled that all the hotels were full and that Viktor and Alexander were not likely to find housing other than her apartment for at least a week. By the time she pulled into her parking space she had a roaring headache.

Frank drove his car just behind hers but didn't get out. She went through the motions of gathering her purse and jacket, as if she would be going inside. Frank sat behind the wheel with his engine idling and his window down. ''You want me to wait until you're inside?''

Relieved he didn't want to come up, she didn't to speak right away.

"Let me just park the car and I'll come with you," Frank offered.

Natalie moved quickly to his window before he could put words into action. "No! No, that's okay. It's late. You should get home, too. I'll see you tomorrow."

He looked quizzically at her a moment, then smiled and gave her a jaunty salute. Finally he drove off with a "See you tomorrow" called over his shoulder.

Natalie stood where she was in the center of the parking lane, thinking about what she should do now. Glancing up at her apartment, she saw that all the lights were out. It didn't take her long to assess her options for the night. She could either go inside or sleep in the car. The latter seemed downright silly. Looking up and down the street to be certain Frank was really gone, she grabbed her gym bag and the uniform on its hanger from the back seat of the car. With a deep, fortifying breath, she headed for her building.

She let herself in, entering as silently as she could, easing the door closed to avoid the usual squeak of hinges. Even so, the click of the lock sounded like the report of a gun. She stood still and stared at the closed bedroom door, waiting for him to come investigate. Nothing happened.

She looked around, a stranger in her own home, and crept across the room to set down her bag next to the sofa. If she went to the second bathroom off the hallway, she would be less likely to wake either of her guests. The last thing she wanted to do was scare them with her unexpected presence.

Moving stealthily, she walked through the living room. On the way, she noticed her caller ID machine blinking. She took a minute to review her callers because she knew the machine made no sounds as it clipped through the data. Her mother's name was displayed at least six times. She'd called nearly every half hour. Frank's showed up several times, too. Natalie stifled a groan as she stared at the blinking light on her answering machine. The unit had been set to blare the caller's message throughout the apartment so that Natalie could hear it wherever she might be. The idea was to screen her calls if she was busy with something else. No doubt Viktor had been treated to an earful from both her mother and Frank, she realized as she made her way down the hall on tiptoe and entered the bathroom.

She turned on the light only after the door was closed. The instant the glare assaulted her eyes, a chilling thought crossed her mind. What if Viktor or Alexander had actually answered the telephone?

This horrible possibility did not bear close review. If only she could play her messages, she'd know whether her mother knew about Viktor. But there was no way Natalie would risk listening to them now and waking her housemates. She brushed her teeth as quietly as she could, then doused the light and walked out quietly.

As she passed the door to the guest room, she heard youthful murmuring. She stopped, wondering what the little boy was dreaming. He made a few more sounds, and Natalie began to worry that he was having a nightmare. The door was cracked open, so she pushed it a little way open and looked in. Alexander seemed small and helpless with the big comforter tucked up to his chin. His brown hair tossed as his head shifted from one side to the other fitfully.

Unable to help herself, Natalie went into the room. Very softly, she began to hum as she ran her cool hand over the boy's forehead. The tension in Alexander's brow eased almost immediately, but Natalie stayed awhile and hummed a lullaby she remembered from her own childhood.

When she finished and had left the peacefully sleeping child, Natalie thought for a time about her mother and how she had always made a point of singing her daughter to sleep. By the time she was lying on the cozy sofa, Natalie remembered that her mother had been exceedingly domestic—loving to cook and sew and garden. And she'd loved her only child, too. It wasn't until Natalie had decided she wanted to join the Army, following in her father's footsteps, that the relationship between mother and daughter had become strained.

Maybe it was time to make a bigger effort with her mom, Natalie mused as sleep slipped ever nearer in the darkness. Just before she drifted off, she marveled that she could sleep at all, given the wild events of the day. But she couldn't deny how safe and comforted she felt with Viktor and Alexander in her home. That welcome sense of security allowed sleep to claim her after only a little tossing and turning over memories of a stolen kiss....

She awoke to the sounds of feet padding along the floorboards. Night still clung to the room, but Natalie's inner clock told her morning was near. Disoriented, she wasn't sure where she lay until a light switched on in the hallway. Ah, yes, she'd gone to sleep on the couch because...because...

A large man came into view clad in boxer shorts. And nothing else.

Natalie sat straight up, throwing her legs over the edge of the sofa.

Viktor leaped a good two feet into the air and twisted himself on the way back to earth so that his back was against the wall and his body stood coiled into a defensive posture, ready to strike. She froze. And gazed appreciatively at the body poised for her inspection.

VIKTOR THOUGHT HIS HEART might never beat normally again. It was one thing to be primed for surprises when on a mission, it was quite another to have an intruder inside your home. And worse to have an intruder inside a home you have only borrowed. The instant he landed on his feet, he realized the identity of the unexpected invader. But not soon enough to avoid appearing very foolish.

As quickly as he could, he relaxed his muscles and stood straight. He stared at her, speechless.

"I...I came back," she said, as if that explained everything.

He found his voice. "I see that."

The moment seemed absurd, but for the life of him, he could not think of what else he should say. But he was alert enough to notice she wore a T-shirt and, although the blanket still partly covered her lap, her legs were bare. He could see the entire length of one calf and part of the other.

"Um...the hotels were full," she added.

"What happened with Marie?"

She ran her hands through her blond curls as she said, "I

went to her place but she already had company. Why are you up so early?"

He waved vaguely toward the guest bedroom. "I thought to run before Sasha wakes. We will be visiting Dr. Brennan later this morning. I will not find another opportunity."

She sat up straighter. "Were you going to just leave him here alone?"

It was clear to Viktor that "yes" would not be the correct answer. He said nothing.

"What if he woke up in the dark and found you gone?" she added reproachfully.

"Well, I...no," he concluded. "I was going to—" he turned partly toward the kitchen and suddenly remembered what he was wearing—or rather, what he was not wearing—and embarrassment flooded him as he searched for a reason to retreat "—leave Sasha a note. I frequently run in the morning. He would expect it. I usually return before he wakes. But should he find me gone, he would know where I go. And the note..."

He knew he was babbling, so he snapped his mouth shut. He stared at her, wondering what she was thinking. At least she did not seem to be aware of his near nakedness. He thought he should be grateful for that, but somehow he felt mildly irritated that she apparently did not notice his body.

"I will go and...." He pointed back toward the bedroom. But instead of saying that he would go and dress, which would draw attention to the fact that he was currently undressed, he simply began to move in that direction.

She stopped him short with her next words. "I'll go with you."

His eyebrows shot upward and he froze. There were hopeful movements from regions of his body he did not want to find activated at this particular moment, for surely he had misunderstood.

"I can show you a good route to run," she added, wilting the hopes of free-thinking parts of him.

He glanced her way. He would enjoy her company, but she had already helped him so much.

She read the look on his face. "Unless you prefer to go

alone," she said, suddenly sounding less sure of herself. "I could just tell you which turns to take."

"No," he assured her. "I am glad for your company."

Her face brightened. "You go into the kitchen and write the note for Alexander while I get my running clothes out of the bedroom. There's pen and paper by the phone." She stood, and his body tensed in expectation of seeing what she was wearing, but she pulled the blanket over her shoulders and around the front like a cloak as she made for the bedroom.

IT WAS THE ODDEST THING, going into her own bedroom after someone else had claimed it. She stood just over the threshold and stared at the rumpled sheets between which Viktor's long body had recently lain. His bag of clothes sat on her rocking chair with a T-shirt hanging over the edge of it, half in and half out. A confusion of clothes had been discarded on the floor, and she recognized his uniform shirt among the items of underwear. The sock that stuck out from the pile, so recognizable, seemed too intimate and she looked away.

But as she passed her own bed, she smelled his light cologne, which clung to the sheets. She couldn't resist sucking in a deep breath of that tantalizing man-smell. She'd forgotten how nice it could be to have a guy in her life.

As she moved to the far end of her room, she reminded herself that she didn't have a man in her life now. Viktor was only passing through. He would be gone in a month. Back to the country that was her nation's former enemy. Back to his little town, halfway around the world.

Natalie ruthlessly crushed the flicker of wishfulness that crossed through her mind at the possibility of something keeping Viktor from returning to his homeland. She wanted the best for Viktor and Alexander and surely it was better for them if they returned home. But she couldn't deny that the idea of the pair of them staying awhile in America held a certain appeal for her.

And then what? she asked herself as she sorted through the clothes in her drawers, choosing a running outfit.

The fact remained that Viktor would eventually return to his native land. As a Russian Army officer, he had no choice. And, call her old-fashioned, but Natalie couldn't have a casual affair. When she decided to sleep with a guy, it was because she was falling in love with him.

And she wasn't about to allow herself to fall in love with Viktor.

As she changed her clothes, she realized that it would probably be best if she reconsidered running with him and went straight to work. The more time she spent with Viktor, the more involved in his life she became. But she didn't stop getting ready to run. Instead, she told herself she would simply treat Viktor like a brother and Alexander like a nephew. That way, she could enjoy having them in her home without falling victim to deeper feelings. She was a disciplined officer and could remain in control of the situation as long as she was vigilant.

So she went into her bathroom to finish preparing and stopped. His stuff was everywhere. A toothbrush rested on the edge of the sink near a half-used tube of what she presumed was toothpaste, although the wording on the label was beyond her limited understanding of Russian. His shaving kit sat on the countertop. A used towel rested over the back of the toilet. The room wasn't messy—everything was carefully placed. He hadn't dropped the towel on the floor and left it, for example. Still, his presence was pervasive.

And, God help her, she liked it.

BY THE TIME VIKTOR HAD the note written out in his neat Cyrillic, Natalia was back in the living room, dressed in shorts and a T-shirt. She sat to tie her running shoes. Without a word, he went into her bedroom to dress, glad to be done with parading before her in his underwear.

Out on the pavement, he watched her stretch and did this himself. She did not seem to be in the mood to talk, so he kept quiet. Though they had a hundred things to discuss about where he would live and how he should proceed, he was grateful for a respite from it all. At least for the moment. When she straightened and asked if he was ready, she looked young and very pretty, and he thought of their brief kiss and wished he could find an excuse for another. But then they were off and he managed not to think at all.

The pavement and sidewalks over which she led him were gently sloped here and there. The grass and trees dappled the ground and scattered orange light as the sun rose over the horizon. He felt the pressure beneath his feet as he took each stride, aware of the beating of his heart and pumping of his lungs. He was also aware of the woman running at his side.

She ran with wide, sure strides, and he slowed his normal pace only slightly to accommodate her. "This is exactly two miles," she said between breaths when they made a turn down an oak-lined street.

He remembered that physical training programs in the American military involved a two-mile run, some push-ups, and sit-ups. He determined that Natalia must do quite well for herself in all three categories. He could see the definition in her leg muscles, and her arms did not appear soft or weak like so many women's. As he saw this, he also saw the car that did not make a complete stop at the intersection. He pulled Natalia back from the vehicle just in time and they both stopped, catching their breaths and silently considering the near-miss.

"I'm not as worried about that lousy driver as I am about the car that's been following us," she said after a few seconds of jogging in place.

She did not look in any single direction, but somehow he understood that she meant the roadway to her left. He bent over at the waist as if he were winded and looked up through the fall of his hair. Sure enough, a car had pulled over and sat idling at a curb half a kilometer down the street.

"Let us go," he said, heading back the way they had come. But as they approached, the car turned off onto a side street. "Did you recognize the vehicle?"

"No, but it reminded me of something I can't quite latch on to," she admitted as she kept on running. "Maybe I'm imagining things, but the car seemed to pace us for a few blocks."

"I think that your instincts are good." He remembered the man standing by the parking lot the previous night and wondered if there was a connection. "We should keep our eyes open for such things."

She waved her hand, dismissing the incident. "I'm just jumpy. Who would follow us?"

Viktor could think of several groups from two separate governments who might be interested in his activities. But he could do nothing about it now. He would simply remain alert and do what he could to keep Alexander and Natalia safe.

They came to within a half mile of her apartment building, and he suggested they walk from there to cool down. It was time to talk about the day ahead and plan for the coming weeks.

"I am regretting to have involved you in this. You cannot like the idea of being watched or of having us in your home."

She glanced at him, looking shy for the first time since he had met her. "I don't like being followed, but it's kinda nice having you and Alexander around. I don't get much company."

He grinned at her, unable to help himself. These might be serious times, but he could not be unhappy about her comment. He liked being with her, too.

NATALIE COULD NOT IMAGINE what had possessed her when she'd told Viktor she liked having him around. It was as if some demon resided inside her, pushing her to misbehave. But she'd said it, and now there was no turning back.

"Should we report this incident with the car?" she wondered aloud, trying to think what she would say and to whom.

"Will we tell the authorities we noticed a blue car that seemed to be following us? We cannot further identify the vehicle. It was not close enough to see the number plate. It turned away when we approached." He shook his head from side to side. "I think we should wait."

She nodded. Maybe she'd made too much of what she'd seen. The car might not have been following them at all. The driver could have been lost, slowing down to look at street signs or addresses. She didn't want to worry about it anymore. There were other problems to deal with at the moment.

She stopped in the center of the sidewalk. "Look," she began, hands on hips. "Since all the hotels in the area are full, we aren't

likely to find a place for you and Alexander. So we're going to
have to make the best of it, with you staying at my place until
he's admitted into the hospital. Okay?''

She eyed him, wondering why she felt so defensive. She was
offering a solution to his most immediate problem, yet she felt
as if she had to convince him that staying with her was the right
thing to do. Or perhaps she needed to convince herself.

"That is very kind of you," he said. He had gone a few paces
ahead of her when she'd stopped so abruptly. And now he stood
before her, very straight and tall, with his back to the street.
"My debt to you grows very quickly."

She waved her hand as if to sweep his debt away. "Pay it
forward," she said, and began to walk again. He looked puzzled
and she would have explained about the movie with that title
that she liked so much, but his next words emptied her head of
all previous thoughts.

"Your mother called last night," he announced.

"I know." She cringed, dreading to hear what might have
happened the first time the phone rang.

"I knew that I should not answer your telephone."

Relief flooded her. "That's good."

He looked straight ahead, avoiding her eyes as he added, "But
I did not have the foresight to explain this to Sasha."

She nearly choked on her own spit. "You mean…"

"He was standing very near when it rang. He picked it up as
a matter of habit," he explained.

"Yes," she said in a strangled voice. "That would be anyone's reaction."

"I moved quickly and replaced the receiver. But he had already said hello." Viktor paused and Natalie closed her eyes
against what she suspected was coming next. "In Russian," he
finished.

"Naturally," she said.

"I did not know who had called. I hoped that the person
would assume he had reached a wrong number. But the phone
rang again and we heard your mother through the machine. She
said something about using speed dial, so she knew she had not
dialed incorrectly."

Unable to take another step, Natalie came to a standstill once more and clasped her forehead in her palm as if she were coming down with a fever. "What must she be thinking?"

Viktor gave her an odd look, half sheepish grin and half worry. "Listen to the machine and you will know what she imagines."

Natalie stared at him a moment, trying to picture where her mother's imagination might have taken her. She started walking again. "Frank said he called, too," she said.

"Yes."

Natalie heard a distinct chill in Viktor's voice as he delivered that solitary syllable. Afraid Viktor might attempt to repeat what Frank had said on the answering machine, Natalie held up her hand to stop him. "I'll listen to the machine for that, too."

A few silent strides later, Viktor said, "You will wish to reconsider your offer to allow us to stay in your flat. We will manage. You should not take on our cause when we have already brought you trouble."

"You're right, I shouldn't. But the truth is, you won't manage without me. The important thing is to get Alexander taken care of."

Viktor nodded. He clearly hated being in debt to her. And yet, he was man enough to admit he needed her.

Inside her apartment, Alexander called happily to his papa from the kitchen. He appeared on the threshold saying something in Russian. Then he fell abruptly silent when he saw Natalie.

"Say it in English, Sasha. We must practice."

"Mmm...tea I cook," he tried.

"Very good." Natalie praised him as if he'd gotten it right. "I've made tea," she gently corrected him, never indicating that he hadn't said exactly those words and trusting that his syntax would improve just by listening.

Viktor smiled at her. That warm, handsome smile that made her want to...want to... She gave up trying to find a conclusion to the thought and moved to the kitchen.

"Let's see what's for breakfast." She opened a cupboard. "Cheerios, Sugar Smacks, Pop Tarts, or..." She pulled a box from the shelf and eyed it dubiously. "I could make these chocolate chip muffins."

Both Viktor and Alexander stared at her, speechless.

"What?" she asked, wondering why they didn't make their selection. They had to be as hungry as she was.

After another moment of staring, Viktor finally consulted his wristwatch. "It is still early. If you will allow me, I will prepare breakfast. Give me a moment to clear my things from your room. You may listen to your telephone machine and then take a shower. When you are finished, the food will be cooked."

"Cooked?" she repeated. Viktor disappeared into her bedroom while Alexander gave her a puzzled look and set himself to foraging for supplies in the refrigerator.

With a shrug, Natalie went to the answering machine and hit the playback button.

Her mother's voice whispered out of the speaker as if she'd subdued her usually strident voice to keep from being overheard by anyone but her daughter. "Natalie, for God's sake, pick up the phone. I know you're home and that someone is there with you. The least you can do is give me the courtesy of an explanation...."

The messages only got worse from there.

CHAPTER SEVEN

TWO HOURS LATER, when Natalie entered the Pentagon, she noticed there was a spring in her step. This, despite the fact that her career had recently taken a wrong turn—not to mention that she'd just taken a Russian officer into her home, imagined someone was following her and had an interfering mother to contend with. It was the food, she knew. There was nothing like starting off the day well fed. Those fried eggs had been heavenly. She would worry about the cholesterol some other time.

"Good morning," she said to Emmy as the secretary grimly handed over a copy of the day's schedule.

Natalie glanced down at it and her good mood evaporated. "What's this?"

"Your schedule for the day," Emmy responded unnecessarily. "The changes came in right after you left yesterday."

"On whose orders?" The schedule listed Natalie in charge of an Australian visit taking place that day. It was a duty that any first-year protocol officer could handle. Not only was it easy, but it would take her away from the preparations she needed to make for an upcoming—and much more important—visit of a Taiwanese delegation due to arrive in a few days. She had a hundred phone calls yet to make for that gig.

Emmy refused to make eye contact. "Colonel Freeman's orders, I was told."

Natalie looked at her and squinted, sensing something strange. "Who said that?"

Emmy shifted in her seat and glanced toward Barbara Dwyer's open office. "Um..."

"Never mind. I don't want to put you in the middle. I'll figure this out on my own.'' She marched purposefully to Dwyer's office, only to find it empty.

That left her only one choice. She'd have to ask Colonel Freeman himself to explain. It was clear to her that something was going on. If it kept up, her hopes of building a military record that would see her promoted to major would be napalmed. Her chances of that NATO assignment were nil without the promotion.

She'd be damned if she was going to give all that up without a fight. But first she had to know what—or whom—she was fighting. This subtle, insidious shift in her assignments would be impossible to overcome if she couldn't figure out the underlying cause.

Taking a few moments in her office to collect her thoughts, Natalie remembered the last time she'd been in to see Colonel James Freeman. He'd dismissed her concerns as meaningless and had reminded her that every officer, even the rising stars, had to do some of the grunt work occasionally. He'd said it kindly and with a slight smile, but she couldn't risk that he might not be so benevolent if he decided she was becoming a complainer. Colonels hated whiners in their ranks.

What she needed was a strategy—a way to approach him without appearing to be barking up the same tree as before. As she thought about this, she reviewed the calendar of assignments for the office over the past several weeks. The bad part was, she could detect no obvious pattern. Sometimes she got crummy assignments and sometimes the others got them. Sure, she'd gotten more than her share lately, but what did that prove? The Colonel would assume that others in the office would get their fair share of the less challenging jobs when their schedules permitted it.

She blew a gust of air upward into the curls that hung over her brow. Leaning back in her chair, she felt irritation well inside her. She needed to figure out exactly who was responsible for the shifts in assignments and why.

She wanted to blame Constance. That woman had never liked Natalie, even though she'd always been falsely friendly in public. But Natalie wondered if Constance was capable of thinking up such a cleverly subtle campaign. The only other possibility seemed to be Barbara Dwyer. But why would Captain Dwyer start this war between them when things had been going fairly well for both of them? They hadn't exactly become friends—the competition between them prevented that—but they had behaved maturely, helping each other on a few assignments in accordance with the concept that an officer's first objective should be the good of the nation rather than achieving personal goals. Natalie did not want to believe Barbara was involved.

Besides, neither Barbara nor Constance had the power to change the assignments without help. Nonetheless, she checked the personal calendars of each woman for the last few weeks to see if she could detect any benefit falling to one or the other as a result of the changes in assignments. These calendars weren't necessarily private, and as the senior officer in the suite, Natalie had every right to go through them. But she found nothing of consequence.

She thought about Viktor and how much worse things would be for her if anyone found out about him. The mischief he'd involved her in could be used against her and twisted in a way that would ruin her future in the Armed Forces forever.

Just as her inner turmoil reached a boiling point, she realized she was running out of time—at least for the day. She had to get busy on the Australian visit within the hour. So, armed with nothing but her certainty that something was very wrong, Natalie went to see Colonel Freeman.

He was willing to see her immediately, which seemed like a good sign. If she were in ill favor with this man, he'd make her wait. He smiled his warm, fatherly grin and bade her to take a seat. "What brings you to this end of the corridor today?"

"Sir," she began, taking a more formal approach than she normally would. "I'll be working the Australian visit today." She paused to see if he would react.

She wasn't disappointed.

"Why would you do that? Can't one of the junior officers handle it?"

She nodded gravely. "Yes, sir, that's what I thought, too. And with the Taiwan visit next week, I have plenty to keep me busy.'' She let that sink in for a minute, then added, ''I was told you had ordered the change in assignments, sir.''

Freeman scratched the back of his neck and peered off into space with his crinkly eyes squinted. ''Did I?'' he asked the air.

''That's what I was told.'' She waited some more, fighting impatience.

''Well, maybe I did.'' He picked up some papers and set them aside. ''Hard to keep everything straight with the Secretary of the Army running off on visits and having people come in to see him every five minutes.'' Shuffling through some loose sheets, he found the one he wanted and brought it to the top of the pile. He stared at it a moment, then remembered to put on his reading glasses. ''Ah, yes. I remember now. That young Lieutenant Safford is out with the flu. Figured you were the only one who could pull off the visit on such short notice.''

''Safford has the flu?'' This was the first she'd heard of it. She was usually better informed. But she'd been distracted by Viktor yesterday. Otherwise, perhaps she'd have known already about an illness in the ranks. Another sign of the danger Viktor posed to her future.

''Yep. Someone left a note.'' He waved the sheet in his hands. ''He's on quarters for at least a week, maybe more. Sorry, Natalie. This isn't up to your usual level of assignments, but who else was I going to choose?''

''I'm glad to help, sir.'' And she meant what she said. ''Thank you, sir. I just stopped by to make certain this is what you want me to spend my time on today. You've answered my question for me.'' She stood to go.

''You're always welcome, Natalie. How's your mother?'' Colonel Freeman had met the irrepressible Pauline at Natalie's last promotion. The unlikely pair had joined a mutual admiration club right off the bat. They were of an age, both widowed, and it didn't seem to matter that one was black and the other white. For a while, Natalie had believed there might be a little romance blooming. But then Pauline had returned to New York and nothing more had been said other than the occasional inquiry on the part of the Colonel.

Natalie remembered her mother's phone messages and re-

sisted a cringe. She still hadn't contacted her mother, mainly
because she hadn't yet thought up a plausible explanation for
Alexander answering her phone and then hanging up. And even
if she dreamed something up, it would be a lie. She'd already
vowed not to let Viktor's scheme turn her into a liar.

"Mom's fine. You should call her sometime. She'd love to
hear from you."

Colonel Freeman smiled warmly. "Maybe I'll do that. Meantime, you tell her I retire in another six months."

Natalie dropped back into her chair. "What?"

Freeman nodded his head. "Yep. Need to pick a time. Six
months from now seems like a good season. Leaves blowing,
maybe snow falling. I've done my duty to my country. Thirty-
five years of my life. Proud of it. Time to give it up and enjoy
what's left."

Natalie was stupefied. The man spoke as if he were old. He
couldn't be more than... She honestly had no idea how old
Colonel Freeman was. He certainly didn't look old. He still ran
the two miles in a period of time that put younger men to shame.

"What...what will you do?" Natalie herself couldn't picture
life without the Army.

The Colonel gave her one of those penetrating stares he was
so famous for—the one that seemed to ask how anyone so mindless could be allowed to wear the Army uniform. "Oh, I suppose
I'll do some fishing. Maybe spend some time with my kids. And
their kids," he added with a grin. "Might give your mother a
call, too."

He said this last part with a hint of defiance. If he thought
Natalie might object to such a phone call, he was mistaken. She
grinned broadly to let him know she wouldn't mind at all.
"She'd like that." She put her hand to her throat, already feeling
the tug of separation from this man who had been a mentor and
father figure to her for many years. "I'd like to think I won't
lose touch with you after you retire," she confessed.

His smile widened. "Not a chance. Someone's gotta look out
for you."

"Thank you, sir," she said with real sincerity. "For everything."

He waved away her gratitude, as he always did. "That's what I'm supposed to do. Bring young officers along. It's just that in your case, it's been a pleasure. Rarely get to see an officer take to a job the way you have. You were meant for protocol. You could see a hockey team through a tea party, and everyone would have a good time."

High praise, indeed, and Natalie knew it. Colonel Freeman tried hard to avoid playing favorites, so he rarely gave out compliments. His words made her glow inside. Suddenly, she felt more certain of herself. Her assignments didn't seem so out of the ordinary. There was even an explanation for this recent job with the Australians.

Natalie left his office with her good mood restored. If it hadn't been for running into Constance as she reentered her office suite, the morning would have been reasonably enjoyable. But Captain DiSanto had some gloating to do.

"Australians, huh?" Constance said.

"Someone has to take care of them. Just because they speak our language, more or less, doesn't mean we should treat them with less care."

"But it doesn't take a rocket scientist to deal with people whose culture isn't all that different from ours," she countered.

"The job would be ideal for *you*, then, but I'm afraid you couldn't handle the extra work on such short notice." Natalie knew she was being childish engaging in such a ridiculous spitting contest with a fellow officer, but her last jibe wiped the smirk off DiSanto's face. It was hard not to be pleased by those results.

She made a few calls to ensure that the caterer had the menu straight for the Taiwanese formal dinner and that the reservations were secured for the tour of the city the group would take. She checked the meeting schedule and sent reminder e-mails to a few people who were expected to deliver briefings to the visitors. She asked Emmy to call a few of the local invitees who hadn't yet responded.

With those wheels set in motion, she turned her attention to the Australians. They were due to arrive in an hour, and she'd need to greet them on the steps of the Mall doors to the Pentagon. This entrance was closest to the Secretary of Defense's office and offered a nice view of the river. She wouldn't need translators, just the itinerary. Luckily, Lieutenant Safford had put the plan in the common files as he was supposed to, and Natalie printed it off.

She hoped the briefing packages were ready, too, and went in search of them. The stack of folders sat neatly on Safford's guest chair, ready to go. She'd have to commend him on his efficiency when he came back to work. By preparing ahead of time, he'd made this easy on her. As she picked up the packages, she saw a half-empty cup of coffee on the Lieutenant's desk. Must have been sitting there since before he went on sick leave, she surmised. She'd have to remember to ask Emmy to dump out the contents and rinse the cup before it started growing things.

Just before she left, she noticed a framed photograph on the wall. It caught her attention because the Kremlin stood proudly in the background. Lieutenant Safford grinned from the center of the photo with some others, clearly enjoying his visit to Russia.

The picture reminded her of Viktor and Alexander. She realized then that the two of them had never been far from her thoughts. Alexander's appointment with Dr. Brennan was scheduled for ten-thirty. By that time, she'd be making certain that the Australian visitors and American hosts all sat in their proper places, carefully ordered in accordance with each person's rank. She'd made sure Viktor had her phone number at work so he could call to tell her when Alex could be scheduled for surgery, but she wouldn't be able to take that call. Her day would be taken up with the less-than-challenging details of supervising the visit from one of America's closest allies.

The day was spent in a rapid succession of greeting, guiding, overseeing and catering. These Australians had visited before. They knew the drill. They didn't stop at every painting along the lavishly decorated corridors of the Pentagon and they didn't ask for impossible menu items at lunch. They'd come with a purpose, and it was Natalie's job to see that their goals were met with the least amount of difficulty. Everything went off without a hitch.

By the end of the day, she was feeling pleasantly weary. She wanted to go home. She wanted to go home to Viktor and Alexander.

That realization stopped her dead in her tracks in the center of the Pentagon's second floor E-ring. Was she really so lonely that she longed for the company of a Russian she'd known a few days and a boy she'd met yesterday?

Apparently so.

She continued to her office, mulling over the possibility of getting a dog after Viktor and Alexander returned home, when she saw Lieutenant Safford cross the hall in front of her, passing from her suite to his own. She didn't know the man well, but she was certain it was Safford.

She quickened her step and made directly for his office. Coming to a stop on his threshold, she stared in disbelief as she watched the young officer calmly take a sip from the mug she'd seen sitting on his desk that morning. It was filled to the brim with fresh, hot coffee. She watched the steam slither past his nose as he brought the edge to his lips.

His eyes smiled at her over the cup when he noticed her standing there. "Hey, Captain. How've you been?"

"I'm fine. But what about you?"

"A little head cold, no big deal. Got some extra rest this morning and I'm good to go now. Say, thanks for taking on that Australian group for me, ma'am. You didn't have to do that."

"You were supposed to have the flu."

His eyebrows shot up. "News to me. Isn't it a little late in the season for the flu?"

"You were supposed to be out at least a week."

"Do I get credit for being present for duty?" he asked with a smile in his eyes. "I came in to do the Australians, but my briefing packages went missing. I spent a half hour looking for them before someone told me you'd taken over that job because I wasn't feeling well."

"Who?"

"Ma'am?"

"Who told you I'd taken over for you?"

"Captain Dwyer. She said there must have been some misunderstanding."

"I'll say." But Natalie didn't stay to explain her irritation to the Lieutenant. With a halfhearted wish for his swift recovery from his head cold, she took herself back to her own office to think.

An hour later, she hadn't been able to find out who had told Colonel Freeman that Safford was out sick and she was no closer to figuring out what was going on. She would have to take up the investigation the following day.

Right now, she had a very annoyed mother to call. She couldn't put it off any longer. Grimly, she dialed.

"Hello, Mom," she said, trying to sound light and breezy.

"Is this my only daughter? The child I brought into this world? The very one who doesn't return my frantic calls?"

Natalie rolled her eyes. "Cut it out, Mom. I got your messages and I'm calling you now. How are you?"

"I would be fine if I knew what you were up to. Who answered your phone last night, then hung up on me. And where were you after that?"

Her mother meant well, Natalie knew this. But some days it was hard to be Pauline's daughter. Still, no matter how irritating the woman could be, Natalie didn't want to lie to her.

"I have a friend staying at my place for a few days. The little boy answered the phone by accident." Omitting the fact that the friend was not female could not be counted as an actual falsehood, she told herself.

"And you couldn't pick up the line again after that? I called a dozen times."

"I was out visiting Marie. When I got home it was too late to call. But I'm calling you now," she reminded her mother for the second time. She'd had enough of the guilt trip. But she knew how to distract her mother. "Guess who asked about you today?"

"The Secretary of State," she snapped irritably.

Natalie squeezed her eyes shut as if this might keep her head from exploding, which felt imminent. Half annoyed, half amused, Natalie said, "Your sarcasm would work better if you

could just remember where I work. It's the Secretary of *Defense,*
Mom. I work for the Secretary of Defense. More specifically,
I'm employed by the Secretary of the Army. And, no, neither
of them asked me how you're doing.''

''Well, get on with it. Who?''

''Colonel Freeman.''

Silence shouted from the other end of the line. Natalie could
tell she had fully diverted her mother's attention. She let the
seconds go by without another word until she knew her mother
must be squirming in her seat.

At last Pauline said, ''That's nice.'' Another moment went by
before her mother couldn't resist asking, ''What did he say, exactly?''

Natalie smiled broadly. A little romance between her mom
and her mentor would be just the thing to take Natalie's mind
off her own problems. ''He just asked how you were doing and
said to tell you he's retiring in about six months.''

''He is?'' Pauline was really interested in this news, Natalie
could tell.

''He said he'd call you soon. Is something going on between
the two of you that I should know about?''

''Not that I know of'' came the tart reply. ''James Freeman
is married to the Army.''

''Not for long,'' Natalie pointed out amicably.

''How is Frank?'' Pauline also knew how to take control of
a conversation.

''As you know very well, he's fine.''

''You should marry that man.''

''What?'' It came out like an exclamation. Natalie was truly
shocked by her mother's blunt declaration.

''You heard me. You should marry him. You're thirty-seven
years old…''

''I'm almost thirty-five.''

''…and you need to start a family before it's too late.''

Natalie's thoughts snapped instantly to an image of Alexander's smiling, animated face. Then she remembered how full her
heart had been when she'd soothed his dreams and hummed her
lullaby the night before. For the first time in a long, long time,

Natalie thought about being a mother. She'd be good at it, she suspected.

"I'm not going to discuss this with you, Mom." And she made good on her word by closing the conversation as quickly as she could.

Shaken by the thought that she could be happy following a path other than the one she had been tenaciously pursuing for the last ten years, Natalie sat still for a few moments. She'd always wanted to be an officer in the United States Army like her dad. There had never been another ambition. So when had she started feeling that there might be more to life?

She knew this was another mystery she was not going to solve today. There was nothing left to do but go home. To Viktor and Alexander.

AT THE END OF A VERY long day, Viktor knew he needed a new plan. His carefully constructed strategy for repairing his son's heart had gone up in flames. With his head in his hands, he waited in the antiseptic hallway of the hospital while his boy underwent yet another long test. But no matter how he ground his teeth or worked his temples with his fingers, no solutions came to mind.

He wanted to talk to Natalia. He was beyond caring that he had already imposed upon her more than he should. His son's life was at stake and he would do anything to ensure Sasha's well-being. He was a father. He loved his son.

The day had not started out badly. First, he had found great pleasure in watching Natalia eat the breakfast he had cooked for her. She had eaten with gusto and smiled at him between mouthfuls. She and Sasha talked of ordinary things, and Viktor had understood that he would be truly happy for the first time in his life if only he could enjoy a lifetime of mornings like this.

He and Sasha had made it to Dr. Brennan's hospital offices in a taxi without difficulty. Although Viktor felt as if he knew the doctor well after their e-mail correspondence, this was their first face-to-face meeting. The doctor's kindly manner had put Viktor and Sasha at ease.

"So tell me, Alexander. How are you feeling these days?" he had asked, looking straight into Sasha's eyes.

"Tired most of the time," Sasha said in Russian.

Viktor translated, having no heart to insist that his son try to speak in English. But then his son surprised him by focusing hard on the words he used and repeating, "Tired. Very tired."

The doctor nodded sagely and held up his stethoscope. "I'm going to listen to your heart and your lungs now, if that's okay."

"Okay," Sasha said. This was a word he knew well and a procedure he had become too familiar with over the years. He raised his shirt to reveal his skinny chest. Viktor could count all of his ribs and the sight nearly broke his heart. As it did every time.

When the doctor finished listening, he examined Sasha for other signs of illness. Viktor knew that other than his heart, Sasha was a reasonably healthy child. When the examination ended, Dr. Brennan stood back and looked first at Sasha, then at Viktor. He seemed to be sizing them up in a way Viktor had never experienced with any other doctor.

"The diagnosis you received in Russia appears to be correct. We'll have to do a series of tests, of course." His eyes were warm and kind, making Viktor feel important to this process for the first time since Sasha had been diagnosed years ago.

Viktor nodded. He had expected tests. Tests had become a part of his and Sasha's life over the years.

The doctor seated himself behind his desk and consulted a calendar on his computer. "I think we can get him scheduled for surgery in about a month if we push it."

Viktor's stomach felt like it dropped to his toes. He had not expected to wait a month before the surgery was performed. His country expected him to return to Russia in a month. He could not leave Sasha to face surgery alone. Therefore, he would be required to find a solution to the problem that would allow him to stay with his son.

His expression must have revealed his feelings because Dr. Brennan's brow creased with concern. "I know I said his surgery could be scheduled for the week of your arrival. You were very specific about how important this would be. But we need to make certain we have enough of his blood type on hand. He's O negative, so he can only get that type and we're unexpectedly low right now. It's possible we can draw some of his own blood to have on hand, but that takes time."

"I understand." He collected himself. "Gratitude at your helping my son. I must work on this. Please make all effort to put the surgery soonest." In the strain of the moment, it was as if his ability to speak coherent English sentences had left him along with his hope for a problem-free mission. "What about my own blood for Alexander?" He pulled out his dog tags and held them out for the doctor to see. "This 'O negative' I believe I have."

The doctor peered at the tags for a moment and clearly could make nothing of the foreign printing there. He nodded his encouragement, anyway. "If you're the same type, that would help. We'll have you tested, too. And if you have any friends who are O negative, now's the time to call on them."

Viktor would give every last drop of his blood to save his son, if the doctors would allow such a thing. Instead, there would be this delay—despite his careful planning—because of an unexpected blood shortage. Taking a deep breath he told himself that it was better to have *these* problems than to have any difficulties during the operation. He would find a way to stay in the United States somehow.

"I can see there's a problem. You'll need to tell me what your concern is if I'm to help you," Dr. Brennan said gently.

Viktor glanced at Sasha, unwilling to air the issue in front of the boy. Yet he found his son sound asleep on the examining table, which explained how quiet he had been throughout the discussion. Normally, Sasha would have had many questions to ask.

"I am expected to return to Russia by the end of the month," he confessed. "I must find a way to remain with my son."

Dr. Brennan's grave expression eased. "I'll write you a letter explaining the circumstances. Or better yet, I'll call your embassy to extend your visa. Surely your government will understand...."

Viktor held up his hand and smiled reassuringly. He could

not have this kindhearted doctor contact his embassy on his behalf. The people there would not take well to Alexander being in America with him. "No, no. Thank you. There are complications. I will request your help if I need." He would think of something.

"I'll do my best to move things along for you. If all the tests go well and we find enough blood, maybe we could get him scheduled in a couple of weeks."

The doctor explained the tests that would be required. Several were already scheduled for the day. Viktor accepted the written instructions and directions to the various labs and test centers. Then he woke his son.

"We're going to ask you to do some work today, Alexander," Dr. Brennan had explained to the boy. "You'll be tired, but we won't let you overdo. Trust me?"

Alexander nodded. "My heart you fix," he said gravely. It was not a question but a statement of his youthful willingness to do whatever was required of him in order to get well.

Viktor had wheeled his son through the long white hallways of the hospital from one grueling test to another. Now Sasha was in a room with blessedly dimmed lighting, undergoing an MRI. It was noisy, but at least Sasha was allowed to lie down for the procedure. No treadmills in sight.

Rubbing the back of his neck to ease the tension, he tried to think of ways he could extend his stay in America. There were few options. It had been nothing short of a miracle when he had convinced his superiors to allow him to come here in the first place. They did not want to believe he could learn anything from American soldiers about supply movement. He had gathered evidence from the Gulf War to prove the superiority of this nation's ability to get equipment and supplies where they needed to be. Finally, he had prevailed.

Now he must explain that he needed to stay longer than he had originally planned.

For that, he would require help from Natalia. If she agreed to assist—and she had already done so much—she could tell him what to say to his American hosts in the Materiel Command in order to gain an invitation to extend his stay. After that, perhaps he could tell his superiors at home that he had been asked to remain awhile and could not politely decline the offer. Would that work?

He had no idea.

But Natalia would know. He felt an enormous yearning to be with her, to let her calm, controlled manner soothe his ragged nerves. Odd that he would feel this need now. He had been through missions of far greater danger with many lives at stake. But this time, of course, the life at stake was his son's. And that made all the difference in the world.

NATALIE ARRIVED HOME LATE because she'd had to see the Australians off at the end of the day. She could have passed the remaining duties back to Safford, but once she started a job, she liked to finish it.

As she turned the key in her lock, she recognized that anticipation swirled through her. She could hear muffled voices inside, and knew her men were home already. When she opened the door, her anticipation turned to joy at the sights and smells that greeted her.

Alexander sat perched on the countertop in her kitchen with his skinny legs swinging side to side. He'd been chatting to his father while the elder male cooked. Whatever simmered in the pots made her mouth water. Viktor looked up from a taste test, grinned and set the lid back into place over the food.

"Welcome home. I hope you do not mind that I cook dinner."

"Papa cook very good," Alex declared.

"I can tell he is an excellent cook from the smell." She put her keys onto the side table and glanced at the answering machine. It was her habit to listen to her messages every evening as soon as she got home. But she ignored the blinking light and went straight over to her houseguests. "What are you making?"

"Roast beef. Potatoes and gravy." Viktor said this in a soft, tempting tone. Natalie's eyes slid to his lips. The memory of their kiss stormed the defenses she'd thought were so strong.

"Carrots and butter. Creaming spinach," Alexander added,

obviously practicing words he had just been reviewing with his father.

"But..." she began, looking at the child to clear her mind of unwanted thoughts. How could they have managed all this?

"Food is not expensive in your country. We were—how do you say—'carried away' at the market." He grinned at her, but she could detect the weariness beneath the smile.

"You shouldn't have done all this. I could have ordered something to be delivered."

His face fell and Alexander went very still. Both males stared at her.

"I should have asked your permission first," Viktor said flatly. The fatigue in his eyes seemed more pronounced now that he was no longer smiling. She wondered if things had gone well for his son at the doctor's office. But she knew better than to start asking questions in front of Alexander.

"No, no. You don't have to ask my permission. You can have full use of the kitchen any time you want. But you don't have to go to so much trouble." She wanted him to feel comfortable, but she didn't want him to think she expected him to cook for her. "Just make enough for you and Alexander whenever you need to."

Viktor tipped his head a little to one side and studied her face. "Cooking is one thing I can do, in exchange for all that you do for us. I am good at this. I am glad to do so. Allow me. You will enjoy, I think."

Alex nodded vigorously at this. Then he made a circular motion over his stomach area and licked his lips. Viktor's cooking clearly pleased the boy. Natalie smiled at him and he returned it.

"You like to cook?" she asked.

Now Viktor's smile was back in place, too. "My mother taught me. It is one of my favorite activities."

The penetrating way he looked into her eyes when he said that made her wonder what his other favorite activities might be. She took a step backward, struggling to regain her equilibrium. Pretending nonchalance, she shrugged to indicate her defeat. "Well, it so happens I like to eat, so cook all you want. But I think you have enough food here to feed an army."

When they sat down to the dinner table together an hour later, Natalie realized how seldom she ate home-cooked food. Thanksgiving and Christmas at her mother's house in New York, mainly. The dish Viktor set before her surpassed even those fine meals.

They talked about the tests that Alexander had undergone. Viktor helped his son with his English as the story of their day unfolded. By the time the meal was over, most of the perfectly cooked roast was gone and there were only shreds of creamed spinach left. Not a single carrot remained. Natalie felt sated and happy. Happier than she could remember being in a long time.

She really had been lonely, she realized. For a while, she would have these two for company. When they went home, she would miss them. And she'd definitely need to get a dog. One with deep brown eyes, like Viktor's and Alexander's.

Viktor waited until Alexander was tucked in his bed and fast asleep before he approached Natalie with his newest problem.

He found her in her living room, sitting on the sofa where he would be sleeping this night. There was a cup of something hot steaming on the table next to her and she was reading an official-looking document, but she set it aside as soon as he came in. With her elbows on her knees, she leaned forward and gazed up at him.

"Will you tell me what the doctor said?" she asked with concern in her eyes.

He nodded and sat across from her in the armchair. He took a moment to collect his thoughts. "Dr. Brennan said that Sasha is an excellent candidate for the surgery. Once it is over, he should be like any normal boy. But—" he hesitated, choosing his words carefully "—the surgery will be scheduled for about three or four weeks from now. And that is only if enough blood is gathered by then."

She blinked at him. "But I thought you were going back to Russia in less than a month."

"Yes. So my orders indicate." He let that sink in.

"You need to find a way to stay here longer," she said, grasping the problem quickly.

"Yes."

"How much longer?"

"Recovery and physical therapy will take several more weeks." He ran his fingers through his hair. "I want you to know I had this all planned before I brought him here. Dr. Brennan understood that surgery must take place soon after Alexander arrived. But he did not foresee the shortage of blood."

Her brow knit as she concentrated on the problem. Then she proceeded to ask a series of questions about the type of blood and whether or not that was the only problem. She wanted to know if Viktor had come up with any reasonable excuses for extending his stay in America and what he thought his chances were of getting his superiors to agree. She offered some ideas of her own, but one by one, the possibilities they came up with were abandoned as unworkable.

"So the best thing to do is to try to get people with O-negative blood to donate some for Alexander. And quickly. That way, Dr. Brennan can schedule the surgery sooner."

"That would be a good beginning," he agreed with a measure of relief.

"You can call the people you know in the local Russian community."

He nodded, liking the way she faced trouble with the aplomb of a good soldier, never considering defeat as an option. He would be pleased to have her at his side in any crisis, he decided. Which led to the realization that he might simply like to have her at his side.

The moment seemed long to him as he looked at her and thought about possibilities he had no right to imagine. She returned his gaze for a time, making him wonder if he could lean forward and kiss her. He wanted to do so very much, even though he knew it would be a mistake to become involved with her. This woman could break his heart, he knew.

"You must be tired," she said at last, breaking the silence. "Why don't you go in and sleep in the bedroom again tonight? I didn't have the kind of day you had."

"What kind of day *did* you have?" he remembered to ask. It was selfish of him that he had not thought to ask before now.

"Weird," she admitted with a lopsided grin. Without elaborating, she stood up and retrieved a pillow, sheet and blanket from where they had been tucked away behind the couch.

"I will sleep here and you will go to your own room. That is right. I cannot take your bed again." He would not sleep much, anyway, so there was no sense keeping her from a restful night, too.

She raised an eyebrow and proceeded to spread the sheet over the cushions. She plumped the pillow and laid out the blanket, folding back one corner invitingly. Then she stood back a bit and eyed her work critically.

"You won't fit," she declared.

He moved forward and stood next to her, nearly shoulder to shoulder. Some inner demon possessed him then and made him tease. "You would be surprised where I can fit this body."

He did not look at her, but he knew her head had snapped around to face him. He could feel her surprise and her wariness. He had meant to be amusing but realized she did not understand Russian humor any more than he understood hers. He should not have made such a suggestive remark. He regretted it.

"I have slept in worse places," he added, to take the heat out of the moment. He did not want to offend her and he should not forget that she had the power to put him and his son out on the street.

"I'm sure you have. You should tell me about them sometime," she said softly. "But right now, I'm really tired so you win. Sleep here if it will make you happy." She moved away, skirting the armchair.

"Natalia," he said, not wanting her to go. "Why was your day weird?" If there really was someone following him, perhaps that person had approached her. He wanted to know if this was so. Should his fears become reality, he would remove himself from her life. He refused to be the cause of any danger to her.

Returning to pick up her empty cup, she stopped for a moment and sighed. "Nothing to do with you. I just seem to be getting assignments that aren't at my usual level."

"Like me?" he said, smiling.

She nodded and grinned sheepishly. "Yeah, like you. And today I dealt with a visit from some Australians on the defense minister's staff." She concentrated, looking off into space. "The thing is, I can't figure out who's behind it. And why?"

Now he grew puzzled, too. "You believe someone is trying to hurt your work intentionally?"

She nodded, then shrugged. "Maybe not. I don't know. There are just a lot of strange things happening. Could be just coincidence, right?"

"Do you believe that?"

She raised her eyebrows and looked into his eyes from across the small space. "I don't know. But either way, it's my problem to contend with. You have enough on your plate."

"But if there is anything I could do for you, Natalia, please allow me. I would be happy to return some of the help you have given me and Alexander."

She smiled at him and there was a brightness to her eyes that gave him great pleasure to observe. "The food you've been cooking is all the return I need. Keep it up and I'll be fat. But don't let that stop you," she added as if she were afraid he might actually withhold his cooking from her. "I'll just have to exercise harder."

"I will cook the meals as long as we are together," he promised. Something inside of him tightened, and he worried it meant he was beginning to wish for much longer than the few weeks they would have together.

He watched her walk away, first to the kitchen to set her cup in the sink, then through the rooms in a pattern that must be a nightly ritual. First she turned out the light on the side table, then she checked the locks on the door. Moving to the hallway, she blew out the candle she had lit earlier. With a final "good night," she disappeared into the bedroom but remained in his thoughts long after.

CHAPTER EIGHT

ON FRIDAY, NATALIE KNEW that Viktor would have to go to work. She had stalled as much as she could, giving vague excuses for his absence not only on Tuesday, when he'd taken Alexander to see Dr. Brennan for the first time, but also on Wednesday and Thursday as well. Those days had been spent going to more tests and taking a tour of the hospital unit where Alexander would be staying. She'd spent those days performing her duties at the Pentagon without learning anything useful about who might be behind her recent troubles. And she'd eaten several fabulous home-cooked meals. There had been no more kissing.

Now Viktor needed to begin in the office where he was supposed to be learning something about supply movements. He also needed to continue his efforts to extend his stay in the United States. His phone calls thus far had resulted in nothing but a runaround.

Even so, she didn't have to like the idea of leaving Alexander in the apartment alone, especially when he looked so pale and worn out. Yet she couldn't stay with the boy herself. Calling out of work would be highly suspicious. And suspicion was the last thing they needed to raise.

She wondered if other people felt this tug-of-war between career and children. And Alexander wasn't even her child. Nor was he her responsibility, she told herself as she dressed for work after her usual run with Viktor. But when she emerged from her bedroom and saw the boy sitting on the countertop watching his father prepare breakfast for them all, she couldn't deny the ache in her heart. She liked this boy. He was funny and intelligent, warm and loving. Who wouldn't care for him?

"Get down, Sasha," Viktor admonished, indicating Alexander's perch.

"No, that's okay," Natalie said. "Sit there if you want. I've come to think of that as your spot." And it was true. In only a few days, she'd come to think of certain places and things as belonging to Alexander or his father. This place on the counter was where the boy sat to watch Viktor cook. The armchair in the living room was where Viktor sat to read after Alexander went to bed. The rocking chair in Alexander's room belonged to him, too. And the place in front of the stove was definitely Viktor's.

She sniffed the air but couldn't identify what he was making. She shot an inquiring look at Alexander.

"Oatmeal," he volunteered. When Natalie looked doubtful, he added, "Good oatmeal."

"Whatever you say," she agreed, and Viktor smiled with his eyes as if he knew a secret.

When she sat down and ate what he put before her—the sweetest, smoothest oats, swimming in cream—she wondered how she would ever be able to live without this man's culinary abilities. After three savory bites, she looked up at Viktor and saw him watching her. His deep-set brown eyes twinkled with amusement.

Her heart fluttered and she realized he was seducing her with his formidable skills in the kitchen. And he didn't even seem to know it. All she could do was grin back at him and take another bite. "Who would have ever guessed oatmeal could taste so good?" she said around the next mouthful.

"I spoke so," Alexander noted. But then he began to cough. He'd been doing that off and on since yesterday, but Viktor told her not to worry as he sometimes got a little congested. He always recovered in a few days.

"Yes, you told me so," she agreed with a fortifying smile in his direction when the coughing subsided.

Worst of all was the moment when Viktor had to say goodbye. She stood near the door next to Viktor as they prepared to leave for work. Both wore their everyday uniforms—open-collared shirts with epaulettes and name tags, dark green slacks.

The colors were different, as were the emblems on the epaulettes, but they were both pressed and polished. Strack, as the Marines would say. Heedless of any wrinkles that might be produced, Viktor clasped his son in a bear hug, picking the child up off the floor for a moment.

He murmured to him in Russian and Natalie understood he was reminding Alexander of what to do if he needed anything. They had prepared a list of phone numbers—hers, his, Dr. Brennan's and the ubiquitous 911, which she had explained to Alexander in English and Viktor in Russian to be certain he understood. There was food in the refrigerator, videos on the table, the oldest looking Playstation she'd ever seen—which Viktor had purchased for him in a second-hand shop in Russia and brought with him inside his luggage—was hooked up to the TV. Alexander would be fine, she told herself.

Out in the hallway, she looked at Viktor. Seeing his worried eyes almost made her turn around and go back. He had hidden his concern from his son, but once the door closed behind them, and they stood together waiting for the elevator, his guard slipped. She supposed she was glad he felt he could trust her with his feelings, but one of them had to be strong. She hadn't expected it to have to be her.

"He'll be fine," she assured him. "He'll have the time of his life with the games and the movies. Did he look concerned or upset?"

Viktor stared into her eyes as if he could pull confidence from their depths. "No. He looked pleased with the situation." He gave her half a smile, which was better than none at all.

They didn't speak as she drove them along Route 1 and then onto 395. She assumed he was also lost in thought about how they would pull this whole thing off without anyone getting into trouble. She turned into a parking spot amid a veritable sea of other cars about a quarter mile from the nearest entrance to the enormous building.

"You want to know why CNN figured out we were going to start our first engagement of the Gulf War?" she asked, hoping to lighten his mood.

He looked at her, surprised. "Why?"

"Because these parking lots surrounding the building normally clear out on the weekends. But not *that* weekend. And the number of pizza delivery orders to the Pentagon went way up that Sunday." She smiled and led the way, weaving through the cars toward the sidewalk that led into the building through the north parking entrance.

"Your counterintelligence forces did not think of this?"

She shrugged. "Guess not. But I bet no one gets any pizza here if we get involved in another campaign."

Natalie didn't know if her conversation helped him take his mind off his troubles, but he seemed more at ease by the time they reached the entrance.

"Do you remember how to get to your office from here?" She didn't want to make him feel coddled by walking with him again if he knew the way. He took out the small white card with the map of the interior on it and consulted the image.

"Yes, I remember," he said. He flipped the card over. "And I have your office telephone number." He winked at her. "In case I need you," he said, imitating her words from the day she'd given him the number.

She chuckled as she went her own way. But before she'd reached her office she began to worry she was really liking her Russian Colonel way too much.

THE MAIN REASON AMERICANS were able to move supplies better than Russians, Viktor quickly discovered, was that they spent so much time on recording inventory into a massive computer database. He understood the database—it was similar to one he used every day—but he could not comprehend the enormous number of man-hours devoted to keeping track of everything. Russian soldiers were mostly out suppressing civil disorder or engaged in alliance peacekeeping operations, not sitting in cubicles typing in data or scurrying through warehouses and stockyards checking off boxes of ammunition and numbers of tanks.

After several hours of reading through a manual on standard operating procedures, he had a fairly good idea how things were done. He realized almost immediately that many of the procedures could not be imitated by his own military because of differences in bureaucracy and deep-seated cultural biases. He would never be assigned enough men to even build a database such as the one the Army Materiel Command used. Especially not when the ill-trusted Internet featured so prominently in the scheme. Viktor knew that such a large enterprise needed to be Internet-based. If not, access and input would not take place with the necessary speed and efficiency from all over the world.

So, after only half a day on the job, Viktor concluded there was absolutely no military reason for him to stay. If it were not for Sasha—and Natalia, too, he realized—he would fly home this very evening.

Instead, he asked innumerable questions of his colleagues, endearing himself to them and learning more than he would ever use. He pored over manuals and surfed through page after page of fascinating Internet sites that he never would have had access to from home.

Still, knowledge was never wasted, as far as he was concerned. He knew there were any number of companies around the world who would pay dearly for the computer and language skills he possessed. Not for the first time, he thought about his options. He didn't want to leave the Army, but with things so precarious regarding Sasha's surgery schedule, he decided he needed to keep an open mind about his future.

He was whisked off to lunch with his new American friends, but when he returned to the office, the secretary handed him a slip of paper indicating there had been a call from Dr. Brennan's office. Viktor's stomach knotted with worry. Brennan would not call him here unless it was very important.

"Colonel Baturnov, I have some bad news," the doctor began when he finally returned Viktor's frantic calls two hours later.

"What news is this?"

"Nothing we can't deal with, but we'll probably have to delay surgery for a bit. We have the set of X rays I ordered yesterday and Alexander has a touch of pneumonia. Probably something we call walking pneumonia, caused by a virus, because he doesn't seem to have a fever, which would have tipped us off sooner. If it was the bacterial kind, I'd just order some antibiotics for him and let him stay with you. But given his condition, we should get him admitted to the hospital tonight so we can monitor him, get him on an IV. Can you bring him in?''

Viktor could not answer immediately. He rested one elbow on the desk he had been using and dropped his forehead heavily into his palm. How could this be happening? he asked himself.

''Colonel?'' the doctor queried gently.

''Yes,'' he said after he cleared his throat. ''I will bring him there tonight.'' They made arrangements and Viktor numbly replaced the receiver on the cradle. Then his brain simply shut down. He just sat in the chair behind the desk and stared at the opposite wall. After a number of minutes, Major Jansen walked by his door and then backed up to stare at Viktor.

''You okay, sir?'' Major Jansen was assigned to Viktor's office. He looked concerned.

Viktor blinked, focused, realized he had to manufacture a smile and some coherent words. ''Yes, Major. Thank you. I am thinking about all that I have learned today,'' he lied. ''A great deal to take in at once.'' He indicated his desk covered with manuals, regulations and database material.

''Yes, sir,'' Jansen replied with an understanding nod. ''You let me know if I can be of any assistance.'' Jansen had already been helpful, giving Viktor the data he needed and showing him how to search the computer files.

When the Major was gone, Viktor could think again. He immediately called Sasha to find out how the boy was feeling.

Sasha had learned his lesson and waited until Viktor told him through the answering machine to pick up the phone. He said he was feeling better and that he had been eating well and drinking hot tea all day, just as his babushka used to insist. Viktor was reassured that he did not need to rush to Sasha's side immediately. He had time to think of a plan to stay in America indefinitely with his son.

Eventually, Viktor came upon the only course of action that seemed possible. He would resort to a desperate act.

Standing, he put on the uniform jacket he had brought with him. The dark coat with red trim and all the medals and ribbons festooned on the front gave him extra confidence. For what he was about to do, he needed all the confidence he could muster.

NATALIE MISSED VIKTOR. There was no doubt about it. She knew she should be worried that she was feeling too much for the man. Instead, she noted the late hour with gladness. She would see him soon.

She had already called Alexander twice during the day. He seemed to be doing fine, though he still had that cough. She looked forward to going home. Another half hour or so of reviewing and signing purchase orders and she could pack up her stuff. And she was in a good mood for another reason. She'd gotten an agreement out of Colonel Freeman's military assistant that no changes in assignments would be made without talking to her first. As the senior officer in her unit, she'd easily convinced him this was correct protocol.

Her only disappointment was that she hadn't heard from Viktor all day. Just as her mind wandered over this fact, the man himself walked through her door.

She stood up and smiled, feeling a little foolish at the way the butterflies fluttered in her stomach. "Sir!" she said. At least she remembered not to call him by his first name. Her door was wide open and anyone might hear her.

"I have come to discuss a thing of great importance," he announced.

She noticed then that his expression was more than merely serious. He was dressed in his full uniform. He looked exceedingly dashing, but his expression was absolutely grim. His eyes were very bright and there was a faint whiteness around his mouth. Her first thought was that there was something wrong with Alexander, and her warm pleasure turned into cold dread.

She stood and moved to close the door to her office.

"What is it, Viktor?" she asked with a calmness that belied her anxiety.

He snapped to attention and declared, "I wish to defect to the United States. I have information that may be valuable to your government."

Natalie stared at him. She could not think what to say. Seconds ticked by. "Viktor…" she breathed. "I…"

He didn't look directly at her but continued to gaze straight ahead. "Take me to the authorities who will process my request, Captain."

"I...I can't do that, Viktor." How could she explain this to him without making him feel foolish?

He glanced her way for a fraction of a moment. "Alexander has pneumonia," he explained. "I have to take him to the hospital tonight. He cannot have surgery until this is cured. It will add many days. I must find a way to remain in your country indefinitely."

Her heart went out to him. This could not be easy for him, this choice between his country and his son. She passed her tongue over her dry lips. "The thing is, sir..." She hesitated, choosing her words. Oh, God, what were the right words?

Natalie sat down heavily in her chair behind her desk. She had to just spit it out and let him deal with his feelings by himself.

"The thing is, sir, your country and mine...they aren't enemies anymore, exactly. You can't defect. No one will care about any information you think you can give the United States..." She stopped speaking abruptly when she saw his body sag slightly.

Looking defeated, he took a seat himself, leaned forward to put his elbows on his knees and lowered his head into his hands. She watched him tensely. What was he thinking?

After a few moments, she thought he might be shaking, then she was certain of it. His shoulders quivered almost violently and she realized with rising horror that the man had lost his composure under the pressure.

"Viktor..." she began, her own voice cracking with emotion. Clearing her throat, she reminded herself that she was an officer in the United States Army. She would find a solution to this problem. "Viktor," she said firmly. This time, it came out like a command for attention.

He looked up at her then and she saw that his eyes were bright, but not with tears. His cheeks were flushed, but not with grief.

He was laughing. It was laced with an underlying sadness, but it was laughter nonetheless.

And when he looked into Natalie's eyes, he could no longer hold back his mirth. He threw back his head and roared with it. He had a wonderful, contagious laugh and Natalie found herself smiling. Relief made her giddy. She chuckled. Then she laughed, too.

"Yes, yes" he managed to say. "We are not enemies anymore. Cannot defect. Very true!"

"I'm so sorry," she said as she tried to get control of her own laughter. "I can understand that your desperation would cloud your thinking."

He began to regain his equilibrium, and shaking his head in amused disgust, he tapped at his temple. "I knew in my mind that I would not succeed in this." Then he tapped at his heart. "But my heart will not accept defeat." He grew very serious again, more in control of himself now that his tension had been released through the unexpected laughter, but still clearly burdened by the gravity of the situation. "I must find a way to stay here in your country while Alexander is recovering. I cannot leave him. And by the time this is all finished, how will my own country welcome me? Certainly my military career will be over."

He sat in silence for a time and Natalie respected the moment. Her mind swirled around half-formed possibilities, never quite latching on to a way to keep him in America while still retaining his right to return home. The best she could come up with were ways to delay the inevitable.

"I am prepared to give up my country, if I must," he said after a while. "Is there no way that your government will agree to protect me? Even for a few months?"

"I can ask my superiors, but I doubt they would be willing to take such a risk. Why would America put its relationship with Russia at stake for one man and his sick boy? And once I ask, the truth will be out and you could find yourself returned to Russia immediately. So I think that going to my superiors should be a last resort. I think Alexander will be protected once he's hospitalized. It would be bad publicity for your country to insist upon his return. We can enlist Dr. Brennan's help to ensure he'll support keeping Alexander here until after his surgery."

Viktor nodded sedately. "This is a comfort, knowing his heart would be repaired though I may not be with him." He looked up at her then and she saw the anguish in his eyes.

She did what she always did when she was handed a problem requiring an immediate solution. She broke the problem down into its components and then set to clearing the pieces away with single-minded actions. "The first thing we need to do is get Alexander admitted into the hospital as Dr. Brennan advised. The doctor will guard Alexander's interests from a medical standpoint."

He nodded and appeared stronger than before, now that a plan was being formulated. "I will continue to do what I can to lengthen my travel plan with my military superiors. This will give us more time to consider alternatives. Perhaps I will find a way to go into hiding when my people become determined for me to return."

She looked at him, her heart breaking. "You'd be a deserter," she whispered, finding it difficult to even speak the phrase in a normal voice.

"Yes," he agreed solemnly. "But Sasha needs me."

It was her turn to nod, finding strength in his willingness to do what he must.

She had to find an answer quickly. Any minute now, she would think of a way to keep Viktor legally in the country.

Any minute now...

NATALIA HAD A STEADYING effect upon his soul, Viktor realized. She thought like a soldier—planning, executing, never wavering from her course, no matter the odds. She had taken on this cause for Sasha as if it were her own.

Glancing at her from the passenger seat of her small automobile as they headed to the hospital with Sasha, he vowed he would find a way to repay her for all that she had done. Sasha sat quietly, playing with a handheld Game Boy she had bought for him on her lunch hour. She had insisted he would need it to entertain himself while in the hospital.

A thought struck him suddenly. Perhaps he could help her with a problem of her own. "Tell me about your difficulties with your assignments,'' he urged. ''Who do you suspect is making this happen?''

She shrugged. ''You have enough to worry about, don't you think?''

He shot her a half smile. ''Perhaps your problems will take my mind away from my own for a time. And I may be of help.''

Gradually, he coaxed her to tell him everything she knew so far. He asked for details about the personalities of both Captain Constance DiSanto and Captain Barbara Dwyer. He agreed with Natalia that both had the necessary motivation, but he silently pondered the fact that each had a great deal to lose if caught. Because they were the most likely perpetrators, they probably would not dare.

''Are there any others who would want to hurt you? Who else would benefit from your failure?'' he asked.

She shook her head as she turned the car into the hospital parking lot and headed for the empty spaces at the end of the row. ''I can't think of anyone else. Truthfully, I can't believe either Constance or Barbara would be so daring,'' she admitted with a sheepish grin.

He took all of her information and stored it away in his mind. He would do what he could to help her. He was trained for covert operations, and not just the kind that required stealth followed by brute force. Sometimes, subtle methods of investigation could lead to a better way to conclude an operation. He would use those skills to try to determine who was hurting her. A surge of protectiveness washed over him.

As he pushed Sasha's wheelchair toward the entrance with Natalia beside him, he gave her surreptitious glances, wondering how she would react if she knew his feelings.

One thing he knew for certain, he could not tell her anything about his plans to discover who was behind her troubles at work. Her fierce independence would not allow her to accept his assistance graciously.

At the Admissions desk, a woman dressed in white stepped right up to them as if she had been expecting them.

''I'm the pediatric cardiac nurse, Angeline Lee,'' she said. She spoke more loudly than necessary, enunciating her syllables carefully. "Dr. Brennan asked me to meet you and get Alexander settled in." She smiled at each of them, her eyes nearly lost in the roundness of her cheeks as she did so, but then her gaze shifted abruptly back to Natalia. A look of surprise swept over her face.

"Natalie Wentworth?"

Natalia appeared puzzled, but she looked at the woman more closely. "Yes, I'm Natalie W— Angel?" Recognition lit her eyes. "It's been a long time!"

"I haven't seen you since junior year in high school when your father got transferred and you moved away. How have you been?" Without waiting for an answer, the nurse turned to Viktor and Sasha. "This woman here was one of the very few people in that high school who was nice to me. I was a lot heavier then and you know how kids can be—making fun of others. Well, not Natalie. A smile here and a kind word there. We never got to be the best of friends, but those little gestures made me feel human and got me through those difficult years." She beamed at Natalia.

"I knew what it was like to be left out," Natalia said. "We moved so much because of my father's Army career that it was hard to make friends."

"Well, you were a godsend for me," declared Angeline Lee. "You joined the Army, too, I see." She looked down at Sasha. "And this is your little boy?"

"No, I'm just helping Colonel Baturnov and his son. They're from Russia."

"Well, you couldn't be in better hands than hers," said the nurse, smiling reassuringly at Sasha. "Or mine. The doctor might not be able to see Alexander until the morning, depending on how his evening rounds go."

"Thank you," Viktor said. "Sasha is tired. I would like to have him settled soon."

Angeline's eyes went wide. "My goodness, but you speak English just fine," she said.

Natalia put a maternal hand upon Sasha's shoulder. "Alexander is not as proficient in the language. But he's learning."

"Will you be one of the people looking out for my son, Ms. Lee?" Viktor asked.

"Oh, my, yes," she gushed. "I look after all of Dr. Brennan's young patients. You can call me Angel like everyone else does. Let's get you to your room now. We want to get your medicine started so you can be all better and ready for your heart surgery." She took hold of Sasha's wheelchair and pushed it through the corridors to the elevator.

Viktor followed with Natalia in silence. Angel did all the talking, chatting amiably with Sasha, who probably only understood half of what she said.

It took about an hour to get Sasha checked into his room and settled in his hospital bed with the IV in place and fluids flowing.

"You have a room to yourself, young man, even though there's that other bed over there. We thought it would be better to have you on your own so you can get well quickly. We want to get your heart fixed up real soon," the nurse bubbled.

"May I bring his Playstation and other toys?" Natalia asked. "He'll get bored if he doesn't have something to do."

"Sure." Angeline grinned, making her eyes nearly disappear again. It was such a contagiously jovial expression, Viktor found himself liking the woman immensely. It was a relief to feel he could trust someone here at the hospital to look out for his son.

"But, look what we have here," Angel said as she walked to the cabinet beneath the television. "We have a Nintendo 64, all bolted down so no one will steal it. Just for you," she added, looking at Sasha.

From the gleeful expression on his face, the boy understood the term "Nintendo 64." "Good toy," he said, ending any worries that he would be bored or unhappy anytime soon.

"And we have other activities for him to participate in as long as he feels well enough. Your son will be well occupied when you're not able to be here with him."

After a little more bustling about, Angel reminded them that they could stay for another hour. This was the cardiac ward and visiting hours were limited, even for parents. Viktor could have made arrangements to stay with his son, but Sasha would have none of that. He was not a little boy anymore, his son reminded him. There was no need for coddling. Pride in Sasha's independence warred with his need to watch over the boy. But at last, Viktor relented. It would not be practical to sleep at the hospital under the current complicated circumstances. As Angel bustled out of the room, Viktor wondered if he had made the right decision.

"Woman, I like," Sasha announced.

"Yes, she will be good to you," he agreed. At Sasha's request, he handed the boy the controller to the Nintendo set and stepped back to watch his son's masterful manipulation of a game and equipment he had never seen before.

Natalia placed her warm hand on Viktor's upper arm. "Come sit over here with me so we can talk. I may have an idea."

Intrigued, he went with her to the chairs along the wall near the door. She arranged the seats, turning them toward each other, conducive to a private conversation. He was certain Sasha would pay them no attention, but he kept his voice low nonetheless. "What is your idea, Tasha?"

She smiled wistfully at him for a moment. "I think there's another way for you to remain in the country legally, at least for a while," she began. "You'd still be giving up your career, but you could probably go back to Russia after a few years, if you played your cards right."

"Played my cards right," he said, adding the idiom to his growing repertoire. "I am listening," he prompted when she hesitated.

She chewed her lower lip, drawing his attention there. He did not have the will to pull his gaze from her mouth. He remembered the taste of her, the warmth, the softness…

"You could marry an American," she blurted out, making his eyes widen and his heart step up its beat.

As his blood began to move rapidly through his veins, he stared at her and noticed the blush on her cheeks. Marry an American? Which American? Did she mean that *she* would marry him? The prospect was dangerously appealing to Viktor, but agreeing to do so would ruin her future. He looked at his hands resting upon his knees. The palms had grown damp.

Afraid that he might say something foolish, he remained silent, waiting for her to elaborate on her own.

"I could introduce you to some friends," she continued. "Or we could see if we could make one of those arrangements like in the movie *Green Card*." She was speaking in a rush now. "We would just pay someone to marry you for as long as it takes you to get a residency card from the Immigration and Naturalization Service. Then you could remain in the country for as long as necessary. You'd have to pretend it was for real. It won't be easy. But I've heard that other people do it. Then, after a time, you'd end it and go home. That's what you want, isn't it?" she asked in a small voice. "You want to go home eventually."

Viktor's racing blood eased back to normal as disappointment took hold. But he found himself nodding his head. Yes, he wanted to go home to Russia with Sasha. Unless...

He put the doubts aside before they could form in his mind. He must not desire the impossible. And as he listened to her ramble on about how they might work out the details, he felt foolish for his momentary hope. He was relieved she was smart enough not to involve herself further in his life. This intelligence was one of her most admirable qualities. He let her speak on, admiring her strategic abilities, then he held up his hand to stop her. Her flood of words came to an abrupt stop in midsentence.

"Your idea has merit and I will consider. But to pay someone to marry me... This is...mmm...distasteful, to me and to the bride, yes? My funds are limited. And we must remember Sasha. He would be this woman's stepson. She might have legal rights over him once the wedding was complete."

She nodded gravely, glancing at Sasha as if she had not thought of that aspect of the plan until he had explained it. She gnawed at her lower lip some more, and Viktor resisted the urge to reach out and smooth his thumb over the surface of it.

"But I am willing to meet your friends, to see if there is one among them with whom I could make an arrangement. Perhaps I will find someone..." He stopped, realizing he was about to say he might find "someone like you." "Someone who needs a good cook for a while or who is willing to exchange vows for a reasonable price,'' he finished with a wry grin. "I have little else to offer a woman, under the circumstances."

She put her hand on his forearm, leaning forward earnestly. "I can lend you the money."

He closed his eyes against the conflicting emotions that surged inside of him. Humiliation warred with gratitude. Not only would he be in her debt emotionally, but financially as well. Yet, he could not deny that he might need her assistance once again.

"And you have a great deal to offer, Viktor,'' she added, still touching his arm. "Any woman would be lucky to have you. Even temporarily."

But he noticed she did not seem to include herself in the category of women who would be lucky to have him. She wanted to help, but there were limits to her sacrifice. He understood this and steeled himself to keep it in mind.

She withdrew her hand and sat back in her chair, staring at the television where Sasha's game was coming to a close. He could tell she did not really see what she looked at. He let the silence lengthen, using the quiet to calm his raw feelings. Such inner turmoil was foreign to him. He had been trained for cool, calculated action, devoid of emotion. Yet he had found himself unable to remain in that sterile frame of mind when his son's life was at stake. Or perhaps he had simply lost the knack for coldness in the years since he had departed from special forces.

The Nintendo game ended, and Natalia rose from her seat to take the controlling device from Sasha's hands. The boy was sleepy and did not protest when she pulled the covers to his chin and tucked him in for the night.

"We'll stay until you fall asleep, Alex," she said. "Nurse Lee will be right outside your door if you need anything in the night."

Sasha nodded and smiled. "Angel," he said. In Russian, he added softly, "I will be well, Papa. This is a very nice hospital with very nice people. Do not worry about me. Worry about being nice to this one," he said, indicating Natalia. Clearly, Sasha would not be opposed to her remaining a part of their lives.

Viktor's heart constricted. "My fine son, you are my pride," he whispered as he bent forward to kiss his soft cheek.

He moved away to allow Natalia to say good-night. Sasha's eyes drifted closed as she stroked his forehead with a gentle hand. As Viktor stood with Natalia, waiting for his son to slip toward dreams—lured there by Natalia's soft humming—he told himself that even if she were to offer, he should not accept her as a temporary wife. The possibility of falling irrevocably in love with her seemed very high.

Those odds would go higher still if he were lawfully wed to the woman.

FOR NATALIE, SUGGESTING that Viktor marry an American had been agonizing. She'd struggled to find a way to say it without leading him to believe she was offering herself as the bride. Then she'd felt guilty about *not* offering, even though she knew she'd already done more than enough. After the guilt had come a flood of jealousy as she thought of this man married to someone else. The fact that she should feel such a strong emotion regarding a man she hardly knew rocked her to her toes.

In the end, she'd spelled out her suggestion in a babble of words. He'd been quiet, listening to her intently. To her relief, he hadn't proposed. But when he'd reminded her that Alexander's fate had to be considered, even in a temporary marriage, she had nearly blurted that she would volunteer.

Only her hopes for her career had held her back. That, and the fact that marriage between them would be one more thing they'd have to keep secret. The secrets were already nearly unmanageable. Frank clearly suspected something was going on. And if Constance or Barbara got wind of a secret marriage to a Russian officer—worse still, a Russian deserter—they'd never let her overcome the taint on her career.

All the way home from the hospital, she was lost in thought. Viktor gave her the silence she needed. That was one of the characteristics she liked best in him. He knew when to be quiet.

As she walked beside him down the hallway of her building, a terrible thought crossed her mind. Frank had a key to her apartment. He'd made himself comfortable inside in the past and could do so again at any time. Even now.

She stopped dead in her tracks.

"What is wrong?" Viktor asked, scanning the corridor.

"Can you wait here a second?" she asked him.

He nodded, accepting her request without question. She took out her key and opened the door slowly as if she expected bees to suddenly swarm out and attack. The place was as dark as they'd left it. The TV was silent. She let out a pent-up breath and motioned Viktor forward.

"Remind me to have the locks changed tomorrow morning," she said as she threw her keys to their usual place on the credenza by the door. "And I'll give you a key of your own, too."

She started to walk to the kitchen, but stopped when she noticed him still standing by the half-open door, looking uncomfortable. He gazed down at his own feet, clearly uncertain.

"What?" she asked, perplexed.

His eyes lifted to hers, his expression unreadable. "I should go to the BOQ now that Sasha is staying at the hospital."

She stared at him, shocked that she hadn't thought of that herself. Somehow, she'd grown so accustomed to having him in her apartment, it hadn't even crossed her mind that he didn't need to be here anymore.

"I did not think of it until now," he admitted.

As if in protest of all the meals he would not cook for her, there was a small gurgle from her stomach. "But…" she began. She would analyze her reasons for wanting him to stay some other time. Right now, it simply seemed imperative that he remain. "Your clothes are all here now. And Alexander's things. It's silly to keep moving them back and forth. And…and we only gave the hospital this phone number. Besides," she added, feeling more certain now that keeping him here was rational and not simply based on a selfish desire to prevent loneliness from returning, "you don't have a car in case you need to get back to the hospital for something in a hurry."

He gazed into her eyes a moment, then said, "I will also need you to take me to the hospital in the morning so that I may donate blood and look in on Sasha."

She smiled, satisfied that it all made perfect sense. "See? I have an appointment to give blood, too. I'm not O negative, but I thought I should donate. So, there you go." She continued toward the kitchen again. Over her shoulder she said, "You might as well sleep in the guest room as long as Alexander isn't here. You'll be more comfortable there." She flicked on the stove burner beneath the kettle she always kept filled with water. "You want some tea?"

She waited several long seconds for his answer and knew he was thinking over the wisdom of staying alone with her in the apartment. But her arguments for remaining must have made sense to him, too, because at last he said he would join her in a spot of tea, sounding more English than Russian, as he often did.

"Why must you change the locks?" he asked. He'd moved to the threshold of the kitchen.

"Because Frank has a key to the place." She couldn't make herself look at him as she confessed this. "It's important that he doesn't find out about you. And Alexander," she added belatedly.

He nodded and moved quietly away, gathering his things to move them from the corner of the living room into the guest room.

When she reached into the cupboard to get down some cups, her hands shook. Ignoring this, she fixed Viktor's tea the way she knew he liked it. As she went to the living room with both cups, she pretended she wasn't looking forward to an hour of quiet companionship with her Russian Colonel before retiring. But when she thought about going to bed, she was honest enough to wonder how she would manage to sleep—with him in the next room, only a few feet away.

FREE GIFTS!

NO COST! NO OBLIGATION TO BUY!
NO PURCHASE NECESSARY!

PLAY THE
Lucky Key Game

Scratch gold area with a coin.
Then check below to see the books and gift you get!

336 HDL DH2S
135 HDL DH2J

YES! I have scratched off the gold area. Please send me the 2 Free books and gift for which I qualify. I understand I am under no obligation to purchase any books, as explained on the back and on the opposite page.

NAME   (PLEASE PRINT CLEARLY)

ADDRESS

APT.#   CITY

STATE/PROV.   ZIP/POSTAL CODE

🔑🔑🔑🔑 **2 free books plus a gift**

🔑🔑🔑 **2 free books**

🔑🔑🔑 **1 free book**

🔑 **Try Again!**

The Harlequin Reader Service® — Here's how it works:

Accepting your 2 free books and gift places you under no obligation to buy anything. You may keep the books and gift and return the shipping statement marked "cancel." If you do not cancel, about a month later we'll send you 6 additional books and bill you just $4.05 each in the U.S., or $4.46 each in Canada, plus 25¢ shipping & handling per book and applicable taxes if any.* That's the complete price and — compared to cover prices of $4.99 each in the U.S. and $5.99 each in Canada — it's quite a bargain! You may cancel at any time, but if you choose to continue, every month we'll send you 6 more books, which you may either purchase at the discount price or return to us and cancel your subscription.

*Terms and prices subject to change without notice. Sales tax applicable in N.Y. Canadian residents will be charged applicable provincial taxes and GST.

If offer card is missing write to: Harlequin Reader Service, 3010 Walden Ave., P.O. Box 1867, Buffalo NY 14240-1867

BUSINESS REPLY MAIL
FIRST-CLASS MAIL   PERMIT NO. 717-003   BUFFALO, NY

POSTAGE WILL BE PAID BY ADDRESSEE

HARLEQUIN READER SERVICE
3010 WALDEN AVE
PO BOX 1867
BUFFALO NY 14240-9952

NO POSTAGE
NECESSARY
IF MAILED
IN THE
UNITED STATES

CHAPTER NINE

SHE COULD SWEAR she could hear him breathing. If she listened any harder, she might start to hear his heartbeat, too. Thump-thump, thump-thump… Impossible. But as she drifted in and out of fitful sleep, she felt his presence pressing upon her.

A heavy warmth swarmed inside her and she squirmed on the sheets to find a cooler spot. Had she been too long without the comfort of a man? she wondered as she tossed and turned. Or was she falling in love?

She groaned aloud, wondering what dark well that last question had sprung from. Pulling the second pillow over her face, she reminded herself that the subconscious played all sorts of tricks when a person roamed in that place between sleep and wakefulness. She yanked the covers back up to her chin and closed her eyes again.

Morning seemed to arrive too soon. Having slept so poorly, she snuggled down into the covers, hoping for a few more winks. It was Saturday, after all. She could sleep as long as she wanted.

Except she had to take Viktor to the hospital. She squinted at the clock. It was seven-fifteen. He was probably out running. Or maybe finished with that by now and waiting for her to get out of bed so he could start his day. This was his only flaw, she decided—he was an early riser. With a sigh, she got out of bed, shrugged into her ragged bathrobe and decided that coffee would be well in order before her shower.

There was no sign of him as she padded to the kitchen. Everything was dark and still. Curiosity got the better of her, so she made her way very quietly to the guest room. The door stood slightly ajar. She listened at the opening but heard nothing. It figured that she would seem to hear his breathing all through the night, but now that she wanted to know if he was awake, she couldn't detect a single sound.

If he was still asleep, he would want to be awakened so he could go to the hospital. She knocked lightly, hoping to wake him without startling him. The door slid open on silent hinges very slowly. She held her breath and froze. Feeling very wicked, she couldn't help but look in.

He was there, still in bed with the blankets only half covering his body. He wore boxer shorts like the pair she'd seen him in before, but this time he also had on an olive-green T-shirt. He lay with one arm over his head, the other nearly dangling off the edge of the mattress. He looked vulnerable and handsome and very, very sexy.

Then he tossed his head to one side and mumbled something that sounded very urgent. He looked exactly like his son when she'd come upon the boy in the throes of his nightmare. Her heart constricted with sympathy.

He clutched at the sheet tangled around one leg and grunted as if in pain. She could see that his brow gleamed with a sheen of sweat. His torment drew her closer. She wanted to comfort him, as she had done for his son, but she was aware that this was a full-grown man—big and powerful and trained to kill. Wary and ready to beat a hasty retreat, she reminded herself she had to wake him so they could go to the hospital, and proceeded carefully forward.

"Viktor," she called softly from a distance of a few feet. His head tossed back and forth, his brow knit. His eyes remained tightly closed. "Viktor," she tried again, creeping closer.

He went still, except for his lips, which moved as if he were mumbling something. She leaned over him, drawn to listen more closely. Naturally, his muttering was in Russian, and she could make nothing of it. She started to move away, wondering if she should nudge him awake.

In the blink of an eye, he grasped her upper arms and immobilized her. She was so startled that only a little yelp came out of her. He gentled his grip. Then she saw that his eyes, though open, were still unfocused. They looked black and fathomless, and she knew he wasn't really awake.

She uttered his name again, soothingly. As he relaxed he murmured some sibilant words in Russian and drew her to him. He lifted himself a little higher off of the mattress with the strength of his abdominals. Pulling her, raising himself, his face came nearer. "Tasha," he whispered as he brought his mouth toward hers.

She had sense enough to know she must pull back—should have, could have. But she didn't resist. She didn't want to. The memory of their one previous kiss scattered her good intentions to the wind. Would this kiss be the same? Would it be better?

Her mouth found his, warm and commanding and sensual. He caressed her lips gently at first, sliding smoothly back and forth and then teasing lightly with his tongue. When a little sound of pleasure slipped past her guard, he took that as permission to deepen his kiss. Hot and slick and penetrating, his tongue worked magic upon her nervous system until she forgot where she was or why she shouldn't be there.

He no longer held her by her arms, but encircled her shoulders with his embrace. And she willingly sprawled across his hard chest. Her palms spread over the thin cotton covering his flesh so that when she flexed her fingers, she encountered firm, taut muscle. She wanted to feel more of him, without the barrier of his shirt. She wanted to touch him and be touched. She wanted...

But when the phone rang, reality crashed over her desire like a great wave of icy water. She jerked back, found herself imprisoned, then struggled free. His arms fell away, one onto the bed, the other to cover his eyes. A groan escaped him. She took another step back, fearful that she would succumb again to his magnetism. The telephone continued to ring, then stopped abruptly. With a click, a voice rang out.

"Natalie. Natalie," her mother's voice called. "Pick up the phone." There was a pause. Natalie watched Viktor closely. The way he rubbed his eyes, it was almost as if he were still not awake. Impossible, she thought.

"Natalie, where could you be this early on a Saturday morning?'' Pauline demanded. ''I hope you're not out running. Too much hard exercise can interfere with a woman's ability to have babies.'' There was a slight pause, then ''Call me when you get home.'' There came the purr of the dial tone, followed by blessed silence.

Viktor blinked a few times and then turned his head in her direction. Through squinted eyes, he focused on her face, but said nothing.

''I came to wake you,'' she explained, still feeling hot and tingling and confused.

''Da,'' he said in a sleepy rasp. He blinked a few times and shook his head a little to clear the cobwebs that clearly clung to his mind. ''Katory siychas chas?''

She knew the word for time, so she took a shot at an answer in Russian. ''Syem' tritsat' chisof.'' Seven-thirty, she hoped she'd said.

''Spasiba, Natashyenka,'' he said, and grinned at her.

The endearment was not lost on her. She found herself standing barefoot in the center of his room, flush with excitement from his torrid kiss, with her pulse leaping and her thoughts reeling. Oh, how she'd like to kiss him again now that he was fully awake. What would he do if she acted upon that fantasy?

The possibilities took her breath away and she backed up two more steps. An alarm blared inside her head. She heeded the warning and beat a hasty retreat.

''I'll make coffee,'' she called over her shoulder. As she passed the answering machine with its blinking light, she knew she would have to call her mother back soon. In the kitchen, she put coffee on for herself and set the teakettle to boiling for the man who'd been sleeping in her guest room and who had kissed her as if there was no tomorrow.

There *was* no tomorrow for them, she remembered. Why couldn't she remember this when she needed to be strong? Why did she forget all the reasons they couldn't be together the instant he was near?

Because he was nearly impossible to resist. And she was human, with all the failings of a normal, red-blooded female in the prime of her life. But she would have to try harder. It was bad enough she had him sleeping in her apartment. Falling for him would be the biggest mistake of her life.

A new worry popped into her head just then. If she got in any deeper with the foreigner, her top-secret clearance might be at stake, and she couldn't do her current job without it. So she needed to keep a level head, stay cool, remember to focus on her aspirations. He was only an ordinary man, after all.

But then that ordinary man, sleep-tousled and clad in a T-shirt and jeans that hung low on his hips, came shuffling into her kitchen. Her heart skidded to a stop. Then it began to beat again harder than before, keeping pace with her careering emotions.

There was something about him. Even sleepy-eyed with his hair sticking up, he made her ache with longing. She sighed, feeling defeated. It would be so damn hard when he left for home. She'd only have these images of him then. So she stood staring at him, memorizing his features and physique.

He must have noticed her doing so, because he stopped spooning sugar into his teacup and turned fully to stare back at her. He didn't speak or move. Standing there silently holding her gaze, he didn't seem fazed by the tension that she could feel all around her, pulsing, growing, pulling. Then she noticed that he'd raised his eyebrows in question and seemed to be prepared to take a step toward her. What would he do if she let him approach? Would he kiss her again?

She forced herself to look away, and he immediately eased back, taking the unspoken cue. After a moment, he resumed his activities with his tea. He said nothing about their kiss. She was grateful to cling to the excuse that he had done it in his sleep, that it wasn't real, that it should be forgotten.

"You're not running today?" she asked, trying to sound normal and failing miserably, at least to her own ears.

"Not today. They take blood today."

"Yes, that's right," she said. "Me, too. We should eat a good breakfast."

She dared to glance at him and saw he was grinning. "Do you want me to cook you something?" he asked.

This was more like it. Light and friendly and teasing was far better than the dark, earnest yearning that had built up between them this morning. She would follow his lead and pretend nothing unusual had happened between them this morning.

"Yes, please." She nodded her head vigorously for added effect, which made him smile more broadly, showing his white, even teeth. If she couldn't have what she really wanted from Viktor, at least she could have his wonderful cooking.

"I have to call my mother back," she told him, glad for an excuse to escape his presence until she could steel herself against his charms. "If I don't, God only knows what she'll imagine happened to me. She'll call out the National Guard to look for me."

She started to ease out of the kitchen, but his words stopped her "We must respect our mothers," he advised solemnly. He looked puzzled and somewhat surprised. "The National Guard?" he asked. He went back to mixing something in a bowl. With a spoon.

She smiled for the first time since she'd awakened and felt some of the tension ease out of her. "It was a figure of speech. Not something to take literally. I only meant she'd stop at nothing to make sure I'm okay. I have a mixer for that, if you want," she offered, eyeing the rapid churning of the spoon dubiously.

He paused his energetic stirring and shook his head. "Muffins are not for blending. Only for gently mixing. Your mother to me sounds good, no? She cares for you even though you are grown."

She sighed. "Yes, you're right. Sometimes I just wish she wouldn't care quite so much."

"We have a saying—'take care with wishes.' Go please and call this mother of yours. These must bake for twenty minutes."

She snapped to attention and gave him a sharp salute, made ridiculous by the bathrobe she wore. Performing a precision right turn, she marched to her bedroom to make the phone call.

Five minutes later, she wished she'd found a way to resist Viktor's order. She stuck out her lower lip and blew air upward, making ringlets of hair dance on her forehead. "Mom, I am not going to marry Frank Lezinski, no matter what he told you. Please…"

Pauline talked right past her without taking any note of Natalie's words.

"Mom," she said, trying a firmer tone. "Mom! Listen to me." She enunciated each word, and finally her mother ceased her prattle. "I am not going to marry Frank. Do you understand?"

"Is there another man, then? Is that it?"

Natalie's mind launched itself straight toward an image of Viktor. In her shock over where her thoughts had gone, she didn't answer her mother's question right away. That fraction of a second's hesitation was all it took. "No, there is not another man" was spoken over the top of her mother's voice insisting the opposite.

"I knew it! There *is* another man. I'll bet it has something to do with that person who answered the phone the other day using that strange word. A *foreigner*, Nat?" she asked.

Natalie held the phone out in front of her and examined it as if she could tell from that inspection how her mother managed to figure out so much on so little information. She was an amazing woman. And so damn accurate, it was scary. "There is no other man," she insisted. She was back to enunciating her words again.

"When are you going to introduce us? Should I plan a visit?"

This time Natalie answered too quickly. "No!" blurted out of her mouth before she could temper the edge of panic from her voice.

Silence greeted her from the other end.

"I mean," she amended. "I can't have you visit right now. I'm up to my eyebrows in work. I wouldn't have any time to spend with you. What would you do all day?"

Another measured silence elapsed, no doubt calculated by her mother to exhibit hurt without being so long as to seem childish. Pauline was a master at this sort of game. "I am perfectly capable of amusing myself while you are at work, Natalie. I could come on a weekend, for one thing. And perhaps I would spend an afternoon with James."

"James?" Who the hell was James, she wanted to know.

"Colonel Freeman," Pauline provided.

Now it was Natalie's turn to go silent. After a moment she said, "So, it's 'James' now, is it?"

"Please try not to be too shocked by this, Natalie dear, but it's been 'James' for quite some time now."

Natalie grinned. There had been the tiniest note of defensiveness in her mother's voice. It warmed her heart to find that Pauline had a vulnerability after all. "I think that's great, Mom," she said with sincerity. "Really. It's time you found someone."

"If you think that means I won't spend as much time worrying about you, you have another think coming, young lady. If you would just settle down, marry, give me some grandchildren. You're not getting any younger, you know. That biological clock just keeps—"

"Hey, listen, I gotta go," she interjected. "I love you, too," she remembered to say before she hung up, even though her mother hadn't said it first. The sentiment was there. In every nagging word, Pauline told Natalie how much she loved her. Some days it was hard to remember that, but today Viktor's admonishment about respecting mothers reminded her. As she hung up the phone, she realized this was the first time she'd felt good after a conversation with her mother in a very long time.

TWO HOURS LATER, Viktor sat with Natalia in the waiting room of the blood center in the hospital. They had been to visit Sasha, who was doing surprisingly well. Angeline Lee's shift was over, but the nurse who came on duty after her seemed nearly as nice. Sasha had already charmed her into letting him walk to the playroom with his IV bag hanging from a wheeled pole. Viktor had found him there and helped him build a castle with little plastic snap-together units that Natalia called Lego. When the time for their appointments at the blood bank arrived, he left his smiling son, who needed no promises about when they would return.

"You don't like blood," Natalia mentioned as they waited.

"Not to worry," he assured her. But she looked at him doubtfully.

A woman entered the room. "Colonel Baturnov?" she said. "You can follow me."

Viktor stood, glanced back at Natalia's worried face, smiled at her to show he was not afraid and followed the woman into the room. There were tables along the walls where blood donors were to lie. Two were occupied, and dark liquid flowed slowly through tubes into plastic bags suspended below each. This did not bother him until he thought about the fact that his own blood would soon be spilling into a similar container.

"Now, you just come on over here, Colonel, and we'll get you settled up on the table," the woman said. Her name tag read "Suzy." She patted the cushioned surface to encourage him to climb up onto it.

He reminded himself that this was for his son and slid onto the table.

"You're looking a little pale, Colonel. Will you be okay?" she asked.

"Yes. Okay," he managed to say. But he was not sure this was true. A low buzzing sound had begun to hum inside his head. Stoically, he stretched out on the table. He felt a little better now that he did not have hold himself upright.

Suzy moved aside to reach for the things she would use to draw his blood, and he saw that Natalia had entered the room. She was led to a nearby table, and Viktor took heart when she flashed him her smile and gave him a thumbs-up sign. But then Suzy straightened and strapped a rubber hose around his upper arm. He knew what was coming and his stomach turned.

"Now, let me see that arm," Suzy said. Viktor complied so she could check his veins and then turned his head away as she tapped at the inside of his elbow. The needle would be next and he simply could not watch.

"You need to squeeze this ball now," Suzy advised as she placed something round in his hand. "Your veins aren't standing out very well."

He had a difficult time keeping his breathing normal. The urge to pant like a dog gripped him. His fingers had gone very cold.

Suzy spoke to another woman, but Viktor could not make out her words over the hum in his ears, which had grown louder. After a time, he realized there had been no stick of the needle. Afraid that it would come at any moment, he did not dare turn his head. But then he caught a familiar scent and felt a warm hand clasp his cold one. Looking toward the source, he saw that Natalia stood beside him. She gazed into his eyes, steady and reassuring.

"Your vein collapsed in this arm, Viktor," she said softly, as if this were a common occurrence. "Do you want the nurse to try your right arm?"

He swept his tongue lightly over his dry lips and nodded. "Sasha needs the blood," he said, but his voice came out in a rasp.

"Yes, that's right. We need to do this for Sasha. So you have to turn around the other way. Put your head on this end. That's right. We'll move the little pillow down here for you. There you go. And I'm gonna stay here beside you and we can talk, if you like."

He nodded, gratitude spilling forth in great waves.

She kept a relaxed hold on his left hand, which rested upon his chest. With the other, she pointed with two fingers to her own eyes. "Look right at me, Viktor. Tell me about your life with Sasha. When did you first discover his illness?"

He told her about Sasha's contracting rheumatic fever and suffering permanent damage to the valves in his heart. Without emotion, he explained that the boy's mother, who had never taken very well to parenting, did not have it in her to care for a child with a long-term affliction. She'd left them, never to be seen again. They had not even been invited to her funeral.

Somewhere during the story, he felt a prick to his arm. He felt Suzy's hands around his own, indicating that he should squeeze on the rubber ball every so often. He did so automatically while he gazed into Tasha's eyes and told her about his son. The dizziness faded, his fingers were no longer cold. He would get through this. He would manage to give the blood his son needed, as long as he had Tasha at his side.

When it was over, he had succeeded in donating two pints, which was all that was allowed in one sitting. Because of the great need for O-negative blood, he would be permitted to give again for his son in another two weeks. Suzy explained that Alexander might be able to donate for himself in order to speed things along. Viktor remembered that Dr. Brennan had suggested this.

"Sit up slowly, now," advised Suzy. "You don't want to become light-headed all over again."

Viktor wished he could deny that he had experienced so much as a twinge of light-headedness, but he knew such protests would sound ridiculous, given his unmanly performance here today. So he kept his mouth closed and sat up slowly and dutifully drank all the juice that Natalia brought over to him. She smiled gently and patted his shoulder as if to console him, which only made him feel worse about his weakness.

She must have seen this, because she withdrew her touch and looked into his eyes with frank curiosity. "How does a man in special forces develop a squeamishness for his own blood?" she asked.

He thought about ignoring the question, thereby saving some measure of his dignity. But then he gave up on pride and decided he might as well explain it to her. "The last time I was wounded, I was in Africa, trapped in the midst of a rebel stronghold after completing my mission. Some flying shrapnel cut an artery in my leg, very small. The blood seemed to flood out of me. I am thinking as I watched my leg bleed, I will not see Sasha again. My work for the military seemed quite pointless then. And the blood just kept coming, soaking my fatigues, filling my boot. I did what I had been trained to do, though there was little hope. My men told me later that they found me unconscious, still gripping the tourniquet I had fashioned. I awoke in an American Army mobile hospital, which was fortunate, as the doctors there made the effort to save my leg."

He paused and glanced at Natalia to see how she was absorbing the information. She shook her head as if overwhelmed. "Is that what you were dreaming about this morning?"

"Dreaming? This morning?" The only dream he remembered was one he could not speak of. He had been only half alert when he had begun to kiss her, but by the time the telephone had interrupted them, he had been fully awake in more ways than one. Knowing she would not want another kiss between them, he had realized he should never mention the heated kiss nor give any sign that it had happened at all. The strategy had helped them past the awkwardness of the morning. Yet now she blushed a pretty pink and looked away.

"I thought I heard you having a nightmare," she said, almost apologetically. "How has your leg been since you were injured?"

"My leg was fine after the surgery. Almost no scar. But since then, I am unable to bear the sight of my own blood. This weakness convinced me to change jobs in the military, something I had been considering for months because of Sasha's needs. Good that I had put in the papers to make this change, as my mother died shortly afterward, leaving Sasha without his *babushka*. It took only weeks instead of months for me to transfer to a position that allowed me to care for him myself."

"So there's a bright side to all this, after all," she noted with a wry smile.

"Yes," he agreed. "A silver lining, as you Americans say."

"Well, you got through the blood donation for today, and if you want me to come with you next time, I'd be glad to do that. In two weeks, did she say?"

"Yes, two weeks," he agreed. He could not deny that he was enormously pleased by the prospect of planning future events with Natalia. Two weeks from now, he would still be in her company. This was another good thing to come of his bizarre affliction.

As they retraced their steps to find Sasha again, Viktor found yet another benefit to his blood-phobia. Natalia felt it necessary to hang on to him as they walked, giving him the excuse to retain her small, warm hand in the crook of his elbow. He decided he could come to terms with his phobia if these were his rewards.

NATALIE WOULD HAVE PREFERRED to stay with Alexander in his hospital room all day Sunday, eating hospital food and playing endless Nintendo games. Instead, she was forced to consume gourmet food at a four-star restaurant in the company of a dashing foreign officer with a sexy accent and charming personality.

Marie was with them.

Her friend had agreed to meet Viktor on the chance that the two of them could come to an agreement about a temporary marriage. Marie was Natalie's only friend who was not in the military. All the other possibilities had been eliminated because the women were either married or serving in the military and as likely to turn Viktor over to the authorities as they were to cooperate with the marriage scheme. Marie had been willing to join them for dinner, but Natalie didn't have much hope. The conversation so far had served to bolster her skepticism.

"What do you do for your job, Marie?" Viktor asked politely over the appetizers.

"I'm a nail designer. But I'm studying for hair."

Natalie sighed. Viktor had stopped chewing as he tried to sort out what Marie had said.

"She paints fingernails for women," Natalie explained. She tapped the table with her short and unadorned nails. "She wants to cut hair for a living but hasn't gotten her license yet. But she has a master's degree in English literature. She could be a teacher or a book editor or a writer, if she wanted to."

Marie made an unpleasant face at Natalie. They had been through this before. Natalie thought Marie should use her brains while Marie felt it was far more important to be happy. For the life of her, Natalie could not understand why Marie couldn't do both.

"A person needs a license to cut hair?" Viktor asked, looking perplexed.

At this, Marie rolled her eyes. "Well, you wouldn't want just anyone cutting your hair, would you?"

Viktor looked at Natalie as if to ask whether or not this was a joke. She pressed her lips together against any hint of a smile so he'd know Marie was serious. He nodded almost imperceptibly, and Natalie marveled at how they were able to communicate so effectively without words.

Just like an old married couple.

Once this thought formed, Natalie's brain seemed unwilling to let it go. It rattled around inside her head while Marie chattered on about the requirements for a beautician's license, sounding silly and brainless. Viktor pretended to give Marie his undivided attention throughout the meal, giving Natalie the chance to glance frequently at his profile as her thoughts continued to dance around how well the two of them got along together.

Suddenly she realized that he knew she'd been looking at him. His body had shifted slightly toward her. His gaze slipped lazily over her hands and along her arms and almost to her breasts, lingering upon her person but never lifting to her face. He wore that handsome half smile he seemed to reserve for her alone. And although he never made eye contact with her, every fiber of her being knew he was focused upon her.

"So, I understand you need a wife," Marie said unceremoniously, suddenly sounding more like her frank and forthright self.

Viktor looked taken aback. His eyebrows went up and he stared a moment at the woman who had spoken nothing but mindless babble for the last half hour. But then he grinned gamely at Marie and nodded his head. "Yes, I am needing an American wife. Do you know someone suitable?" he asked with a twinkle in his eye that might have made Natalie volunteer on the spot if it had been directed at her.

Marie grinned at his playfulness. "I might," she said coyly, reverting to airhead mode.

"It would have to be a real marriage in almost every way," Natalie felt compelled to point out. "You'll have to be able to fake it with the Immigration and Naturalization Service, prove to the investigator that the marriage isn't just a sham to stay in the country."

Marie shifted her attention away from Viktor long enough to look directly into Natalie's eyes. "I thought the situation was desperate, and he wasn't going to be very picky. Now you've suddenly got *rules* on how this will go?"

Natalie squinted at Marie. Most of the time she could count on Marie to cut to the chase with precision. It was her quick mind and her razor-sharp ability to get to the point that made Marie such a good friend. But right at the moment, Natalie wasn't feeling very appreciative.

"I just want you to understand what's involved," she explained, knowing full well she sounded defensive. "It won't be easy to fool the INS. They're good at spotting these scams. So you have to be able to pretend you really like and understand each other. You have to know each other's habits and talents and desires.''

"Really," Marie said. She drawled the word. "I think I could manage it." She looked at Viktor. "How about you?"

This made Natalie's blood come to an instant boil. A hundred caustic remarks flew through her mind and a temptation to throttle her best friend nearly overwhelmed her. "I have to go to the bathroom. You two can plan your wedding while I'm gone," she said, with a touch of acid dripping from her voice.

As she slid from the booth, she couldn't help but notice that Marie shot Viktor an apologetic look, shrugging her shoulders and tipping her head toward Natalie as she got to her feet. "I'll go with her," Marie volunteered, as if Natalie were in need of a keeper.

She wanted to kick herself for succumbing to such a childish fit of jealousy. Nonetheless, she couldn't get a grip on her annoyance with Marie. They wound their way between tables and entered the ladies' room.

"Why are you acting like such an idiot out there?" she demanded.

Marie raised her eyebrows but said nothing.

Natalie tried again. "I mean, what's with the airhead routine? You're supposed to be helping me. The man needs a wife, remember?"

"I remember," she said without inflection.

Natalie stared at her. "Then why are you doing everything in your power to turn him off?"

Marie gazed at her steadily for a while. "You really don't see it, do you?" she whispered.

"See what?" Natalie snapped, but there was a sinking feeling in the pit of her stomach.

Instead of answering, Marie turned to face the mirror to fuss with her hair and smooth her makeup.

Frustrated, Natalie turned to the sink and splashed cool water onto her cosmetic-free face. Drying herself with a paper towel, she peered into her own eyes over the damp white sheet. What she saw reflected back scared her to her toes.

"Uh-oh," she said to the shocked face staring back at her.

"There. You see? So now who's been acting dumb?" Marie asked.

"What do you mean?" Natalie asked hesitantly. She did not want to put her own thoughts into words.

Marie smirked. "You want me to spell it out for you?"

Natalie nodded, albeit very reluctantly.

"It's obvious, girl! You've fallen for the Russian. Hard."

She felt the blood drain from her face. It was true. She had gone and let that man into her heart.

"You think I could move in on your man and marry him, even temporarily? What kind of friend would I be?"

Natalie groaned and passed her hand over her face. "You don't understand. I can't marry him myself. My career would be over. And besides," she added mournfully, "he isn't staying. I couldn't marry him only to have him leave me to go back to Russia."

Marie stared at her again. After a moment, she said, "I'm not buying the 'career would be over' part. Your career might take an unexpected turn, maybe, but it wouldn't be over." Marie moved behind her to pat her shoulder consolingly. "You might have to take a big chance here, Nat. You might have to do something wild and crazy, for once. If you don't, you'll regret it for a long time." She gazed knowingly into Natalie's reflected eyes.

Could she exchange vows with her Russian Colonel and then let him go? Not without her heart being broken. Could she marry him and try to keep him with her, holding him back from returning to a country he loved? Not without his heart being broken.

"No, it just wouldn't work," she told Marie's mirror image. "Too risky on a variety of levels."

"Well, then you're going to have to find some other temporary bride because I'm not about to say vows to that guy. Not when he's as madly in love with you as you are with him."

Natalie blinked as she watched Marie leave the ladies' room.

Her friend didn't usually make mistakes about men. Could she possibly be right about Viktor's feelings? Love that erupted in a matter of days was not a lasting thing. It couldn't forge a real marriage. It couldn't be strong enough to make Viktor want to give up his country.

As she walked back to join her dinner companions, she told herself this several more times. Unfortunately, this conviction was battered by her worry that she alone would be able to make the INS believe that Viktor's marriage was real, that they were in love, that he wanted to stay in America forever.

If only all that were true, she admitted. Then she might be tempted to go for it.

VIKTOR HATED NOT BEING with his son during the workdays. But at least his time had been put to good use. In the week since Sasha was admitted to the hospital, Viktor had studied the attendance records of officers in the protocol division in an effort to determine who might be trying to hurt Natalia's career. He had carefully put the information into a database constructed for this purpose, hoping to eventually query it for coincidences that would lead him to a suspect. In addition, the American officers with whom he worked were amazingly forthcoming. When he asked some of the men about the lovely Captain Wentworth, the male officers were more than happy to oblige with information. It appeared Natalia was a common topic of conversation and a frequent object of lust among the men who worked in the Army section of the Pentagon.

Major Jansen smacked him on the shoulder and offered some commiseration. "You won't get anywhere with the ice queen. She's only hot to look at. Try making a move and she'll freeze you where you stand."

Viktor nodded as if this were sage advice, even though the description was a far cry from the woman he knew. Her response to his kisses had been the opposite of cold. "She has a man already?"

"Hell no!" Jansen said. "But Major Lezinski seems to think he's got dibs. They knew each other in school or something and he's got it in his head that she belongs to him."

"How do you know this?" Viktor asked mildly.

"Because he lets everyone know at just about every chance he gets. Last week I overheard him at O'Malley's betting he'd get her to accept his marriage proposal within the month." Jansen made it clear by his expression that he did not think this was likely.

"Why would he pursue her if she is not interested?"

"Oh, she's not completely cold to Frank. He's the only one she's given any encouragement to. And maybe Frank likes the challenge." Jansen grinned wolfishly. "I would, if I thought I had a prayer."

Viktor managed to fake a good-natured laugh, even though his pulse surged with the desire to hit something. Not only should Jansen be more respectful of Natalia, but the idea that she had history with Frank made him burn inside.

He made himself wave dismissively. "Well, she is clearly not worth the time. What about the other two lovely women in her office?"

Jansen scowled slightly. "Captain DiSanto is yours for the asking, I'd say. She goes for big guys like you. Often. Easily," he added as if Viktor could have somehow missed that Constance had a reputation for willingness. "But Barbara—Captain Dwyer—she's got someone."

Viktor eyed the slight blush that tinted the man's cheeks. "I had not heard," he admitted. "With whom is she connected?"

Jansen shifted his stance, spreading his feet slightly apart and easing back his shoulders. "Me," he said defiantly.

Viktor grinned and held up his two hands, palms outward to show his acquiescence. "Okay. I understand."

Jansen relaxed and grinned back. "'Course, she doesn't know it yet," he admitted as his blush deepened.

Viktor laughed out loud at that. "She is a beautiful woman. Perhaps you should not wait too long to make yourself known to her."

Major Jansen nodded thoughtfully. "I'm working on it," he said. He glanced at his watch. "Hey, I gotta get back to work. You want me to come by and get you for lunch?"

"Yes, Major. That would be appreciated. I am still less certain of these corridors than I would like to be." This was a blatant lie, as Viktor had made a point of reconnoitering the hallways of the Pentagon during the week. But he felt it was to his advantage to remain in the company of people who could help him learn things that might lead him to the person causing Natalia her difficulties with assignments.

Jansen nodded and began to walk away only to stop short and turn back. "Oh, yeah, I almost forgot. There were a couple of guys looking for you. One was an old guy, cranky. Said he was General Schmidt or something."

"Schwinn," Viktor said with an exasperated hiss.

Jansen brightened. "Yeah, that's the guy. Schwinn. A retired general or something. A bit senile, if you ask me. What's he want with you?"

Viktor decided to be honest. Major Jansen had been an ally so far and might prove to be helpful in thwarting Schwinn. "He used to command Fort Drake. He is not pleased by my presence. Cold War and such. I am Russian and he does not like."

Jansen nodded his understanding. "You want us to steer him in the opposite direction? You don't need that kind of trouble while you're trying to learn this stuff." He gestured toward the reams of database printouts and regulations littering Viktor's desk.

"That would be helpful." He waited a fraction of a second, then prompted, "And the other person looking for me?" His guts told him that the second man might be the far greater danger.

"Oh, yeah, the other guy. Civilian. Creepy sort. Not much older than us. The guy got my attention for some reason, so when he left, I asked the secretary if he'd given his name." Jansen shook his head back and forth as if puzzled. "Nope, never said who he was or what he wanted." He looked straight at Viktor then. "Is this some sort of trouble we should know about?"

Viktor called upon years of training to keep his features neutral. Maintaining eye contact and forcing his expression to reveal mild curiosity and confusion, he said, "I am not aware of trouble. Should I be concerned?"

Jansen relaxed. "No, probably not. For all I know, he could have been a reporter from the Pentagon newspaper looking for an interview. Those guys are weird. If he wants to find you, he will. Forget about it."

But even hours later, Viktor could not forget about it. He did not like the coincidence that this man would come looking for his office during lunchtime when Viktor was most likely to be away. He remembered the man watching from the shadows of the parking lot when he had retrieved Sasha's clothes from the BOQ. And there was the blue sedan that he and Natalia had noticed following them when they went running. Just yesterday, he had observed the vehicle again. It was clear someone was tracking him.

And that meant someone besides him and Natalia knew about Sasha.

CHAPTER TEN

NATALIE REALIZED SHE WOULD have to ask Viktor to move back into the BOQ. If she didn't, it would be only a matter of time before her desire for the man overcame her better judgment. He was in her thoughts almost constantly.

Dropping the pile of books onto her desk with a heavy thud, she eyed the stack and sighed. She should be spending her free hours studying and testing for the correspondence course she needed to complete in order to be promoted to major instead of obsessing about the Colonel. Even though her points toward promotion were high, she wanted to be certain the deck was stacked in her favor when the decisions were made. But that promise had been made to herself before Viktor and Alexander had come into her life. She'd been decidedly distracted since then. Just this morning, she had found herself skimming through Viktor's personnel file. When she'd stumbled upon the section containing his many medals and citations, she hadn't been able to put it down. Viktor had failed to mention that when he'd been wounded in Africa, for example, he had saved the lives of a whole group of stranded embassy civilians. They weren't even the civilians of his own embassy he'd gone in and rescued, but from the French embassy, which happened to be located in the heart of the fighting.

As a woman, combat positions were denied her. That's how Frank had been promoted ahead of her. Although she had consoled herself with the fact that the Army couldn't accomplish its mission without support and services behind the lines, Natalie had great admiration for the men who risked their lives performing heroic deeds. Men like Viktor.

She supposed this was why she wanted the NATO assignment

so badly. She'd be close enough to feel the pulse of real action over there. Her work would make a difference to the world.

She'd never questioned her single-minded focus on this goal before. But today, as she'd leafed through Viktor's file, she realized that there might be other, equally rewarding differences she could make in her lifetime. Making Alexander laugh, for example, had taken on a meaning for her that she never would have thought possible. The boy was very good-natured but needed more reasons to laugh. When he held her hand so trustingly as he drifted off to sleep in his hospital bed each night, her heart swelled with love and satisfaction.

"A dollar for your thoughts," Viktor whispered from the doorway to her office. He leaned casually against the jamb, looking very handsome in his foreign uniform. His smile was tender and melting.

"A dollar? That's a high price to pay," she said, trying to pretend his nearness didn't make her pulse quicken.

"Is it? Did I say the American idiom wrong, then?"

"A *penny* for your thoughts," she suggested as she took her seat behind her desk. Having something solid between them seemed advisable.

He pulled himself lazily upright and then eased into a guest chair opposite her. "Ah, yes, a penny," he agreed. "But I would pay a dollar for *your* thoughts, Tasha."

She shook her head, unwilling to make up a falsehood and unable to tell him the true nature of her thoughts—especially when he called her Tasha in that breathy way of his. "They wouldn't interest you," she said, wishing that were not true. "What can I do for you today, sir?"

"I wanted to let you know that a man has been looking for me. Or perhaps the location of the office assigned to me. He didn't leave his name."

This was serious news. She lowered her voice to avoid being heard. "Could he be from your embassy?"

Viktor nodded, glancing into the outer reception area for possible eavesdroppers. "Possibly. General Schwinn made no secret of his desire to have the CIA watching me."

"Geez," she said, alarmed. "What would they want with

you? You haven't done anything..." She looked at him, searching for any sign that he might be hiding something from *her* the way he was hiding things from his government.

He held up one hand. "I assure you, I have done nothing that would especially interest the CIA. At least not since I've been in your country," he said with a glint of defiant amusement in his eyes. "I do not tell you about this man to frighten you, but only to ensure you remain on your guard." He hesitated a moment, looking intently at her. "You must promise me you will do nothing that would compromise you in the eyes of your government. If you are approached and asked questions by someone in authority, you must answer honestly."

"I'm not telling anyone anything. If someone finds out what we've been up to, there is little likelihood that I'll be able to convince them I was somehow duped into my involvement. So I'm already compromised, Viktor."

"I will move back into the BOQ tonight after I visit with Sasha," he declared. "This will put distance between you and me. Protection for you must be primary." Then he said something in Russian that she had no hope of understanding.

"What does that mean?"

"How do you say it in English? Believable denyness?"

She smiled, despite the dire nature of their conversation. "Plausible deniability," she offered. "Yeah, that worked so well for everyone who's used it in the past."

He shrugged at her sarcasm. "I have brought you enough trouble. You must not continue to help us. You are putting yourself at risk."

Natalie didn't know what to say. Yet, she was suddenly, inexplicably unwilling to abandon Viktor and his son. "Let's go see Alexander."

He made no move to get up from his seat, but sat staring at her. He clenched his jaw stubbornly.

"I am not going to just depart from his life without saying anything to him, Viktor. And all of his things, and most of yours, are at my apartment. So you're stuck with me for a little while longer."

He nodded then. "Yes, you must say goodbye to Sasha. And tonight I will clear my things from your flat."

"It's four-thirty already. No one will care if we take off for the day."

This time, he rose from the chair. "I will meet you at your car after I collect my things from my desk. We must not be seen together so often."

"I'll see you at the car at exactly four-fifty," she said, tempted to add that maybe they should synchronize watches.

He seemed oblivious to the hint of teasing in her voice. With a grim expression, he left her office.

VIKTOR WATCHED HIS SON with Natalia and mourned that she could not remain in the child's life. She was very good with him—never mothering him too much, making him laugh, coaxing him to cooperate even when he preferred to do something else. They had forged a bond, these two. It was sad to separate them. But he had no choice.

"Time for your supper, young man," said Angeline Lee as she bustled in with a tray. "The game goes off until you eat everything on your plate."

Sasha groaned. "Bad guy killing, I am good," he protested as he worked the controller feverishly in an attempt to complete the round before Angel turned off the machine.

"You've played this thing for three solid hours," she noted, then mercilessly clicked off the power just as Sasha was about to conquer his electronic nemesis.

"You are cruel," he said, using proper English syntax for the first time in Viktor's memory.

Viktor scowled at the boy. "Respect, Alexander," he reminded the boy.

"Oh, it's all right. He's practicing his English. That's something he learned from a cartoon." Angel smiled warmly at the boy.

"From *Dexter's* Lab-*or-a-tory*," Natalia said in a strangled accent. "You are cru-ell," she repeated in the same strange tones. "This is my greatest in-*ven*-tion!" she cried dramatically with upraised hands like a mad scientist, obviously imitating something from television and making Alexander laugh out loud.

Viktor shook his head. "I have never seen you watch television and yet you know much about the shows and movies. This is…mmm—" he searched for the right word "—mysterious."

She shrugged, clearly not in the mood to explain herself. She smiled for Sasha, but Viktor could detect the element of sadness beneath. It was almost time for her to say her final goodbye.

"I believe it's nearly the right time for our favorite cartoon," she said, giving Angel a pleading look and nodding toward the television.

"Oh, all right," the nurse said, handing over the remote control.

The instant Angel slipped out of the room, Natalie clicked on the television and surfed through the channels until she had located the one she wanted. She and Sasha exchanged gleeful looks as the words Cartoon Network flashed across the screen. The next minute, the announcer stated that *Dexter's Laboratory* would be next.

"I have a surprise for you," she said as she lifted a bag containing an ice-cream sundae from McDonald's. "It's a little melted."

"Yes!" came the enthusiastic response from Sasha. "Melted not much."

"But you have to eat all the chicken and the salad, okay?" she bargained.

"Okay." Then he tore into his dinner with enthusiasm.

"I wish I could make him home-cooked meals," Viktor said as he moved away from Sasha's bed to converse quietly with Natalia by the door. "He should eat better food."

"You heard what the doctor said earlier. He's doing well. His test results indicate he's a good candidate for this surgery. His pneumonia is clearing up. He's going to be fine." As she spoke, she rested her hand on his arm to reassure him.

Instead, Viktor felt her touch in a carnal way. His thoughts careered to the memory of kissing her passionately in the guest room of her flat. He had tried unsuccessfully to convince himself that he would forget that kiss in time. But the way she looked at him sometimes, the way he felt when he was near her, convinced him there was something charged between them. Something unforgettable. She felt it, too, he thought as he watched her drop her gaze to the floor and remove her hand abruptly. Her fingers trembled slightly as she pulled away.

From where they stood on the far side of the room, she watched Sasha for a moment and her eyes went misty with emotion. "How can I say goodbye to him? He needs me. Doesn't he?"

Viktor could no longer resist touching her, and so he moved to stand behind her, rubbing her arms to soothe her. "Yes, he needs you. But you cannot help him if you are in jeopardy." She did not pull away, so he rested his hands on her shoulders.

"I think you're overestimating the danger. The worst that can happen is I'll have to find a different job. What is that compared to abandoning Alexander when he most needs someone to mother him?"

Astonished by her words, Viktor said nothing. He simply continued to knead her shoulder muscles slowly, hoping to ease her torment. The contact with her body created a torment of its own—at least inside him. After a moment, Natalia sighed and relaxed against him and he slipped his arms loosely around her. He wished he could hold her like this forever. But their time together had to end.

He could see no alternative. Someone was watching them and probably already knew of Natalia's involvement.

"How will you buy the time with your superiors and with the people in the Materiel Command without my help?" she said in a sad voice, still leaning against him, still watching Alexander. Their hopes of finding someone to marry him were quickly evaporating, although Marie had promised to find a candidate or two from among her civilian friends.

"How will I buy that time even *with* your help?" he countered.

She said nothing for a while, but simply stood there with him, pressed against him back to front. "We have to think of somehing, Viktor. I can't just walk away from the two of you right now."

He looked at his son, already eating the ice cream that Natalia had brought. "If only it were me lying there with the heart condition. I would give anything to change places with…" He stopped speaking the instant he realized his emotions threatened to crack his voice if he said another word. Clenching his jaw, he ground his teeth, not even realizing he was doing it.

"Stop it," Natalia said quietly. "You'll break your teeth."

The fact that she could tell what he was doing without looking at him startled him. But her gentle nagging sounded so wifely, he managed a smile. This was only one more example of how well suited they would be, if only… "The tension grows," he admitted, making a conscious effort to relax his jaw muscles.

"Yes," she agreed. After a few minutes of contemplation, she pulled out of his grasp and turned to look at him. "I know this is a terrible idea, but you've made me think of something." She looked at her feet as if she were ashamed of what she was about to propose. "If we could convince your American co-workers that you've had a heart attack or something and pretend it's you in the hospital instead of Alexander, then you'd get some of the time you needed. They'd contact the Russians for you and stall any effort to send you home until you'd recovered."

He stared at her, astonished. "Tasha," he said gently. "Brilliant as your plan may be, I must point out the fatal flaw. I cannot contact them myself and tell this grand lie. I would have to ask someone else to do this for me. I will not do that."

She shuffled from foot to foot and glanced around the room as if she were searching the air for assistance with her moral dilemma. But at last, she calmed herself and stood still. "I'll make the call for you."

"You will *not*," he commanded with gentle firmness. "You are already involved enough. How would you explain yourself if you were caught in such a lie?" He shook his head when she looked as if she would protest. "You will not do this, Natalia. I will not cooperate even if you try."

"Viktor," she pleaded. "The situation is serious now. Finding a temporary bride will take time. And even if we find you some one, there are a hundred ways it can all go wrong before the vows are spoken."

He began to pace, feeling trapped. "I know this," he snarled wishing she would not be so blunt. She was forcing him to see the precariousness of his position. He stopped pacing and looked at her.

"I will not involve you further, Tasha. You must honor my decision in this. You will say goodbye to Alexander tonight and not return. And I will remove myself from your life before you are hurt by my presence."

For a moment, he thought she would defy him. Her mouth worked and her eyes flashed.

"I'm a superior officer, Captain. And this is a lawful order. Do not involve yourself further."

Her shoulders sagged, and Viktor wished he did not have to witness the defeat in her eyes.

"Please, Natalia. Say goodbye to him. Then leave us. I will stay here tonight." He indicated the armchair in the corner of the room. "If you would be so kind as to bring our things to the BOQ in the morning, I will explain to Specialist Murdock that the suitcase had been misplaced by the airline."

"How will you get to work in the morning?"

"I am familiar with the taxis now. They are not so different from our own. And there is the Metro. I will be quite all right."

"Viktor, I…"

Angel rushed into the room. "Well, it's all settled, so you two can stop arguing."

Both Viktor and Natalia stared at the woman without comprehending.

She smiled hugely and slapped her hands together as if dusting off crumbs. "I called a Major Jansen at the phone number you gave me for your work. I told him you're here on the cardiac care ward and asked him to tell your co-workers. He was more than willing to take care of letting everyone else know about it."

Dumbfounded, Viktor stared. "What have you done?"

"I bought you some time, didn't I?" she said confidently.

"You didn't want anyone to lie for you, but I took it upon myself. I wanted to give something back to Natalie. And I didn't exactly lie. I told him Colonel Baturnov was in the cardiac care unit due to a heart condition. And that's true, in a way. I had to do *something* to keep you and your son together while he goes through the surgery."

"Angel," Natalia began, but then she stopped as if she did not know what else she should say.

Viktor understood. He couldn't decide where to begin with his questions and protests. "How…?" was all that came out of his mouth.

"Oh, I'm not deaf, you know. The nurses' station is just outside the door. I can't shut my ears off. You two have been plotting and scheming for days about how to keep the Colonel in the country long enough to see Alexander through this operation and recovery. That may take longer than you might think. So when I overheard that it would help if people thought the Colonel was the one in the hospital instead of the boy—well, I made a call. Seemed simple enough and it was."

"But Major Jansen…?"

"Nice man. He was the one who answered. I wasn't sure I'd get an answer this late in the evening, but the Major picked up after a few rings. I figured I should take care of it all right away. If I'd waited until tomorrow, you might have accidentally shown up somewhere before I could tell you to lie low."

Viktor still could not understand how the Major had become involved. His puzzlement must have shown on his face, because Natalia explained. "He was probably the officer on duty tonight."

"Well, the Major said he'd be sure to tell everyone who needed to know in your Army, too, and he asked me to tell you he hoped you'd get better quickly. He indicated that a heart attack would spell the end of your military career, but the way you two have been talking, I was certain your hopes of going back to Russia on happy terms with your employer were slim to none. This way, there's at least a chance you can stay. And maybe you can have a miraculous recovery later," Angel concluded, clearly quite proud of herself.

"Papa?" Sasha called from his bed. He looked from his father's shocked face to Natalia's and seemed unable to decide if he should be worried.

"Everything is fine, Sasha. Nurse Angel has taken our fate into her hands."

Natalia stared blankly at the woman. "You should have talked to us first," she said to the nurse.

Angel waved her hand as if to shoo the notion away. "You would have forbidden me to get involved."

"Papa, you not go," Sasha said firmly. By the wary expression on his face, Viktor knew his son needed reassurance.

"No, I will not leave America," he promised his son. "Not until you are well again."

Natalia saw where she was needed most and went to the boy and held his hand. She smiled down at him and talked to him softly about the cartoon on the television. Soon Sasha was smiling again.

"I cannot decide whether I should thank you or curse you," Viktor said to the nurse.

"Oh, you should thank me, of course. Natalie clearly needs you, and this is the least I could do for her. If it weren't for me, you'd be pushing her out of your life tonight. You don't really want to do that, do you?" She smiled, making her look far too adorable to be the same woman who had so recently duped two separate and rather formidable Armies with a single phone call.

"It is all very complicated," he said, looking at Natalia with his son. The ache of hopeless longing grew nearly unbearable. To himself he said, "I will not be going home with her in any case."

Angel heard, despite his lowered voice. "Well, you can't stay here. Hospital rules for this ward unless you make special arrangements. You can't go back to the place you were staying or Sergeant Citallio might get to wondering why you aren't in the hospital."

"I could tell the Sergeant that it was all a mistake." It unsettled him that she had taken control of his life this way. Despite the benefits of her actions, he had a perverse desire to undo what she had done.

"You could," she said agreeably. "But then you wouldn't be able to spend the next few days with Alexander while he goes through the last of his tests before his surgery. Did I forget to tell you we have it scheduled for Tuesday?"

Viktor ran his fingers through his hair. "Yes, you did forget to tell me. This is good." He gazed at Sasha, who was finishing up the last of his ice cream and joking with Natalia in between bites. "Is there enough blood?"

"There will be enough blood by then, don't you worry. All those people you sent in from the Russian-American community have really come through. They've been donating in Alexander's name in droves. Dr. Brennan would never agree to start the operation if he didn't think there would be plenty. You can give your blood again tomorrow, if you like. Every pint helps."

Viktor was glad that Mr. and Mrs. Petrov had made good on their promise to alert their fellow Russian immigrants to Sasha's plight. But he knew he had gone pale at the thought of giving more blood himself. He said nothing. He would do it.

Angel tapped the face of her watch. "Nearly time to go, you two. But at least you can come back, Colonel, and spend the whole of each day. Just make sure none of your friends from your offices catch sight of you."

The cartoon ended, Sasha yawned, and Natalia lowered the bed and tucked the covers under the boy's chin. Viktor stood nearby, taking in the picture of Sasha's small hand nestled in Natalia's. Sasha trusted her like a child trusts a mother. Soon, the child turned on his side and closed his eyes.

"Visit tomorrow?" he whispered to Natalia, needing one last reassurance. This side of Sasha was something Viktor rarely saw. At twelve, he had grown very independent and resisted most of Viktor's efforts to nurture him. Alexander Viktorovitch wanted to be a man in front of his father. This was one of the reasons Viktor had not insisted on staying at the hospital against his son's wishes. Sasha would not have appreciated the coddling coming from him. But coddling from a woman was apparently something else entirely.

"Yes, Alexander, we'll be here tomorrow," she answered,

glancing at Viktor and begging him with her eyes not to contradict her.

Viktor moved silently to the other side of the bed and gave in to the urge to treat Sasha like a little boy instead of a young man—just for this one moment. He reached out and stroked his son's hair, then leaned forward and kissed him on his cool, smooth brow. Sasha smiled ever so faintly, then relaxed into sleep. "Good night, Sasha. Sleep well," he whispered.

Together, they left Sasha's room and walked through the hospital corridors. Viktor remained silent until they reached the hospital lobby. Then he stopped and turned to her. "What were you thinking, Captain, to make a promise to my son about seeing him tomorrow? If you continue your acquaintance with me and my son, you will not be able to—"

"To claim plausible deniability," she finished for him. "Yes, I know. But I won't abandon Alexander. I can't." She placed her hand on his arm, making him instantly aware of her physically. "I won't abandon you, either," she added softly. "You need me."

He turned abruptly away and stood there for a moment, collecting himself. His chest felt overfull and his throat had gone tight. He seemed unable to think clearly when she was touching him, so he put a little distance between them by moving to the row of empty seats arranged in the lobby for visitors. The fullness around his heart did not diminish. "We are being followed," he reminded her. "The blue car, the man who came to my office—"

"But if he wanted to turn you in for bringing your son here, he could have done so a long time ago. If he wanted to get me in trouble for helping you, he could do that at any time. Whoever is watching us must be interested for some other reason," she assured him.

"What reason?"

"I don't know. I only know that he hasn't reported either one of us to our superiors yet. I figure it isn't our efforts to save Alexander that he's interested in."

Viktor could not dispute this logic. Or perhaps he simply did not want to disagree with her anymore.

"Besides, I'd rather not be left all alone if there's really someone watching my house," she added. He looked at her, wondering if it was possible for this confident, independent woman to be afraid for her own safety. The steady gaze she returned told him nothing of her inner feelings.

The idea of protecting her was just the excuse he needed to give up his campaign to end things between them. Especially when she looked at him with a softness in her eyes that he simply could not resist. "Come home with me, Viktor. I want someone with me and you should get some rest. Alexander will need you in the morning."

After a moment, she gently took him by the hand and led him outside. He followed her without further protest, thinking of the night ahead when he would sleep in the room next to hers and remember the warmth of her touch and the heat of her kiss.

AS SHE DROVE HOME with Viktor from the hospital, Natalie kept the conversation focused on the best way to proceed. They needed to work out how Viktor would come and go with the least likelihood of being seen by anyone who might recognize him as the man who should be in the hospital with a heart condition. And then they needed to talk some more about finding him a bride. Angel's lie would only keep the military at bay for a few weeks at best.

"You'll just have to be careful as you come and go. Use evasive procedures, vary your routes, wear disguises if you have to," she said.

"You want me to wear disguises?" he asked with an interested glance.

She appreciated his effort to lighten the moment, but she wasn't in the mood to cooperate. "I want you to keep yourself safe. If you won't at least try, then you might as well go into the Pentagon tomorrow and tell everyone about Alexander. We can't forget that there's someone following you."

His expression grew serious again. "I do not forget."

She pulled into her parking area, reassured that no one had turned into the lot behind her. She scanned the vicinity for a blue sedan. The darkness kept her from seeing any sign of their pursuer. But both of them were wary and tense as they made their way to the building. Viktor checked over his shoulder twice.

"The most maddening part is wondering why this mysterious follower hasn't turned us in to the authorities yet," Natalie said as they rode the elevator to her floor.

Viktor nodded thoughtfully. "This is in my thoughts, also," he admitted. "But I will gladly accept all the time he gives us." He followed her to her flat, his mind quickly shifting to less ominous thoughts.

"I will make omelettes for us," he announced as they entered. If he could not make love to her, at least he could feed her.

She made a sound that seemed to indicate agreement, but she kept on walking toward her bedroom. "I'm going to take a shower," she said over her shoulder. Her departure had all the indications of a hasty retreat, as she uncharacteristically failed to push the button on her answering machine with its blinking light indicating a call. She went right past it and closed her bedroom door securely behind her.

VIKTOR STOOD LOOKING at that door for a few seconds. It was such an insubstantial barrier. She probably had not even locked it against him. He would never trespass into her room uninvited, of course. But the knowledge that he *could*…

He took a deep breath and let it out slowly. Determined to clear his mind, he set about making the omelettes. He diced some leftover ham and a bit of onion and tomato. Finding some spinach, he chopped that up, too. He had noticed that Tasha seemed to like everything he made, never once admitting that she did not care for certain foods. So there was no hesitation as he threw ingredients together. He stood at the stove, trying hard not to fantasize as he cooked the eggs and filled the house with a pungent aroma. Then he heard the click of Natalia's bedroom door opening. The sound brought his fantasies roaring back.

She would be coming to the kitchen next, fresh from her shower. What would she be wearing? How would she smell? Would her hair be damp? Would her skin be pink from the heat and cascading water?

He heard her feet cross the carpet to the kitchen entrance.

"Hi. I feel better now," she said in an easy tone that contrasted sharply with his stretched nerves.

He did not look up or turn around. He did not dare. If he did, she would know what had been on his mind—what *remained* on his mind. He grunted a greeting and continued to cook.

Her feet were bare. He could tell by the soft padding sound she made on the linoleum as she entered. She leaned casually against the counter behind him. He could not resist sneaking a glimpse of little naked toes peeking out from beneath her bathrobe. That slight shift of his head brought her scent to him. She smelled like the strawberry shampoo she favored. He longed to inhale deeply, but knew better than to torture himself that way. The tension inside him was already at the breaking point.

"I'm glad things are working out for Alexander. With his surgery on Tuesday and everyone believing that it's you in the hospital—you should manage to hold out until you can both go back to Russia," she said.

"Sasha will have a few weeks of rehabilitation. If everything goes exactly as we hope, we will not be able to leave America for at least another month. And there could be complications. Sasha may require extended care. So my problems are not over." He tried to say this in a casual, uncomplaining voice. He did not want to worry her. But neither did he want her to give up her quest to find him a bride. As repugnant as the idea of marrying a stranger was to him, he could not see another way.

"Oh," she said. "So you still need to marry?"

"Yes. If only…" He trailed off before he could say something they might both regret. "I plan to mail my military discharge request on Monday. I will not be able to return to my position in the military without all the lies surfacing. If I remain an officer, the first thing that will happen upon my return will be a physical examination. I cannot hope to convince anyone of a 'miraculous recovery,' as Angel suggested. I must get out of the Army before the truth is discovered."

He shifted to the left and slid half of the enormous omelette onto one plate. "I have served well and for many years. Together with what the embassy will have heard about my heart, I believe the discharge papers will be processed without difficulty. In this, Angel has helped me." He slid the other half onto another plate.

He did not have to explain to her that the INS would require medical verification of his heart condition in order to exchange his current permit to stay in the country with one suitable for a civilian. He could not provide that verification, and he would not want anyone to falsify such documentation. His plan was to use Angel's lie about his heart to deal temporarily with the American and Russian military departments. But the only way to gain the extended time he needed to stay in America was to fool the INS through a marriage.

"But what will you do when you're not an officer anymore?"

"I will find other work. My language ability and computer skills will be useful, yes? By leaving the Army, perhaps my activities will not be discovered. Perhaps I will be able to return to Russia someday with Sasha without trouble," he said as he turned one hundred and eighty degrees to put the frying pan in the sink.

Instead, he crashed into the woman who had been standing much closer than he had realized. The remains from the frying pan spilled all over her. He feared the stuff was hot, so he threw the pan onto the counter and grabbed a dish towel.

"It's okay," she said, as he began to swipe at the front of her bathrobe with the cloth.

"*Prastite,*" he said, forgetting to apologize in English. He saw she was not hurt, but his heart continued to hammer and he could not seem to stop himself from trying to put her to rights. "*Prastite,*" he said again as the ties to her robe came undone as a result of the onslaught from his towel.

Everything seemed to move in slow motion after that. The ties slid slowly apart, the sides of her robe gaped, the little white T-shirt and panties she wore conspired to reveal more than they covered. She was more than he had imagined. It took less than a second for him to silence the warnings of his mind and to listen instead to the thrumming desire of his body.

He reached out slowly, dropped the towel to their feet, and spanned her waist with his hands.

SHE SHOULD HAVE KEPT her robe from opening, but she didn't. She should have turned away, but she didn't. She should have told him to stop, but she didn't.

She wanted him to touch her, to kiss her, to remind her of those feelings she'd so long suppressed in the pursuit of her career.

As his palms slid around her waist, those feminine feelings melted through her like sunbaked honey. Everything went warm and slick. He didn't pull her against him as she'd expected, and the way he seemed to linger over each tantalizing movement made her liquefy with desire. He seemed to shift his hands only a fraction of an inch at a time, making her tremble with anticipation.

Her nipples hardened as her labored breathing made her chest rise and fall against her T-shirt. She wanted him to touch her there, to remind her of that indescribable sensation that only a man's hands on a woman's breast could produce. But he merely hovered at the brink, as if he were trying to memorize her fragrance. His eyes were closed, his lips were parted, his nostrils flared. The intensity of his focus seemed electric, and a delicious shiver ran up her spine.

He didn't speak. He didn't look into her eyes. Closer and closer he leaned, until she thought she would die of want if he didn't pull her to him. Yet she held herself in check, resisting the urge to throw herself against him or to stroke his chest where his shirt still hung open. She kept her hands at her sides and allowed the tantalizingly erotic dance to continue at whatever pace he selected.

At last, he nuzzled her ear, sliding his nose along the side of her neck, nipping at her sensitive skin, tasting her. Waves of lust coursed through her until she was weak-kneed and aching with desire. Then his palms moved to her back, slipping stealthily beneath her T-shirt to connect with bare flesh. The heat of his touch made her groan. Gently, he pulled her closer until her breasts pressed against his chest. All the while, he nibbled and tasted her throat, along her jaw, her cheek—and at last, her mouth. She quivered with excitement.

Delicate kisses, meant to galvanize her desire; hands that

softly stroked and gently kneaded, meant to make her yearn for more—these conspired to drive her to do what she knew she shouldn't. She leaned into him, encouraging him and felt his breath escape in a rush as she pressed against his arousal. Spreading his hands over the cheeks of her bottom, he pulled her firmly to him. He moaned softly.

She wrapped her arms around his neck to hold him as tightly as he held her. She wanted him to understand that she, too, could no longer resist. His mouth became insistent and demanding upon hers. His tongue invaded and retreated, dancing with her own. Suddenly it seemed inevitable that they would be together, making love in this fevered, passionate way. This was right, this was good, this was…

"Tasha, I want you," he rasped into her ear. "Not just for this moment, but for tomorrow and the next day and the day after that." He nibbled at her earlobe. "It would tear me apart to marry someone else when I feel this way about you." He pulled away to look into her eyes. "Marry me, Tashyenka," he begged.

He stole her breath. She couldn't speak for lack of air and couldn't think past the thunder in her ears. *Yes,* her heart wanted her to shout. But nothing came out of her except the sound of her gasps.

"Tasha," he began earnestly.

Then the telephone rang, sounding unbearably loud because it hung only inches away from her shoulder. But even its insistent ringing couldn't douse the heat coiling low in her belly. She clung to Viktor.

"*Chort,*" he barked as he slid his lips along her jaw, down her throat and into the crook of her neck. "*Eta tvaya mat',*" he growled. Then he translated. "That is your mother."

Still breathless, she struggled to speak. "H-how do you know?" she managed to ask.

"A guess," he said in a half-strangled voice, as if he, too, could not easily command his speech. His respiration seemed as hitched and labored as hers. When he put his forehead on hers, leaning against her as they each struggled for control, she felt the telltale sheen of perspiration on his brow. Then she became aware of the dampness all over her skin and particularly between her legs. She knew that she would have willingly let him take her, right there in her kitchen, if they hadn't been interrupted. Hell, she might still be willing…

The answering machine finally picked up the call. Viktor's hands slid from her spine to her backside, holding her possessively. His gaze held hers.

Her mother's voice broke free from the answering machine. "Natalie? I know you're there. I just talked to Frank, so pick up the phone."

Viktor went very still, though he didn't let go of her.

"Speak to her," he urged.

With a shaking hand, Natalie picked up the receiver and pressed the star button to turn off the recording machine. "Mom?" she croaked. Then she cleared her throat and added, "How are you?"

NATALIA TURNED AWAY FROM HIM, and it was all Viktor could do to keep his hands from continuing to wander over her. The surprise of the phone call had done little to abate his lust for this woman before him. She was everything he had imagined and more, and he wanted her desperately. Even now, he could not take his eyes away from the delectable vision of slim hips and perfectly shaped bottom. He wanted to caress those exquisite curves. But he held himself back, admiring her from the distance of a few feet and wishing he could brush her bathrobe aside for a clearer view.

"What was I doing just now?" he heard Natalia say into the phone. "I was…I was, uh, busy in the kitchen. I was going to call you back, but you sounded upset so I picked up. Is everything all right?"

Viktor sucked in a breath as he watched her lean onto the countertop and put her head onto her palm. Her movement presented her derriere to him in a way that was nearly too exciting to resist. He wished he could help her with whatever seemed to be draining the strength out of her, but he had to keep all his efforts focused on regaining his self-control.

"Mom, I am not being difficult with Frank. I just don't want to marry him." She sounded exasperated.

Viktor grunted his approval. The idea of Natalia marrying Major Lezinski made him want to hit something.

"Yes, I know you don't really care to whom I wed. You just want me married and reproducing before I'm too old to give you grandchildren. I've heard. But I have plenty of time. And I'm concentrating on my career right now," she said into the phone.

Viktor wondered if she remembered that he had just asked her to marry him or whether she had been too swept away to register the words. He doubted her mother would approve of her daughter marrying a Russian officer on the run from his government.

Suddenly, Natalia spun around to face him, her eyes were wide with shock at whatever her mother had said. She looked right into Viktor's eyes. "Why would you ask if someone was here with me? Come on, Mom."

He held her gaze for another minute while she listened to her mother. He realized that the implications of what they had been doing here in the kitchen were beginning to sink in.

Viktor's heart sank. Unable to bear the bleakness of her gaze, he turned his back on her. Mechanically, he put the spices he had used back onto the rack by the stove.

He heard Natalia move out of the kitchen and he risked a glance in her direction. She went into the wide space between her dining area and living room and dropped to her knees in the center of the carpet, sitting there in the open as if she needed to get some air. "Mother, I appreciate your concern for my unwed state," she said in clipped tones. "I even understand that I'm taking a risk by waiting to have children. If I promise to try harder to remedy the situation, will you lighten up?"

Viktor realized that even if she accepted his proposal, she probably wouldn't mention it to her mother, given that it would be a temporary union. Then his thoughts skittered off in the direction of what it would take to keep this woman married to him forever.

"Okay, listen, I have to go now," she said into the phone. "My dinner is getting cold."

Viktor eyed the two plates in front of him. He could not face the eggs right now, so he wrapped his up and put it in the refrigerator. But maybe Natalia needed to eat. He put her plate into the microwave.

It took her another five minutes to extricate herself from the phone call. By then, the food was reheated. As he carried it to the table, Viktor watched Natalia sitting motionless on the floor with the phone still in her hand, a thumb pressed to the disconnect button. Her head was bent downward as if she were thinking hard and he dreaded to hear what she was planning to say to him.

"Come to eat, Natalia," he urged gently.

Without further prompting, she stood and walked to the table. She avoided his gaze, but she took her seat in front of the food he had placed there.

"How does my mother always know things?" she asked as she stared at the food.

"What does she know?" He slowly pulled out a chair and eased into it.

"Things." She looked up at him then, right into his eyes. "She knows you're here. Or at least, she knows someone's here."

This stunned him for a moment, but then he pieced together the bits of information Mrs. Wentworth had at her disposal and he could see how she had drawn her accurate conclusion. "She is a wise woman and she knows her daughter well."

"She's friends with my commanding officer. Close friends," she said, still staring into his eyes. "What if she mentions you?"

"Perhaps we should tell her the truth. Enlist her to be silent."

She snorted at that and looked down at her food. "I don't think so. She's never been able to keep a secret in her entire life. And the only way she would approve of you being here is if we were getting—" She stopped speaking abruptly and Viktor knew that she had been about to say "if we were getting married."

She blushed and took a large bite of her eggs. He waited.

Would she pretend the kissing had not taken place and make believe he had not proposed?

It was what he had done regarding the kiss they had shared earlier.

He did not think he could do so again. Not this time, with the memory of her passion burned so indelibly in his heart. This time, she had responded to him thoroughly and he had found her very, very arousing. It was not something he would be able to pretend away.

"Viktor," she began. The sad expression on her face and the shine in her eyes told him she was about to make a speech he did not want to hear.

He held up his hand to stop her. He would savor the memory of this night, at least until morning. Meanwhile, he would give himself the time to think about what he would be willing to sacrifice for her. He needed to search his heart before he made promises. And he needed to brace himself for the possibility that she might reject him anyway, unwilling to give up her career even if he was willing to give up his country.

"Please, Tashyenka. Let us not discuss anything until tomorrow. I want to take my memories of this evening to bed with me just this one night." He stood. Retreat would be the kindest thing right now, for both of them, he decided. "Sleep well, Natalia," he said as he made his way to her guest room, where he was certain he would not be able to sleep at all.

CHAPTER ELEVEN

NATALIE SAT AT THE TABLE for a long while after Viktor left. Eventually, she realized she wouldn't solve anything this night.

She needed something to read, but the novel sitting on the end table wouldn't hold her attention. With a sigh, she decided to go down to her car and get the books for her correspondence course. Maybe she would be able to study.

She slipped on the loafers she'd left by the door, coaxed her raincoat over her bathrobe, then picked up her keys and trudged out. The silence around her made the hum of the elevator sound louder than usual. When she got to the door of the building, she looked out at where the cars stood lined up in rows and squelched a shiver that ran down her spine. The streetlights didn't brighten the area much. There were shadows everywhere.

Taking a deep breath, she headed out, telling herself that the spooky chill she felt was a product of the cool night air and her overwrought nerves. Then she stopped dead in her tracks.

Just behind her car was the blue sedan, lights on and engine idling. She saw now that it was a Buick and the license plates were from Virginia.

The passenger-side door stood open and someone—the passenger?—was at the driver's side of her parked car. His head was bent so she couldn't see his face, but she watched in amazement as he opened the door of the car she knew she had locked. He leaned inside, but the interior light only showed her the color of his hair—brown. He bent down as if he were stretching across the seat. Was he doing something under the dashboard?

Anger at his audacity made her foolhardy. "Hey!" she called. "Hey, that's my car!"

She saw the driver of the blue car shift in his seat. The man shouted something to his partner and a head popped into view from inside her car. The face turned her way. A flash of recognition crossed her mind, but she couldn't place exactly where she'd seen him before.

"What are you doing to my car?" she called out. Remembering her training, she took cover behind another parked car. "Get away from my car!" Apparently the man who had been inside her vehicle heard her. He slipped into the Buick, and it sped off.

It was then Natalie realized that she hadn't caught the entire license plate number. She cursed and gave chase, but the car was too fast. Suffused with embarrassment at her own stupidity, she turned back.

Catching her breath, she walked to her car. She realized she was shaking violently as adrenaline pumped through her. All she wanted to do was check her car to be sure no permanent damage had been done, then get her books and hurry back to the safety of her apartment. Despite all the trouble he'd brought her, she was mighty grateful that Viktor was there so she wouldn't have to be alone during the night.

Perhaps it was the thought of Viktor that stayed her hand as she reached for the handle to open the car door. She hesitated, thinking over what she was about to do and imagining all sorts of things that could happen as a consequence. What had that man done inside her car? She backed away without touching anything.

Forgetting her weariness, she ran to the building, punched the elevator button repeatedly until the doors finally slid open, then hit the number for her floor.

She nearly dropped the keys as she fumbled to put the right one into the lock at the entrance to her apartment. As soon as she was inside, Natalie went straight to Viktor's bedroom door and knocked loudly. She paused, then rapped again, but right in the middle of her frantic effort, the door swung wide and Viktor appeared.

"Natalia, what is it?" he said with a worried scowl.

It was all she could do to keep from throwing herself into the safety of his arms. Now that he stood before her, exhibiting all his nearly naked masculine strength, the fear that had been barely suppressed came crashing to the surface.

"There were men," she began, still a little breathless. "I went to my car. To get some books I'd left there. The blue sedan. I don't know if it's the same one." She knew she wasn't making sense yet, but he didn't patronize her with suggestions that she slow down or confuse her with questions. He took a second to grab a shirt and slipped it on.

She calmed herself with a deep breath and started again. "I went out to get the books I'd left in my trunk so I could study. But when I got there, a blue sedan was parked behind my car. There was a driver inside it, but the passenger had gotten out. He jimmied the door of my car. I thought he was going to try to start it so he could steal it, but I'm not sure that makes sense. If they'd wanted to steal my Focus, the blue car wouldn't have been blocking it, right? So, I shouted at them and they sped off. Then I started thinking maybe they weren't actually going to steal it. Maybe...maybe they did something to it."

"Your car, you did not touch it?" he asked gently after a few seconds.

"No. I started to, but then I didn't think I should. I came to get you on the assumption you know more about this sort of thing than I do, being a former special forces guy, and all." She tried to smile and wondered if it looked as forced as it felt.

He smiled grimly back. "You did the right thing. I will be able to detect whether these men were merely thieves or something else entirely. Do you have a light stick?"

"Sure." She went quickly to the kitchen and returned with two flashlights. "Here you go," she said, offering one to Viktor. "Maybe we should call the police," she suggested, suddenly worried that Viktor might get hurt if he tried to look the car over.

He gave her his boyish grin. "I assure you I know far more about these matter than your local police."

She sighed, letting some of the pent-up anxiety leak out of her. She was out of her element and she knew it. There was nothing else to do but trust him.

FIFTEEN MINUTES LATER, Viktor was dressed and standing with Natalia at the car. The night was hushed and lit eerily by the streetlights. The cool air danced over his shirt and chilled his skin. But inside, he burned with frustration and anger. Whoever had been tracking him had touched Natalia's car. If he ever got his hands on the guy...

With great care, he inspected the outside of the car, then lay on his back so he could slither beneath it as he went over the chassis in minute detail. After a while, he concluded that nothing had been done to the brake lines and nothing had been attached to the undercarriage. The tires were intact and there were no signs of tampering with the wheels. Still beneath the vehicle, he hitched his way along so that he could peer up into the engine compartment. Nothing.

He crawled out from beneath the car and stood up. "Let us take a look inside now," he said in a calm, reassuring tone. He did not want her worried that the thing would explode as soon as he worked the latch. Such devices were highly ineffective and rarely used outside of certain circles in the Middle East and South America. She handed over the keys without hesitation.

As he knew would happen, the door opened uneventfully. The lock and window were undamaged. A very professional job. He shone his light over the darker portions of the interior and saw nothing unusual. Before he climbed into the seat, he checked thoroughly beneath it.

"Tell me again how the man sat in the car?"

"Well, he sat behind the steering wheel for a minute, but then he leaned over as if he were lying down on the seats or something."

Viktor slid sideways until his shoulder rested on the passenger seat. "Like this?"

"Maybe. It was hard to see from where I was standing."

He stayed where he was and gazed at the dashboard thoughtfully for a time. He tried to imagine what a person could do to a car from this position. After a while, he ran the light beam beneath the dashboard. No wires dangled, no panels seemed loose. He ran his hand underneath and behind the plastic covering of the dashboard and felt the many wires hidden there. They all seemed as if they ought to be there.

After searching every nook and cranny inside her car, he said, "I believe your car was only being searched."

They looked at each other for a moment and he said "CIA" at the exact same time she said "INS."

In his surprise he blurted out the first thing that came into his head. "Your immigration agency would do this?"

She shrugged. "I don't know. I just figured they were the only ones who would be after you right now. If they've been following us, they know you're not the one in the hospital. Maybe they want to prove you're trying to stay in the country illegally."

"Would they go to such trouble over one Russian?"

She raised and lowered her arms in exasperation. "I have no idea. But it sure makes more sense to me than the CIA. I mean, aren't they supposed to stick to spying on foreigners?"

He smiled grimly at her. "I *am* a foreigner," he reminded her gently.

"Well, I'm not and it's my car! I'm an American!"

He laughed out loud at that. "Ah, now, those are the magic words, so your people believe."

She gave him a disgusted look. "What do we do now?"

He turned in the driver's seat and turned the key in the ignition. The engine hummed quietly. He backed out of her space and drove around the parking lot, testing the brakes. Then he pulled back in and shut off the engine.

"There is nothing else to be done. Your car is safe. I wonder what they were looking for?" He followed her up to the apartment again, wishing he could put his arm around her shoulders or hold her hand or make some other show of how protective he felt toward her. But he did not touch her.

He watched her lock the apartment door, then shifted from foot to foot where he stood between the kitchen and living room. Though he was certain he betrayed no outward sign, his nerves were frayed with tension.

"I will not sleep anytime soon, Natalia. Where are these videos you keep telling me you will show to me? Perhaps watching a movie will help me relax.'' He eyed her warily, then decided to ask her for what he longed for. ''Will you join me in this?''

Her gaze slid from his face to the couch as if she could imagine them sitting there together. She chewed her lower lip, making him want to kiss her. ''Okay,'' she said, but she sounded uncertain.

She went to the cabinet and opened the doors. Behind them, she stored at least two hundred videotapes and DVDs. From one end, she retrieved a paper that had been slipped into a clear plastic cover. ''This is a list of most of the films in my library. I haven't updated it in a while.'' She handed it to him. ''Pick one.''

''You choose,'' he said, holding up his hands to refuse the list and making a face that said he wouldn't have any idea how to make a selection.

She put the list back and pulled out *Toy Story*. ''I remember when we toured the Air and Space Museum.''

He remembered, too. ''That seems a very long time ago.''

''To infinity and beyond,'' she quoted.

He smiled at her. ''There is nothing beyond infinity.''

She grinned back. ''You'll see,'' she assured him.

An hour and a half later, Viktor admitted that he had enjoyed the movie even though he did not always understand the American humor. But he got far greater pleasure out of having a sleeping Natalia leaning on him, trusting and peaceful. She had begun to doze during the second half of the film, and although he had silently vowed to keep his hands to himself, he had found that drawing her into the circle of his arms so she could rest against him was natural. She had cuddled close without hesitation.

With his free hand, he eased the remote control from her fingers and pressed the power button. The television went black and the room went silent. Natalia stirred, but she did not waken.

He thought about carrying her to her bed, but immediately rejected that notion as too dangerous. Instead, he propped a pillow behind his head and closed his eyes.

The light of dawn woke him. Somewhere in the night, Natalia had turned over to face him. She lay sprawled across him with her arms wrapped around his waist. He grinned. Despite the crick in his neck, this felt like paradise.

After a few minutes, she began to wake up, too. He had no idea what to expect when she realized her position, but the sleepy smile that kissed her lips was more than he could have asked for. "Good morning," she said as she crawled off of him and sat on the opposite end of the couch. "Sorry I used you for a pillow. You should have woken me."

"I did not mind," he admitted. He looked at her, bemused by the disarray of her hair and the pink crease along her cheek where her face had pressed to a wrinkle in his shirt. She was beautiful. And he was madly in love with her.

"Are we going running today? I'd give anything to get another chance at memorizing the license plate of a particular blue sedan."

"I give blood again today. And I ask you not to run without me. At least for today."

"Okay. I won't run alone," she said. "At least not until we figure out who those guys are."

Relieved, he unfolded himself from the couch and stood up, stretching cramped muscles along the way.

"I just remembered something." She frowned. "The man who messed with my car looked familiar," she said. "But I can't recall where I've seen him before. I see so many people. Maybe he's someone I've worked with." She stared into his eyes a moment. "That doesn't make sense. Does it?"

"I do not know, Tasha. Many strange things have happened. Anything is possible."

BY SOME UNSPOKEN AGREEMENT, neither of them raised the issue of what had happened between them in the kitchen. The time never seemed right to talk about it, given all they had to do. But that didn't stop Natalie from thinking about it all day long. While she helped him through the ordeal of donating blood again, she thought about his kisses. Listening to Dr. Brennan explain the details of Alexander's impending surgery, she thought about his marriage proposal. She spent the afternoon with Alex, playing board games and reading from a book of short stories. But she kept thinking about watching the movie with Viktor and then sleeping cradled in his arms.

Wouldn't it be nice if she could enjoy those things every day for the rest of her life?

"I'll make dinner," he said as they entered the apartment together at the end of the day.

"And we'll talk while we eat," she said, eyeing him for a reaction. She could not go on pretending that those passionate moments in her kitchen had not taken place the night before.

He sighed and his shoulders sagged slightly. He looked very tired suddenly and her heart ached for him. She watched him go into the kitchen, and although she hated leaving him to do all the work, she knew she would be more hindrance than help. Instead, she went to her answering machine and played her messages. Her mother was among the callers, of course. Natalie closed her eyes as she listened to the usual. Then Marie's voice rang out.

"I might have somebody, Nat. This woman I know, she might be willing to marry Viktor. It's complicated, though. I'll need some time. Don't ever say I'm not a great friend after this. Though I still think…well, you know what I think you should do about Viktor."

"Great," Natalie said to herself, feeling defeated even though she knew she should be happy that a solution could materialize soon.

"What does she think you should do about me?" Viktor asked. She hadn't heard him come over to the hallway table.

She turned to him, struck anew by his bearing and clean-cut good looks. He was wiping his hands on a dish towel, which had the unexpected effect of making him seem even more masculine. She liked it best when he was smiling, though. He wasn't smiling now.

"She thinks she might have found you a bride."

He straightened his spine and squared his shoulders. Looking right into her eyes, he said "I already found the bride I want." The penetrating gaze he fixed upon her made it clear whom he wanted for his bride.

Her eyebrows shot up at this open declaration. "But…"

"I have not yet sorted out all the details, however."

Details? "I need to think," she said, fighting the stammer that threatened to infiltrate her words.

A slow grin spread over his face. It lit his eyes. "At least you are thinking about it. That is better than an immediate rejection," he said. "Should I attempt to persuade you?"

She held up her hands to ward him off, even though he made no move toward her. "I don't need any more persuasion, thank you. I just need to think." She took a few steps away, putting some protective distance between them. Problems and options began swimming through her mind. "Even if I accept, it would be a temporary marriage. If we don't tell anyone but the INS, my career might survive. People keep marriages secret all the time, at least for a short time. It's no one's business." She began to pace as she thought about how things could work out. "We'd only have to be convincing for a few weeks. Then Alexander will be all better and the two of you will return to Russia. Before you go, we can annul the marriage or get a divorce, and I can get on with my life." She paced back again, then stopped when he stepped into her path.

"What if Alexander Viktorovitch and his father agree to stay in America?" he asked softly.

She looked up at him, her heart leaping at the prospect. At the same time, visions of a ruined military career flashed before her eyes. "Stay?" she asked in a small voice.

If he stayed, there would be no way to keep her marriage to a Russian military officer secret from her superiors. Yet, a real marriage with Viktor sounded wonderfully appealing. She was in love with him, after all. And every second she continued to look into his warm, brown eyes, she fell a little bit more in love with him.

Expression had drained from his face at the one questioning word she'd uttered. His body stiffened and a coolness seemed to descend around him. "I beg your pardon. I realize your career is important to you. You have worked hard. You must protect it. I should not have made such a suggestion." His gaze seemed to harden. "Still, I want to be honest with you. I would stay with you in America—though it means Alexander will grow up far from his homeland. I would live a true marriage with you. If you want me.''

Heart hammering now, she couldn't think straight. The man was offering everything she'd secretly hoped for. Yet she couldn't accept without giving up everything she had worked so hard to accomplish. She put her fingers to her temples. ''I don't know! I'm confused. I need to think.''

After a few seconds, she heard him move away. ''I will finish in the kitchen,'' he said as he went.

She drifted to the living room and fell onto the couch. Her books for her class sat on the coffee table where he'd put them. Angry with herself and the situation, she roughly flipped one open. The words on the page seemed to swirl and blur. She couldn't focus.

''I think I should meet this woman Marie has in mind,'' he said as he came out and placed dishes of steaming and fragrant food on the dining table.

''I agree,'' she said wearily. ''But I'd like to know why you think so.''

He looked in her direction but his features were inscrutable. ''I am not certain I could engage in a temporary marriage with you, Tasha. Once I say vows to *you*, I doubt I could bring myself to undo them.''

She let out a rush of air all at once and then couldn't seem to take any back in. ''I feel the same way,'' she admitted in a whisper.

He raised one eyebrow, managing to appear surprised and skeptical at the same time. ''But your military career...''

She pushed the fingers of both hands through her hair and grabbed fistfuls of the curls. ''I know! I know!'' she shouted.

He gave her a weak smile, his expression sympathetic. ''I cannot encourage you to make a decision that would not benefit you, Tasha. Do not think of it now. Come eat. Perhaps things will seem clearer in the morning.''

THINGS DID NOT SEEM CLEARER in the morning. Nor did they sharpen into focus that evening when they got home from the hospital. The day had been a strain for her as she'd thought about what she wanted most out of life. It was clear she would have to choose one goal over another.

She ate the food Viktor cooked for her and talked with him about Alexander, but she felt as if she were in a fog. "I have a headache," she told him when silence had filled the room for several minutes. "I'm going to bed."

She didn't feel any better when the door of her bedroom closed behind her. She stripped off her clothes and left them in a trail on the floor. She grabbed a T-shirt and put it on. Then she scanned the room and looked at all the familiar things. There was the quilt that her mother had made for her in honor of her college graduation and the jewelry box she'd gotten from her grandmother. Yet she didn't feel comfortable. She could not relax.

The knock on the door made her jump. "Yes?" she called. Her voice quavered slightly. She hoped he hadn't noticed.

"I have medicine and water for your head," he said.

It was hard not to be warmed by his thoughtfulness. But she knew in her heart of hearts that it would be a mistake to open the door. "I..." She had ibuprofen in her own bathroom, but she pictured him standing on the other side holding a glass and some pills and she couldn't bring herself to send him away.

She swung the door open. "Thank you," she said as she accepted his offering.

As soon as he'd passed the cup and Advil into her hands, he took a step back. Clearly he felt the danger, too.

"Good night, Tasha," he said softly. Then he turned and walked away.

She pushed at the door with her foot as she headed to the bed with the glass and the tablets. Popping the capsules into her mouth from her right hand, she lifted the glass with her left one. It shook and she scowled. He was only a man, she told herself, just as she stepped onto the little bedside carpet that lay on the hardwood floor next to her bed. An article of discarded clothing made her shift her balance awkwardly.

The carpet slipped, the glass flew out of her hand, and she went down hard. The glass landed after she did and shattered into a hundred pieces. She closed her eyes in time, but shards sprayed all over her. The sound made her head feel as if it had split.

"Damn!" she yelled as she got onto her feet, and her toe made contact with a jagged chip.

"Don't move," Viktor said from the doorway.

She surveyed her surroundings. There were crystalline sparkles everywhere she looked. "Okay," she agreed readily.

"I'll be right back."

A moment later, Viktor reappeared on the threshold of her bedroom. This time, he wore his loafers and was armed with a broom and dustbin. "Your knight in shining armor," he spoofed.

It was right about then that Natalie realized he wasn't wearing any armor. In fact, he wore nothing but his boxer shorts and loafers.

"You first," he said, handing her the little brush from inside the dustpan. "Brush yourself off."

"I'll need a hairbrush, too" she said, nodding toward her bathroom.

He went where she told him and came back with a comb. Bending over at the waist, she freed a few glass shards from her blond curls. Then she straightened and gently brushed off the rest of her, all the while finding herself excruciatingly aware of Viktor's presence.

He wouldn't allow her to move until he'd carefully swept all around her. Then he ordered her to the bed. From her perch she could inspect her cut foot, but as soon as she extricated the sliver of glass from her toe and swabbed the blood away with a tissue her gaze was drawn to Viktor again. He moved the broom in a measured pattern so as not to miss a spot. His spine was straight and the tendons on either side of it were thick and defined. She had a wonderful view of etched triceps along the backs of his arms.

At last, he gathered the final pile of shattered glass into the dustbin. He set the thing carefully aside and turned to her. "Your foot is cut?" he asked, eyeing her position.

"It's fine," she said. "I got the glass out, and it's not even bleeding anymore.

"May I see?" he asked. But he hesitated only a second before he sat on the edge of her bed and lifted her foot into his hands. "Just a small cut," he agreed as his left hand encircled her ankle. His long fingers splayed along her calf, supporting her leg. His right hand held her ticklish foot, then massaged the arch gently as he looked at her toe.

It was a vulnerable position she found herself in, especially when she remembered she was wearing only underpants and a well-worn T-shirt. Though his gaze seemed focused entirely on her cut toe, Natalie knew there wouldn't be much left to his imagination if his eyes wandered.

"Only a single drop of blood," he said, his voice raspy and seductive. His left hand slid ever so slightly upward along the underside of her leg so that the tips of his longest fingers grazed the tender, sensitive skin at the back of her knee. A shiver passed over her, and her skin tightened and nipples puckered.

He lifted his gaze to hers and then very slowly raised her foot higher. She was mesmerized by the depth of desire she saw burning in his eyes so she didn't see what was coming until his lips parted. She caught her breath as his tongue appeared. Her heart began to hammer wildly as he gently, slowly licked the drop of blood from her foot and then took the tip of her toe into his mouth and suckled gently.

"Oh, dear God," she whispered, fighting the erotic pleasure that swept from one extremity to all the others. It didn't seem normal to react this way from a man doing such a strange thing. But she couldn't help the moan that rumbled in her throat, and when his hand slipped farther up her leg to her inner thigh, all she could think was *Don't stop.*

CHAPTER TWELVE

VIKTOR'S BRAIN HAD GONE AWOL and his body was in sole command of the situation. He could not explain why suckling her toe seemed so utterly erotic. He only knew it made him think of giving the same treatment to other parts of her body, too. He kissed the arch of her foot to see what she would do. When she did not pull away, he nipped his way to her ankle with growing determination.

If Tasha did not stop him soon, there would be no turning back. Yet he dreaded the possibility that she might come to her senses at any moment and ask him to leave. When her lips parted, his heart skittered with panic. He slipped his hand a little higher on her thigh, teasing her sensitive skin, distracting her. But she spoke, anyway.

"You...you don't like blood," she said.

Relief flooded him. "Only my own blood, Tashyenka," he reminded her in a sensuous whisper.

He was driven to lean forward by something strong and primitive, keeping one hand on the bed near her waist to hold himself over her, he stroked the full length of her leg to the edge of her panties. They provided no barrier. And her T-shirt did almost nothing to hide her shapely breasts. In fact, the garment had inched up to reveal abdominal muscles nearly as strong as his own.

Acting on instinct, he began to kiss those tightly flexed stomach muscles while his free hand slowly slipped just under the edge of her panties. When she moaned her pleasure, his breath caught and his blood surged and he had to nibble at that sensitive flesh some more.

He felt her hands rise to his shoulders and smooth over his

skin, stroking him, fanning the fire inside him. "Tasha," he murmured as he raised himself up again and pushed a little higher until he suspended himself directly above her. She had parted her legs for him and his knees were between her thighs, perfectly positioned for what he longed to do. "Let me love you," he begged.

She did not speak, neither granting him permission nor denying him access. Her eyes were closed and her head was tipped back, arching her throat. Her palms moved across his shoulders and down to his biceps, swept over the straining muscles that held him above her and then slipped back the way they had already traveled. She must feel it, too—the unrelenting pull of desire.

The knowledge that she wanted him played upon his passion like a potent aphrodisiac. He could not wait for her to give her consent. Acting on the most basic impulse, he dipped his hips so that his erection stroked slowly along the soft cleft at the crest of her pelvic bone. The sensation was enough to drive him mad with wanting, but when her hips tipped up in welcome, he knew he was on the right track. Perspiration formed on his brow and it required all his self-control to go just as slowly when he performed the movement again.

"Oh, please," she moaned.

Her eyes were still closed. He wanted her to feel transported, but he needed to know she would take him with her wherever she was going behind those tightly closed lids of her. "Look at me, Tasha. Tell me. Do you want me?"

Her lids lifted very slowly, as if awakening from sleep. Her unfocused gaze found his and then recognition snapped her into the present.

"Yes," she said breathlessly.

The last of his blood departed from his brain and headed south at a frantic pace.

It took him less than a second to discard his shorts. And no time at all to strip her of the bits of cloth she wore. When she was naked, he stared at her.

"*Prokrasnaya kozha, gladkaya kozha,*" he murmured, praising her lovely, smooth flesh.

He discovered the intensity of her reaction when his palms grazed one taut nipple, so he took the peak into his mouth, making her moan and shudder. He gave the other one the same treatment and felt her tremble. Suddenly the instinct to join with her overcame his self-control. Seeming to understand his need, she reached for him and he made his way eagerly into position.

Entering her was excruciatingly pleasurable. Holding her gaze, he felt her wrap her legs around him to draw him deeper. The hot slickness and heavenly snugness brought him to that tingling state that foreshadowed an imminent climax. The need to let it happen pulled at him tenaciously.

Nyet! Too soon! He stopped moving, steeling himself against the insistent urge to thrust. But she did not know that he teetered on the precipice and kept on stroking his shoulders with her hands and encouraging him with a rhythmic movement of her hips. "Please," he begged. "Move not."

She ceased, but he could tell it cost her as much as it did him. "A moment only," he assured her, and she answered him with a tender expression, melting his heart.

"I love you," she whispered to him.

He groaned and knew there was no holding back after that. He began to move again, this time with a purpose that would not be denied, and her breath slid from her lungs in a long sigh. The sound had the effect of a bellows on a flame, spurring him to move a little faster, then a little harder. Setting a rhythm, he nibbled at her throat and along her jaw, nuzzled her ear and then found her mouth with his own. His tongue played with hers even as his body urgently sought satisfaction.

Faster. Harder. Closer. Higher.

"Oh, Viktor!" she cried between gasps for air. "Please, please," she begged.

"Zaznoba maya," he cried, wanting her to know she was *his* woman to love and no one else's. Then he was at the crest. An effervescence built and pulled and swelled beyond bearing. "Tasha!" he cried as he climaxed with such intensity he thought surely he must die of it.

But after a bit, his lungs began to work again and his heart ceased its violent pounding. There were no regrets except one.

He had not been able to wait for Tasha, but had gone careening over the edge into ecstasy without her. Now he knew what he must do.

Nothing on earth could have persuaded him otherwise, certainly not her soft murmurs of protest when he withdrew from her; not her gently grasping hands trying to hold him next to her; and not her murmured assurances that she was fine, that she did not need him to…to…

The long, quavering groan that vibrated in her throat and cut off her words when he touched her with one carefully placed finger would have been reward enough. But when she relaxed for him and gave herself over to the sensations his evenly circling touch produced, when he felt her legs tremble and heard her soft cries of pleasure, he discovered he was excited all over again. She was close, he felt certain, and he continued his gentle rhythm to bring her closer still. She tossed her head back and forth on her pillow and every muscle in her body seemed to strain with need.

"Oh, yes! Oh, Viktor!" She cried out and arched and seemed to pulse and throb. He knew she rode the waves of her orgasm. "I love you. I love you," she shouted as she clasped him tightly.

After a moment she eased up enough for him to raise his head. He propped himself on one elbow and looked down at her with so much love in his heart he could not contain it.

"Bozhe moy, ya lyublyu tebya," he confessed. Then remembering to speak English, "My God, I love you, too."

She smiled up at him and the sweetness of her expression made his eyes sting. So he kissed her on the mouth and then kissed her some more, and then started all over again making love to his Tashyenka.

NATALIE TOOK THE INITIATIVE in their lovemaking the second time. She liked the sound of his laughter when she heaved him over onto his back so she could explore his body with her eyes and hands. He was wonderfully made, with wide shoulders and a broad chest. She traced her finger over a scar that ran along his ribs and frowned.

"I was not always as clever as I am now," he explained. "That injury taught me to be much smarter."

"How did it happen?" she asked as her touch trailed gently down to his flat abdomen. His muscles tightened when she reached the spot just below his navel. "Are you ticklish?"

He answered her by sucking in a breath when she made featherlight strokes over the sensitive area. But he did not stop her. He gritted his teeth and spoke through his clenched jaw. "Something blew up. I was stupidly in the way. War is hell."

"I'm glad you won't be doing anything so dangerous anymore," she said as she grasped his erection and reveled in the strangled sounds he made as she stroked him.

"Do you like that?" she asked, as if she weren't already certain that he did.

"Mmm," he said, and the sound rumbled in his throat. His eyes were tightly closed and he seemed to vibrate with tension.

"Do you want me, Viktor?" she asked seductively. She wiggled closer, preparing to climb on top of him when he said "yes."

"You are already mine," he said unexpectedly.

She laughed and climbed on top of him, anyway. Straddling him, she positioned herself and then eased him inside.

"Aah," he sighed. *Ni astanavlivaysa! Do not stop!*"

"I wouldn't dr—"

The phone rang, cutting off her promise.

Viktor growled and clamped his hands on her thighs to hold her in place. "That is your mother," he declared. "Do not answer."

She laughed and squirmed against him sensuously, making him moan with pleasure. "You can't possibly know that my mother is on the phone." She let the thing ring.

"Whenever I want you, your mother calls. She is… mmm…psychic."

Natalie slid her body back and forth, to their mutual pleasure, and told him he was imagining things. Just then, she heard her mother's voice call out from the answering machine, though the words were unintelligible.

"You see?" he crowed triumphantly as he lifted his hips with wonderful effect.

"Shh," she said as she moved faster, distracting him thoroughly from the insistent voice coming from the other room. Continuing the motion, she propped herself up on stiffened arms so she could look down at him. "Tell me you love me."

"I love you," he said promptly, then he raised his hips in perfect time with the descent of hers, deepening their union. "And I'll show you now." He slipped his thumb in between where their bodies joined. He circled once, twice, three times, and her entire body quivered with immeasurable sensation.

Oh, this was so good, so intense, so consuming....

She found the precipice, and with one more circle of his thumb, she went over the edge, falling, falling, falling into sheer pleasure. Every muscle in her body joined in the rejoicing and even her toes curled and tingled.

And the best part was that Viktor found his own release immediately on the heels of hers. So when she fell upon him, all sated and sweaty, she knew he was just as content.

She curled up beside him and snuggled into the security of his arms, but she lay awake for a long time after that. She'd meant what she'd said about loving him. And he'd said that he would stay in America and make a life with her if she wanted him to. That sounded almost perfect to her—exactly what she wanted, in fact. She shouldn't feel even a modicum of discontent.

But she was worried, anyway.

It wasn't that she was unwilling to make sacrifices. If this wonderful man could give up his country, the least she could do was accept some changes in the military career she had envisioned. The NATO assignment would probably not be possible. She'd have to be content with what she was currently doing, concentrate on getting promoted to major, try to find a tour of duty that wouldn't conflict with her marriage to a foreigner.

But she had problems apart from her job. There was the concern over the mysterious men following them. And she wasn't confident about the Russian authorities' willingness to let Viktor out of the military. And, most important of all, there was Alexander's surgery coming up. So many things could go wrong.

Dreams crept up to her in the night. She tossed and turned, but found Viktor's soothing warmth beside her each time she awoke. At last, she drifted into a deep sleep, free of troubled visions.

"Again with the phone!" she complained as the incessant ringing dragged her from the depths of a deep, dark sleep. "I'm gonna get rid of them all."

But she reached for the receiver, cracking only one eye slightly open as she did so. "Hello?" she said groggily.

"Where the hell *are* you?" said a woman's voice. "Are you sick?"

"What?" Natalie said, still drowsy. She squinted at the clock as she tried to make sense of things. The illuminated digits read nine o'clock. "Damn!"

She sat bolt upright as the voice on the phone said, "Yeah, you got that right. You better be here in time for our ten o'clock staff meeting."

"Staff meeting," she muttered. "Right. I'll be there on time. Thanks, Constance."

"Don't mention it," Captain DiSanto said before hanging up.

Natalie leaped out of bed but stopped dead in her tracks after three steps. There was a telltale dampness between her legs that brought back a flood of memories from the night before. She looked down at her nakedness and then over her shoulder at the bed. Viktor was not there.

Undoubtedly, he had gone to be with his son at the hospital. He would undergo the last of his tests before his surgery tomorrow, she remembered. Why hadn't Viktor awakened her?

She dashed through her shower and was out the door in less than twenty minutes. Her stomach growled and she mourned the lack of one of Viktor's well-cooked breakfasts. She'd have to find food later after she had scrambled through an hour's worth of work in ten minutes.

She had no time to think over what had happened with Viktor the night before. She didn't even think about whether or not anyone was following her. Traffic took all of her attention, and then the only available parking space was in the last lane about a half mile away from any entrance to the Pentagon. She checked her watch and saw she would only make it in time to pick up her notebook and get to the meeting if she ran all the way to her office. The day was already warm, but she had to risk the sweat as she jogged the distance.

Emmy greeted her with "You're late," when she arrived breathlessly in the office suite.

Barbara came out of her office and leaned against the jamb, looking at her watch and lifting one eyebrow. "Five minutes to get your act together before the meeting," she commented dryly.

Natalie didn't spare her so much as a glance. She fell into the chair behind her desk and took a couple of deep breaths while she turned on her computer. Then she drummed her fingers rapidly on the desktop as she waited for Windows to launch. Finally, her programs came up on the screen, and she checked her calendar and e-mail messages. Twelve had to do with the Taiwanese visit, but she didn't have time to read them. She printed her calendar and her task sheet so she could make some kind of report at the meeting if she was called upon to do so, then she dashed out.

The meeting was in one of the conference rooms that had been preserved in the old style of decor despite the recently completed renovations of the building. Natalie eased herself into a chair not too near either end of the table, uncharacteristically trying to be as unnoticeable as possible. Barbara took the chair opposite her and Constance came in a few seconds later. She scanned the room, sized up Natalie's odd choice of position, then took the place Natalie usually occupied.

Great! She'd made herself conspicuous by changing her normal behavior. That was not what she'd had in mind, and the mistake made her feel hot and damp again. But she had no time to worry about it. Colonel Freeman strode into the room with his deputy on his heels.

"Good morning, everyone," he said cheerfully. He didn't seem to notice anything amiss, and he began the meeting with some administrative announcements.

"Can I hear your reports, please?" he requested a few minutes later. "Anything to tell us, Captain DiSanto?"

"Yes, sir," Constance said. Then she began to explain a complication that had come up with the Secretary's trip to Guam.

Natalie found it impossible to keep her mind trained on what Constance was saying. Even when the next person began to speak, she couldn't stay focused. She kept drifting to thoughts of Alexander and Viktor, wishing she could be with them at the hospital. She'd need to take some time off tomorrow to be with Alexander during his surgery. And maybe a few days after that to help with his recovery.

"Well, Captain Wentworth, how's your Russian?" This was from Colonel Freeman. But she was certain she hadn't heard him correctly.

"Excuse me?" she asked.

He eyed her with his brows knit. "How's your Russian?"

Her mind skittered to images from last night when her Russian had been very fine indeed. She felt certain this information was not what the Colonel sought. "Um. Fine?" she tried.

He stared at her for a moment, then looked to his deputy. "All right, then, if she can speak Russian *fine*," he said, with an odd note to that last word, "then I suppose she should go with the Deputy Secretary to Moscow in September. Put her on the calendar."

Russia? In September? Her mood darkened. Would Alexander and Viktor have returned to their homeland by then? Perhaps she would have the opportunity to see them while she was there. But as soon as the possibility entered her mind, she rejected it. Either she would marry Viktor and build a life with him here or she would have to give him up forever. There could be nothing in between.

Still as undecided as before, she simply nodded and tried to pay attention to the rest of the meeting. It seemed endless. When it was her turn to report, she consulted her notes and delivered the data mechanically. Finally, the meeting broke up and she kept her head down so as not to make eye contact with anyone as she made her way out.

She sat down at her desk and her stomach growled. The cafeteria wouldn't reopen for lunch for another half hour. She pulled out her desk drawer and found nothing but a half-eaten candy bar.

"Captain?" Emmy stood in her doorway. "You might want to take a look at this before I put it into Barbara's mailbox," she said, handing her a pack of stapled papers.

Natalie took it and immediately noticed that her own name had been crossed out at the top and Barbara Dwyer's name added. It was an assignment packet. A quick glance revealed that it was in regard to a trip to Belgium. Two days at NATO headquarters were included.

It would be a perfect opportunity to get in good with the protocol office over there. Natalie's gaze drifted back to the top of the page. There were initials after the change—JMF. James Malcolm Freeman, her commanding officer.

Forcing her features into neutral, Natalie handed the papers back to her secretary. "Thanks."

Emmy didn't depart as quickly as Natalie had hoped. "What are you going to do?" she asked.

"I have no idea," Natalie answered honestly. Four weeks ago, she would have marched into the Colonel's office and demanded an explanation. But today, she had other things on her mind.

Emmy stood still, apparently perplexed. "Really?"

Natalie looked up at her, realized she should make some attempt to behave normally, and said, "Not really. You know me, Emmy. I'm gonna kick someone's butt over this. It's my assignment, not Dwyer's."

Emmy smiled, reassured. "'Kay, then," she said happily. "I'll make a copy for you and put the original in Barb's mailbox."

"You do that." She was relieved when Emmy bounced away. Lowering her forehead into her hands, Natalie tried to clear her mind of everything.

Barbara appeared outside her door. "So, how come you overslept?"

The truth was not something Natalie was about to share. "I forgot to set my alarm last night." She shrugged. Did Barbara know about the changed assignments? Was she the cause?

"You forgot to set your alarm?" It *did* sound outrageous, given Natalie's usual attention to detail.

"Long story."

Barbara shifted from foot to foot and her gaze wandered back and forth. "Look, I know we've never been friends. But I wanted to ask you about something."

"Yeah? Well, come in and ask."

Barbara took a seat. "I wondered if you knew anything about Major Jansen."

"Jansen? Um, let me think." Natalie was puzzled. She knew the guy only vaguely. She thought he worked down in… "Hey! Didn't he work with Vi—" she caught herself just in time. She took a breath. "I think he works in the Materiel Command."

"So you don't know him?"

"Not really. Why?"

"He's been hanging around our corridor lately. I just wondered if you knew what he was up to. Sometimes he seems to be watching me." She shrugged. "I'm probably imagining it."

Natalie frowned. "You haven't asked him what he's doing?"

Barbara shook her head. "He kind of disappears whenever I head in his direction. Maybe he's just shy, but he creeps me out a little."

"I've seen him before at O'Malley's. Maybe you could catch him there sometime."

She thought about that. "Yeah, I'll try to do that." She nodded. "Well, look, I'll let you get on with your day."

Natalie watched her go. She sat for a few seconds, wondering if Viktor might shed some light on Major Jansen's activities, but she had work to do. Mercifully, Emmy brought in coffee and a bagel with cream cheese an hour later. "Barbara said you could use some food."

Natalie smiled her gratitude and fished out some bills to pay for the food.

"Don't forget that protocol regulation you're supposed to review. It's due by Friday," Emmy reminded her.

Natalie groaned. As if she didn't have enough to worry about right now. "Listen. Can you clear my calendar of appointments for the rest of the week, reschedule everything? I've got this family thing happening. It's kind of important. I might have to ask for a couple of days off.''

Emmy frowned. ''You sure you want to do that right now?'' she asked carefully.

''I don't have a choice. Things come up, you know. Just because I don't have a husband and kids doesn't mean I never need time off to take care of family matters.''

Emmy held up her palms in surrender. ''Hey, you're singin' to the choir, Captain. I don't care if you take time off. I just think things are kinda screwy around here and you might want to stick around to get 'em back on track.''

Natalie knew the younger woman was right. But she would have to worry about all that later. Her most immediate concerns involved keeping a Russian Colonel out of trouble and praying for his son during heart surgery. Nothing else could get in the way.

Another thought struck her. ''Emmy, have there been any guys coming around asking about me—men you don't recognize?''

''That Major Jansen was down here last week. Why?''

''What did *he* want?''

''He asked if you were in because he was looking for that hunky Russian dude and thought you might know where he was.''

''Oh.'' Weird that the guy's name would come up twice in one day. ''Anyone else?''

Emmy looked at her with confusion knitting her brow. ''Other than Frank? He was here this morning before you got in, asking where you were.''

''Anyone else?''

''No. Should there be?''

Natalie waved her hand. ''No, no, but if anyone should ask about me, don't tell them anything, okay?'' At least the men from the blue Buick hadn't come prowling around her office.

''Okay,'' she said hesitantly. ''If you say so.'' She started to walk out, then turned back. ''Are you in trouble of some sort?''

''No, I'm not in trouble,'' she said in the most reassuring tone she could muster. *Yet,* she added silently. "Don't worry about me."

"Well, what if these men show badges or something? What should I do then?"

Natalie resisted the urge to roll her eyes at the woman. "You know what? Just forget I said anything. It's not important."

Emmy smiled back and looked relieved. "'Kay!" She went out of Natalie's office with her usual perky stride, all cares apparently forgotten.

Somehow the rest of Natalie's day went by too quickly for her to accomplish all that she was supposed to do. Yet at the same time the hours seemed to drag so slowly, she thought she would never escape.

VIKTOR SAT AT HIS SON'S bedside in the military uniform he no longer had the right to wear. He was a Russian deserter now. He clenched his jaw, then caught himself grinding his teeth. If not for his memories of the night before, he would not have been able to keep himself from drifting into a black depression.

While Sasha played a fierce Nintendo game, Viktor thought about Natalia and the wondrous hours they had shared in her bed. Yet he knew she had a golden future without him. He had little to offer her in exchange for giving up that potential success—almost nothing to offer, except for his undying love and his wonderful son. Looking at Sasha as he whooped with glee over a success in his game, he thought maybe this sweet boy would be enough of a gift to make up for all she would lose.

And yet, Sasha might not live.

This possibility had been creeping into his mind at random intervals throughout the day. He forced it away, but it kept coming back. Each time, Viktor's heart constricted with doubt and fear.

Was he doing the right thing to insist on this surgery? Or was he giving up months, even years of Sasha's life on the chance he might be cured? He wanted a normal future for his son, but was he sacrificing what little time Sasha had left because he could not accept his son's infirmity?

No, he told himself. He only wanted the best for his boy. The doctors had assured him this was the right thing to do. Dr. Brennan had explained how common this surgery was in America and that he should not worry.

But he worried, anyway.

And so it went, through the long hours of the day as he kept his son company, his mind tugging him back and forth between dread and hope. When he was not worrying about Sasha, he found himself dwelling on Natalia. He missed her.

As if he could read his father's thoughts, Sasha spoke suddenly and asked when Natalia would come. "I like her," he added, reverting to Russian.

"I like her, too," Viktor admitted.

Sasha's head whipped around to skewer Viktor with a penetrating look. His brow knit. "Why not marry her?" he asked.

Viktor chuckled. "I am working on it."

Sasha grinned, then nodded his approval. "She will make a good Russian."

Viktor's smile faltered, but Sasha had already turned. Now was not the time to suggest to the boy that they might not be going home, that their countrymen might turn against them when they found out what they had done. If he married Natalia, he would not return home for a long time. Perhaps not ever.

"At ease, men" came a feminine voice pretending to be deeply masculine. Viktor turned to see Natalia framed in the doorway. She looked crisp and professional, standing there in her military uniform. Without thinking, he stood and went to her. Without asking, he swept her into his arms and held her hard against him. He buried his face in the crook of her neck and stayed there a moment, breathing in her wonderful scent.

"I'm glad to see you, too," she said, erasing any worry that she might reject his advances. Her arms stole around his waist as if she sensed how much he needed her in this moment. She squeezed him in return and Viktor knew he would not lose his sanity during this last day before Sasha's surgery as long as he could rely on Natalia's comforting embrace.

"Papa, stop. Natalia must hello me also," said the boy in an exasperated tone.

Viktor smiled at his son's English and released Natalia, then felt a deep, comforting joy when she kept his hand in hers as she approached his son's bed and kissed the boy on the forehead. "Hello, Alexander. How are you doing?"

"I am fine," he said while nodding his head and grinning. "See?" He pointed proudly to the television, which displayed his final score from his Nintendo game.

"Yes, look at that!" she exclaimed. "You did it! You're getting really good."

"Really good," Sasha repeated.

"Sir, you can't go in there!" they heard Angel call from just outside the door. "Sir! This is a cardiac unit! You cannot just barge in and…"

Viktor looked over his shoulder to see what the commotion was about. When he saw what was happening, he completed the turn and squared his shoulders, standing protectively in front of Sasha and Natalia, guarding them as best he could behind his body. Angel had taken on a similar stance in the doorway, blocking entry to the man who was determined to get in.

"What's going on?" Natalia asked as she tried to see around Viktor.

"Schwinn" was all he needed to say.

CHAPTER THIRTEEN

"I'LL DEAL WITH HIM," Natalie announced after a moment to recover from her initial shock. She scrambled off of her perch on the edge of Alexander's bed and slipped past Viktor.

"No, Natalia!" Viktor called. But Natalie ignored him.

"I see you in there, Red!" the General called angrily. "I know you're up to no good." He shook a fist, while Angel valiantly blocked him from doing more. "Supposed to be at the Pentagon, they said. Supposed to be learning things. Ha!"

"General Schwinn, sir," Natalie said as she approached. "I have the Russian in my custody, sir. There's nothing to worry about. I haven't let him out of my sight." She put a comforting hand on Angel's shoulder. The nurse relaxed her posture slightly, but remained where she was so that the General could not barrel into the room.

Natalie slipped around her, effectively forcing the General to take a few steps back. Viktor had been right behind her as she'd approached the door, but he'd obviously decided to remain back a few paces when he'd heard what she'd said. If they could convince the General that Viktor was in her custody, perhaps he would leave peacefully. Wanting to separate the two angry men, she said, "Come into the hallway with me, sir, and we can discuss what should be done."

"Done? Done? That man is a Russian spy and needs to be locked up. Permanently," Schwinn shouted as he allowed her to ease him across the wide corridor.

"He's in my custody," she said again. "I have everything under control," she assured the old man.

Roscoe P. Schwinn looked her over from head to toe with an

expression of disgust on his wrinkled face. "You're a woman!" he declared.

"Yes, sir, and I'm an officer, too. I've been assigned to Colonel Baturnov. He can't spy while I'm watching him."

The General gestured in Viktor's direction. "Look at him! He could overpower you in the blink of an eye," he declared.

This was undoubtedly true, so Natalie didn't bother to argue about it. She chose a different tack. "What are you doing here, sir?"

The General grinned smugly. "I've made it my business to learn his habits since he's been CONUS," he boasted, meaning that he must have been following Viktor since he'd arrived in the continental United States. "I figured out he was coming here, but I couldn't get away from those MPs who're always looking over my shoulder. But I managed it today, though. You think I'm stupid?"

Fleetingly, she wondered how many people were following them and noted—not for the first time—how much like a spy movie her life had become. "No, sir. You're not stupid." In fact, for a crazy old man, he'd certainly put two and two together.

She glanced over her shoulder at Viktor standing in the doorway beside Angel. Anger simmered just beneath his cool expression. The General saw this, too, and made a lunge at him. Natalie stepped into his path and pushed him back, leveraging herself with a stance she'd learned in basic training.

"He's up to something, and I want to know what it is!" the General shouted. "Why is he here? Who's in that room behind him? What's going on?"

In her peripheral vision, Natalie saw some people come bustling around the corner about ten yards away. The woman among them yelped when she spied them in front of her. "There he is!" she called. Natalie took her eyes off of the General long enough to recognize General Schwinn's wife. She had hospital security and two military police officers with her. "Roscoe! Thank goodness we found you. If it hadn't been for these nice young men…" she said, indicating the MPs walking beside her. "What are you doing here?"

But Roscoe did not take his attention off Viktor for so much as a second. "I'm calling the Russian embassy to find out about you and why you aren't where you're supposed to be, mark my words. Then I'm going to call the CIA and see what they have to say about all this."

Mrs. Schwinn reached her husband and put her hand on his arm to gently lower the fist he shook at Viktor. "Ros, come on home now. Leave these nice people alone." One of the MPs moved to the General's other side and began to ease him away from where Natalie stood.

"Don't mind him, ma'am," said the police officer with a sad smile. "He's harmless. We try to keep an eye on him for the missus and this isn't the first time we've helped her find him."

"It's a good thing I noticed him driving off the post and tailed him," said the other man. Natalie would have laughed at the image of everyone following everyone else, except that the General's next words reminded her of the seriousness of the situation.

"I'm calling the Pentagon!" he shouted. "You're supposed to be there, but you never are! You're supposed to be at Fort Drake at night, but you're not there, either!"

The hospital security guard said to the MPs, "You need to take him out of here right away. He's causing a disturbance." The MPs calmly nudged him a little faster down the corridor. Mrs. Schwinn murmured encouragement as she held on to the General's arm and urged him into a steady walk. Natalie realized how far out of their jurisdiction the MPs were. She supposed they'd rather catch up with Schwinn themselves than have the General embarrass the Army by getting himself arrested. Undoubtedly, they'd insist on some sort of restraint against the General's wanderings after this. But that didn't mean the man wouldn't be able to make good on his promises to call various authorities.

What he threatened next chilled her to the bone.

"I'll call the immigration people, that's what I'll do! They'll want to know about you and whoever's in that hospital room.... Another Red, I bet. They'll want to know!" He shouted this last bit as he was pushed and pulled around the corner and out of sight.

Natalie growled in frustration and turned to look at Viktor and Angel. "We're running out of time, Viktor," she said.

He nodded, holding her gaze. He must have felt the same despair that had crept into her soul, but he hid it well.

"Papa?" called Alexander. Then he asked something in Russian.

"Everything is fine now, Sasha," said his father as he turned back toward the bed. "That man is gone." Viktor returned to his son's side, and Natalie could hear their voices as they talked softly to each other.

She faced Angel. "We need your help again," she said.

"Just let me know what I can do for you" came the prompt reply.

"We need to have a wedding here as soon after Alexander's surgery as you think we can. He'll want to be able to witness it, but I don't want anything to interfere with his recovery, so you'll have to help me decide the right time."

"Who will be the bride and groom?" Angel asked, looking as if she already knew the answer.

"Viktor will be the groom," she said. But she couldn't quite bring herself to say who the bride would be. She wasn't one hundred percent certain herself.

THERE WAS NO QUESTION that he would spend the night at his son's bedside. This time, Angel made no attempt to evict them when visiting hours ended. Viktor did his best not to let on that this was his plan because he did not want to make Sasha more nervous on the eve of his surgery. He and Natalia played card games with the boy until late, which resulted in great fun for them all. They laughed about the rules that Natalia seemed to make up as she went. They laughed about how well Sasha could hide his thoughts before a winning play. He had a poker face, Natalia said, and they laughed at that strange American idiom, too. When he was losing his third round, Viktor made a great show of pretending to cheat, and more hilarity ensured. He thought some of their silliness stemmed from the fear none of them wanted to acknowledge.

Sasha's upcoming ordeal was such a frightening prospect that they could not talk about it, nor could Viktor even think about it without feeling as though his own heart were being torn from his chest.

Better to play cards together as if nothing were out of the ordinary. Then tuck Sasha under the covers when he grew sleepy, kiss him on his smooth forehead, ruffle his hair as he had done a thousand times before. Gazing down at his child, he could not keep from resting his large hand on the small chest to feel the living heat and the rise and fall of the boy's rib cage as he breathed. God grant that this not be the last night Viktor would know a father's joy.

Natalia moved to stand beside him. "May I stay with you?" she asked softly. Clearly, she understood his need to stay with his son.

"You must go to work in the morning. You should go home and sleep."

"I couldn't sleep, anyway. I'll make myself go to work for a bit tomorrow so that no one gets suspicious, but please let me stay tonight."

He looked down into her face and said, "I would be grateful for you to remain." If she left him alone with his morbid thoughts, he might go mad. He felt halfway there already.

In reply, she slipped beneath his arm and leaned against him. She was warm and she smelled heavenly and he was very relieved to have her company during this most difficult time.

"I brought my books to study," she said. "Do you want me to get you a magazine or something else to read?"

"I have my computer with me. I have some data I need to enter, some queries to run." He kissed her gently on the cheek and released her. The least he could do was continue his inquiry into who might be trying to hurt her career.

NATALIE STAYED THE ENTIRE NIGHT with Viktor and Alexander. She knew with deep certainty that she belonged with them. By morning, she was more sure of their place in her life than she was of her military career.

She and Viktor had slept uneasily in fits and starts, propped in chairs. Dr. Brennan's arrival at seven o'clock rescued them from further torture in those uncomfortable seats.

"Good morning, everyone!" he said cheerfully. "It's a beautiful day for fixing hearts."

Sasha rubbed the sleep from his eyes and grinned, but then his expression grew apprehensive. Natalie went to him and tousled his hair.

"You're going to be good as new after this," she assured him.

Angel came in and offered her own words of encouragement. She patted Viktor on the shoulder and ordered him not to worry. "Dr. Brennan is the best," she said. Then she went to Alexander's bedside. "I'll visit you in ICU to make sure those nurses take good care of you after your surgery. Okay?"

Sasha nodded. He looked very young and vulnerable as he did so, and Natalie felt her throat go tight. Dr. Brennan took out the plastic valve he kept in his lab coat pocket and once again reviewed with father and son what would happen in the operating room. He pointed to where Alexander's incision would be, explained again how his chest would hurt from being opened up, that his scar might not look so good at first but would fade over time. He assured them all that Alexander would be up and taking his first steps with his repaired valve within thirty-two hours.

"I'm looking forward to this, guys," he said in that calm and friendly tone that seemed natural to him. "You're going to feel so much better than before, and I can't wait to see you up and about, doing what boys your age usually do."

"Make trouble," Alexander offered, cracking a smile. The way his lips lifted more on one side than the other reminded Natalia of his father and her heart filled with love for both of them.

Viktor laughed at his son's joke and the doctor chuckled and patted Alexander on the leg. "Not until after the surgery, if you please," he quipped. "I'll see you in the operating room."

He winked at Viktor, then squeezed Natalie's fingers reassuringly, and he was gone. Less than a minute later, nurses and orderlies arrived to put medication into Alexander's IV and shift him onto a gurney. Viktor refused to let go of his son's hand and the boy clung to him with white knuckles as the party began to move through the corridors of the hospital.

"I'll be at your side when you wake up, Sasha. You're a brave soldier, my son, and you will come through this very well." Natalie thought perhaps Viktor said these words more for himself than for his son. But they had the right effect on Alexander, too. Determination replaced some of the fear on the youthful face. The steel in those young brown eyes matched that in his father's.

As they approached the doors through which Natalie and Viktor could not go, the medical personnel slowed and then stopped. "How are you feeling, Alex?" the kind-looking nurse asked.

He said something in Russian, and Viktor translated that he'd said he was very sleepy. Viktor spoke with him in Russian briefly, then Alexander's eyes drifted closed. "I love you, Sasha," she heard Viktor say. Then he kissed his son before the medical team wheeled him into the operating room. Natalie's heart ached as she saw the smaller fingers slipping gently from the larger ones as the sleeping boy was moved away.

THE WAIT WAS AGONIZING.

As the hands of the clock began their slow journey around the circle of time, Viktor repeatedly told himself that this was no different from the many other life-threatening situations he had faced during his military career. But the reality was that though he cared a great deal for the welfare of the soldiers under his command, he had always been exceedingly successful at maintaining an emotional detachment from his men. Doing so was necessary to the missions and to keeping everyone alive. But detachment simply was not possible with Sasha.

When his boy had been taken into the operating room, Viktor wanted to howl like a wounded animal. He wanted to weep. He wanted to call back the nurse and demand his son's immediate release from this place where his chest would be cut open and his heart would be tampered with.

Instead, he held these emotions inside and turned away, fighting off a deep frustration that he could do nothing but wait.

Natalia was there, quietly standing by to take his hand in hers and lead him to a seat in the waiting room. That human contact was all that kept him from shattering, so he clung to her for a long time. But after a while, he rallied himself enough to point out that she ought to be at work.

"I don't want to leave you alone," she said.

"Dr. Brennan said it would be evening before he completes the surgery. Please, Tasha. Go to work as if nothing is out of the ordinary."

"I know you're right," she said. "If I stay, people will wonder what's going on." Her eyes gleamed with a telltale shine, but she made herself stand up.

He stood, too, and wondered if he would be able to maintain his composure once she was out of reach. Hoping to collect enough strength to make it through the day, he pulled her into his arms and held her close. She wrapped him tightly in her embrace, and before he was able to make himself let her go, he felt a dampness seep through the cloth of his olive-green shirt and knew she was crying. She managed somehow to wipe her eyes before she drew apart from him. She even smiled.

"Dr. Brennan is a great doctor. Alexander will be fine." She picked up her purse, jacket and military cap and only one small sniff exposed the depths of her emotions. "I'll be back as soon as I can get away." She walked resolutely to the exit.

He thought she would go without a backward glance. When he had first met her, that is exactly what she would have done. The soldier she had been had no time for sentimentality. But the woman she had become hesitated on the threshold. Then she glanced over her shoulder, smiled tremulously and whispered, "I love you," just before disappearing.

The air seeped from Viktor's lungs in one long breath, and for a moment he was not certain his chest would expand to take in more. His heart felt heavy, his limbs weak. So he sat down and concentrated on taking in oxygen and expelling the carbon dioxide. It was an effort and it kept him busy for a long time. He might have dozed. The next thing he knew, a young woman gently shook his shoulder.

"Colonel Baturnov?" she asked.

"*Shto? Kto?*" he murmured. Then he shook himself fully alert and grasped the woman's arm. "What is wrong?"

She gently patted his hand reassuringly. "Everything will be fine. Dr. Brennan wanted me to give you a report. The surgery is going well. Everything is proceeding normally."

"How much longer?" He let her go and eased back into his chair.

"We're about halfway through."

"Halfway," he said softly. It seemed as if an eternity had already passed. "Thank you for the message." He attempted a smile, knew it fell short, and was glad when the young woman departed again.

That's when he began to pace.

Viktor had never been captured by any enemy in his entire career. But he decided this must be what it was like to be a prisoner of war. The room seemed smaller with every lap across the floor. The walls seemed to close in around him. He counted his steps, just to be certain the distance from one end of the room to the other remained the same. Then he counted again. And again.

A movement outside the entrance made him stop dead in the center of the room. The door swung open. Natalia stepped into view. And Viktor smiled sincerely for the first time all day.

"I am glad you came back," he said. "You did not give me the chance to tell you I love you, too."

She did not say a word, but walked straight into his arms and hugged him fiercely. "How is he? Have you heard anything?"

Viktor looked at the clock, surprised to see how many hours had passed since he had last been visited by the nurse who brought him updates. "We should hear soon," he assured her. He found he could be more confident for himself when he also had to be confident for someone else.

She backed up a little and looked at Viktor. "I have something to show you," she said to him. She fished in her purse and then handed him a folded paper.

He opened it and read the English words. It was a Maryland marriage license. His name appeared on the document right next to Natalia's. His heart beat a little harder. He stared at it a moment as if it might disappear if he took his gaze away. His pulse throbbed in his ears.

"You still want to?" she asked gently.

In a flash, his attention went to her face. Her eyes were filled with worry and doubt. He needed to erase them.

"Yes, I still want to. Very much." His gaze went from her face to the paper in his hands and back again. "But..."

"It's a good thing I still had your dossier. I needed to provide some facts about you in order to get the thing processed. Funny that it only takes one party to acquire a marriage license in this state, don't you think? It got a little dicey when I couldn't give them a social security number for you, but when I explained you were Russian, they had me fill out a bunch of special forms. And then..."

In two steps, he brought himself close enough to swoop in with a kiss. His mouth sealed hers, stopping the tumble of words that spilled from her. She tipped her head up eagerly, shifted her stance to press her body against his, and grasped the front of his shirt in a tight hold as if to prevent his escape. When he knew she would not again resort to a cascade of information in order to avoid what must be discussed, he released her mouth and tucked her head against his shoulder and beneath his chin. Such a strange picture they must make, he thought, as he considered the disparate uniforms they wore.

"Your career will suffer, Tasha," he reminded her gently.

"You and Alexander are more important."

"Did something happen to make you decide you must make this sacrifice?"

"Yes."

His heart sank. He wished that she was making this decision because she loved him and his son. But he knew that was too much to hope for. "What happened, Tashyenka?"

She tipped her head back just enough so she could look into his eyes. "I realized how much I love you," she said softly.

He caught his breath, and his pulse stepped up its pace. He could find no words to express what he was feeling.

"I want you to be my husband, even if it isn't forever."

He found his voice. "I want it to be forever," he said with conviction. He had never been more sure of anything in his life.

"Your government might not allow it, Viktor." She pulled away from him and turned toward the window. "Some people from your embassy were asking questions about you today. They talked to Sergeant Citallio and to the guys in the Materiel Command. Frank came by to tell me. I could tell he was watching me closely for a reaction of some sort. I tried not to give anything away."

Viktor moved to stand behind her and raised his hands to her shoulders. "You have done nothing but try to help us, Tasha. You do not owe us anything else."

"It occurred to me that if your government decides to take you home all of a sudden, we should have a plan for Alexander." Viktor felt her gradually relax against him. Then her right hand rose to cover his where it rested on her shoulder.

He sighed, weary to the bone from the tension and strain. Tired of being afraid and feeling hunted and wondering if he would celebrate his son's thirteenth birthday with him. "Yes, we should have a plan for Alexander," he agreed.

"I want to be his stepmother as much as I want to be your wife."

"He loves you like a mother already."

She turned around suddenly and looked up at him with shining eyes. "Does he? Do you really think so?" Her voice broke on the last syllable.

"Yes, Tasha. He loves you like a son loves his mother. I see it in his smile each time you sing him to sleep at night." He watched a tear leak from her eye and drift slowly down her cheek.

Impatiently, she swiped it away. "If we marry and you are forced to go home, then at least we can keep anyone from trying to send Alexander back to Russia before he is well. And you will have a better chance of returning to us later.''

"My home is here with you now," he said. "Together we will—"

He did not finish the sentiment because the doors to the operating room whooshed open and Dr. Brennan stepped through them. There was a smile on his face that made Viktor want to go down on his knees and give thanks to God.

"Everything went well!" the doctor announced. He looked exhausted but pleased. "He's in recovery now. It'll be a while before he wakes up, and I bet you haven't eaten all day."

Viktor nodded numbly. He had lost sensation in his fingers and he could not be certain of his legs. The relief flooding through him had the effect of a narcotic and amphetamine mixed together. Fortunately, Natalia stood beside him beneath his left arm, leaning into him and smiling broadly.

"Thank you," he managed to say to the doctor as he shook the man's hand. "Thank you so much."

THEY STAYED BY ALEXANDER'S bedside in intensive care, amid the myriad machines that beeped and thrummed to the tempo set by the boy's vital organs, waiting for him to regain consciousness.

"He seems so still," Viktor noted.

"But see how his chest rises and falls evenly. And the machines have a rhythm that tell us he's doing well," she said.

He nodded and said no more for a while. Then he shifted suddenly. "His fingers moved," he announced a little breathlessly.

Natalie leaned closer. She saw the child's eyes move beneath the lids. In another moment, they fluttered open and their deep brown color seemed bright and alive.

"Sasha," Viktor sighed. Natalie put her hand on his broad shoulder to steady him. "How do you feel, son?" he asked in Russian.

"Hurts," the boy said in English.

Natalie saw that Viktor grinned from ear to ear. If Alexander could remember to speak in English at a time like this, then clearly everything would be all right.

Angel came into the room and checked everything over. She told Alexander he could have a little water. "His throat probably hurts the most right now. The tube for the breathing machine leaves it feeling raw," she explained. She held a straw to Alexander's mouth, and he sipped a little from it. Then smiled.

"You did it, Alexander," Natalie said. "Your heart is fixed! The hard part is almost over. I know it hurts, but you will be better soon."

Alexander didn't try to answer. He quirked his mouth again in satisfaction, then let his lids drift closed. He was asleep again in minutes.

"He'll sleep a great deal for the next few days. That's a good thing," Angel told them. "We'll move him back to his room on my ward tomorrow or the next day."

Viktor nodded and the gratitude in his eyes made Natalie want to weep. She held Sasha's small hand and kept his father company during the night-long vigil by the bed.

For the next few days, Viktor spent every possible moment at the hospital, coming home to shower and catch a few hours of sleep in the guest room. Natalie went through the motions at work, drifting through her duties at the Pentagon like a machine while her mind remained on the boy at the hospital and the man she was going to marry. They had agreed to wait awhile before taking their vows to make sure Alexander would be well enough to witness the ceremony. But soon Viktor would be her husband.

As she got off the elevator after fetching breakfast on Sunday morning, she tried to imagine the ways her life would change once she was married, but found that it made her head spin. She focused on the present instead of what loomed in the murky future. Alexander was moved to his previous hospital room without incident. A haggard but happy Viktor clasped Natalie's hand throughout the process. She felt needed and loved and grateful to be a part of this wondrous miracle that Dr. Brennan had performed.

When she returned that evening from a dinner-run to the cafeteria, she knew the minute she saw Angel that something was wrong. And Angel must have seen the worry on Natalie's face, because the nurse rushed forward to reassure her that Alexander was fine.

"But something's wrong."

Angel nodded. "Someone claiming to be from the Pentagon has been calling the hospital today looking for you two. Sally down at the reception desk told me. He was pretty insistent, but she didn't give anything away. Told him she couldn't give out any information about patients and their families."

"Did he give his name?"

"No. Should I ask Sally to find out if he calls back?"

She shook her head. It didn't really matter who it was. The only important part was that someone was looking for her here at the hospital. Things were rapidly growing very difficult.

"There's more," Angel said gently.

"More?"

"Someone from Immigration called, too. He wanted to know if the Colonel was the one in the hospital. Sally told him the truth. So now they know."

She groaned. If the INS was on their trail… "Remember that wedding ceremony I mentioned to you the other day?"

Angel nodded. "I can have the hospital chaplain here in the morning. Alexander ought to be up to watch the big event by then."

Natalie breathed a sigh of relief. "Good."

"And do we have a bride yet?" she inquired as if she didn't already know.

"Oh, we figured that out a few days ago." Natalie smiled. "I've decided to make an honest man of him."

VIKTOR WANTED TO MARRY Natalia Wentworth with every fiber of his being. He needed no other reason than the yearning of his heart. But for her sake, he would have preferred to wait until he could secure his discharge from the Russian Army and help her sort out what was going on with her career. But she had been adamant that if someone could be found to join them in matrimony, then the deed would be done immediately. So now he stood before a beleaguered chaplain—stolen away from his breakfast by an insistent Angeline Lee.

As if in a dream, he listened to the vows the chaplain intoned and realized that Natalia had repeated them to him. She looked right into his eyes as she spoke, almost as if she doubted he would believe she meant them. He thought of the night they had spent in each other's arms, of the way she had kissed him and made love to him. He thought of her standing by him while he awaited the results of Sasha's surgery. He could not doubt her feelings for him.

With wonder and joy, Viktor stared back into Natalia's eyes and began to pay close attention to the words she said.

"…to love and honor you, in sickness and in health, from this day forward," she said. His heart swelled with pleasure and love. He wanted to kiss her very much.

But then it was his turn to repeat vows. Her clear blue eyes searched his, a hint of uncertainty in their depths. He wanted to reassure her, so he reached for her hands and held them both.

As he listened to the chaplain, he suddenly realized how strange this must seem to the minister. With Natalia in her American Army uniform and he in his Russian one, they were as mismatched as any two people could be. Add the boy who reclined nearby with a beatific smile on his face and tubes and wires attached all over his body, the Asian nurse who looked on with the pride of a mother-of-the-bride shining in her eyes, the doctor who had performed a miracle for Sasha only the day before, the orderly who had brought a ring to the ceremony on Angel's request, and the myriad other hospital staff members standing with tears in their eyes, and Viktor wouldn't have blamed the chaplain for wondering about the wedding. He gave a half smile that brought an answering one to Natalia's lips and he wanted to kiss her again.

The chaplain had stopped speaking, and Viktor realized with a start that it was his turn to say his vows. His heart did a little lurch as he tried to remember the simple phrase the chaplain had just given him to repeat. Then it came back to him all at once.

"I, Viktor Mikhailovitch Baturnov, take this woman to be my lawfully wedded wife," he said. And there were many more words after that. He repeated them dutifully, felt their meaning deeply, but didn't really hear them clearly through the pounding of his pulse in his ears.

And his gaze kept dipping to the perfect pink bow that her lips made. When the chaplain said he could kiss his bride, Viktor swooped down eagerly as if he had waited a lifetime for this one kiss. It did not end until he heard his son clapping, and Angeline sniffing and the chaplain coughing. Even then, Viktor was reluctant to pull back. He loved the feel of her mouth beneath his, the taste and warmth and texture.

But then he could feel her lips flex into a smile and noticed the slight quaking of her shoulders as she chuckled. He had no choice. Her joy was his and he had to smile, too. He discovered it was impossible to kiss someone when both parties were laughing, so he lifted his head and contented himself with smiling into his bride's eyes.

Everyone was laughing by then. Backs were slapped and congratulations offered. Viktor and Natalie went to Alexander's bedside and each kissed him. Sasha smiled up at them.

"Pazdravlyayu, Mat'," Sasha said to her, and Viktor could see that Natalia understood that Sasha had not only congratulated her, but had called her mother. Her eyes flooded and she smiled, then gently kissed the boy again.

After a while, the chaplain managed to get everyone to sign the certificate in the proper places and then smiled at them and bade them goodbye. Viktor began to put the marriage certificate into his inside breast pocket, but Natalia plucked it from his fingertips before he could. Already she was acting the managing wife, and he found himself grinning foolishly as he watched her put the document into her purse.

"Oh, Natalie, what have you done!" A male voice called this out from the threshold of the room. Angel moved to him quickly, demanding that he leave the room and pushing him back.

But Frank would not be quiet. "Natalie!" he called from outside the room where the relentless Angel had driven him. "Natalie, you need to hear what I've found out. You don't understand! He's already got a wife in Russia!"

CHAPTER FOURTEEN

"FRANK, WHAT ARE YOU DOING here?" Natalie demanded angrily as she stormed toward him in the corridor outside Alexander's room. "For God's sake, this is a hospital. That child back there just had heart surgery! Are you insane?"

"You need to listen to me, Nat. That guy duped you. He's already married." Frank sounded genuinely concerned. Natalie grasped his elbow and made her way farther down the hall. "Did he tell you they were divorced? Did he say she was dead?" Glancing over her shoulder, she saw Angel watching them. Viktor was still inside the room comforting his son. Alex was still groggy from his pain medications so maybe he hadn't heard Frank's accusation. But she knew Viktor would need to make certain the intrusion had not caused him any upset.

"How could you do something this stupid and impulsive?" Frank accused. "To let the man live in your house, then to up and marry him…"

"How do you know he's been living at my house?"

"That crazy General has been walking the corridors of the Pentagon telling everyone."

Her shoulders fell and a long breath gushed out of her.

"There have been some other guys asking about the two of you," he added. "You've made a mess of things, Natalie."

She had known this confrontation with Frank was inevitable eventually, but had hoped it wouldn't come this soon. The best she could do now was stall for time. She decided she should begin with his comment about Viktor having a wife. "Viktor's first wife is dead, Frank, so you can stop worrying about that."

"Is she?" He smirked at her, clearly in possession of information he had not yet revealed. "I checked his background. You told us at O'Malley's he was married with children. Well, he still is! According to the records, her name is Katarina and she lives in Yaroslavl.''

Her jaw tightened in anger. How dare this man pry into Viktor's life and then make these terrible allegations. ''You're mistaken. She's dead. She died when Alexander was very young.''

''That's what he *told* you.''

She was seething with anger now and wanted to pound her fists into him. But she also recognized that her emotions were out of proportion to the situation. If she didn't believe what Frank was saying, she should simply dismiss his assertions as nonsense and tell him to mind his own business. Clearly, there was a part of her that struggled with the possibility that he could be right. ''I believe what he told me,'' she said, more to herself than to Frank.

''Then you're a fool. He's used you, Natalie,'' he said emphatically. ''He needed help with his son and he needed a way to stay in the country. He figured out right away that you had the biggest heart around and he used you.''

The words were venomous and she wanted to pay them no attention. But her brow furrowed as she tried to remember exactly what he had told her about his first wife. He had said that she was *myortvy* and although the Russian word was unfamiliar, the way he'd said it had convinced her it meant dead. Was it possible that even though he hadn't seen her in years she was still alive and well in Russia? ''Oh, God'' slipped from between her lips before she could stop them.

''Yes, you should be very worried, Natalie.'' Somewhere in the conversation Frank had taken hold of her arms and now he shook her gently. ''This is a mess.''

''Take your hands off her,'' Viktor commanded from nearby. Natalie's head snapped up and she looked right into those brown eyes that had been so warm only a little while ago. They were cold and distant now.

Frank's hands dropped to his sides. Viktor took another step nearer and she saw that his fists were clenched at his sides.

''Don't believe him, Tasha,'' he said. Natalie's gaze lifted to his again.

His jaw muscle flexed once, twice, and she knew he was grinding his teeth again. She wanted to tell him to stop, but she didn't know if she should say something so intimate to him. Was he capable of using her the way Frank claimed?

Yes, it was possible. The man was a ruthless special forces operative who would do anything for his son.

Natalie felt tears pricking the corners of her eyes. But she would not demean herself by letting them fall in front of either of these men.

"The military attaché at the Russian embassy knows about all this," Frank added. "He doesn't know where you are yet. It took me all night to find out which hospital you were in after I heard Baturnov was supposed to have had a heart attack. But the Russians are demanding that the Pentagon turn him over immediately." Frank looked at Natalie as if he expected something from her. When she just stood there, trying frantically to make her mind work out a solution—or at least some sort of plan to find a solution—he took a step toward her. "If he'd lie to his own government, he'd lie to you, too."

Viktor bristled visibly, leaning forward and glaring at Frank with a dangerous glint in his eyes. Frank fell short of touching Natalie, and for this, she was grateful. She couldn't bear this man's hands on her. He'd ruined her wedding day, ruined her hopes for her future, ruined her life. Whatever his motives might be, she hated him.

"Let me take you home, Nat. We can sort this out together. Tomorrow, I'll take you to Colonel Freeman, and we can explain how you were taken in by this asshole. Freeman will help you deal with the authorities, and you can save what's left of your career."

The last remark brought Natalie to her senses. "You're the last person I would turn to for help, Frank. I'm beginning to wonder if you aren't the one who's been messing with my assignments all along! You always wanted me to be more dependent on you. Maybe you want to wreck my future in the military." She swept her hand in front of her to indicate Viktor. "All of this probably plays right into your plans."

The stunned look on his face could not have been feigned,

she decided. Maybe she was wrong about him being behind her troubles at work, but she was not mistaken about his happiness with the current situation.

"You have done enough for one day, Major. Leave us," Viktor said in that voice that brooked no disobedience.

Frank squared his shoulders and glared at him. "I'm an *American* officer and I don't answer to you," he spat. "And I'm not leaving her here with you to—"

Natalie stepped between the two men just as they appeared to be headed toward a physical altercation of some sort. Viktor immediately saw that this was neither the time nor the place and took a step back, regaining control of his temper instantly. Frank, however, attempted to grab Natalie's arm as if he would haul her out of the hospital with him whether she liked it or not.

She evaded his grasp. "I'm not going with you, I'm not going with anyone. I'm fully capable of dealing with this situation without a man to help me. If you come within ten feet of me, Frank, I will not be held accountable for my actions."

She executed a perfect about-face and glared at Viktor. Then, seeing the hurt lurking in the depths of his eyes, she softened a little. "Tell me none of this is true, Viktor," she said evenly.

"I searched for Katarina for years after she left us. She went first to her family, then drifted with friends from one town to another. There was a great influenza where I heard she went last. There was every indication she died there with hundreds of others. When I inquired with her family, I received a letter from a cousin confirming my suspicions. But I never bothered to correct my military records. It just never seemed important."

She stared at him for a long moment, her heart pounding in her chest as she realized he could not confirm his first wife's demise. "You have no other documentation?"

"Russia is not like America. There is much documentation for the living, but not so much for the dead." His accent had grown thicker as he spoke, the only indication of his distress other than that shadow of concern in his eyes. "I never had any reason to make the authorities declare her death official. Why should I trouble myself when I never intended to marry again?"

She nodded, feeling as if the life were being sucked out of her. "What about us?"

He took a step toward her, reached for her, but then stopped himself. She was grateful for his reticence. She wouldn't be able to think if he touched her.

"Tashyenka, please believe me. What we have is very real. I have not duped you. I have no intention of leaving you. You are my wife forever." He let his guard down for a moment and a sorrowful yearning crossed over his features. He glanced toward Frank and seemed to recollect they weren't alone. The mask of detachment snapped back over his face almost before she could be sure of what she'd seen.

"I want to believe you, Viktor. But right now we have two of the greatest armies in the whole world really pissed at us. I have to go to my superiors and see what I can do to salvage something for us." A plan formed as she spoke it. She would go to Colonel Freeman and make him listen to her. "You need to stay with Alexander." She eyed Frank, still standing by the wall and listening.

She wiped the sly expression off of his face with her next words. "And you need to keep messenger boy here with you for a while so he doesn't follow me."

Viktor didn't grin, but the feral look of pleasure that lit his eyes would have worried her if she had been the target. "Don't kill him or anything," she admonished. "That would just make things worse. Just keep him here for an hour or so." She looked at her new husband and decided she would not judge him yet. "We'll sort out the issue of your first wife later. Right now, I need to keep my tail out of military prison and do what I can for you regarding that Russian attaché."

He nodded once and moved into place to effectively block the sputtering Frank from following her down the corridor. Natalie ignored Frank's protests and forced her legs to carry her down the wide hallway and out of the hospital. She was already driving away before she remembered she hadn't said goodbye to Alex. The ache in her chest made her breath come in little gasps, but she was determined not to cry.

She couldn't face Colonel Freeman with red-rimmed eyes. If ever there was a time to behave like a soldier, this was it.

"You will remain here with me if you can be quiet," Viktor said to a fuming Major Lezinski.

"You can't do this!" the major cried. "I'm an officer! An *American* officer! You can't hold me here against my will."

"In accordance with every military code in the world, I still outrank you," Viktor snapped. "Be silent!"

Perhaps it was the lethal stance Viktor had taken on, maybe it was the tone of his voice. Regardless, Frank closed his mouth while his face grew very red. Enraged, he lunged at Viktor, who easily sidestepped the man. Lezinski crashed into the opposite wall, his fist making an enormous dent in the surface.

Several loud expletives came out of Frank's mouth. A man in a white hospital uniform came out of one of the rooms to see what the commotion was about. When Lezinski made another effort to strike Viktor, the newcomer moved to restrain him.

Surprised, the Major did not have the sense to be still. Instead, he shouted threats and struggled, forcing Viktor to immobilize him. He grasped one of the Major's arms and pinned it behind him, bending it so that any movement would be painful. The cursing and threats continued unabated.

"You want me to call hospital security, Colonel?" Angel asked, eyeing Lezinski as if he were a long-legged insect.

"That would be helpful," Viktor said calmly. "Perhaps they would be so kind as to lock him up for a few hours for us."

"Oh, that can be arranged, after the ruckus he caused up here," said the orderly who eyed Lezinski suspiciously.

Viktor grinned over the top of his captive's head, though he was fairly certain the smile did not reach his eyes. The Major did not say another word until the security guards showed up. Viktor remembered one of them from the incident with General Schwinn and he nodded to the man.

"I would like to go back to my son," Viktor said to Angel.

"You can stay another few hours," she assured him. "He'll sleep through the night, though. He's doing fine. You know you can't keep staying here with him through the night. You need to get some rest yourself. But we'll take good care of him."

Viktor nodded and went back to Sasha's room. The boy was asleep. Sasha had been determined to witness his father's wedding, but the event had taken a great deal out of him.

Viktor sat down in a chair and lifted his laptop to his knees. Now, more than ever, he wanted to uncover the source of Natalia's changed assignments. As much as he hoped it would turn out to be Lezinski, he now believed the major was not involved. The look of surprise on Lezinski's face when Natalia had accused him had been genuine.

So who else could it be?

Viktor had input all the data he could gather and he had eliminated several possibilities. Surely he was missing someone who ran in Natalia's circles and had the necessary motives.

One query after another failed to reveal anything relevant. Twice the stubborn machine had flashed Lezinski's name as the culprit. But Viktor knew that was not right. He had missed something somewhere. If only he could think it all through from a different angle.

Angel came to the door. He looked up at her and noted that her expression appeared to be one of a concerned parent. "Everything will be fine, Colonel. You'll see. Love has a way of overcoming great odds."

"Love may not be able to overcome Mother Russia," he said grimly. "I have a great deal of knowledge about my military that my government would not like to lose to the Americans. The Russian Army will go to any lengths—"

He broke off in midsentence and thought about what he had said. An odd notion had popped into his head.

"What is it?" Angel said.

"A different way of thinking about things has just come into my mind."

"Good! This must be the beginning of everything working out."

He smiled at her, touched by her optimism on their behalf, and then began to work with his database, hoping that his hunch would prove fruitful.

When Natalie walked into Colonel Freeman's office, she knew trouble had preceded her. The Colonel sat ramrod straight behind his desk and stopped her in her tracks with a penetrating scowl. Almost automatically, she came to full attention, stiffening her spine and clamping her arms to her sides. But she didn't take her gaze away from the Colonel.

"Sir, permission to speak."

"I think I've heard all I want to hear about you for one day, Captain," he barked. Then he stood up and leaned a bit forward, emphasizing the depths of his anger. "I treated you like the promising young officer you gave every indication of being. I did everything I could to promote your career. And this is how you repay me?"

Natalie knew better than to speak when he had explicitly told her not to, but it was very hard. She wanted to ask what he'd been told, wanted a chance to defend herself before he condemned her, and wanted to beg his assistance. The latter possibility began to fade the longer Freeman glared at her across his desk.

A long silence passed while he forced her to stand there, resisting the nearly overwhelming urge to squirm or blurt something out in her defense.

Finally, the man relented. "What have you to say for yourself, Captain?"

"Sir, I don't know what you've been told but I assure you I have done nothing to dishonor this uniform."

He snorted at that. "I'd say consorting with a spy would be pretty dishonorable."

She let her gaze connect with his. "He is not a spy. In fact, he is a guest of the American government. As the protocol officer assigned to him, I helped him with his problems, both official and personal."

"My God!" cried the Colonel. "You are not supposed to get involved personally with any visitors! Are you insane? You've ruined your career!" He came around his desk, but stopped himself short of grabbing Natalie and shaking her as he clearly wanted to do.

"My career was in trouble before Viktor arrived here, sir. I believe I've tried to discuss that with you on a few occasions and…''

"Viktor? He's Viktor now?"

She nodded, fighting the impulse to take a step back from the furious man who towered over her. "We were married this morning, sir," she said softly. "I believe I should refer to my husband by his first name."

"You…you…! Don't you dare make such a smart-aleck remark when your entire career is on the line and mine along with it because I was your advocate!" The man looked as if he might have a stroke, so Natalie tried her best to look contrite.

She didn't feel contrite, though. The entire interview was her worst nightmare and she wanted to lash out and fight against the unfairness of it. Who had gotten to Freeman? What had that person said against her? Was it Frank? Was it someone else? Perhaps the person hell-bent on ruining her career?

The only thing that kept her in check was the Colonel's comment that his own career could be tarnished in some way by her actions. She hadn't thought of that before.

Freeman made a visible effort to calm down. He took a few steps away and walked toward the window. With his back to her, he said, "You married him?"

"Yes, sir. The INS seemed to be catching up to us. Marrying him was the only way I could keep him in the country to be with his son while the boy recovered from heart surgery. General Schwinn threatened…''

"That old coot?" The Colonel half turned at the mention of Schwinn's name.

"Yes, sir. He's been threatening Viktor almost since the Colonel disembarked from the plane. The General made it clear he would engage the INS, among others. He can't seem to accept that the Russians aren't the enemy anymore."

"Well, they're not exactly our friends, either."

"Viktor is no one's enemy," she assured him.

The Colonel shook his head. "Natalie, Natalie. Listen to yourself. This man, this Colonel Baturnov—he's been a loyal Russian soldier for most of his life. He's a trained killer, ten times more deadly than the average military man.'' He pierced her with a glare. ''Your Viktor is *everyone's* enemy.''

Unwanted doubts flashed through her mind as she recalled the accusations that Frank had shouted to her. Had Viktor lied to her? Had he used her for his own ends the way he would use someone when conducting a mission?

''He is not *my* enemy,'' she said with less conviction than she would have liked. ''He wanted to defect, he wants to stay here in America.''

This got Colonel Freeman's attention. ''When did he say that?''

She tried to remember. It seemed so long ago. ''A week or so ago, I think?''

''Why didn't you tell me?''

Her brow knit in consternation. ''First, the idea of him defecting seemed laughable given that he's on a friendly visit to train with us. Second, I couldn't trust anyone to take him seriously and worried that he would be sent home immediately while his son was about to have heart surgery. How could we risk that?'' Eyeing the Colonel dubiously, she asked, ''Do Russian soldiers still defect?''

''No, but there are some in our government who might make an exception for a former special forces officer with interesting connections to an Army that still remains largely a mystery to us.'' He looked out the window again. ''Still, if your objective was to keep him in the country, you probably did the right thing.''

Natalie was confused. A moment before, the Colonel had been ready to bite her head off for her involvement with Viktor. Now he seemed to be affirming her decisions and expressing satisfaction in her reasoning ability. She decided to take advantage of this new mood.

''Sir, I need your help.''

He swung around to her, eyes flashing, jaw set, shoulders squared. He was every inch the formidable Colonel who had led troops into battle. ''You need my help! I've been helping you since the day I met you, Captain Wentworth. And you return the favor by throwing it all away on a stranger from around the world and his pathetic son!''

That was too much. No one got to call Alexander pathetic! ''My stepson is not pathetic. You know nothing about him, so don't you dare speak of him.'' She clenched her fists at her sides and her entire body trembled with the force of her outrage.

Unexpectedly, the Colonel's eyebrows shot up. ''Is that so?'' he asked calmly.

She made her muscles relax and her stance return to a deferential pose. It would be insane to let her temper get away from her when this man could help them if he chose. ''Yes, sir,'' she said softly.

''I apologize for maligning a child. I'm upset.''

Natalie stared at him, trying not to show her surprise and confusion. ''You have cause, sir.''

He gave a rueful laugh at that. ''You bet I do,'' he agreed in a calmer tone.

Natalie eyed the clock attached to the side wall. Time was slipping away. ''Sir, Major Lezinski said the Russian authorities were aware of what Viktor has done and were looking for him. It's only a matter of time before they track him down and take him away.'' Her voice cracked. Doubts about Viktor might nag at the recesses of her mind, but the fact remained she loved him and wanted him safe.

''He'll need to deal with his military as best he can. You have your own troubles.''

She shook her head and took an urgent step forward. ''Please, Colonel. You can help us. All I ask is that you do what you can to keep him in the country. He's put in his papers for a discharge. He has a son in intensive care at Montgomery County Memorial. He's married to an American. Clearly he has no desire to leave the United States. And you said he might be a valuable asset to us....''

''Stop!'' He made a slicing motion with his right hand and Natalie had the sense to close her mouth. ''You should be worried about yourself,'' he said, eyeing her.

Her shoulders sagged. ''Honestly, sir, I don't care what happens to me if I can just keep Viktor here with his son.

"You're in love with him?"

She gave him a pained half smile. "Yes, sir, I am."

He stared at her for quite some time, and Natalie suddenly remembered that this man had given every indication of being infatuated with her own mother. Perhaps Pauline could be enlisted to help convince Colonel Freeman that Viktor's case was a worthy cause.

She dared to say some of what she'd figured out on the drive to the Pentagon about her own situation. "As for myself, sir, I haven't broken any laws or disobeyed any orders. I just helped someone who needed to be helped even though I knew my career would probably suffer. It just seemed to be the right thing to do."

He glanced at her and walked over to his desk. Sitting down heavily in his chair, he picked up a pencil and tapped it against the desktop. "I can't think of any charges I can level upon you, though I'd sorely like to right about now. You might as well go home while I think about what to do with the new Mrs. Captain Wentworth-Baturnov."

She winced at the ridiculous title, but took heart that the Colonel was at least willing to let her go. Still, it was not enough. She needed him to help her save Viktor. "What will we do about Viktor and the Russians who are after him?"

Freeman continued to tap his pencil, faster than before. "I'll see what I can do," he said.

Natalie took a breath to plead some more, knowing that she needed a more certain commitment out of this man. But the Colonel held up his hand abruptly to stop her.

"Don't say another word, Natalie," he said. "Just get out of my sight. I gave the Taiwanese visit over to Barbara Dwyer, so you might as well go home to your new husband." He picked up a random sheaf of paper and made a great show of sorting through the top documents. "I have work to do. Dismissed."

Frustrated nearly beyond endurance, Natalie executed an about-face and marched out the door. The minute she was out of sight, she began to hurry through the enormous hallways of the Pentagon toward the north parking exit. She had to get to her car as quickly as possible. She couldn't risk making a personal call on her office phone where any number of people might hear. Instead, she would call her mother from the cell phone she'd left in her vehicle.

AFTER TALKING WITH HIS SON and making certain the boy would not miss him too much during the night, Viktor took a taxi to the flat, which he had come to think of as home. He hoped Natalia would be there. He wanted to talk to her, make her understand that he loved her. He could not allow her to think that what Frank Lezinski had said was true.

He let himself in with the key she had given him and then threw it onto the side table, exactly the way he had seen her do many times. Sighing deeply, he remembered that this was his wedding day, that the sun was setting, that he should be with his bride making love to her. But he could tell by the gloomy silence that she was not home. He wondered where she had gone. Probably to her superiors to see what she could salvage of her career.

At least he would be able to give her the name of the person he'd identified as responsible for the changes to her assignments, he thought as he wandered to the kitchen. If his computer program had not given him the same name three times, he would never have guessed.

He passed his hand over his face and acknowledged his weariness. A shower would feel good, so he went to the guest bathroom. It felt very good to step out of the uniform he had spent the last few days in. A small pleasure to be in clean clothes, but one he might not be able to enjoy often in the future. He paced the apartment in jeans and a T-shirt, wondering what he should do next.

Ultimately, he knew he had to find a way to prove to Natalia that he was her husband, that Katarina was dead. He would need to elude the authorities until he could accomplish that much. He went to his room and packed some necessities into a bag, then threw in some food items from the kitchen, just in case. He stowed his laptop into its case and took care to put his keys inside one of the pockets. Then he put everything onto the fire escape.

He looked at his watch for perhaps the thousandth time and cursed. It would be many hours still before any offices were open in Russia. He needed official documentation regarding his first wife, but he was unlikely to interest any officials in his homeland to help him. Now, if he could make contact with those offices from inside the Russian embassy, using secure communications, he might convince them that the matter was urgent....

The idea took hold in his mind. He thought about the likelihood of being caught if he went to the embassy. But then he thought about how much harder it would be to survive a prison in eastern Russia if he could not prove to Natalia that he loved her. He simply could not go back without convincing her that he had only one wife.

He took his cup of tea to the living room and set it on a coaster on the table. Then he sat down on the sofa to think through how he would get in and out of the embassy, how he would get access to the computer he would need, how he would deliver the information to Natalia. After a while, he stretched out and closed his eyes, certain it would be impossible to sleep as he listened to every sound that came to him from beyond the apartment walls. He would need to wait until after midnight when Russians at home would be just waking up and going to their jobs. At that hour, the embassy here would be lightly staffed. He would use his credentials as a colonel and wear his special forces medallion on his uniform. There would be just enough time...

"Mom, I got married," Natalie said without preamble.

"What!" came the expected cry. "Without me there! How could you?"

Natalie wanted to laugh but was afraid it would come out sounding hysterical. Instead, she sighed deeply. "It was sort of an emergency."

Her mother was silent a moment. Then, "You had an emergency wedding?" She didn't sound convinced. "Unless you're nine months pregnant or terminally ill, I just don't see how your wedding could be an emergency."

"Yeah, well, when you hear the story, you'll understand."

As succinctly as she could, Natalie told her mother about Viktor and Alexander and the Russians and the current state of her career. "So, you see, Mom, I'm in big trouble."

"I'll be on the next train down there," her mother said with fierce protectiveness.

Natalie smiled and felt like crying at the same time. "Actually, I don't need you to come down here just yet, although I hope you'll get to meet Viktor and Alexander soon." Silently she acknowledged that she'd be lucky if Viktor managed to remain in the country through the end of the week. "But I *do* need your help."

"Tell me what to do."

"Would you call Colonel Freeman for me?" She felt a little guilty. It went against everything she believed about earning your way through the ranks without special treatment. But this was for Viktor's freedom, perhaps his life. Pride would have to take a back seat when the stakes were so high. "I need you to try to get him to help Viktor. He knows a lot of powerful people, but he isn't convinced he should use his influence to keep Viktor in the country. By the time he decides, it may be too late."

"I understand, Natalie. Don't you worry about a thing. I'll make sure he pulls out all the stops for my new son-in-law."

Natalie felt her eyes sting with unshed tears. "Thanks, Mom," she croaked.

"You go find your husband. It's your wedding day."

She nodded at the phone, unable to say anything more than "Bye."

Then she put her car into gear and pulled away from the Pentagon parking lot. She would stop at home first and change her clothes. If he wasn't there, she would go to the hospital to find him. They had a lot of talking to do.

THE SCRAPE OF THE KEY in the lock jolted him awake, and in a flash he was on his feet poised to fight or flee. Then his sleep-fogged mind realized that if a key was being used, it must be Natalie returning home. As the door swung inward and he heard the familiar sound of keys being dropped onto the table, Viktor shook the tension from his body and stepped forward to greet his wife.

She saw him and stopped all of a sudden, as if she were a rabbit caught in a beam of light. He could see that she had been crying, or perhaps trying too hard not to cry. He wanted to go to her and wrap her in his arms, but he hesitated.

"Natalia," he said in a gruff voice.

"Hello, Viktor. How is Alexander?"

"He is well, they tell me. I am to get some rest while he spends another day mostly sleeping."

She nodded. "That sounds like good advice."

He had no idea what to say next. He took a step toward her, giving in to the growing urge to touch her. She barely moved, but the wary expression that crossed her face nearly broke his heart.

"I need to take a shower in the worst way," she said. "We'll talk after that."

He nodded and retreated back to the couch.

He had done a great deal of waiting since he had begun this American sojourn. Now he waited for Natalia to shower. This was much worse than waiting for her to come home. For now he imagined her in the shower, wet and surrounded by steam, sliding soap over her body and running her fingers through her soaked hair. He wanted to strip off his own clothes and join her. He wanted to wash her from head to toe and then kiss her everywhere.

He wanted her the way a groom wants his bride.

But she would not welcome him. Lezinski had made her doubt him. A woman as intelligent as Natalia would need to give the accusations due consideration, regardless of what her heart told her. Viktor ought to be respectful of that.

Unfortunately, his body had other ideas. And by the time she came back, his good intentions had been overtaken by a deep desire to coax her into his arms once again—perhaps for the last time before the authorities tracked him down.

She was wearing her old, ragged bathrobe and nothing could have been more erotic. He remembered how it would gape open when the tie was undone and how the opened sides framed her exquisite body. Heaven only knew what she wore under it, and when she tugged the lapels more securely closed, as if she could tell that he was undressing her in his mind, he had cause to hope she wore nothing beneath it at all.

He stood to greet her and noticed he had gone breathless and warm. He wanted her. He wanted her now. So he took a step toward her, watched her stiffen, and noted she did not move back or say anything to stop him.

He took another step. His pulse quickened and he could feel the blood pumping through his veins. He held her gaze and saw a flash of defiance in her eyes.

Her chin went up a notch as she said, "We need to talk about things, Viktor."

"You must trust me, Tasha. They will come for me soon." Her eyes filled with pain. He wished he could have saved her from the truth, but he knew there was no sense in trying. "You must simply believe me when I tell you..." He took another step toward her. "That you are..." He stood directly in front of her, close enough to feel her warmth and catch her scent. "My one true wife." He raised his hands slowly until they were to the level of her shoulders, then he touched her. Gently, he pulled her toward him.

She made him gasp with surprise and relief when she suddenly flung her arms around him and clutched his neck. She pressed herself to him, and he could feel her breasts against his chest and her abdomen against his erection. He had not thought it would be possible to love her more than he had moments ago, but he found out he could. Desire flooded him.

He scattered kisses along her neck and jaw, making hungry sounds as he felt her skin grow warmer. When his mouth found hers, he knew he had never known anything as sweet as her lips.

"Tasha, I love you," he said, as if the words had been wrenched from his very soul. "I will always love you."

He felt a wrenching sob shudder through her, but her hands continued a feverish exploration of his body. She seemed to want him as much as he wanted her, so he lowered her to the soft carpet. Yes, her bathrobe had came undone again! Its sides lay to the right and left like wings while Natalia's body rested in the center clad much the same as before. One firm tug, and the thin fabric of her panties gave way and the cloth was removed from her body.

He could not bear it if he were forced to return to Russia without ever having tasted her intimately, without giving her such pleasure to remember him by. So he began a slow journey southward, beginning with her mouth. Then he kissed her throat, her collarbone, the slope of her breasts. Pushing her T-shirt up, he latched on to one nipple and suckled. He heard her moan and felt her writhe, but it was not enough for him. He gave the same treatment to her other breast, but then he had to move lower to kiss her flat stomach. He licked the sensitive skin at her navel, making her suck in her breath and plead with him.

"Please, please, please," she whispered.

He slid lower over her smooth skin and she grappled at his shoulders, kneading his muscles with her fingers, whimpering. Yes, this was what he wanted. Every electrified nerve in his body wanted her squirming with desire, lusting for him, needing him.

It seemed imperative that he bring her to a searing climax in the surest possible way. And when he tasted her for the first time, he knew he could not let it be the last.

He felt her legs begin to tremble. Her pleas and muted whimpers became more frantic as her need grew. She flexed and strained and cried out his name, begging for what he could give her with his mouth. Viktor knew he would bring her where she wanted to go, and the knowledge filled him to overflowing with transcendent ecstasy. And his arousal intensified with each moan and gasp.

So close, he knew. So very close...

Then someone knocked on the door.

CHAPTER FIFTEEN

VIKTOR TENSED, BUT DID NOT LET her go immediately. One last kiss. He had to have that. He nudged her chin upward with his finger and pressed his lips gently to hers. He savored it, this final kiss, while the knocking continued and grew more impatient.

Finally, Major Lezinski's voice could be heard from beyond the door. "Natalie, I know you're in there. You need to open up and talk to this guy I brought."

"Oh, that bastard," Natalia growled. "How could he bring them to my door like this?"

"He is doing what he thinks best, Tasha. He worries that I have taken advantage of you."

"But you haven't," she said fiercely. Her certainty made him smile, despite the seriousness of the moment.

"I love you, Tasha," he said, and he could not keep the hitch out of his voice. "I have my things ready to take with me down the fire escape. For your protection, I must leave now.

"Wait. Don't go yet." She sounded desperate and he hoped she was not afraid. He would not be able to leave her willingly if she feared for her own safety. "Maybe he didn't bring any Russians. Maybe he's just trying to get me to let him in." She walked to the door and peered through the peephole. "Oh, God," she said. "There's a man with him. But he's in civilian clothes."

"There is no sense in taking a chance, Natalia. Wait until I'm gone, then open the door," he said calmly.

Her eyebrows shot up, but she nodded her agreement and he slipped on his shoes. He moved toward the sofa and slid open the window above it. "I will prove to you that we are properly wed, Tasha. Do not allow anyone to make you doubt me."

"I have no doubt now. And it doesn't matter," she assured him. A new worry crossed her mind and she rushed to him. Grasping his hand, she said, "Don't you take any extra risks to get information about Katarina. Promise me, Viktor."

He smoothed his other palm over her cheek in a soothing gesture. "I will take great care," he said.

"Where will you go? How will you know when it's safe to come back?"

"Don't worry, Tasha. I must do this. I have to gather information, talk to people in Moscow. Things will go as they will," he said softly.

The pounding on the door became insistent. "For the love of God, Natalie, open the door. You don't want these guys to have to get a warrant, do you?" Lezinski called.

"I must go," he said. "Be careful. Alexander needs you, so do not get yourself in more trouble because of me."

She nodded. "When will I see you again?"

"I will contact you as soon as possible," he said, wondering if he would ever be able to speak with her again. He kissed her quickly and climbed out onto the fire escape. She closed the window and drew the shade so that Lezinski and his friends would not see him.

Viktor scanned the dark alley below but saw no sign that anyone was keeping watch on this unexpected exit. Silently, he slipped the straps of his bag over his shoulders and then climbed down the ladder, heading toward where the last of his freedom would be found.

NATALIE CHECKED OVER HER shoulder to be sure he was out of sight, then she opened the door.

"It's about time!" Frank roared as he moved to enter the apartment. Natalie stood in her bathrobe directly in his way, blocking his path. "You're not going to let us in?" He sounded incredulous.

Natalie simply stared at him, trying for an aloofness that she didn't feel. Inside, she was red-hot with anger and aching with worry for Viktor.

"What do you want?"

"This is Mr. Hodges. He's with Immigration," Frank said, indicating a short man with the balding head. He seemed weary and put out so Natalie smiled at him, hoping to win some points.

Hodges flipped out a typical Federal ID, let her read it, then put it back in his pocket. "I understand that Mr. Baturnov is staying here," the man said.

She didn't respond to this, stalling for time to think, and was saved when the elevator doors slid open and an unfamiliar man stepped into the hallway. He smiled at them cordially and walked toward them. "And you are?" she asked of the newcomer. Frank turned to give the civilian clothes a disdainful once-over and seemed as curious as Natalie.

"Federal Agent Norton. I've been told I might find Viktor Baturnov here." His eyes and lips smiled, but she felt certain the expression was a mask. He did not show her any identification.

"Get in line, buddy," said Mr. Hodges.

"Colonel Baturnov is not here," she said evenly to them all. Then she closed her mouth and waited to see how they would react.

Frank flapped his arms in exasperation. "Natalie, the jig's up. Just let us in. I know he's here! I saw him come inside, and he never came out."

She said nothing to that, but glared at Frank. How dare he spy on her home!

Federal Agent Norton stood back and watched Natalie with a practiced eye.

Mr. Hodges gave a long-suffering sigh. "If he's not here, do you know where I could find him?" he asked. He looked at his watch, then shot a scathing look at Frank. "We've been getting calls about this guy all week. Folks keep trying to turn him in, saying his documents for remaining in the country have expired. I'm supposed to talk to him and find out what all the bother is."

Natalie managed to smile at the beleaguered man. "There's nothing for you to worry about. Colonel Baturnov and I are married now and we'll be in to see someone at the INS in a few days to straighten out his documentation."

"Married?" said Hodges, looking both deflated and relieved. "That's good, then."

"That's a lie!" cried Frank. "He's married to someone else."

"Married?" asked the Federal Agent. He looked past her into the apartment, scanning rapidly for something. He wasn't looking for a person, though. His gaze was too low. He seemed to be looking for an item on the tabletops or on the floor.

Natalie casually angled the door to limit his view. She turned her smile on Norton. "That's right. Major Lezinski is mistaken about Viktor's previous marriage. His first wife is deceased. I have our marriage certificate right here." She rummaged in the purse that sat on the table by the door. "Here it is," she said, holding out the paper for them to see and hoping no one would notice her trembling hand. Hodges and Norton both studied the document with interest while Frank sputtered that it was all nonsense and none of it was legal.

"Frank, please calm down," she said. "Your accusations are groundless." She turned her attention back to Mr. Hodges and found it easy to give him a pained expression. "Frank is an old boyfriend. He's having trouble with the fact of my marriage."

Frank roared with indignation. "What! That is not true. I'm trying to look out for your welfare and…"

Natalie ignored him and continued to speak calmly to Mr. Hodges, who was nodding his understanding. "If you like," she said, "I could make an appointment with you now for us to meet in your office. My husband and I are eager to get things started to secure his permanent residency in America."

Mr. Hodges smiled up at her. She was doing everything she could to make his job easier and he seemed to appreciate that, just as Natalie had hoped.

"No, that won't be necessary," he said, handing her a business card. "Just call when you get a chance." He scowled at Frank. "It seems I've been led on a wild-goose chase tonight." He turned to go, muttering something about being kept from dinner and not being paid enough to work this much overtime. He punched the elevator button and waited, still muttering.

Frank drifted halfway down the hall toward him, complaining that Hodges should stay and arrest Baturnov, who was clearly an illegal alien, and what did it take to get government employees to do any work these days?

Meanwhile Norton kept his gaze locked on Natalie's face. "Would it be too much trouble if I came inside to talk with you privately, Mrs. Baturnov?" he asked in a low, smooth voice.

Natalie pulled her bathrobe more securely around her, smiled and shook her head. "I'm not prepared for guests at the moment. This just isn't a good time. If you'd give me your number, I promise to call you, too. What agency did you say you're representing?"

He didn't answer her question but took out a business card that had only his name and a phone number written on it. "It would be to your benefit if you and your husband spoke with me soon." He glanced over his shoulder to ensure that Frank was still engaged in his argument with Hodges. "I might be able to help you and Colonel Baturnov," he said quietly.

Natalie was interested in help from any corner. "Perhaps if you told me what you could do or what you want, I could discuss it with my husband," Natalie prodded.

Norton stared hard into her eyes. "I simply want to talk to the Colonel. I have reason to believe he might have something that belongs to us. He may not even realize he has it. In exchange for it, I could possibly help him with all this." He swept his hand around to include Frank and Mr. Hodges.

Again, Natalie felt as if she were in the middle of a movie. "I'll talk it over with my husband," she said, fingering the uninformative business card.

Norton smiled wanly at her comment, then turned toward Frank, who was still arguing with Mr. Hodges, trying to prevent the man from getting into the elevator that had finally arrived.

"Major, I believe we have come at a bad time," Norton said. "Captain Wentworth would rather we left." He walked up to Frank as he was speaking.

Frank clearly did not want to leave, but Norton was heading down the hall to the elevator, and by spreading his arms he urged both men through the elevator doors.

"This isn't the end of it, Natalie," Frank called. "I'll be back. Maybe I'll bring that Russian attaché with me next time."

Natalia slammed the door and shot the dead bolt into place. She leaned her forehead against the door for a moment, then turned toward the window. She wondered if she'd ever get the chance to tell Viktor what Federal Agent Norton had said tonight.

And what could Viktor have that the Feds might want?

A call from the hospital kept her from thinking clearly about this or about where Viktor might have gone. A man who said he was on the night shift with Angeline Lee told her that Alexander was awake and asking for his father.

"No, there's nothing wrong with him and he's not in more pain than should be expected, but we thought it was best if we call you. Maybe you and the Colonel could come back for a few hours to keep the child company until he falls asleep again."

Natalie frowned. This seemed odd in some way she couldn't quite put her finger on, but if Alexander needed her, she didn't want to delay. "My husband can't come right now," Natalie said, with more calm than she felt. "But I'll be there in under half an hour."

She hung up and dashed to her room to dress, focusing all of her energy on Alexander. She could do more for the son than she could for the father right now. At least she could be of use to someone.

WHEN VIKTOR LEFT NATALIA'S home, he slipped through neighborhood alleys for about five blocks before he decided he was not being followed. He hailed a taxi and went directly to Fort Drake. As soon as he entered the BOQ and Specialist Murdock saw him, Viktor could see the younger man was agitated.

"There've been guys here looking for you, sir," the Specialist said. His brows furrowed in concentration for a moment. "I thought you were in the hospital with a heart problem." he added.

"Your doctors are very good here," Viktor said.

Murdock smiled. "I'm glad you're feeling better now."

Back to the subject, Viktor thought. "About these men who have been looking for me..."

"Oh, yeah. There was the Russian dude, begging your pardon,

sir. An officer, by the look of his uniform. And then there were these two others…''

''What did they want?''

''Just looking for you. Said it was important that they talk to you. They left their business cards.'' Murdock handed them over.

One included the seal for the Russian Army and provided the name of the attaché stationed at the embassy. Viktor might be able to use that name to get past the clerks when he sought the use of the embassy computers. The other card had very little on it. Just a name and a local phone number.

He thanked the Specialist and said goodbye, then took the stairs toward his room three at a time. Once inside, he looked around the small space in which he had spent only a few nights four weeks and an eternity ago. Even so, he noticed some things out of place. The room had been carefully searched. Since there was nothing he could do about that, he went to the closet, where there was a garment bag with an extra dress uniform inside. It was this he had come for. He also could make some phone calls in relative privacy to prepare for what he would do later at the embassy.

It took him a while to make the telephone connection through the Internet provider he used. He connected his laptop to the line in his room, set up security measures to obscure the nature of the call for anyone who might have tapped the BOQ line, donned his headset and dialed the international number. At last he was able to speak to his cousin in Yaroslavl, who forgave him for waking her before dawn. He was required to report on Alexander's successful surgery before he could get her to focus on what he needed her to do.

''Trouble has found me here,'' he said to her. An understatement, but he did not want to alarm her unnecessarily. ''You can help me. You must go to my home and find a letter.'' He described the location of the envelope. ''Take it with you and I will call again in a while to tell you where to send it by facsimile.''

She became agitated about how to do such a transmission even to a location within Russia, but he soothed her and explained with as much patience as he could muster that she would be able to fax the document from the local government offices for a fee, which he would make up to her. If everything worked out the way he hoped, he would give her all of his furnishings from his home in Yaroslavl. This would repay her for her help these past months with Sasha and for doing this for him with the letter.

After concluding his call, he made a search to locate some government offices, jotted down numbers and refined his plan. Then he changed quickly into his uniform.

When he slid the wool jacket over his shoulders, he caught sight of himself in the long mirror attached to the back of the door. He paused, staring at his reflection with mixed emotions. The pride he had once taken in wearing this uniform was overshadowed by an unexpected sadness. He would never wear it again after this. Indeed, he had no right to wear it now. Soon, he realized, he would be folding it into a cedar chest in Natalia's apartment or exchanging it for prison garb in Siberia. The latter prospect brought a leaden feeling to his stomach. He ignored it, tugged the jacket down for a smoother fit and lifted his chin to ease the pinch of the shirt collar.

It was nearly late enough for him to go to the embassy. He wanted to time it perfectly. He did not want to be in the building any longer than he had to be.

Truly, he did not want to be inside the Russian embassy at all, but he could think of no other place where he could accomplish his tasks. An hour later he found himself striding through the front doors, easily passing the guards who made a thorough inspection of his Russian identification documents but who were friendly and unsuspecting. It was the uniform that helped him gain access to such a highly secure building. Which was why he had risked going to the BOQ. And he had needed a relatively safe place to leave his laptop. It held the very important proof Natalia would need regarding her career.

Having been cleared by the guards at the door, he made his way to a reception desk and put a great deal of authority into his voice. "I require the use of secure communications, both phone and Internet," he said to the receptionist in Russian.

She blinked at the credentials he held out for her to examine. It was very late and she was likely unused to such requests being made at this hour. She looked up at his face, which he knew was set in cold, hard lines, then she sent him down the hall to a particular office where she thought he might find someone to help him.

He went where she told him and found the room lit by only one small desk lamp and unoccupied. At this hour, he would have been surprised to find anyone around. But beyond the small outer office, he saw another room with desks holding computers and twin sets of phones. If things were set up here like they were back home, the tan phones would be the secure lines, which he could use freely. But in order to use the secure computers, he would need a password.

He approached the larger back room and called out, but no one answered. So he walked through the semidark space, eyeing each of the desks with their pictures of loved ones upon them. He selected a desk with a photograph of a smiling husband and two small children. There was a rolling index of phone numbers sitting to one side. He followed his hunch and leafed through it. When he got to the Russian letter for *P*—for *parol* or password—he found a card containing a series of random letters and numbers. He smiled at his good fortune even as he shook his head at the lax security. Then he turned on this unknown woman's computer.

"YOUR FATHER IS TAKING CARE of some important matters," Natalie said. "Remember that your friends at home awaken at a different time than you do here, so he must contact people there when it is the middle of the night here." As she explained this, she wondered what risks he might be taking while she sat comfortably at his son's bedside.

Natalie watched the boy play with an electronic chess set Viktor had purchased for him the week before his surgery. He played chess very well and she could not keep up with the intricacies of the strategy he worked against the machine. Her mind drifted over all that had happened throughout the preceding weeks and some of the information began to emerge as clues.

Federal Agent Norton was clearly one of the individuals who'd been following them. Perhaps in the blue sedan. And he wanted something that Viktor might not realize he had.

While she was deep in thought, Alexander asked if he could play with his Game Boy. When she reached inside the bedside drawer for the toy, Natalie noticed a group of CD cases that didn't go with either the Game Boy or the chess game. They appeared to be Playstation games and she glanced through them, confirming her suspicion by reading the names of the games— Final Fantasy, Tekken, Ridge Racer. But one CD case stood out in the pile. It had odd markings on it so she picked it up.

"What's this?" she asked Alexander when she realized the cover didn't provide a title. The markings were in some sort of Middle Eastern or Arabic writing.

Alexander made a face to indicate that he didn't know. "A game of Playstation, Papa tells to me. I do not know it."

She thought about that a moment. "Your father thinks this is a Playstation game? Where did it come from?" She flipped it over in her hand, examining the back, but found no clue as to its contents.

"Evo kampyuter," he said, gesturing to indicate that he'd found the thing inside something else.

"With his computer," she translated.

He nodded. "He holds the…mmm…games to give me here." He gestured weakly to indicate the hospital room *"Vot tvai ee-graee,"* he said in a deeper voice, imitating his father.

Natalie searched her limited vocabulary. "Here are your games," Viktor had said to his son.

She nodded her understanding and handed Alexander his Game Boy.

"Eta eegra," he said, looking at the disk in her hand, "work not." He shrugged slightly, dismissing this game that didn't work, and turned on his toy, which chirped a lilting tune.

While he played with the handheld unit, she continued to stare at the CD case, trying to understand why it wasn't better marked and why it didn't work in the Playstation unit. She opened the case.

Inside was a disk with no writing on it. She knew that Playstation games were always marked in either Japanese or English. This one had neither. It was plain, silvery plastic without so much as a picture imposed onto its surface. Natalie knew for certain this was not a game disk.

Agent Norton had told her that Viktor might have something they needed. And in exchange, Norton said he would help Viktor.

She closed the lid and tapped thoughtfully on the outside of the CD case. Time was passing very fast now, and she was no closer to finding a way to save Viktor from the Russian authorities. Perhaps she should take a chance.

Another hour passed before Alexander drifted off to sleep again. She kissed his forehead and left the room with the CD in her hand. On her way out, she stopped to speak with Angel, who told her that Alexander was doing fine. He would begin physical therapy in the morning, even though he'd already taken several walks and even managed a few physical tasks.

"Be sure to thank the person who called me tonight," Natalie said. Angel looked confused, so she elaborated. "The man who called me to tell me Alexander was awake and needed me."

"Man?" Angel looked even more puzzled. "Someone called you? That explains why you came here so late. I didn't have the heart to tell you visiting hours were over."

Natalie's heart missed a beat and then throbbed with urgency. "There was no man working on the ward tonight? A nurse, an orderly, maybe a doctor?" She should have gotten his name, she realized. She should have asked more questions, been more suspicious. Someone had deliberately tried to get her out of her apartment. Were they searching the place right now, just like they searched her car?

With purposeful strides, Natalie walked through the hospital, out to the parking lot and over to her car. She started the engine but didn't drive away. Instead, she picked up her cell phone and dialed the number from the card Norton had handed her.

"Yes" came a masculine voice almost immediately.

"Agent Norton, if you're inside my home, I'm going to be very unhappy," she said through gritted teeth.

There was a slight pause, then, "What makes you think I would be inside your apartment?"

She took a breath, prayed her guess was correct. "You searched my car and you're probably searching my house. Or maybe you're finished by now. You didn't find anything, did you. That's because I know what you're looking for and where you can find it."

She eyed the CD case she held in her free hand. Should she keep it with her or leave it somewhere safe? What if this disk wasn't even what they wanted? Yet, it made sense to her. Norton had said Viktor might not realize he possessed what they needed from him. If someone had put it with the other games he'd carried into the country for his son, then he wouldn't have noticed it. He would have been an unwitting courier.

"I see," said Norton very evenly. "What is it you've found?"

This was it. In a moment she would find out if she held the bargaining chip that would buy Viktor some help. "I have the disk," she said simply.

"What kind of disk?" Norton asked carefully.

Her heart tripped over itself, but she smiled slightly. She must be on the right track or Norton would already have hung up by now. "Can we stop the spy-drama nonsense and get to the important part? I need you to help me keep Viktor out of the hands of the Russians and in this country. You can do that, can't you? If you do, then I'll give you the disk."

"You'll have to be more specific about what it is you have, ma'am. There are a lot of disks in the world."

Damn. She would have to describe the thing to him and risk that she didn't have the right one. "It has writing on it that I don't recognize. It looks like it might be Arabic. The disk itself has no markings."

"I see," Norton said again, but she could hear a note of excitement in his voice. "You have it with you right now?"

She looked up and scanned the dark parking lot, wondering if someone was watching her. She dropped the disk into her lap and out of sight. "Of course not," she said, feeling suddenly vulnerable. "I put it somewhere safe." She nudged the disk to the floor of her car and scooted it beneath her seat with her foot.

"When you help Viktor, I'll give it to you." It sounded good. Would he believe it?

"Okay," he said amiably. He probably did this sort of thing all the time, she thought. "But it's going to take me a while to get things going in the right direction regarding Viktor. You could try to keep the Russians from flying him out on the next plane."

"What do you mean? Do you know where Viktor is right now? Do they already have him?" She knew she sounded panicky, but she didn't care.

"I'm not certain they have him, but he walked into the Russian embassy an hour or so ago, and we don't believe they'll let him simply walk away again. Did he think he could negotiate his way out of this? Or was he giving himself up?"

Natalie's stomach churned with anxiety. Why had Viktor gone to the one place he should have stayed away from? She knew the answer before the question was fully formed. He had gone to get documentation about Katarina, and perhaps to see what he could do about his military discharge. "Oh, God," she said softly. "I told him not to take chances."

"Tell me what you know, ma'am, and we might be able to help each other."

Knowing she had no other choice but to trust Norton, she explained why she thought Viktor had gone to the embassy. Norton asked a few questions, then told her to wait for further orders. He didn't ask for her cell phone number and Natalie assumed that he must already have it. He seemed to know all sorts of things.

Even though she'd agreed to wait, the minute the conversation was over, she put her car into gear and headed home to put on a uniform. She wanted to look the part of an American military officer when she drove to Embassy Row in the heart of the District of Columbia. She needed to find Viktor. She needed to demand that the Russians release him into her custody. At the very least, she would do what she could to ensure what Norton had originally suggested—somehow she would keep the Russians from flying him out of the country before help could arrive.

THROUGH THE INTERNET, Viktor had found a high-level government office in Moscow capable of giving him the document he required. He had talked by secure telephone to a person in the office who was willing to validate a death certificate if he could see the letter that Katarina's relatives had sent him. Viktor acquired and passed on the fax number to his cousin and then waited through for her to transmit the letter to Mr. Nikitin in Moscow. Had Viktor not called from the embassy, he might not have met with any measure of success. But Mr. Nikitin seemed to be impressed with the origin of the call and promised to fax the certificate as soon as it was ready. It had been worth the risk to come here.

Unfortunately, Viktor could find no trace of his discharge papers. He searched military records while he waited for the fax and made several phone calls, but these efforts resulted in nothing but frustration. He did come across the documents in his file that had led Lezinski to believe Katarina was still alive. Viktor made the corrections and saved the new records.

At last, he heard the beep and burr of the facsimile machine. The sound seemed overly loud in the thick silence. No one had come into the office during the time he had been there. He had worked quietly even when speaking into the phone. Only the gray light from the computer screen gave away his physical presence. But the chirping of the fax could draw someone, so he shut down the computer and went to the area where the machine sat, the paper emerging with exquisite slowness. He could see no way to make the thing work more quietly or faster, so he stood beside it, spring-loaded with tension.

He listened for other sounds, but heard nothing. The page inched forward. What he could see of it looked official. It would not have a raised seal, but surely it would be enough to convince anyone that his first wife was truly dead. Soon he would be able to give it to Natalia and erase her doubts.

"Who are you?" asked a man in Russian from behind him. Viktor turned quickly, surprised he had not heard him approach, and saw him silhouetted in the center of the door frame. Backlit as he was, his features were obscured and there was no way to tell whether he wore a uniform or not.

"Polkovnik Baturnov," he said, deciding that he could not give a false name after showing his identification earlier. He might be asked to show it again and he did not want unnecessary suspicion.

"And you are?" Viktor added with a touch of arrogance in his voice. With casual and economical movements, he retrieved the completed certificate from the tray of the facsimile machine and folded it up. Then he tucked it into the inside pocket of his uniform jacket.

"What have you got there?" the man demanded, sounding a bit more strident.

Viktor took several steps forward, stalking toward the man in an effort to intimidate. "I asked who you are," he said, coming to a halt only inches away. Viktor could see now that the man was young and none too sure of himself. He wore a suit, not a uniform. Viktor was sure he'd be able to get past him with little or no difficulty. If worse came to worst, he would be able to overpower the younger man, who was much shorter and had a slight build.

"I am Kirill Sidorov. I work here. But you do not." Despite Viktor's physical advantage, Kirill stood firmly planted in the doorway, looking up with his jaw set stubbornly. It was admirable, really, this young man's determination.

"At ease, Kirill," Viktor said as he placed his hand on the youth's shoulder in a comradely gesture. "I was directed by the receptionist to use this equipment. Shall we go ask her to verify that so your fears are allayed?"

Kirill thought about this a moment, nodded stiffly and stepped aside to let Viktor pass. As he went into the smaller outer office, Viktor tried to put Mr. Sidorov's mind to rest. "I am glad to see you here. It is not good security to leave the office open and unattended. Have you worked here long?"

Kirill shrugged and some of the tension seemed to leave him. "The morning shift will arrive soon. I have been at the embassy a year now."

"How do you like working in America?" Viktor asked as he proceeded down the hallway toward the exit. If he could ease this man's concerns and then claim to be pressed for time, perhaps he could escape.

"I like it here. These Americans live well, yes? Why are you here in the United States, sir?"

Ah, the young man had given due credit to his rank at last. The battle for trust was over with Mr. Sidorov. "I study supply movements. I am to learn from the American Army." He chuckled so as to share the irony with the younger man, who was not yet old enough to know that such an exchange would not have been possible in previous years. Viktor paused at the reception desk and the woman there confirmed that she had cleared him.

Viktor held out his documents for Mr. Sidorov to inspect, all the while planning his walk to the nearby exit. He would reduce suspicion with sure steps and a straight spine.

"Viktor!" A woman's voice. A familiar voice. Viktor looked up and saw Natalia in the main entrance where the armed guards had detained her. They stood shaking their heads at her and indicating she must leave, while she stared straight at Viktor from across the open expanse of the foyer. Dear God, what was she doing here? His escape was within his grasp. If he acknowledged her, she could confuse the situation. If he did not respond, she would likely continue to call to him.

"Viktor Baturnov," said Kirill, thoughtfully looking at the identification card he still held in his hands. "I have heard your name recently."

"Excuse me, Mr. Sidorov. This is an American colleague who requires my attention," he said as he gestured toward Natalia.

"One moment, if you will, Polkovnik Baturnov. I remember now that our attaché has asked to speak with you. We are to take you to him at once if we see you."

Viktor's heart began to beat very fast. His jaw tightened and he ground his teeth together momentarily. "Allow me to speak to my associate for a moment," he said evenly, hoping to have just enough time to pass Katarina's death certificate to her, tell her the location of his computer, reveal the name of the person at the Pentagon who was trying to ruin her career, and perhaps kiss her goodbye.

Kirill nodded graciously and motioned to the guard to let the woman pass through.

CHAPTER SIXTEEN

NATALIE WANTED TO TOUCH HIM. If only she could hold his hand or rest her palm against his cheek. But they were in the expansive entrance hall of the embassy and the armed guards and the other Russian were observing them closely. She kept her hands to herself.

"I can't believe you came here, of all places. But I've found a way to help you," she said softly. For once, she appreciated the Russian habit of standing close to converse, a cultural difference that had sometimes strained her nerves. But standing ten inches from Viktor while they talked gave them some semblance of privacy.

Viktor did not respond to her comment. "Tasha, I must speak quickly to you. There is much to say and no time to say it."

"I won't let them take you back to Russia. I figured out what those creepy guys who searched my car were after. They're going to help us in exchange for it."

His eyebrows shot up. "What is this thing?"

"A disk. It was in with your computer along with some other disks you carried for Alexander. You thought it was one of his Playstation games."

His expression hardened. "I will not provide your government with Russian secrets in order to save myself, Natalia. You must not do this thing."

Her mind went blank for a moment. She hadn't foreseen this protest. The writing on the disk was not in Cyrillic. "But it isn't Russian. The writing on the case is unfamiliar."

"You do not know what this disk contains. You must destroy it."

She tried not to show him how deeply she opposed this decision. If the disk contained information her government needed… "Whatever we decide to do with the disk, the fact remains that there are people working toward keeping you out of custody," she assured him.

He grasped her arms then and tightened his grip just enough to make sure she understood the seriousness of the moment. "I am already in custody, Tasha. This man has been ordered to take me to the attaché. He may not yet understand how serious my circumstances, but I am certain I will not be allowed to leave."

She groaned softly and felt her knees go weak. But when he let go of her, she forced herself to stand tall. "I was told to keep the Russians from putting you on a plane. Will you be able to tell me when they plan to transport you?"

"Probably not, but I will try. Listen to me now." He leaned even closer. "There is this document." He paused a moment and shifted his position slightly so that his broad shoulders blocked her from the young Russian's view. From inside his jacket, he slipped a folded paper into view. With a quick but surreptitious gesture, she took it all the way out and then tucked it beneath the hem of her uniform shirt and between her skin and her skirt's waistband.

He gave her a small smile of approval. "It is Katarina's death certificate."

"Oh!" she said, then pressed her lips tightly together to keep from railing at him about taking such risks for something so unimportant. He must have seen the anger flare in her eyes because he attempted to soothe her.

"It is important that our marriage not be challenged. If you are to free me from Russian custody, I must be your husband without doubt. I also searched records and made calls about my discharge papers and was unable to find out the status. As my wife, you will have a right to continue to pursue those discharge documents."

He hesitated when the Russian appeared to be listening to their conversation, but when he became distracted by the arrival of someone coming in for the day shift, Viktor spoke in a rush. "There is something else important I have discovered tonight.. Major Jansen appears to be the person who alters your assignments. If you find any of the notes left for your Colonel, you will see his handwriting."

She stared at him as surprise made her brain stop working for a moment. But she quickly recovered and accepted what he'd found out. She nodded her head. Someday she would have to ask him how he made this discovery. Jansen had never been one of her suspects.

"My computer is at the BOQ. I left it there for you because I knew you would be able to retrieve it from there. It contains information you may need to prove Jansen has targeted you and why." He paused and looked at her as if searching her soul. The young Russian shifted from foot to foot, clearly growing impatient. Viktor dropped his hands to his sides.

She glanced at the man in the suit and wondered if she could convince him to let Viktor go with her. With a tip of her head, she indicated the Russian and said to her husband, "I can tell him I've come to bring you to an important meeting with the American Secretary of Defense...that we can't keep the Secretary waiting." Viktor was already shaking his head, and she felt panic gathering in her stomach and around her heart. "Let me try to persuade them to let you go with me now," she pleaded. Her desperation was mounting and it was difficult to catch her breath.

"He has his orders, Tasha. Do not complicate things. There may still be a chance I can talk my way out." He paused for the barest second, then pierced her with a searing gaze. "This disk you speak of. I do not know what information it contains, but if it had to be smuggled out of my country, it cannot be good for Russia. Do not make me a traitor to my homeland by giving it to your agents, Tasha. I am trusting you."

She closed her eyes briefly against the flood of conflicting moral responsibilities. When she opened them again, he was still staring at her, searching her eyes now, waiting for her promise. If her country wanted the foreign disk, could she turn her back on a request from her government? And yet, she knew it would be unforgivable to betray Viktor by giving the disk to Norton without knowing what information it contained.

"You can trust me," she said, praying that some solution would come to her.

The Russian civilian cleared his throat, indicating they had talked long enough. Natalie wondered if he understood what he was doing to their lives. Viktor took a single step back from her, but it felt as if he'd put an impassable chasm between them. Her hand lifted of its own accord as if she could keep him from going, then it fell back to her side.

"Tashyenka, please take care of Alexander for me," Viktor said as he took another backward step toward the waiting Russian. "Please make him know that I did not leave him willingly." His voice had gone rough and his eyes held a telltale shine. Before he turned, he managed to say, "Make him know I love him." He put his right hand over his heart and his lips pressed together as if to hold back his emotions.

Natalie felt something warm and wet slip down her cheek. She brushed it away impatiently, but could not find her voice. There seemed to be too many things to say and the words became jumbled in her mind.

"Thank you for coming, Tasha. It eases my heart that I have said these things to you." She watched him walk away with pride in his steps, realizing now that she hadn't been able to tell him she loved him or to hear those words from him. The Russian listening to them might have heard. Bad enough he'd heard what Viktor had said about Alexander.

She straightened, tugged her military uniform into place and turned to leave. She would not allow this to be the last time she saw him. There were a thousand things to do before she would despair. It was almost dawn. Soon she would be able to call Colonel Freeman to see if her mother had cajoled him into securing Viktor's military discharge papers. She needed to get to the BOQ for Viktor's laptop and she decided to make her calls from there. Specialist Murdock would keep anyone from bothering her if she asked him to.

She was tired and afraid and moving like a robot. At last, she found herself inside Viktor's room. He'd left his jeans and T-shirt on the bed. She left them where they were, fearing that the scent of him on the cotton would break her control.

She located the computer and scanned the information Viktor had stored there for her. Then she called Colonel Freeman.

"We think his discharge papers may have been sent to the Pentagon," he told her. "He's been officially released from the Russian military, but he'll have a hell of a time proving that to the folks at the embassy unless we can find those documents."

"I'll go there now and find them," she said.

"I have people looking. You need to stay put. I don't want you any more involved than you already are," he told her. "Now, give me that Agent's phone numbers so I can work things out with him myself. You won't do your husband a bit of good if you don't stay out of trouble."

He was right, of course, but sitting by and waiting while Viktor's future hung in the balance did not appeal to her. During the long, endless hours of the day, she found many duties to occupy her. She spoke by phone to Mr. Hodges about obtaining a green card for Viktor. He said that getting the card would not be difficult, given that she had Katarina's death certificate.

Using Viktor's laptop attached to the BOQ phone line, Natalie also researched airline schedules from the D.C. area to Russia. There were a lot of them from both Dulles and Baltimore-Washington International. Methodically, she worked her way through the list, making note of the most likely flights. Then she started on foreign military flights out of Andrews Air Force Base. Two diplomatic departures were scheduled to leave for Russia that day. Of course, Viktor might fly out on a smaller plane to New York or some other American city and then depart for Moscow. But there was nothing she could do about that possibility.

She called the hospital and asked if she could be with Alexander while he underwent his first rehabilitative therapy, and when she was told she was allowed, she packed up the computer and drove to the hospital. Before she went in, she made certain the foreign disk was tucked safely into her purse. She would not let go of the thing for so much as a second.

It was hard to watch Alexander do the physical challenges he was asked to undertake. Despite his obvious pain, he smiled valiantly and did everything with amazing fortitude. When she tucked him back into bed later on, he looked at her with anxious eyes. "Where is Papa?" he asked softly in Russian.

Natalie fought back a tide of sorrow and met his worried eyes directly. Her ability with the Russian language was not refined enough to speak in subtleties, so she responded in English, hoping he would understand. "He is trying to make his way back to you, Alexander. My friends and I are helping him. We hope he will be here to see you tomorrow."

He held her with a steady gaze. "Papa go to Russia, not me," he said. It was a statement, not a question. It was said with resigned certainty, without reproach or anger.

"He is doing his best to stay in the United States with you. He loves you and always wants the best for you." God, this was the hardest conversation she had ever had.

Alexander nodded his understanding. "Yes. He give me you," he said calmly. "The best for me."

Natalie felt the sting of tears in her eyes. The joy she would have felt by this child's acceptance of her could have healed any wound except the one inflicted by Viktor's absence. She tried to smile to show Alexander she understood.

He squeezed her hand gently and told her everything would be all right. "Papa will make it right," he assured her. Then fatigue must have caught up with him. His eyes began to drift closed. By the time Natalie had control of her rioting emotions, he was already asleep.

She sat beside him and watched him for a time. The room grew too warm and her own eyes threatened to close. Except for a brief nap, she hadn't slept in more than thirty-six hours. She needed to keep moving or she would fall asleep. She needed to sleep or she wouldn't be able to keep moving. After another few minutes, fatigue overwhelmed her fear and determination and she lowered her head to the bed next to Alex. Her lids drifted downward.

The insistent burr of her cell phone awoke her. She searched for it in her purse, fumbled with it a moment in her hurry, then flipped it open and put it to her ear. "Yes?"

"Dulles airport," Norton's voice said without preamble. "A special executive jet brought in especially for him and departing at 2100 hours. It's leaving from a special terminal for smaller aircraft, not from the gates where flights usually depart.''

She looked at her watch. There was plenty of time to get to the airport, but could she find the terminal and the plane before it left? And if she managed to do that, how would she stop anyone from taking Viktor away?

"Meet me outside of Customs and I'll take you to him. You bring me the disk and hand it over to me at the airport and I'll do what I can to convince the Russians to leave Baturnov behind," Norton promised.

"Yes," she said. There were no guarantees of success. She pocketed the phone and scrambled to her feet, shaking off the torpor of sleep as she began to gather her things together. She decided to leave Viktor's laptop in Alexander's room. She doubted anyone wanted it now that the disk was no longer with it. The information about Jansen would be safe here.

Looking back toward the sleeping boy from the doorway, she made a promise. "I'll bring your papa back with me, Alexander." She hoped it was the truth.

It took her longer to get to the airport than she'd anticipated. It took forever to find a parking space. There was an interminable walk to the main terminal and then to the customs area.

Then there was an endless wait for Agent Norton.

He wasn't where he'd said he'd be, and minutes ticked by without any sign of him. Natalie looked around the area, making several complete circuits of the perimeter. Just like when she'd come here to meet Viktor for the first time, there were a great many people. But no Norton. After her third lap, she tried dialing the phone number he had given her. No answer.

Why hadn't she gotten more information from him? she asked herself. Too late, too late. She had only half an hour before the plane was scheduled to depart. That wasn't much time in an airport this size. Natalie made a decision to try to locate the gate herself.

She had to ask at least six different people for directions. Nowhere in her journey through the huge complex did she stumble upon Agent Norton. She took the shuttle to another terminal, hoping she was getting closer to her destination.

At last, she arrived at the smaller building. The moment the doors hissed open, she broke into a trot toward the nearest counter.

"I need to find an airplane that's leaving soon," she said in a rush to a woman in a dark blue uniform. She gave what little information she had about the plane.

"All the planes affiliated with the embassies use a few specific gates," said the woman. She gave instructions on how to find the area.

Natalie thanked her breathlessly, checked her watch for the hundredth time and ran.

As she approached the gate at last, she accepted the fact she was on her own. There was no sign of Norton and no sign of Colonel Freeman, who had agreed to come with the discharge papers if he found them in time.

And without help, Natalie had no idea what to do to keep Viktor off that flight.

Fear coursed through her as she made for the doorway marked with the number she had been given. She'd never felt so powerless, so enormously out of her element. But she kept moving forward. She put her trembling hand on the handle of the door. She would get on that plane herself if necessary.

There were stairs behind the door and she rushed down them and through the next exit. She found herself outside under the night sky. Lights from the airport lit the area, but beyond their reach, the darkness stretched endlessly. An executive jet that had seen better days sat on the pavement in the distance. There were stairs leading up to the open hatch. Even from so far away, she could see that a Russian military man stood at attention at the bottom of those stairs. There were no other planes in sight.

"Where is Norton?" she asked herself. She wanted to wail it loudly to the heavens, but instead she headed for the plane, hoping some kind of plan would begin to form.

Two other Russians in military uniforms were escorting a group of civilians toward the airplane. They approached it from a different angle, as if the group had come out a different door. They parted slightly and she saw the person in the middle had on a Russian officer's uniform and held his hands oddly in front of him as if they were bound together. Though his hair was covered with his military hat and it was too dark for her to see him clearly at this distance, she knew it was Viktor.

Natalie held on to her beret and broke into a run again.

VIKTOR LOOKED UP WHEN he heard her calling. He thought at first that he was simply imagining her voice, a figment brought on by the depths of his despair. But when her voice became louder, more urgent, closer...

He turned his head and saw her. He would get one last look at his Tashyenka after all.

"Stop! You must stop!" she called to them. Then she managed to say it over again in Russian, though her accent was so bad, it made one of his captors wince. But the leader of the group stopped, and the entire procession halted with him.

When she saw that they were no longer moving toward the plane, she slowed to a purposeful walk, looking very regal and certain of her authority as she approached. After a few more paces, he could see the set of her jaw and the determination in her eyes and Viktor wondered what she could possibly be up to. Surely she would not attempt to gain his freedom at this point. As glad as he was to see her, he suddenly feared for her. The last thing he wanted was to bring her more trouble. And these men could give her a lot of it if they wanted to.

"Are those handcuffs really necessary?" she said in English. He could tell she was angry by the flush of her cheeks and the glint in her blue eyes. The light from the plane made them seem cold and steely, but he remembered how they looked smoldering with desire. That was how he wanted to remember her eyes.

She didn't wait for an answer before launching into what she had come to say. "You can't take him. There are unsettled matters regarding this man. My government sent me ahead to ensure you don't remove him until we can sort things out. The others will be here any minute," she declared. Viktor glanced quickly at the surrounding area but saw no one coming to the rescue. Natalie had come here by herself. He could not imagine how she had found him, but here she stood, dignified and defiant and very, very alone.

Everyone stared at her in silence. She held herself very still and glared into the eyes of each official in turn, daring them to ignore her when she claimed to be doing official business of the United States. Viktor's heart filled with pride.

At last, one of the Russian officials said in clipped, British-sounding English, "This is highly irregular. You cannot actually mean to keep us from boarding the airplane. What interest could the United States have in this man?" He said "this man" as if Viktor were not fit to polish his shoes. But at least he had deigned to speak to Natalia.

"All I'm asking is that you wait awhile. You don't need to take him immediately," Natalia said.

The English speaker checked his watch, then looked her up and down disdainfully. "We are scheduled to depart quite soon. Who are you exactly? Whom did you say you represent, precisely?"

She was losing his interest. Her gaze faltered and her spine was not as stiff. "I'm an officer with the protocol office of the United States Army," she said. "In that respect, I represent the Secretary of the Army." Those words seemed to bolster her courage and Viktor saw her straighten herself once more. "I request that you refrain from removing this man from American soil for a few hours until matters of interest to the United States can be resolved."

Viktor wondered what she thought she could gain by such a ploy. But he knew he would not find out. The English speaker gave a curt order in Russian to the soldiers who were with them, and in a heartbeat Viktor was grabbed by his two elbows and pulled along toward the airplane.

"Wait!" Natalia cried. "Do you want to cause an international incident over one man?"

The argument was a good one, but his keepers were no longer listening. Having decided he must be more important than they had realized, they were whisking Viktor to the relative security of the airplane as quickly as possible. Without realizing it, Natalia had made his plight worse by her plea. He would be questioned relentlessly about this, as if he were hiding something from them that involved their American "friends." They would not rest or allow Viktor to rest until they had the information they sought.

Though he knew it was hopeless, he could not go to such a fate without some sort of struggle. So he dug in his heels, twisted first one way and then the other, and shook free of the soldiers. Crouching and backing up, he glanced around to gauge where all of his countrymen were located. There was nowhere to run—he would simply be caught again by the agile soldiers, who were not encumbered with handcuffs. At best, he could hold them off for a while by dodging their efforts to recapture him.

Then he heard it. The sound of engines speeding in their direction. The headlights of more than one car appeared in the distance. They grew larger, merged, filled the area with their light. Viktor did not dare take his eyes off of the people who would try to put him on the plane, even though help had arrived. He circled out of reach just as one of them tried to grab him.

Natalia seemed to be nearly dancing with eagerness for those vehicles to arrive. She might have been calling something to them, but his concentration remained centered on the young soldier smiling at him from a distance of a few yards. The soldier wanted to be a hero today. Viktor could not allow him such glory. Not if he ever wanted to see Sasha again or hold Natalia in his arms.

The black surfaces of the sedans gleamed in the lights of the airplane as they stopped abruptly nearby. Engines were kept running and headlights lit. Men emerged. From the lead vehicle, two civilian males stepped forward. From the other, came Colonel Freeman, whom Viktor had seen at the Pentagon. The civilians stood to one side while the Colonel conferred with Natalia a moment. Then Freeman and one of the civilians walked briskly toward the English speaker among the Russians. After a few words were exchanged, the English speaker made a sharp movement with his hands and angrily snapped an order to desist. The soldiers backed off. The smile left the face of the nearest one, replaced by a disappointed scowl.

Viktor stood up straight again. Slowly, he edged toward the Americans, still half expecting his countrymen to come after him again. One of the American civilians met him halfway and introduced himself as Federal Agent Cofflin. Viktor recognized him immediately. He was the man who had watched from the shadows the night Sasha arrived. He was also the one Viktor had chased down at this very airport when he had first arrived in the country. This was the man who had attempted to steal his computer. But for Viktor, there were no hard feelings. Cofflin had come to the rescue just when things were most grim. Viktor would forgive him almost anything.

And then his vision was filled with the sight of Natalia, running toward him. Though she smiled, the tension had not yet eased from her pretty face. He understood. The arrival of the Americans did not guarantee escape. But at least he would have this moment. He walked in her direction and lifted his arms to embrace her, forgetting his wrists were bound. He dropped his hands and satisfied himself with a searching look at her features.

"Get these off him!" Natalia demanded, staring with disgust at his handcuffs. But before anyone responded to her order, she looked up at the American with whom he stood.

"You!" said Natalia, noticing him for the first time. "You're the guy who searched my car!"

"Yes, ma'am," Cofflin said amiably in one of the many lazy American accents Viktor had heard at the Pentagon. "I knew you'd seen me, so Norton had to be the one to make contact with you if we were to keep you from getting too stirred up. But now it doesn't really matter if you put it all together." He gestured for one of the Russian soldiers to hand over the key to Viktor's handcuffs. While Colonel Freeman continued his heated discussion with the Russians, Cofflin unfastened the bonds and Viktor was free again. "At first, we thought we could just grab the thing, get the disk we knew our operative had put into the bag, and be done with it," he volunteered. "But you two proved to be a real pair," he said ruefully. He looked Viktor over from head to toe. "You move real fast for such a big guy," he said with a grin, clearly referring to when Viktor had tackled him. Cofflin rubbed his chin as if it had made painful contact with the cement sidewalk that day. "After that, it seemed as if you just about slept with that little computer bag of yours. We watched you, but you never seemed to let the thing out of your sight.''

"Why not enter the flat and take it when you observed we were both out running?" Viktor asked, interested in why these men had gone to so much trouble when brute force would have done the trick.

Cofflin's eyebrows shot up. "Colonel, this is America! There are laws against entering an American citizen's home."

"Yeah, right," said Natalia with disgust. "That didn't stop you from searching my car."

Cofflin grinned again. "We had a warrant to search your car, ma'am. We hoped you might be leaving that bag there at night. No luck. But by the time we had the warrant to search your house, you had already begun taking it to the Pentagon with you. It never seemed to be unguarded." He turned to Natalia. "It was the disk we wanted, Captain. I believe you have it. We've done our part, so you can give it to me now."

She shook her head. "Not until we're away from here."

Viktor's heart began to beat hard again. "Tasha," Viktor whispered to her. "You cannot give it to him at all. I will not give him Russian secrets."

She moved closer to him then and he could smell her unique scent again and feel her warmth. He wanted to wrap her into an endless hug, but knew he could not. The danger was not yet behind them and he must remain ready for anything. None of these other people were his friends, not even these Americans who had come to save him. They wanted to turn him into a traitor as the price for his freedom. This Viktor could not allow.

Natalia stood shoulder to shoulder with Viktor when she turned toward Cofflin. "I don't understand how Viktor became a part of getting this disk to you," she said. "Why would you use someone unsuspecting to transport it."

Cofflin shrugged. "Desperate situations require desperate solutions, Captain. The disk came out of a country along the southwestern border of Russia. The only safe route to get it to us was through Moscow, a big city where a man can lose himself. But our operative became convinced that he was identified at the airport there. We happened to have information about Colonel

Baturnov's flight plans that we could pass on to him. Your Russian Colonel was in the right place at the right time."

"Or the wrong place at the wrong time," she corrected him. "You used him without his knowledge. You put him in danger he didn't know he should guard against."

Cofflin gazed at her with a hard gleam in his eyes. "We do what we must in the interest of national security. We knew Colonel Baturnov could take care of himself. Did you know that military officers with the proper identification are almost always passed through Customs without having their bags checked? It was a fact that played into our decision to 'accidentally' bump into him and drop the disk into the Colonel's carry-on bag. That, and the fact that our Agent noticed he had other disks with him in the case. Ours blended in quite nicely."

"Is your Agent an elderly man named Mr. Zurtin?" Viktor asked softly. Cofflin said nothing, he just looked blandly at them and kept his lips sealed. "What information does this disk contain?" Viktor asked, trying hard not to show his anger at being so badly used.

Before Cofflin could respond, the other civilian walked over to them. He looked weary and impatient. "Let's have the disk, Cofflin," he said, holding out his hand expectantly.

"She won't give it to me," he said, gesturing toward Natalia. Viktor edged closer to her in case these men realized they could overpower her and take what they wanted.

"Where the hell were *you!*" Natalia cried, bristling with anger. "You were supposed to meet me by Customs, Norton!"

Norton held up his hands, palms out, as if to fend off her tirade. "Just give me the disk, Captain, and I'll explain everything."

She backed up a step. "I don't have to give you anything. Colonel Freeman is the one taking care of Viktor's release. You didn't do a single thing except show up too late."

Viktor's eyebrows shot up at such bravado. He watched warily to see what the civilians would do next.

Norton scrubbed his fingers through his hair in obvious frustration. He took in a breath and let it out again slowly, as if he needed to take a moment to compose himself. Then he looked at Natalia with cold eyes. "It's like this, Captain. I was late getting here because I was talking myself hoarse trying to convince my superiors that we should share the information on the disk with our friends here." He slanted his head toward the group of Russians still in deep conversation with Colonel Freeman. "I put my career on the line so I could trade information of mutual interest for this man." He glanced at Viktor and nodded. "Now, I'm just about out of patience. Give me the disk!"

She squared her shoulders and looked as if she would not give in without a fight. "You're going to share the data with the Russians?"

He nodded.

"When?"

He squinted at her, and Viktor's muscles tensed in readiness in case the man's control snapped. "If you give me the damn disk," he said in a deadly whisper, "I will make a copy right now with the equipment inside the car. They won't let Colonel Baturnov go unless I do."

She looked at Viktor, seeking his opinion with her eyes. There was no guarantee that Norton would not take the disk and drive off in the car, leaving them behind to deal with furious Russians. Viktor took Norton's measure, assessing him as he would an enemy across a battle line. He decided he would have to trust the man.

Viktor gave Natalia a slight nod and he thought he heard a pent-up breath slip past her lips. She opened her purse and lifted out a CD case with writing that looked Afghani. She passed it to Norton, and Viktor felt as if his life had just been handed over to the Agent. Stomach tight and churning, Viktor watched Norton stalk to his vehicle. When he went to the back door instead of opening the driver's door, he felt a little of his tension dissipate. Norton motioned one of the Russians to step closer to observe his actions. A telltale glow of a computer screen lit their faces and Viktor surmised they were reviewing and copying the data on the disk.

Another of the Russians, who had been listening to Colonel Freeman, turned to Viktor and called out, "You married this American woman?" He was clearly incredulous.

Both Viktor and Natalia faced him as if they were one unit. "Yes, I married her," Viktor said. "I wish to emigrate to America to be with my wife and my son."

The Russian shook his head. Beyond him, Colonel Freeman concluded his discussions and handed over a set of documents. "Here is your copy of his discharge papers. He is no longer under the authority of the Russian Army."

"If he is alleged to have committed a crime, he must be held in military custody regardless of any discharge. It is the same in your own military," the English speaker said, but it was clear his arguments were for show. He kept eyeing Norton, who remained half in and half out of his car. Apparently the Russian diplomat was keenly interested in that disk.

"You have no evidence of any crime," Colonel Freeman responded calmly. "He brought his son here, that is true, but he did it lawfully. He might have bent some regulation or other, but now he's on American soil and has an American wife. The United States has chosen to welcome him as a resident." He displayed the last of the papers he held.

As one, Viktor and Natalia moved forward to get a look at the new document. It was an INS letter that informed Viktor Baturnov he'd received conditional residency. It was signed by Mr. Hodges.

"He's the man from Immigration that Frank brought to the apartment last night—or was it the night before? Frank wanted Mr. Hodges to declare you an illegal alien or something." She smiled up at Viktor, clearly enjoying the twist. Looking down at her lovely face, glowing with relief and happiness, Viktor knew Mr. Hodges had never had a chance if she had turned her smile on him.

Norton emerged from the back of his car. His Russian companion nodded his head to indicate everything was in order. A second disk, unmarked this time, was passed to the English speaker in the Russian group.

The man accepted it with a slight bow, then straightened quickly. "We will not press this further today," he said to Colonel Freeman. He eyed Viktor with only a hint of disdain. In Russian, he said, "I hope you do not come to regret your decision to remain with these people, *Polkovnik*. At least you have chosen a good wife, fierce in her protection of you. She could almost be Russian. If you will excuse me, I have a plane to catch.'' He put his fingertips briefly to his forehead in a salute. Calling the order to embark, he stepped smartly toward the plane and was followed by all the others.

He left Viktor on the tarmac with his wife and the other Americans.

WHEN VIKTOR BROUGHT Alexander home after weeks of rehabilitation, it was to a little three-bedroom house in the suburbs he and his bride had purchased only a few days before. If they ever managed to get all the boxes emptied and the contents put away, it would be a perfect place to raise a child. It was enormous by Russian standards, with room for a large garden in the yard. There were families with children living all along the street. He and Sasha had been teasing Natalia that she needed to produce some infants if she wanted to keep up with the neighbors. Natalia always laughed and shook her head whenever they conspired to convince her to have a baby soon. But in the privacy of their bedroom, she had already confessed to him her hope that she would be pregnant with his baby before long. She said it would be a perfect reward for the ordeal they had been through.

If only her ordeal were over.

Major Jansen's court-martial would be concluded in another week, she had told him, but to Viktor it seemed endless. It still amazed him that Jansen would cause someone so much trouble in the name of love. He had fallen for Captain Barbara Dwyer and somehow thought if he advanced her career for her, she would give him more than a brief greeting occasionally. Captain Dwyer had not been amused when her name was linked with what had been happening to Natalia's career. She had assisted gleefully in the prosecution.

Viktor knew that he had helped his wife with Jansen. This was the one fact that kept him from despairing over all the hurts he had caused her. She had been forced to find another Army job outside of the Protocol Office—because of him. She was enduring an investigation into her activities—because of him. Her promotion to major was in jeopardy—because of him.

He rubbed his temples. His head hurt every time he thought of how much trouble he had brought her.

"Papa?" Viktor hadn't heard his son come into the room.

The smile he gave his son was genuine, despite his worry over Natalia. There was nothing like the sight of his boy, rushing from one youthful pursuit to another, to cheer him. "Yes, Sasha?"

"I go to play outside with neighbor childs," he said, practicing his English as they had agreed he would.

"Did you finish your chores?"

Alexander shifted from foot to foot, obviously searching for an excuse to play instead of doing the tasks he had been asked to complete.

The front door opened. Viktor heard Natalia in the foyer, home from work.

"Viktor? Alex?" she called.

"Come to the kitchen," he said.

She appeared in the doorway, and Alexander gave her an exuberant hug. "I go to play, yes?" he said.

Natalia nodded before Viktor had a chance to protest. "Have fun," she said as he skipped away. Viktor heard his son's footsteps going rapidly to the second level, probably to get his beloved baseball cap, and did not have the will to stop him. It was such a pleasure to see his son enjoying the fullness of life.

But then Natalia turned to him and smiled. His heart tripped over itself, something that still happened when she bestowed her attention on him like this. Surveying the condition of the room, she sighed.

"I suppose you want me to help," she complained with a playful pout.

"Not at all," he answered. "You have made it clear that the kitchen is my domain. So I will find places for these things as I see fit."

She smiled again. "Good. I didn't really want to help, anyway. I don't even know what half this stuff does." She picked up a garlic press from the countertop and eyed it dubiously.

He moved closer and took the device from her hand, then pulled her into his arms. "Good afternoon, wife," he said, kissing her on the neck in the spot he had come to think of as belonging to him. "You are home early." He tugged her uniform shirt from the waistband, slipped his hands beneath the hem and slid his palms over the bare skin of her back.

She snuggled closer. "I spent the morning learning my new job. Personnel administration is more interesting than I thought. And I like being in charge of an office, even if it's small." A delightful quiver ran through her body when he began to nibble at her neck. "I had to go over to Jansen's trial to answer more questions. No one understood how Jansen got Colonel Freeman to make the changes in assignments until I showed them the note about Lieutenant Stafford having the flu. It was in Jansen's handwriting. He'd been slipping Freeman notes like that to get him to reassign things. Sometimes Jansen would simply change the names himself, crossing off my name and replacing it with someone else's. Anything to help advance Barbara's career." She looked at Viktor. "When the prosecutor was done with me, I came home."

"I am glad. You can begin to put away the books in the library," he suggested. With her face pressed against his chest, he sensed that she smiled. She never failed to be amused by the name he had given the spacious room just off the kitchen. She had laughed when Viktor declared that there was no need to have a family room *and* a living room. His many books had already begun to arrive from his cousin. Boxes of them were stacked along the matching bookcases he had paid a carpenter to install before they moved in.

His wife hugged him tighter and sighed contentedly. "I still can't believe we can afford this," she said.

He huffed next to her ear playfully, wanting to prolong the moment of happiness. "I assure you that my new job pays very well. I must support you in the manner you deserve, after all. What sort of husband would I be if you could not rely upon me?"

"Give me a break."

"I give you a house, now you want a break?" he teased.

"What next? I may not be able to afford you?" They had been over this before, starting on the day after he had been released from Russian custody and informed her that he had received an offer for a job with Raytheon, one of the largest defense contractors in America. He was to begin in a week, but already they had given him a healthy signing bonus that had gone a long way toward paying down their mortgage and Alexander's hospital bills.

"I'm so very proud of you for landing such a perfect position—great pay and reasonable hours—doing something you really like."

"They are intrigued by my computer skills combined with my language ability. I told you they would be," he reminded her. But it was the six-figure salary that had stunned and pleased her. This unexpected financial success helped keep him from sinking into depression over all that she had sacrificed for him and his son. He longed for a conclusion to the entire debacle.

She sensed his unease and pulled back from him so she could look into his eyes. "Everything will work out in the end, and..." she began. But she was stopped when the doorbell rang. The sound was something he still was not used to, but he liked it.

Alexander's footsteps were heard pounding down the stairs to the foyer. As Sasha was no longer slowed down by an overtaxed heart or lack of oxygen, his natural exuberance had begun to emerge physically for the first time in his life. Every day brought improvements.

"Papa!" Alexander called. Whoever was at the door was not one of his son's many new friends.

Together Viktor and Natalia went to investigate.

"Colonel Freeman," Natalia said. She sounded surprised, and Viktor remembered that the Colonel was not due back from New York for another few days. Then Viktor heard his wife mutter to herself, "James. He's James now...about to become my stepfather. I have to remember to call him James."

Viktor smiled as she stepped forward to greet him. It was difficult to remember that this man no longer wore the Army green, was no longer anyone's superior officer, and would soon be related to them by marriage.

"Come in, James. When did you get back from New York?" she asked. Freeman had put in for retirement a little ahead of schedule, deciding life was too short to "dither around," as he put it. As soon as he had been released from active duty, he had gone north to woo Natalia's mother. He must have done a good job, because they had announced their engagement by phone a week ago.

"I got in last night and look who I've brought!" James cried. He stepped aside and let Pauline Wentworth into the house.

"Mom!" Natalia threw herself into her mother's arms and hugged her tightly. "I'm so glad to see you!"

"I decided I should spend some time with you before my wedding. I have a new son-in-law to get to know and a grandson to spoil," she said, smiling down at Alexander, who watched with keen interest. Viktor had no doubt that Pauline and his son would become fast friends in no time at all.

Natalia stepped back and spread her arms. "And look, there's plenty of room for you to stay with us!" She beamed with pride in her new house.

"It's beautiful. Perfect for children," Pauline said, smiling into Viktor's eyes. Somehow, he felt that he had passed some sort of test with his new mother-in-law. Maybe Natalia's obvious happiness had convinced Pauline he was worthy. Some of his tension seeped away. At least he could do one thing right.

"I have another surprise for you," James said. He reached into his back pocket and pulled out a folded envelope.

Puzzled, Natalia took it. She pulled on the ends so it flattened out. Viktor peeked over her shoulder and saw the return address was for the Judge Advocate General's Office. The two of them stared at it a moment, all levity suddenly gone. Viktor moved closer to her, sharing the dread he knew to be weighing heavily in her stomach. The document inside could mean the end of her military career, and Viktor would be hard-pressed to bear such news with his composure intact. He had been the cause of this.

She looked up at her former commander. "What does it say?" she asked.

"Open it," James responded. His blank expression made Viktor more nervous.

Her eyes lifted to Viktor's and held there a moment as if searching for strength.

She gave a stoic little smile, took a deep breath and pulled out the single sheet of paper, holding it so he could read it along with her. He skimmed the opening remarks, concentrating on the second paragraph. Then a lightness filled him and he let himself breathe again. "Yes!" he cried as he pumped the air with his fist in victory.

"It is good?" Alexander asked. He gazed up at Viktor with a delightful mixture of confusion and amusement in his eyes.

Viktor pulled him into a one-armed hug. "Very good," he said. "Your new mother is cleared of wrongdoing. The lawyers found no reason to charge her with anything." Then he translated the complicated meaning into Russian—something that had become increasingly less necessary—so that Alexander could fully enjoy the moment with them.

"Really good!" the boy said with a broad smile.

"Thank God it's over," Natalia said with a sigh.

"Thank James, you mean," Pauline said, with a smile at her betrothed.

"Yes," Natalia agreed, looking up at the man who had worked another miracle on her behalf. "Thank you, James." In a rush, she went to him and hugged him tightly a moment.

Viktor could tell Freeman was uncomfortable with this unexpected show of appreciation, but after a second he grinned and patted Natalia's shoulder. "Well, yes, that's fine, just fine. It's the least I could do after being duped by Jansen, so don't mention it. Viktor helped, too, you know."

"He did?" Natalia asked, releasing the man all at once and turning an intense gaze in Viktor's direction. "How?"

"I only gave a statement, Tasha," he said, uncomfortable with praise when he had only tried to undo some of the damage he had caused. "I explained things to the authorities."

"You had a hand in all this, too, Mom. If it weren't for you, I'm not sure those discharge papers would have been found in time." Natalia looked at her mother with eyes full of love.

"Well, James wasn't very hard to convince, so it was really nothing. You did what I wanted and got married before you turned thirty-five, so it was the least I could do," Pauline said. Then a puzzled look came over her features. "Whatever happened to that Frank person?"

"He made a formal apology to Viktor for accusing him of bigamy and he decided to resign from the Army," James explained. "His view of zealous protection of a fellow officer didn't compare favorably with mine," James said. "He had no business interfering with Natalie and Viktor."

"You're sure he won't bother you anymore?" Pauline asked.

"I am sure," Viktor volunteered. All eyes focused on him suddenly. He realized he had said too much and now he would be required to explain. He shrugged. "I spoke with him. We came to an understanding just before he left for his new job in St. Louis," he added with a smile. He said no more.

Natalia grinned at him, then glanced down again at the paper in her hand. "I may not be going to NATO—and I'm actually kind of glad about that, since this is such a good place to raise a family." She winked at her mother. "But at least I can keep my dream of wearing this uniform until I retire."

Viktor heard the emotion in her voice and went to her. He pulled her close and she rested her head against his shoulder. He was so damned relieved and grateful that her record had been cleared, he was nearly overcome himself. But he held together and gave her the moment against his shoulder that she needed to compose herself. When she was ready, she pulled back and there was a smile lighting up her face. Viktor suddenly thought of the night ahead when they would celebrate their good fortune in bed together. It would be the first time they would make love without a dark cloud looming.

He returned her smile and silently counted the hours until nightfall.

"You just make sure you stay out of trouble now," James said. "I can't go around getting you two out of jams all the time—even if you *did* find that disk and get it into the right hands in the end." There was a twinkle in his eyes.

"I'll do my best, sir," Natalia said as she straightened her spine and snapped her former commanding officer a respectful salute.

"Come, dear," Pauline said to Freeman. "We need to take Alexander for a nice, leisurely walk so he can show us his new neighborhood while we get to know one another."

"But we just got here," James protested, looking confused.

Pauline sighed dramatically. "Must I spell it out for you?" Freeman stared at her blankly, so she whispered, "I think we should give the newlyweds a moment alone to enjoy their good news."

"Oh. Oh! Yes, let's go for a little walk. What do you say, Alexander?"

"I say many things now. My English goes very better." Viktor laughed as he watched Sasha lead the way down the sidewalk.

Natalia turned to face him then. "Alexander's very better English reminds me of something," she said.

"Shh," he whispered as he moved into position and lowered his head to bring his lips within a centimeter of hers. "Our troubles are over. We are alone. Let me kiss you, my Tashyenka."

He slid his mouth gently over hers, then played upon her lips with his tongue. He made slow work of increasing the pressure, teasing her—and himself—by clinging to self-control even as the passion mounted inside him. She shattered his tenuous hold on himself when she slid her tongue into his mouth and made little sounds of eagerness. In one quick motion he swept her up into his arms and headed for the stairs. To hell with waiting until nightfall. The time to celebrate had arrived.

As he carried her up toward the bedroom, she pulled back slightly and looked at him. He could see that she was thinking—and not about making wild, passionate love. He groaned and took the last steps two at a time. He must not give her time to think.

She yelped when he tossed her onto their wide new bed. But even when he pounced onto the mattress with her and covered her with his body, she clearly had not let go of whatever was on her mind.

"What is it?" he asked in exasperation, convinced now that she would not be distracted.

"There's still one thing bothering me," she said.

"Only one?" he asked as he began to kiss her ear and along her jaw.

She sighed happily, but still she continued. "You never told me what you said in Russian at the airport when we first met. You realized I couldn't really speak your language and quickly spouted a flood of Russian. What did you say?"

He drew back in surprise. He had not expected this. And as his words came back to him, he realized he did not want to translate them for her. "I do not recall the exact…" he began.

"Don't give me that," she protested, pushing at his chest with no effect. "You remember every word." She pushed harder.

Defeated, he rolled onto his back and lay spread-eagle on the thick quilt. He was also embarrassed. His comments had been foolish in the extreme. But he had been so tired and so alone. She had appeared before him as if from a dream, so beautiful he could hardly breathe.

"If you had understood me, I would not have been happy. It was unwise of me to say such things. You might have understood some of it and then you would not have favored me with your friendship."

"That comment just makes me want the translation even more." She propped herself onto her elbow beside him, giving every indication of settling in for however long it took to exact the information. He glanced at the clock and wondered how much time they would have alone. Discussing this with her was definitely not how he wanted to spend the remaining half hour.

"Some things are better left unsaid, Tasha," he argued. But she gave him a look that said she would not be content with evasions. He sighed and closed his eyes, deciding to get it over with.

"I said that I hope you are as kind as you are beautiful because I might need your help before long if my superiors ever found out what I was plotting."

She did not respond, so he opened his eyes and found her staring down at him with suspicion on her face. "Is that all of it?" she asked with doubt in her voice. "You rattled off a great

many words in Russian and I hardly think it was this one sentence.''

He shook his head, smiling. ''I may have also elaborated on
your most favored attributes. Just a little. But this is the...
mmm...I give a basic meaning and it is all you need to hear.''
He twisted suddenly so that she was beneath him again. ''I have
given you your answer. Now you must give me what *I* want.''

She laughed and kissed him. Then she gave him everything
he wanted and more.

The Shannon Sisters

A Trilogy by C.J. Carmichael
The stories of three sisters from Alberta whose lives and loves are as rocky—and grand—as the mountains they grew up in.

A Second-Chance Proposal
A murder, a bride-to-be left at the altar, a reunion. Is Cathleen Shannon willing to take a second chance on the man involved in these?

A Convenient Proposal
Kelly Shannon feels guilty about what she's done, and Mick Mizzoni feels that he's his brother's keeper—a volatile situation, but maybe one with a convenient way out!

A Lasting Proposal
Maureen Shannon doesn't want risks in her life anymore. Not after everything she's lived through. But Jake Hartman might be proposing a sure thing....

On sale starting February 2002

Available wherever Harlequin books are sold.

Bestselling Harlequin® author

JUDITH ARNOLD

brings readers a brand-new, longer-length novel based on her popular miniseries *The Daddy School*

Somebody's Dad

If any two people should avoid getting romantically involved with each other, it's bachelor—and children-phobic!—Brett Stockton and single mother Sharon Bartell. But neither can resist the sparks...especially once *The Daddy School* is involved.

"Ms. Arnold seasons tender passion with a dusting of humor to keep us turning those pages."
—*Romantic Times Magazine*

Look for Somebody's Dad in February 2002.

HARLEQUIN®
Makes any time special ®

Visit us at www.eHarlequin.com

PHSD

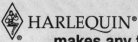

HARLEQUIN *Super*ROMANCE®

Old friends, best friends...

Girlfriends

Your friends are an important part
of your life. You confide in them,
laugh with them, cry with them....

Girlfriends

Three new novels by Judith Bowen

Zoey Phillips. Charlotte Moore. Lydia Lane.
They've been best friends for ten years, ever
since the summer they all worked together at a
lodge. At their last reunion, they all accepted a
challenge: *look up your first love.* Find out what
happened to him, how he turned out....

Join Zoey, Charlotte and Lydia as they
rediscover old loves and find new ones.

Read all the *Girlfriends* books! Watch for
Zoey Phillips in November, *Charlotte Moore* in
December and *Lydia Lane* in January.

HARLEQUIN®
Makes any time special ®

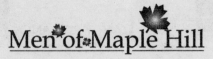

Men of Maple Hill

Muriel Jensen's new trilogy

Meet the men of the small Massachusetts town of Maple Hill—and the women in their lives:

Hank Whitcomb, who's back in Maple Hill, determined to make a new life for himself. It doesn't take long before he discovers he wants his old high school flame, Jackie Bouregois, to be a part of it—until her long-held secret concerning the two of them gets in the way!

Cameron Trent, who's despaired of ever having the family he's wanted, until he meets Mariah Shannon, and love and two lonely children turn their worlds upside down!

Evan Braga, who comes to Beazie Dedham's rescue when a former employer threatens her life. Then Beazie learns the secrets of Evan's past, and now the question is—who's saving whom?

Heartwarming stories with a sense of humor, genuine charm and emotion and lots of family!

On sale starting January 2002

Available wherever Harlequin books are sold.

HARLEQUIN®
Makes any time special ®